gone to ground

John Harvey is the author of the richly praised sequence of eleven Charlie Resnick novels, the first of which, *Lonely Hearts*, was named by *The Times* as one of the '100 Best Crime Novels of the Century'. His first novel featuring Frank Elder, *Flesh and Blood*, won the CWA Silver Dagger in 2004, and a Barry Award for the Best British Crime Novel published in the US in 2004. In 2007 John Harvey was awarded the CWA Cartier Diamond Dagger for sustained excellence, and in 2009 he was awarded an honorary degree, Doctor of Letters, by the University of Nottingham. For more information about John Harvey visit www.mellotone.co.uk

Praise for John Harvey

'John Harvey is not just a fine crime novelist but a fine writer, and an adornment to his chosen genre. Great stuff'
John Connolly

'If the title – King of Crime – is to go to the male writer who is at the summit of his form and writing some of the best crime fiction this side of the Atlantic, the crown is John Harvey's'
The Times

'Just when you thought Harvey couldn't get any better, up he pops with yet another brilliantly constructed, coolly written, chillingly sharp and utterly contemporary procedural'
Daily Mirror

'Harvey's Resnick novels are f...
British polic...

'Sharp plotting, great characterisation and a powerful narrative;
it's as good as they get'
Observer

'As ever, John Harvey's writing is cool, light, and beautiful'
Stella Duffy

'Harvey's fleshed-out characters and sure grasp of the complex
emotional underpinnings of society generally, and individuals
in particular, make him a favourite among crime writers and
readers alike' *Daily Mail*

'Visceral, engaged and yes, unputdownable'
Independent

'In John Harvey's sure and practised hands, police procedural
novels achieve new heights in grainy reality ...
The writing is thrilling and atmospheric'
Guardian

'An impassioned, at times heartbreaking story about love and
violence and the breakdown of contemporary society
and it confirms Harvey as one of our most
accomplished writers in any genre'
Sunday Telegraph

'Everything is just as it should be in a classic
modern British crime novel'
Times Literary Supplement

'Harvey is as excellent on human relationships
as he is on police procedure'
The Times

'Without doubt the best cop on the Britcrime beat, Harvey has
set a bench mark which the genre must now measure up to'
Literary Review

John Harvey

gone to ground

arrow books

Reissued by Arrow Books in 2013

1 3 5 7 9 10 8 6 4 2

First published in Great Britain in 2007 by William Heinemann

Arrow Books
Random House, 20 Vauxhall Bridge Road,
London, SW1V 2SA

www.randomhouse.co.uk

Addresses for companies within The Random House Group Limited can be
found at: www.randomhouse.co.uk/offices.htm

The Random House Group Limited Reg. No. 954009

A CIP catalogue record for this book
is available from the British Library

ISBN 9780099585626

The Random House Group Limited supports the Forest Stewardship
Council® (FSC®), the leading international forest-certification
organisation. Our books carrying the FSC® label are printed on FSC®-certified
paper. FSC is the only forest-certification scheme supported by the
leading environmental organisations, including Greenpeace.
Our paper procurement policy can be found at:
www.randomhouse.co.uk/environment

Typeset by Palimpsest Book Production Limited, Falkirk, Stirlingshire
Printed and bound by Great Britain by Clays Ltd, St Ives plc

For Jill Dawson & Meredith Bowles

Home is where the heartbreak
Wraps cold around my bones

Beth Orton: 'Safe in Your Arms'

1. EXT. COAST ROAD. NIGHT.

A blank screen. Dark. Little more than pinpricks at first, we see two lights amidst the blackness, gradually coming closer, until we realise they are car headlights.

As the car – a dark 1950s saloon – gets nearer and we hear the sound of its engine, the road along which it is speeding begins to take shape and we can just see that it is narrow and winding with dark trees to one side and what appears to be a cliff edge to the other.

The headlights become larger and brighter until they dominate the screen and dazzle, then the car is gone and for several seconds we are left looking at the empty road along which it has travelled. We hear the sound of the car accelerating away, gaining even more speed, until there is a sudden squeal of brakes, followed moments later by the sounds of the car crashing down the side of the cliff.

Cut to the car, viewed from above, as it strikes the

water and, for a moment, seems to disappear below the surface.

From a closer angle, we see the car being thrown around by the force of the waves, then cut to a close shot of the windscreen which has been shattered by the impact.

Over this we see the first of the credits, the title, superimposed . . .

SHATTERED GLASS

Behind the title, we see that the water is rising inside the car. A woman's face moves close to the shattered windscreen, a strange smile, almost of triumph on her face.

The second credit is superimposed over this image . . .

STARRING

STELLA LEONARD

. . . before a wave splashes across the front of the car and it disappears back into the sea.

2

1

Will Grayson had been awake since a little after five, the light leaking through the curtains like spoiled milk. An hour earlier, maybe more, Jake had cried out from the middle of a dream, and although Lorraine had stirred beside him, it had been Will who had pushed back the covers and barefooted into the adjoining room. The four-year-old's pyjama top was soaked through with sweat, his skin slick to the touch, breath sour on Will's face as he held him close. A dream about wolves. Some animated film to blame, Will thought, wolves, slinky and grey, sliding down between tall silvered trees.

'It's all right,' Will had murmured. 'It's okay. They're not real.'

For a moment, the boy's eyes had seemed to focus on Will's face, taking in the words, and Will had kissed his damp forehead and lowered him back down.

'It's early. Go back to sleep.'

He stood there, watching, until he heard the boy's breathing change.

Nestled against the warmth of Lorraine's back, he fell asleep again almost immediately, only to be woken when the baby began to cry and Lorraine, half-blindly, lifted her from the cot and into their bed, fingers unfastening the nightgown at her breast.

'I'll go down,' Will said. 'Make some tea.'

5:09.

Easing back the curtains, he saw not a wolf but the blurred outline of a fox, tail up, head high, making its dainty way along the edge of open field beyond the garden end.

By the time Will had showered and shaved, made a fresh pot of tea and some toast, Lorraine, wearing a sweatshirt and jeans, hair pulled loosely back, had come downstairs.

'She's gone off again.'

'And Jake?'

'Still sleeping.'

Will poured the tea.

'I saw a fox,' he said.

'The same one as before?'

'I think so. It's difficult to tell.'

Lorraine nodded, absent-mindedly. 'I was talking to Penny Travis. In the village. You know, she does some childminding. I mentioned her before.'

Will looked at her, set aside the knife.

'She says she might have a vacancy later in the year; for Susie. Once Jake's started school proper.'

'We've been through all this,' Will said.

'I know. But I still think . . .'

'And I thought we'd agreed.'

'You'd agreed.'

Will sighed. 'I think you should stay home with her a little longer, that's all.'

'How much longer?'

'Longer than you did with Jake.'

'There's nothing wrong with Jake. Nursery's been good for him, you've said so yourself.'

'That's not the point.'

'Well, then, what is?'

'I just don't think Susie should be with somebody else, not this soon. It doesn't seem right.'

'Fine. You stay home with her then.'

'How'm I supposed to do that?'

'Take time off from your job.'

'I can't.'

'Then get another job.'

'Now you're being stupid.'

'Am I?'

'Yes.'

'Okay, then. That's what I am.'

Lorraine slammed the door behind her, feet heavy on the stairs. Will poured what was left of his tea down the sink. Minutes later he was in his car and driving south, the radio turned up loud, no idea what he was listening to or why. When Lorraine had first become pregnant with Jake they had decided to move out to the country — a larger house, more garden, a nicer environment in which to bring up kids. For Will it meant a longish commute, forty minutes when the traffic was with him, often more, a pain at first, but worth the stress.

Helen Walker's blue VW was in the car park before him, but she was not at her desk. Outside, Will thought, sneaking a cigarette. He had given up himself two years before and no amount of mints could disguise the smell on her breath.

They had worked together in the Major Investigation Team for close on three years, Helen and himself, and for much of that time they'd been based at Histon, a couple of miles north of Cambridge. The police station there was fairly recent, a brick-built, two-storey building with a car park too small for its needs and a stairway that was wide enough for a half-decent game of five-a-side. Now, however, they were close to Cambridge city centre, in a building that was a testament to the ugliness of most mid-sixties architecture in general and concrete in particular.

Will, as detective inspector, held the higher rank, but, most of the time, that wasn't how it seemed: he and Helen were more like partners; sometimes one would lead, sometimes the other.

'You look tired,' Helen said. She was balancing two Styrofoam cups of coffee, one on top of the other.

'I'm fine,' Will replied.

'Baby keeping you awake?'

'I said, I'm fine.' Sharp as ice.

Helen set one of the coffees on his desk and studied his face. 'You and Lorraine had a row?'

'Jesus!' Will exclaimed.

'All right,' Helen said with a grin. 'You want me to mind my own business, that it?'

'Yeah, mind your own fucking business.'

Helen laughed. The phone rang on Will's desk and she picked it up. After listening for several moments, she reached for a pen and wrote a name and an address on the back of her wrist.

'Right,' she said, putting down the phone. 'You want something to take your mind off things? This might do the trick.'

Will's first thought when he saw the man's face: it was like a glove that had been pulled inside out.

The upper part of the face, in particular, had been beaten almost beyond recognition.

Blood had coagulated around the ridged base of the shower stall and patterned itself in darkening arcs upon the walls; the plug hole was blocked by what Will assumed to be tissue, hair and skin. The shower curtain, wrenched down from the rail, had become entangled round the man's naked body, entwined between his legs and draped across his chest like a plastic shroud. One hand cradling his sex.

In the doorway, Helen was talking to the crime scene co-ordinator, while one of the SOCO team readied a video camera in the adjoining room. The photographer, who had set up his tripod close to the body, had stepped back when Will had arrived, and was now waiting patiently to resume. Other officers, clad head to toe in white coveralls, gloved up, were beginning their search of the rest of the house.

The cleaning lady, who had discovered the body when she started work that morning, was sitting inside one of the neighbours' houses, a police officer in attendance, sipping sweet tea. It had been only her second day at this address, the first time she had used the key. The proverbial wild horses would not have dragged her back inside.

Helen came and stood at Will's shoulder, looking down at the body. 'Lovers' tiff?' she said.

Will looked back at her, uncertain. 'Could be,' he said.

Uncertain or not, the words came easily to his mind: *You do this and I never want to see your face again. Not ever.*

It was a two-storey terraced house in a road of similar houses just a short distance from the centre of the city, fronts covered in a pastel wash of varying shades, this one a paleish grey. Estate agents, Will reasoned, would describe it as a cottage, going for that homely, almost rural feel. And close enough to most of the colleges for junior lecturers to cycle in at ease, even walk if they'd a mind. Not cheap then, he thought, not that anything in Cambridge was. Not any more.

Inside, gentrification had taken hold: the extended kitchen-diner replete with a six-foot Smeg refrigerator and a deep white butler's sink, units faced in brushed aluminium, a butcher's block big enough to bone a side of beef.

The furniture in the downstairs living room reminded Will of stuff his parents had inherited and then tossed out, all plywood arms and metal legs. Utility, is that what it had been called? Probably worth a fortune now.

The front room upstairs had been turned into a virtual library with floor-to-ceiling bookshelves on three walls, one of them crowded not with books but with videos and DVDs; magazines in piles on the floor – *Cineaste*, *Film Comment*, *Sight and Sound*. A copy of *Shepperton Babylon* had been left open, face down, on the arm of one chair, a young Dirk Bogarde in shiny black leather trousers and improbable black hat staring out from the cover. Perhaps the victim had been reading it when he had been disturbed; when someone had called.

There was a flat-screen TV in one corner of the room, digibox and other accoutrements alongside. Framed film posters back down in the hall and on the stairs.

The middle room, with a window looking out over the side passage leading towards the garden, functioned as a study. Will doubted if it was usually in as much disarray. The lower section of a tall, three-drawer filing cabinet had been pulled open and a number of files lay close by on the floor; two of the desk drawers had been upturned, their contents strewn to all corners; papers were littered across the floor.

Someone searching for something worth stealing, Will wondered, or a wanton act of destruction?

There was a Hewlett-Packard laser printer to the left

of the desk, an empty space where a computer might have stood. A mains lead hung loose towards the floor. Resting against the side wall by the desk's edge were several slim computer manuals, amongst them the white-fronted *User's Guide to an Apple iBook G4 laptop*.

Worth stealing certainly.

But worth killing for?

The main bedroom, at the rear, had been made en suite, a small dressing room leading into the bathroom where the body had been found. Here again, everything was in turmoil. Cream-coloured sheets had been torn from the bed; the contents of both the wardrobe and the chest of drawers hurled haphazardly across the room. Shirts, jackets, boxer shorts, jeans. Some of the shirts had been ripped almost in two. A small photograph, that might once have stood on the bedside table, had been pulled from its frame, the glass splintered and smashed, the photograph itself torn in half and then half again.

With care, Will picked up the pieces and reassembled them on the bed.

Two men in shirtsleeves, arms on each other's shoulders, smiling. Squinting a little because of the sun. One man, the older of the two but not by much – mid-thirties, nothing more – was stockier and dark-haired; the younger man was taller, lean, a fold of fair hair falling over his face, reminding Will of one of the posters on the stairs: Montgomery Clift or James Dean – he was never sure which was which. His mother had once confessed to having had a crush on one of them when she was younger; she had watched his films on the television on weekend afternoons. He thought it might have been Montgomery Clift.

Will looked at the photograph again, the way the couple's smiles radiated happiness.

What had Helen said? A lovers' tiff?

When he went outside, easing off his gloves and reaching into his pocket for a mint, Helen was standing on the far pavement, smoking a cigarette. It was cold, cold enough to see her breath.

'My lungs for your teeth,' she said, seeing him pop the mint into his mouth.

'You can live without teeth,' Will said.

'Clever sod,' Helen said and poked out her tongue.

'Where do we stand with ID?' Will asked.

'Early days.'

'Wallet? Driving licence? Passport left lying around in some drawer?'

Helen shook her head. 'Not so far. No sign of a wallet at all.'

'Neighbours?'

'First name's Stephen – they think. Been living here less than a year. Keeps himself pretty much to himself. That's how the cleaning woman knew him, apparently, Mr Stephen.'

'That's all? No surname?'

'That's all.'

Without meaning to, Will crunched the mint between his teeth. 'How d'you want to do this? You want to stick around and talk to the pathologist or shall I?'

11

'It's Danebury?'

'Danebury.'

Helen shrugged. 'I could stay.'

Edgar Danebury had once made reference, with a nod in Helen's direction, to officers endowed with, as he put it, pulchritudinous plenitude. Next chance she got, Helen had brought her boot down hard enough on Danebury's instep to make his eyes water, since which time he had kept any extraneous remarks to himself.

Back behind his desk, Will switched on his computer and accessed first the electoral roll, then the council tax records held at the Guildhall: the householder was one Stephen Bryan. Stephen Makepeace Bryan, to give him his full due.

Some forty-five minutes later, one of the Scene of Crime officers at the house found a pink British Library card bearing the name Bryan, Mr S M, inside one of the books in the upstairs room, and Helen had it biked round to Will's office. The face in the small square photograph matched that of the dark-haired man from the photograph Will had found in pieces in the bedroom. Matching it to that of the murdered man would not be so easy. And, without visual identification by a relative, and lacking any obviously identifiable external marks on the body – scars, birthmarks or tattoos – they could not be one hundred per cent certain that Bryan and the victim were one and the same.

A DNA match with the dead man's mother, or, failing that, with siblings, might give them the desired result, though Will thought dental records could be their quickest and best bet, the lower part of the face not having suffered as badly as the rest. An initial check of dentists in the area, however, failed to show Bryan as a patient, meaning they would have to look further afield.

All those books on film, Will thought, magazines, DVDs – a hobby or something more? A quick check on Google told him there were more courses in the area involving some kind of film studies than he would have thought possible. Having noted the numbers of the various departments, he began ringing round and struck pay dirt on his fifth call.

Stephen Bryan had been appointed to the Department of Communication Studies at Anglia Ruskin University in the autumn of the preceding year, and was currently teaching courses in British Cinema, Class and Culture, and Sexuality, Gender and Identity.

No, he did not have any classes that day.

Just as well, Will thought, all those students missing a lost hour of vital education. More time to lounge around in bed, sad bastards.

He rang back the department administrator and learned that prior to taking this post, Bryan had done some part-time teaching at De Montfort University in Leicester. Yes, the woman said, her accent pleasantly northern, not East Anglian at all, she believed Leicester was where Mr Bryan had lived before. As for a previous address, well, it was, of course, outside normal university policy, but in the circumstances if she could call him back . . .

Within ten minutes, Will had Bryan's old address in

the Clarendon Park area of Leicester and very soon after that the name of the dentist with whom he had been a patient. Or should that nowadays, he wondered, be customer? No matter. A copy of Stephen Bryan's dental records would be put in the post that afternoon, guaranteed delivery by 09.00 the following day.

Will rose from his desk and stretched his arms, thought about fetching coffee from the machine, changed his mind and sat back down, reaching for the phone.

'Mr Bryan,' he asked the administrator, 'you don't happen to know if he was married or anything, do you?'

'Oh, no,' the woman said, something of a smile in her voice, 'I don't think he was anything like that at all.'

'He's gay, then,' Helen said. 'That's what you think?'

They were in the police station car park, standing close to Helen's VW, the end of a long day. Headlights were showing clearly now on most of the passing cars. The moon like a thumbprint, faint in the sky.

'Don't you?' Will said.

'Based on what? One photograph? A little bit of innu-endo down the telephone?'

'When you first saw him . . . the body . . . it was what you thought then.'

'Yes.'

'And why?'

Helen shrugged. 'The scene . . . the force with which he'd been bludgeoned.'

'Bludgeoned?' Will raised an eyebrow. 'That's a good old-fashioned word.'

'You know me, Will. Just an old-fashioned girl.'

He grinned. 'Home by eight, a little gentle needle-point before Ovaltine and an early night.'

'That kind of thing.'

'Not what I've heard.'

'Oh, Will,' fluttering her lashes, 'you'll never know.'

'Can we,' Will said, 'get back to the matter in hand?'

Helen grinned. 'In hand, certainly.'

'A lovers' quarrel, that was your suggestion.'

'Or the obvious.'

'Which is what?'

'A bit of rough trade. Bryan goes out cruising, picks up some bloke and brings him home. Things turn nasty round about act four.'

'You don't think that's a bit of a cliché?'

'Clichés are clichés for a reason.'

Will nodded. Sexuality, Gender and Identity: perhaps there were a few lessons to be learned there. 'The wallet turn up?' he asked.

'Not so far.'

'Credit cards? Cash?'

Helen shook her head.

'The laptop would be too much to hope for.'

'Wouldn't it just?'

'Robbery the motive, then, you think?' Will said. 'Or a little add-on after things went wrong?'

Helen pointed towards the back seat. 'Maybe we'll know more once I've been through those. Letters and diaries from the house.'

'You want me to take half?'

'No need. Go home and be nice to Lorraine and your kids.'

Halfway across to his car, Will turned. 'First thing tomorrow, if those dental records match, we're going to have to track down the family, next of kin.'

'I know.'

As he waited for a gap in the traffic he could see her behind the wheel of her VW, lighting another cigarette.

Will drew the car slowly on to the gravel, locked it and walked towards the house, the downstairs curtains already drawn against the dark. Lorraine was sitting in the half-light, the sound of the Cowboy Junkies, languorous and slightly spaced out, coming low from the stereo; Jake was curled on the settee beside her, his head in her lap, the baby held high against her shoulder, sleeping.

For a moment, Will thought his heart had stopped.

Lorraine turned towards him in slow surprise, and, as he reached down to take the baby from her, his fingers grazed the back of her neck and then the baby's face was against his, the familiar musky smell of her breath, the bewildering smallness of her bones.

Lorraine lifted Jake, the boy barely walking, and together they carried the children up to bed.

'You know how long it is,' Will said, unhooking the fastening at the back of her blouse, 'since we made love?'

'A long time?'

Will laughed. 'Unless you count a couple of assists.'

She dug her elbow sharply into his ribs and he cried out louder than was necessary and rolled back on the bed, taking her with him, her dark hair, as their mouths met, falling across her face and his.

2

Stephen Bryan's parents had moved from Chesterfield to a new-build bungalow on the outskirts of Kirkby Stephen, pitched perfectly between Swaledale and the Lakes. His father, early retired from a medium-grade administrative post with Derbyshire County Council, was only too happy to potter in his garden, slowly knocking it into shape; a former midwife, his mother now volunteered at the Citizens' Advice Bureau three days a week. Still fit, they walked a good ten to twelve miles each weekend, rain or shine.

The request had come through from the Cambridgeshire Force mid-morning, and the local sergeant had waited until there was a woman officer free from other duties to accompany him. Never a task to be relished and this one, by the sound of it, worse than most.

Delaying the inevitable, the sergeant parked at the end of the street.

Ted Bryan was digging a trench beyond last year's set of onions; his wife, Grace, sitting, coat on, reading a Margaret Forster novel in the weak afternoon sun. As the two officers passed through the side gate, the book slipped from her lap, unnoticed, to the ground.

'Ted, Ted . . .' She called her husband's name, and, resting one foot on the spade, he looked around. 'Oh, Ted . . .'

'Perhaps we should go inside?' the sergeant suggested, as gently as he could.

Reaching out, Grace Bryan gripped the sleeve of his uniform just above the wrist. 'It's Lesley, isn't it? Something's happened. Or is it Stephen? No, it's Stephen. Our Stephen. There's been an accident. Ted, there's been an accident.'

'Mrs Bryan,' said the constable, stepping forward, 'let's go inside.'

'Just tell me, is he all right? He is all right?'

Reading the answer in the young constable's eyes, the older woman's face collapsed inward, like a balloon sucked short of air.

Ted Bryan looked into the sergeant's face, then turned away.

'Bastard!' he said. 'Bastard! Bastard!' Driving the spade hard into the ground.

Helen Walker had begun reading Stephen Bryan's diaries the previous evening whilst eating her supper – a cheese and tomato pizza prised from the freezer and then microwaved, sliced into manageable sections and washed down with a glass of quotidian Chardonnay. Not finding anything either salacious or especially revealing, she had shifted her attention to a batch of some thirty or so letters, stretching back several years and ranging from the sheerly practical – an acceptance by the gas company that he had been overcharged for the first quarter in his new accommodation – through the academic to the more intimate and personal – family, lovers, friends. Helen had saved these for last; poured a second glass of wine, ran a bath.

There was some lengthy correspondence, entertaining and chatty, sent from New Zealand by someone who Helen thought at first might be an old girlfriend, but later realised was Stephen's sister, Lesley; a letter of congratulation from his mother, sent on the occasion of his new university appointment, her happiness allayed by an anxiety that was never spelt out; and finally, some half a dozen love letters, the erotic content in places detailed to the point where Helen felt she was being told more about the specifics of man-on-man by-play than she really wanted to know.

Back downstairs and wrapped in an oversize white towelling dressing gown, the television switched on though she was neither watching nor listening, Helen smoked a final cigarette of the evening, drank instant coffee and went back through what she'd read, noting down those names and dates that seemed, on early sight, to be important. Between midnight and the quarter-hour she felt her eyes closing, pushed her notebook aside, turned the key in the front door, switched out the last of the lights and went to bed.

*　　*　　*

Will had gone for a run that morning, pulling on an old Simple Minds T-shirt and some shorts on the landing, then lacing up his running shoes in the dark of the downstairs hall; as he stepped out through the front door, he slipped an orange reflective vest with Day-Glo stripes over his shoulders: no sense getting sideswiped by some half-awake driver who failed to pick him out in the slow-rising light.

The air was raw in his mouth as he went beyond the furthest edge of the village and turned off along the fen. Mist hung over the blackened water and drifted, wraithlike, above the rutted surface of the fields. It would be another quarter of a mile or so before the knots disappeared from his legs and he could relax into the rhythm, lock off all thought of what he was doing – the need to put one foot down after the other, the slight ache in his side – and let whatever thoughts slip through him, higgledy-piggledy, as they might. The first blows, had they been struck in the shower or earlier? Will saw a man turning under the full spray of water, eyes squinched almost shut, hair splayed out flat upon the dome of his head. He would have felt the impact of the first blow before realising what was happening. And then another: another. More than a fist. Something hard, metallic, possibly. A hammer? Like a leviathan, the bulk of Ely Cathedral rose out of the mist.

Mark McKusick was in good spirits. Confirmation had come through that morning that a £17,000 order from an American couple for equipping their Chester Street house had been confirmed. Both academics, they had taken the house on a long lease, and had wanted the best audio and DVD technology their not inconsiderable salaries could buy. McKusick had first convinced them of the wisdom of investing in a fully integrated set-up, then demonstrated the beauties of a plasma surround-sound system with adjacent Artisan Acoustic speakers supported by a sub-woofer, and compatible speakers in all of the other main rooms. Everything controlled by a simple Philips Pronto universal touch-screen remote. Looked great, sounded great, cost no more than they could afford, and in nine months' time he'd be getting back to them about upgrading to a superior surround-sound amplifier and hard disc soundserver.

He was still counting the prospective commission on that little lot, when the buzzer sounded over the main door and a few moments later one of the other assistants put his head round the door of the multi-room department that was Mark McKusick's domain.

'Asking for you.'

McKusick strolled out into the body of the shop, sizing up the couple at the centre of the floor. A man in his mid- to late-thirties, tall, wearing a dark suit that had seen better days, tie loosely knotted, blue shirt, his brown hair in need of a trim; the woman with him was five or six years younger, black trousers and a black T-shirt under a waist-length leather jacket, little obvious make-up, thick dark hair cut short and not without a certain style: no way they were going to be spending more than a thousand, two tops, and then only if the man could get away with keeping the exact cost secret.

'Morning. Mark McKusick. How can I help?'

Both handshakes were firm, businesslike, her grip, if anything, the stronger; their eyes stayed focused on his.

'Detective Inspector Grayson,' Will said, showing his warrant card. 'This is Detective Sergeant Walker. Is there somewhere we can talk?'

No sale then, McKusick thought. It wasn't until they were seated in the smaller of the two demonstration rooms that it occurred to him this might be about something other than some stolen hi-fi.

'Stephen Bryan,' Will said, 'you're a friend?'

'Yes.'

'Know him well?'

'Yes, yes. Why? Why do you want to know?'

'When did you last see him?' Helen Walker asked.

'Stephen?'

'Yes, Stephen.'

Something low in McKusick's gut was starting to squirm. 'Not . . . not for a while now. A good few weeks, I suppose, a month or so. I'm not sure.'

'But if you're such good friends . . .'

'We . . . well, we decided to stop seeing one another, so much of one another anyway.' McKusick's throat was dry and he could hear, louder than usual, the sound of his own breathing.

'You had a row.'

'No.'

'A falling out.'

'No.'

Will was sitting with his hands held steady, fingers lightly interlocked. Helen's elbows were resting on the arms of her chair, relaxed; she was having trouble marrying the writer of those sexually explicit letters with the man in front of them. But then, with sex you never could tell.

'What's happened?' McKusick said. 'Something's happened.'

They looked back at him without expression, their gaze unfaltering.

'You don't know?' Will said.

'Don't know what?'

'Yesterday morning, Stephen Bryan was found murdered.'

McKusick recoiled as if he'd been thumped in the chest; the colour blanched from his face. Head turned aside, he leaned low over the side of the chair and retched, but aside from spittle and a few thin strings of saliva, nothing emerged. His eyes stung but as yet there were no tears.

'Here,' Helen said, handing him a couple of tissues from her bag.

'How . . . ?' McKusick began, then stopped.

'He was beaten,' Will said, with a slight softening of his voice.

The pain in McKusick's chest was real, something pressing against his breastbone, against his ribs. It was becoming more and more difficult to breathe. 'Where? Where did it happen?'

24

'In his own home.'

McKusick's cry was a wail of pain. Falling forward on to his knees, he began punching himself in the face with his fists.

'Don't,' Will said, catching hold of McKusick's wrists. 'Don't.'

Helen left the room and when she returned with a cup of water, Will was bending over McKusick, holding his arms and talking to him quietly, earning trust.

'Drink this,' Helen said, and Will stood away.

McKusick took the drink in both hands.

'We'll need to talk to you,' Helen said. 'At the station.'

McKusick looked at her vaguely and then nodded his head.

'We should go now,' Will said a few moments later, offering to help him to his feet.

'I shall just have to explain . . . my boss . . .'

'Of course.'

The early morning mist had cleared leaving a wan sky; a breeze, slight for the time of year, barely disturbed the trees, yet McKusick was shivering nonetheless as they led him to the waiting car.

That early in the inquiry, detectives would be working as close to round the clock as motivation and overtime would allow: uniformed officers would be helping with house-to-house, and civilian staff would be setting up files, starting to cross-reference information and accessing it on to computers. As senior investigating officer, it was Will's job, assisted by the office manager, to establish priorities and ensure that all viable leads were followed up. Each move, each policy decision he agreed or set in motion, would be carefully recorded.

For some, this was an invitation to slip behind a desk and demonstrate powers of organisation, delegation, play mastermind. But for Will, the crux of what he did was still what happened out on the street, confronting suspects face to face, the heat, the heart of the action. When necessary, he knew Helen to be the most capable of deputies, but together, he felt, they could achieve more than they could apart.

And these first days were crucial. Without results, the adrenalin would cease to race and the number of officers involved in the investigation would be cut back; not so long after that, someone else would likely be brought in to look over Will's shoulder and pick out what he'd missed, point out where the investigation had gone awry.

He didn't want that to happen.

Detailed results of the post-mortem had been promised for the following morning, along with the first results from samples taken at the scene; until then officers were following up on the names garnered from Stephen Bryan's diaries or letters, together with those of any friends or close colleagues mentioned by either his parents or the university.

Which left Mark McKusick . . .

'What did you think of the show?' Helen asked once they were back at the station and McKusick was safely out of earshot.

'You think that's what it was, a show?'

'Punching himself in the face.'

'He was upset . . .'

'I'll say.'

'Distraught.'

'Careful to miss his eyes and nose, you notice that?'

'He'd just heard someone he cared for had been murdered, what do you expect?'

'Something more than play-acting.'

'If that's what it was.'

A smile crossed Helen's face. 'You ever do drama at school?'

'Not if I could help it. Why?'

'I was the White Rabbit once in *Alice in Wonderland*. This born-again hippy drama teacher reckoned it was all some kind of druggy fantasy, dreamed up by poor old Lewis Carroll on laudanum or whatever the Victorians used to get spaced out on. So that was our school show. Strobe lights and patchouli and lots of stoned sixties music. You know, Grace Slick and Jefferson Airplane. One pill makes you larger, one pill makes you small.'

'Grace who?' Will said.

'Never mind. I was fourteen years old, never done drugs in my life. The occasional drag on someone else's spliff aside. But I had that white rabbit spinning through an amphetamine trance so convincingly, on the second night a drug counsellor came up after the show and practically begged me to make an appointment.'

'And your point is?'

'Maybe it takes a faker to tell a fake.'

*   *   *

Mark McKusick had washed his face in cold water, combed his hair, straightened his clothes; most of the colour had returned to his cheeks. He had asked if he needed to contact a lawyer and been told that at this stage there probably wasn't any need. This was little more than a chat, informal, simply to establish some background. He was doing them a favour by being there, Will was careful to make clear, helping the police with their inquiries. Whenever he'd a mind, he could get up and leave.

Somehow it didn't altogether feel like that, not to McKusick, nor was it entirely meant to.

'What happened?' he said, as soon as Will and Helen entered the room. 'What happened to Stephen, was it . . . I mean, whoever did it, was it somebody who'd broken in? A burglary?'

'All in good time,' Will said. 'All in good time.'

'I want to see him,' McKusick said suddenly. 'Stephen, I want to see him.'

'I'm afraid it's not possible right now.'

'I have the right . . .'

'I know, I know. But you do appreciate the urgency . . . There are questions we need to ask.'

McKusick breathed out slowly. 'Very well.'

'Your relationship with Stephen Bryan, from what you've said, it was long-standing?'

'Our relationship? I don't see what that can have to do . . .'

'Please just answer the question. Your relationship, it was long-standing?'

'Yes.'

'Serious.'

'Yes. But I still don't see . . . ?'

'You'd both signed a contract? A civil partnership?'

'No, not that.'

'Lived together then?'

'Not exactly.'

Will leaned back.

'Look,' McKusick said, feeling the need to explain. 'We spent almost all our free time in each other's company. Evenings, weekends, holidays. We just . . . well, we just didn't live together, that's all.'

'And you were happy with that?' Helen asked.

McKusick was surprised at the question. 'It was what Stephen wanted.'

'Not you?'

Looking at her, he hesitated. 'It wouldn't have been my choice, no.'

'But you accepted it?'

'Yes, of course.' He tried for a smile that didn't quite come off. 'Compromise, you know?'

Bollocks to that, Helen thought. 'And was that the reason you split up?'

'No, not really.'

'No?'

'Look . . .' McKusick bit down a little on the inside of his mouth. 'It's never that simple.'

'So, what happened?' Will asked. 'You had a row or what?'

'Not really, no.'

'Still, some kind of a falling out?'

'If you like.'

'A tiff?'

'Yes, I suppose . . .'

'A lovers' tiff?'

McKusick shook his head. 'It wasn't serious, if that's what you mean. Is that what you mean? It's like I said before. We just decided to see less of one another for a while, that's all. Take a break.'

'And this was mutual?' Helen asked.

'Yes.'

'Mutual,' Helen said nodding slightly, speaking to herself as much as anyone.

They both looked at McKusick and waited.

'Stephen,' McKusick said eventually, 'I suppose it was more his idea than mine. He had all this teaching now, more than he was used to. Since coming to Cambridge. More students. New courses. And then there's this book he's been working on. That was taking a lot of time, too. It was really important. To him, anyway. He wanted a little more space, more time. I mean, it's easy for me, once my job's done, it's done, you know? I don't mean I'm not interested, I am, I like what I do, but at the end of the day . . . well . . .' He gestured with open hands. 'But for Stephen, it's his life. Films, movies, writing, teaching, it's all one. It doesn't leave a lot of room for . . . well, for anything. For somebody else.'

He sniffed and wiped a hand across his face as if he might have been wiping back a tear and Will wondered if that was acting, too; if Helen was right and he had been pantomiming before.

'You were together how long?' Helen asked, looking for a sympathetic tone.

'Three years.'

'That's a long time,' she said. Longer than I've ever managed, she thought. A bloody sight longer. 'You couldn't have been altogether happy with that?' she said. 'That arrangement?'

McKusick all but smiled. 'We did try living together for a while. When Stephen was still in Leicester. I thought it was fine. I really did. I mean, it wasn't perfect, nothing is, but Stephen, he said he couldn't work, not with me there all the time. I wasn't, of course, but that was how it seemed to him.'

'So you moved back out?'

'Yes.'

'You were working in Leicester then?' Will asked.

'That's right.'

'And when Stephen got a job here, you upped sticks and followed suit?'

'Yes.'

'Really, then,' Helen said, 'you put yourself out for him quite a lot?'

'I suppose so.'

'He was calling all the shots.'

McKusick shrugged.

'Come on. You chucked in your job, found somewhere else to live and no sooner had you done all that than he turned round and said he didn't want to see you any more.'

31

McKusick shook his head. 'That's an oversimplification.'

'But it's what happened.'

McKusick didn't answer.

'If that were me,' Helen said, 'if someone treated me that way, I'd be royally pissed off. To put it mildly.'

'So? What? I lost my temper and bashed him round the head? Is that what you're saying?'

'Did you?'

'Don't be ridiculous.'

'Is it ridiculous?' Will asked.

'Of course it is.'

Will took a beat. 'What made you think,' he said, 'that Stephen had been bashed around the head?'

'I don't know. I don't know what happened, do I? You won't tell me.'

'Even so, bashed round the head, that's what you said.'

'And that's supposed to prove something?'

'Let's see,' Will said. 'He could have been stabbed, shot, poisoned, gassed, strangled, strung out from a beam, anything.'

'Crucified,' Helen suggested quietly.

'But you chose beaten around the head,' Will said. 'I wonder why?'

Will fetched two coffees from the machine and, despite the cold, they stood outside so that Helen could smoke a cigarette. For a moment, Mark McKusick had looked surprised when, after the usual warnings about not changing

32

his address, not leaving the country and so on, they had told him he could go. They would, it was made abundantly clear, be wanting to speak to him again. He had looked over his shoulder not once, but twice, descending the shallow steps away from the station, as if half-expecting to be called back.

'You still think he's lying?' Will asked.

'Still?'

'Play-acting, then.'

'Doesn't have to be the same thing.'

'No?'

'No.' Helen drew smoke down into her lungs, held it there, then, head averted, released it in a slow, blue-grey stream. 'I mean, you might behave in a certain way because you think that's what's expected of you, because you want to convince people of what you're feeling. That doesn't mean the feelings themselves aren't true.'

'And in this case? You think he's selling us a bill of goods?'

Helen shrugged. 'It's what salesmen do.' She dropped the end of her cigarette to the ground, swivelled it flat with the sole of her shoe, and grinned. 'But how the fuck should I know? You're the SIO.'

3

Stephen Bryan's wallet was found in a green recycling bin less than half a mile from where he had lived. Most of the contents had been recycled, certainly, only a creased five-euro note and an out-of-date Tate membership card remaining. Of the laptop, there was still no sign and, without sending officers round to every car boot sale in the county and having them check assiduously on eBay, he doubted if there ever would be.

The post-mortem showed that Bryan's skull had been fractured in five places, as a result of having been struck numerous times by a wooden implement which seemed to have been wielded as a club. Several tiny splinters had been found embedded in his skull and were being sent for further analysis.

Initial tests showed that the blood in the shower matched Bryan's and Bryan's alone. If he had fought back, there were no physical signs, no skin trapped under the fingernails of his hands as might then have been the case. It was as if, Will thought, Bryan's attacker had been able to take him completely by surprise.

But how?

Unbeknown to Bryan, had he gained access to the house and climbed the stairs, finding Bryan, naked and unsuspecting and at his mercy? There were no signs of forced entry, which suggested that, were this the case, whoever it was had been in possession of a key. The alternative scenario was that the murderer had been already in the house when Bryan went off to take his shower. Which in itself suggested something about the relationship between them. Not lovers necessarily, but, Will thought, two people who knew one another quite well and were at ease in one another's company.

Despite his protestations, Mark McKusick could easily be made to fit either version of the story.

Paul Irving was the Family Liaison Officer attached to the case, and it was his responsibility to accompany McKusick to the viewing of Stephen Bryan's body. Irving was a slim, bespectacled man with light brown hair and an unassuming expression that could easily be read as sympathetic. Looks aside, perhaps his greatest asset as liaison officer was a voice that was low and warm and, in other circumstances, could have been used to sell toilet paper or personal insurance.

Will had made it clear that he wanted to be present, but if he had been expecting McKusick to break down and reveal something crucial, he was disappointed. Tears came readily to McKusick's eyes at the sight of his former lover's body, but that was all; although visibly shaken, there were no histrionics, there was no more self-flagellation. Instead, for several minutes, McKusick closed his eyes and his lips moved in what Will assumed was silent prayer. Then he turned and, head bowed, walked away.

Irving raised an eyebrow questioningly in Will's direction and Will shrugged and shook his head. Later that day, Irving would be meeting Bryan's family at the railway station and escorting them to see what was barely recognisable as their son.

'Well,' Irving said, 'he didn't exactly break down and confess.'

'That'll be the day when they do.'

'How is it going?'

Will raised a smile. 'Slowly?'

House-to-house inquiries had so far yielded little: Stephen Bryan's neighbours were the type that kept themselves to themselves, eyes glued to the screens of their home computers or, given the demographics of the area, whatever documentaries were being shown on BBC 4. No one had noticed anything suspicious at or around the time of Bryan's murder; nobody had seen what Will wanted: Stephen Bryan entering the house with another man, McKusick or someone else, as yet unknown. Nor had they seen somebody other than Bryan leaving alone.

Will and Helen, separately or together, had had initial

conversations with Bryan's former colleagues in the Department of Communication Studies at the University: Bryan, though not yet all that well known, had been generally liked and respected as someone who prepared his lectures assiduously and seemed to take his departmental responsibilities seriously. His students, by all accounts, had responded well to his manner and his teaching.

'You ever feel,' Will asked as they were driving back from the main campus, 'no matter how far you go, you're not really getting anywhere?'

Helen stared back at him scornfully, as if the question didn't deserve answering.

'McKusick,' Helen said. 'That's where we're concentrating?'

Unable to find a space in the station car park, they found one on the street close by.

'Until someone can show me a better suspect,' Will said, 'yes.'

Helen lowered one of the windows and lit a cigarette. 'The motive being rejection? Bryan calling a halt to the relationship?'

'I think McKusick believed what he told us,' Will said. 'The break-up was only temporary, some kind of breathing space.'

'And Bryan thought otherwise?'

'Who knows? He might even have had his reasons for allowing McKusick to think the door wasn't completely closed.'

'Letting him off lightly?'

'Trying to.'

'But McKusick pushes him . . .'

'Wants a decision . . .'

'Urges Bryan to change his mind.'

'Pushes him too hard until what he finally hears from Bryan is the truth. It's over. Bryan's not going to change his mind at all.' Will clicked forefinger against thumb. 'McKusick finally snaps. Bingo.'

'While Bryan's in the shower?' Helen said. 'They're arguing in the shower?'

'No, the argument's over by then. As far as Bryan's concerned, anyway. Could be he even takes a shower as a way of saying to McKusick, listen, we've nothing else to talk about, I need to get ready. You can let yourself out.'

'Which leaves McKusick fuming.'

'Exactly. And instead of letting himself out, he follows Bryan into the bathroom.' Will brought the back of his clenched fist down into the palm of his other hand with a slap.

'There's just one thing wrong with that,' Helen said.

'Only one?'

'The weapon.'

'What about it?'

'Either it was something Bryan had left conveniently around in the house, in which case what? Or was it something the murderer had brought with him . . .'

'Which argues against a sudden loss of temper . . .'

'And suggests premeditation.'

38

'Exactly.'

For several moments, neither of them spoke.

'You're not thinking of charging him?' Helen said. 'McKusick?'

'Not yet,' Will said. 'We're not even close.'

'But we'll talk to him again?'

'Oh, yes. I think so, don't you?'

That evening, while Will, to Jake's rowdy delight, was sinking half his fleet of bath toys with a mixture of plastic darts and ping-pong balls, Lorraine was downstairs on the settee, trying to keep her eyes open through another episode of *EastEnders*.

Helen, meantime, back home in her small terraced house, was running a bath of her own, opening a bottle of wine, glancing at the paper, getting undressed. A few weeks before she had spotted a CD by a singer-songwriter she liked, Dar Williams, bought it and brought it home and there it had sat, beside the stereo, still in its wrapping, unplayed. When she opened it, the cellophane, as it always did, stuck to her hand and it took her several attempts before she could prise it clear and set the recording to play.

Upstairs in the bathroom, she tested the water with her elbow and then her toes, dribbled in a little more Weleda bath essence, a present from her ecologically minded elder sister, splashed it around and then slowly lowered herself in.

Gorgeous!

One of the greatest pleasures in life and, unlike a

number of others, with any luck and a little judicious scrubbing, you got out cleaner than you went in.

She closed her eyes and went over the day.

Mark McKusick punching himself in the face in a display of grief.

We were in a relationship. A serious relationship. For years.

Living together?

Not exactly.

What had Will said? *You ever feel, no matter how far you go, you're not really getting anywhere?*

Just a little, Will, Helen thought, just a touch.

Eyes still closed, she slid lower in the bath till most of her body was immersed; comfortable, music just audible from below, she remained in that position, more or less, until she felt the water beginning to grow cold around her. Then it was a quick wash and a brisk rub dry before she pulled on sweat pants and an oversize T-shirt and carried her empty glass back downstairs. The CD had finished and, volume lowered, she set it to play again. In the mirror, hair unkempt and still wet, face free of make-up, she could read all too clearly the lines around her eyes. Though she hadn't dialled the number in a long time, she still knew it by heart. She got as far as the final digit before stopping.

You idiot, she thought, you fool, and, lighting a cigarette, she poured herself another glass of wine.

Will stood outside on the low wooden porch, hands in the pockets of his winter coat, scarf wound tight. When

Lorraine had finally fallen asleep in front of the TV, the kids already fast off upstairs, he had taken a brisk walk to the edge of the fen and now, back at the house, he stood quite still, staring out across the dark expanse of fields towards the town, some eight or nine miles off. It was silent in a way the city had never been; more stars overhead than he had ever seen. Their first six months here had been hell.

Will had complained endlessly about the drive, the time it took to and from work, the idiot drivers on the road; when finally he arrived back at the end of a gruelling day, his son, more often than not, was already in his bed, asleep. And Lorraine, still breast-feeding Jake, hormonal, exhausted, shorn of her friends and the easy access to their support, had been bereft; stranded amidst cabbages and clanking farm machinery and people from the village who looked down on her if they bothered to look at her at all.

'You're the one dragged us out here,' Lorraine had said. Yet another evening when Will came home moaning, almost an hour later than he'd promised, the dinner solidifying in the bottom of the oven.

'Don't talk such bloody nonsense,' Will had retorted, kicking off his shoes. 'You were the one wanted to move, more than me.'

'Out of the city, yes. Somewhere nice. Not a God-forsaken dump like this.'

'Well, this God-forsaken dump, as you call it, was all we could afford.'

'Then maybe we should have stayed put where we were.'

41

'Like it so much, why don't you move back?'

'And what'd you do? Stay here?'

'Maybe I would.'

Lorraine let out a loud, humourless laugh. 'And Jake? What about Jake?'

Will pushed past her and pulled open the fridge door, looking for a beer.

'Well?' she persisted. 'What about Jake in this grand master plan of yours? He's not exactly going to stay here with you.'

'Lorraine, for Christ's sake, leave it be.'

'No, come on, tell me.'

Will slammed the fridge door shut. 'You just won't let it alone, will you?'

'What?'

'Anything. Any bloody little thing. On and on. You never know when to fucking stop.'

'And you do?'

Snapping the top from the can, he brushed past her on his way to the door.

'You do, Will?'

Turning, he slammed the beer down on the side. 'Yes, I fucking do!'

A moment later he was on the stairs, taking them two or three steps at a time. When Lorraine, following him, pulled open the bedroom door, he was pushing things into a bag, shirts, trousers, socks, anything.

'What are you doing?'

'What does it look as if I'm doing?'

'Putting on a show?'

'Yeah?' Grabbing hold of a shirt, he thrust it towards her face.

'Does this look like a fucking show?'

'You wouldn't dare.'

'No?'

'Leaving us both, you wouldn't have the guts.'

'Watch me.' Seizing the bag, he started for the door.

'Will . . .'

His feet were fast and heavy on the stairs.

'Will . . .'

He was throwing the bag into the back seat of the car, ducking behind the wheel.

'Will, don't you dare.'

The car door slammed; the engine lurched into life.

He could just hear her shout, her face up close against the glass, inches from his face. 'You do this and I never want to see your face again. Not ever.'

The wheels spun for a moment on the gravel, then caught. Trapped in the porchlight, she was there for a few seconds in his mirror, then gone.

By the time Will reached the main road, he realised he was driving too fast, steadied and slowed. Turning off on to a side road, a farm track and little more, he stopped the car just past a low, dark barn and sat, shaking, one hand still fixed to the wheel. A ring of yellow light clung, narrow, to the horizon, all but blocked out by the dark. Everything he had: everything he had ever wanted. His son. He sat there until the cold slid deep into his bones.

When he let himself back into the house, hours later, everything was quiet, no lights on, up or down. He fully expected Lorraine to be in bed, but she was in the living room, just sitting, legs drawn up.

Will switched on the light.

There was no colour in her face, her hair scraped back.

'Turn it out.'

He turned it out.

After a moment, she swung her legs down and came slowly towards him.

'I'm sorry,' he said.

She slapped him hard across the face.

'Really sorry.'

She slapped him again, once, twice.

Blood trickled from his upper lip and he could taste it in his mouth.

'Lorraine . . .'

He reached for her hand, but she pulled it away, and they stood there, the silence folding around them, not speaking, not touching, until finally they went upstairs to bed.

4

When Will woke and went downstairs, it was closer to three than four. Outside, in the light from the porch, he watched as flakes of snow hazed lazily down and vanished the moment they touched the ground.

Something had woken him and he wondered what it was. The fox again, roving wild? Hungry and wild.

He didn't often think of Helen at times like this, but now he did. Wondering if she, too, were awake. Alone. A while ago there had been a man, though Will had never met him nor heard Helen say his name. Even so, somehow he had known. Just the most cursory of mentions, a few small changes of routine. And then he was gone. Dismissed? Walked off? Will didn't know. He didn't ask.

Things went on as before.

One evening before Christmas when Helen had been to the house for supper, nothing elaborate, lasagne and then ice cream from the freezer, Lorraine had made a remark – not meaning anything, just making conversation, a question, Will supposed it was – about boyfriends, men friends – he couldn't remember the term she'd used – and Helen had bridled, angrily, resentment clear in her eyes and the set of her mouth.

When Lorraine had asked him about it later, without knowing why, he'd claimed not to have noticed.

The snow, such as it had been, had ceased to fall. Lorraine and the children were all upstairs in their separate beds, asleep.

Will stood there a few moments longer before switching off the light and going back inside.

For McKusick, the days since Stephen Bryan's death had not been easy: dreams, nightmares, memories of Stephen's ruined face. Regrets. Plenty of those.

'It helps to talk to someone,' the liaison officer had said. 'Someone else who knew him well.'

He had telephoned Stephen's parents, as much out of obligation as anything else, wanting to be seen to do the right thing. But the conversation with Stephen's mother had been stilted, broken by long silences and uneven breathing. His father had refused to come to the phone. And, of course, McKusick realised, they hadn't really known Stephen, not since he had left home, had hardly known him at all. When Stephen had come out all the way and had finally convinced his father that he was gay, a light had gone out in the older man's eyes. 'Stephen, I'm sorry,' he had said, as if his son had just told him he had something akin to a tumour of the brain.

'You want to meet them?' the liaison officer had asked. 'The parents? When they're down?'

McKusick had declined.

'You don't look so hot, Mark,' McKusick's boss had said, the morning after viewing the body. 'Why don't you take a little time?' But the last thing McKusick wanted was more time on his own. That or Will and Helen walking back into the shop and asking for him by name.

They sat in the same demonstration room as before, a couple of Rega R7 speakers angled towards them, something short of £1,500 the pair and, McKusick would have argued, cheap at the price.

'There were just one or two more things we wanted to ask,' Will said.

McKusick waited.

'When you and Stephen broke up, according to what you said before, that was because of his work, his need for time and space, that kind of thing?'

'That's right.'

'No other reason?'

'Not that I know of, no.'

'Not that you know of?'

'No.'

'So there could have been something else, something that, for whatever reason, he wasn't telling you?'

McKusick shifted a little on his chair. 'It's possible, but, no, that wasn't the kind of relationship we had. If there'd been anything, anything important, he would have said.'

'Even if he'd been seeing somebody else?'

McKusick laughed. 'That's absurd.'

'Absurd that it would happen, or that he wouldn't tell you about it?'

'Either. Both.'

'Yours was an open relationship, then?' Helen said.

'In what sense?'

'Whatever sense you take it to mean.'

McKusick shook his head. 'If you mean were we frank with one another about our feelings, I'd say yes. But if you mean did either of us feel free to live up to the stereotype, then no.'

'Which stereotype is that?'

'Oh, come on.'

'No, please. Tell me.'

McKusick looked at her before answering. 'The one so-called straights are so fond of touting. Promiscuity, cruising, more sex than you can shake a stick at.'

'You mean it's not like that?' Helen said, sardonically.

'Not at all.'

'You and Stephen,' Will said, taking over, 'while you were together, you were both faithful?'

'I don't see that's any of your business.'

'Really? Isn't that a little naive?'

'What do you mean?'

'Your ex-partner's found murdered in his house, presumably by another man, there are no signs of forced entry, and you can't see why we might be asking about fidelity?'

48

McKusick drew breath. 'It's different now.'

'Because you were no longer together?'

'Yes.'

'So whoever did this, it could have been someone he'd met? Somebody new?'

'No.'

'No?'

McKusick shook his head. 'I don't think so. I mean, I suppose it's possible, in theory, but, no, I really don't think so.'

'Why ever not?' Helen asked.

'Because the whole point of our breaking up was to leave Stephen free, like I said, to give him more time and space. Not to become entangled all over again.'

'There are different kinds of relationships,' Helen said. 'They don't all require a lot of time or space.'

McKusick passed a hand across his face.

'And without wanting to get into that gay scene thing you were denying,' Helen went on, 'isn't it possible this was just someone he met for sex? Someone casual?'

'No.' McKusick sounded definite.

'But you can't be sure.'

'I can.'

'How? How can you be?'

'I knew him. I loved him.'

'That doesn't mean . . .' Helen allowed the sentence to peter out.

'Look,' McKusick said, 'the scene, as you call it, it was anathema to Stephen. He hated it. You'd no more get him into a gay bar than you could persuade him to – I don't know – go and see Leicester City on a Saturday afternoon.'

'There are other ways of meeting people, surely,' Will said, 'nowadays especially.'

'You mean the Internet?'

'Amongst others.' Will seemed to remember reading somewhere that the playwright Joe Orton met most of his rough trade on building sites. Hadn't that been in Leicester?

'Let me tell you,' McKusick said, leaning forward, 'a story about Stephen. This happened more than two years ago, close to three, we hadn't all that long been a couple. On this particular night, this was before we moved here, we were in a pub close to the city centre. Not a gay pub at all, nothing like that, but anyway we're sitting there, drinking, and suddenly, out of nowhere, we had this row. I can't even remember what it was about, not exactly, nothing important anyway, and besides, the row isn't the point. There was a bit of shouting, a bit of swearing, and it ended up with me banging down my glass and storming out. Which was when this bloke, he'd been sitting close by, came over to Stephen and called me a bit of a tosser. To which Stephen replied – he told me this later – I had to be good at something. The bloke laughed and asked Stephen if he wanted another drink and Stephen said yes and an hour or so later the two of them went back to this bloke's flat and fetched up in bed. Which might have been all right, except after a bit, the bloke gets up and says he has to go to the loo and a few minutes later the bedroom door opens and it's another guy, someone else altogether, and this one is not good news. He starts to get into bed with Stephen and Stephen says sorry, he's not interested, and then the first bloke comes back and the two of them, they take it in turns till Stephen's bleeding and then they throw him out. He phones me on his mobile, three in the morning.'

'They raped him,' Will said.

'By any definition you care to use.'

'He reported it?'

'What would have been the point?'

'Rape is rape.'

'And gay men getting rougher trade than they bargained for is their own stupid fault.'

'Your words, not mine.'

'But isn't that what you think? What the majority of your colleagues would have thought, even if nowadays they might hesitate before saying it too loud?'

No sense in going there, Will thought. 'These men,' he said, 'do you know who they were?'

'No, and it doesn't matter. Not now. What matters is that after what happened, there's no way Stephen would have taken a risk like that again. He would have been terrified.'

'In which case,' Will said, 'if Stephen did invite whoever killed him into his house, the probability is that it was someone he already knew.'

McKusick repeated a little sideways gesture with his head and sighed. 'I suppose so,' he said. 'You don't know that, though, do you? That it was someone he knew? I mean, just because there were no obvious signs of a break-in, that doesn't mean it couldn't have happened.'

Neither Will nor Helen answered.

'Things were missing,' McKusick said, persevering. 'That's right, isn't it? On the news, it said . . .'

'His laptop appears to have been taken,' Will said. 'Cash. Possibly some papers.'

'What kind of papers?'

'As yet we don't know.'

'But were they important, or . . .'

'As I say, as yet we don't know.'

'In the meantime,' Helen said, 'perhaps you'll be good enough to help us with a list of Stephen's friends and acquaintances, gay or straight, it doesn't matter. There may well be people we haven't spoken to yet.'

'There's a sister,' McKusick said. 'Lesley. In New Zealand, I think. I assume her parents will have told her what happened, but I don't know.'

'Put it all down,' Will said. 'Anyone in particular you can remember him mentioning from work as well.'

'Of course,' McKusick said. 'I'll do what I can.'

Helen offered him a pen.

Will was sure he could remember a time, not so far back, when if someone had told him he'd fork out two pounds for a cup of coffee he'd have called them daft.

'Any cakes or pastries at all?' asked the young woman behind the counter, *barista in training* emblazoned on the front of her uniform.

Will shook his head, pocketed the change from his five-pound note and carried the two lattes over to where Helen was browsing, somewhat incongruously, through a copy of the previous day's *La Repubblica*.

'Didn't know your Italian was that good,' Will said.

'It's not.' Helen reached sideways and slid the newspaper back into the rack.

'You believe McKusick's story?'

'The one he told about Stephen?'

Will nodded.

'Yes, I think so.' Helen sipped her coffee and when she lowered the cup away, there was a faint smear of milk along her upper lip. 'That doesn't mean I agree with his conclusion.'

'You don't think what happened – the rape – you don't think that would be enough to prevent him ever putting himself in that situation again?'

'Certain kinds of pain,' Helen said, 'it doesn't matter how severe they are at the time, how much we swear we're never going to submit to them again, somehow, if we think the pay-off might be worthwhile, we forget, take the risk. Why else would women go on having children, for instance?'

'Hang on, you're not equating childbirth and . . . ?'

'You know what I'm saying.'

'So you think, despite what happened before, he might have gone out cruising and picked up the wrong person?'

'It's possible.'

Will set his coffee back down. 'The way he was

beaten – that amount of anger – it's either deeply, deeply personal or else, I don't know, maybe it's the opposite. Not personal at all.'

'But not just robbery? You're not thinking robbery?'

'No.'

'You think it's because of what he was. Because he was gay.'

'One way or another, yes. Probably.'

'I was thinking,' Helen said, a few moments later, 'that case not so long back, one guy beaten to death on the common – I know it's not the same, but . . .'

'You're right,' Will said. 'It's not the same.'

Helen drank a little more of her coffee. Two women came in with five children and two buggies between them and manoeuvred the buggies so that no one else could easily enter or exit. The place, she thought, was turning into a crèche.

'What McKusick was saying,' she said, 'about people thinking someone who gets raped has been asking for it, you think that's true?'

'It depends on the circumstances, but, yes, I think a lot of people do.'

'People on the force?'

'We're no different from anybody else.'

'Maybe we should be.'

'It's difficult, isn't it?' Will lowered his voice. 'You know what it's like. A young woman comes into the station, early hours of the morning, alcohol levels way over the limit, skimpy top showing everything she's got, skirt up round her waist almost, claiming she's been raped. It's hard not to think to some degree, at least, she's contributed to that.'

'You mean it's her fault?'

'I'm not saying that.'

'Aren't you?'

'What I'm saying, unless she's spent the last ten years living in a convent, she knows what it's like out there, pubs and clubs, Friday, Saturday nights. You get yourself tarted up . . .'

'Tarted up, Will?'

'All right, make yourself as attractive as you can. But then it's cheap lager, cheap drinks, alcopops, Bacardi Breezers, whatever. Next thing you know you're half-pissed and you're putting yourself at risk.'

'And you deserve what you get?'

'Jesus! How many more times? That's not what I'm saying.'

'Well, it's still the way it sounds.'

Will sighed. 'Look, you put your hand in a trap, unless you're really stupid you expect you might lose some fingers. If you're a gay bloke and you go out looking for sex and follow someone into the bushes the same thing applies, you should know the risk. All the risks. And if you're a young woman, out on the town, the same again. I think it's too easy to say men are beasts, no better than animals, shuffle off all the blame. You have to be aware, take some responsibility for your own actions, that's what I mean.'

'And you'll tell your daughter that, when she's of an age? Your son, too?'

'Yes.'

'And when one of them comes home in the early hours, bleeding, raped, what will you say then? You should have known better? You should have known the risks?'

Will's face darkened.

'Well?' Helen said.

'It's time we left,' Will said. 'We've got a job to do.'

He swallowed down the rest of his coffee and Helen followed suit. The car was parked close by. Neither of them spoke again until they were almost at the station.

'Stephen Bryan,' Helen said then, 'there's no evidence he'd had sex before he was killed?'

'None so far. I doubt everything that went off to the lab'll be back for a couple more days.'

'We've got someone out checking the gay clubs anyway? Showing Bryan's picture? Whatever McKusick's just said.'

Will nodded. 'Nick Moyles is doing the rounds.'

DS Moyles was active in the Lesbian and Gay Police Association, and, despite his occasional complaints, was often called to work on investigations in which the gay community were involved.

'I'm sure he'll thank you for that,' Helen said.

Will shrugged. 'Free drinks on our time.'

'But nothing back so far?'

'Nothing.'

For once there was a space in the car park and Will reversed neatly in. The air outside was brisk; the temperature had dropped and would drop again overnight.

'I'll be in in a minute,' Helen said, once they were out of the car. 'I'm just going to have a cigarette.'

Will gave her one of his 'your funeral' stares.

'McKusick,' Helen said. 'You still like him for this, don't you?'

The photograph of McKusick and Bryan came to Will's mind, the frame smashed, the picture itself torn and torn again. *I never want to see your face again.* 'Don't you?' he said.

Helen tapped a cigarette from the pack. 'Maybe. I'm not too sure.'

Will nodded and began to move off.

'I'm sorry,' Helen said. 'About earlier. Riding you like that. I didn't mean to get under your skin.'

Will smiled quickly. 'Yes, you did.' He stepped away. 'See you in a few minutes, okay?'

'Okay.' Helen clicked her lighter and used her thumb to lower the flame.

5

And when one of them comes home in the early hours, bleeding, raped, what will you say then? Will's reflection stared back at him from the glass. After she'd been fed, the baby had failed to settle and, leaving Lorraine to sleep, Will had lifted her from the cot, wrapped the blanket carefully around her and settled her where she liked to be, resting against his arm and chest, her head just above the crook of the arm, against the soft inside. The skin over her closed eyes was the faintest of mauves and wafer thin. *What will you say then?* He touched the tips of his fingers to her forehead, brushing the slightly damp hair aside, and, without waking, she stirred.

Sleep for Will, as was often the case, had been a parlous thing and lying there, attempting to juggle bits and pieces into place, no rest at all. The most recent batch of results from the lab had come through late that afternoon. The shape and size of several depressed fractures to Stephen Bryan's skull – indentations on the bone and grazing on the skin – suggested the use of a quite narrow hard-edged instrument – hard rather than sharp – and wood, they confirmed, rather than metal.

Several hairs not matching Bryan's own had been recovered from the living room settee, some from the bedroom, one from where it had snagged on the uneven edge of the bathroom door. According to the DNA, the majority of the hairs belonged, not surprisingly, to McKusick.

Traces of semen had been found on one of the towels that had been in the laundry basket, waiting to be washed: some was Bryan's, but not all. Not McKusick's either. The sample was being further tested, to see if there was a DNA match with any of the stray hairs that were otherwise unaccounted for. Either way, what the discovery of the semen did suggest, contrary to McKusick's assertions, was that at some point in the previous week, Bryan had had sex with someone as yet unknown.

Someone who might have killed him.

If Mark McKusick did not.

Of course, there was as yet no way of knowing if the person with whom Bryan had sex and the person who killed him were one and the same. They could, as easily, be two different men, men whose identity they did not yet know. And if it were two men, Will wondered, could they somehow be connected? Possibly through Bryan's sexuality? Or were they strangers? Never met?

Susie stirred again against his arm and then settled.

There was condensation, Will noticed, towards the corners of the window; the window itself deliberately wide to take advantage of the view. A broad swathe of sky, surprisingly few stars, the moon veiled in cloud. Fields that angled down towards the fen.

At certain times of the year those fields were busy with men and women, mostly men, bent over as they harvested the crop. Potatoes, kohlrabi, cabbages, beets. Poles, Lithuanians, Slovakians, Latvians, Czechs. Sometimes walking behind clanking machines, sometimes picking by hand. Before deductions, £4.50 an hour at best. At night, in certain months, he would see them, outlined in floodlight, stooped against the clock.

Susie shifted again and made a sound, small and fragile, in her sleep, and Will rested his lips against the top of her head, the fontanelle, the soft tissue where the cranial bones had yet to meet.

Stephen Bryan's skull had been fractured in five places.

Five.

He shifted position carefully, so that Susie's face tipped inwards towards his chest, her breath faint against his heart. The first hint of light at the horizon's edge.

What will you say then?

He didn't know.

The gutter press were living up to their traditions. Official police statements had been sparse, inquiries were ongoing, anyone with information should contact this number, the usual tight-lipped caution. Questions about Stephen Bryan's sexual orientation had been played down and, for the most part, ignored. But this only served to fuel the rumour mill, rather than the opposite; officers within the force, a few, paid back their not inconsiderable retainers with a mixture of fact and fanciful rumour. The more restrained of the media responded by mixing straight reporting with conjecture and innuendo; those to whom restraint was a dirty word printed lurid tales about rough trade and the twilight world of men who trawl for sex. *Cruising for a Bruising* ran one headline, a man's brutal murder reduced to a sub-editor's childish joke.

The truth, as far as Will and Helen could ascertain it, was more mundane, if less immediately useful. Strange faces in gay pubs and clubs tended to be noticed, but Bryan's photograph had so far elicited little positive response. A handful of possibles, a couple of weak maybes, nothing more. As Nick Moyles put it, if Bryan had gone social since moving to Cambridge there was, as yet, little sign. As to the single assignation of which there was recent proof – well, as Moyles said, 'You don't have to go to a gay club to meet gay men.' Adding, with a wink, 'The ready-cooked meal aisle at Sainsbury's is meant to be quite good, Will, if you've a mind.'

The investigation was in danger of stalling. The short list of names McKusick had provided had still be to be checked, but Will hadn't looked at it with any great hope.

He was on his way across the car park when a woman

got out of a somewhat elderly Peugeot and moved to intercept him.

'Detective Inspector Grayson? Can I have a word?'

She was early thirties, Will thought, bright faced, medium height, stocky rather than slight, reddish-brown hair that flicked out at the sides. A blue coat; smart red and grey bag, laptop size, over one shoulder.

'If you have a few moments?' The voice was professional, polite but firm. 'Lesley Scarman.' She was holding out her hand.

He didn't recognise the name, just the manner.

'You're a reporter.'

'BBC Radio Nottingham.'

'A little off your beat.'

'Scarman's my married name. Before that it was Bryan. I'm Stephen's sister.'

He could see it then in her face, enough of a family resemblance, something about the eyes, the set of the mouth.

'I thought you were in New Zealand,' Will said.

'I was. I got back a couple of months ago.'

She had an East Midlands accent, Will thought, tricked out with something else.

'I wanted to ask about the investigation,' Lesley said.

'What exactly?'

'How it's going, what progress you're making. Anything, really. Whatever you can tell me. I was going to come and see you yesterday, after seeing Stephen's body. With my parents. But they were in such a state afterwards, I didn't like to leave them.'

Why didn't Irving tell me? Will was wondering. Perhaps he had, an email or a message Will had not yet seen.

'I'm not sure,' he said, 'I can tell you a lot more than Paul Irving will have told you already.'

'Really?'

'Really.'

She fixed him with a look. 'You are in charge of the investigation?'

'That's correct,' Will said, on the back foot and less than comfortable.

'The liaison officer,' Lesley said, 'Irving? He spelled out the basic facts, gave us the party line, but that's all. He didn't tell us anything about any potential suspects, or which direction the investigation is heading. And it's not as if the police so far have been exactly forthcoming. Which means most of what's in the media, unless it's being fed from inside, is just speculation. Robbery, that's what it said in the papers. Some of the papers. The others are slathering over Stephen's sex life and precious little else.'

A patrol car carrying two uniformed officers pulled out from one of the spaces near where they were standing and they moved to one side to let it pass.

'Look,' Lesley said, 'you can imagine the condition my parents are in. I still don't think either of them can really believe what happened, even now. If there's anything I can tell them, anything positive, it will make a difference.'

Will hesitated, feeling he was being backed into a corner.

'I'm not asking for state secrets,' Lesley said, 'just

a conversation. And in case it's what's worrying you, anything you say, it won't get any further. This is nothing to do with my job, okay? It's personal. You've got my word.'

'You'd better come inside,' Will said.

While most of the CID accommodation was open plan, Will's seniority gave him office space of his own, a cubicle as he liked to call it, though there was room for a modest desk, a two-drawer filing cabinet and a couple of chairs. He asked Lesley if she wanted something to drink, tea or coffee, and, businesslike, she shook her head. Shrugging off the topcoat she was wearing, she hung it, at Will's suggestion, behind the door, over the North Face anorak he kept there against bad weather. The bag she set down at her feet.

'It might be easier,' Will said, 'if you tell me what you do know and then I can try to fill in a few gaps.'

'All right. But it's not a lot. That's the problem. Stephen was killed in his own house, I know that much. Beaten to death. Most likely, some of the papers have suggested, by someone he knew.'

Her voice started to go and, abruptly, she turned her head aside. Will thought she might be about to lose it altogether, break down in tears, but she recovered and carried on.

'Other than the suggestion that the motive might have been robbery, that's about it. That's all I know.'

'As I tried to say before, there isn't a great deal I can add,' Will said. 'I only wish there were.'

'But you must have some ideas? There must be suspects? Leads?'

'There are lines of inquiry we're following, of course.' He realised how lame it sounded; how like the standard anodyne press release.

'What you mean,' Lesley said, leaning back, 'you still haven't got a bloody clue who killed Stephen or why.'

'Look . . .' Will said angrily, then stopped. 'As you say, there is the possibility that burglary was a motive . . .'

'You really think so?'

'Well, your brother's laptop was stolen. His wallet, credit cards and so on. Much of the place had been turned upside down, the office and bedroom especially, as if perhaps whoever it was had been searching for something else worth taking.'

Lesley continued to stare at him, and, even though he partly believed what he was saying, to Will his words sounded hollow.

'One thing's clear,' Will said, 'there was no sign of a break-in. So the chances are whoever was responsible was almost certainly somebody Stephen had invited in. Which might mean it was someone he already knew, perhaps knew well – or it might have been someone he'd just met for the first time.'

'For sex, you mean?'

'Possibly.'

'Well, that's what you're implying, isn't it?'

Will spread his hands. 'It's a possibility we have to consider. That's all I'm saying.'

'And the motive is what? If it's not burglary?'

'I don't know. We don't know. Unless . . .'

'Unless what?'

'Unless it was some sort of hate crime . . .'

'And all this gay-bashing stuff half the media's revelling in is true. Homophobia rules. Stephen went out and picked up the wrong man, simple as that.'

Will sighed and said nothing.

'Is that what you believe?' Lesley asked.

'I keep telling you, I don't know.'

'You must have an opinion, surely?'

'All right, yes, it's a possibility.'

'That's all?'

'A strong possibility.'

Lesley slowly shook her head from side to side.

'You don't believe that?' Will said.

'No.'

'You really don't believe it, or you don't want to believe it?'

'If you're asking me do I like the idea my brother used to go looking for casual sex and that was what got him killed, then no, of course I don't. But if he ever picked up people in that way, for that reason, I just don't know. It's not something he would have talked about. Not to me. Close we might have been, but we didn't exactly have detailed brother and sister chats about our respective love lives.'

The door opened abruptly, far enough for Helen to look in and realise Will had company; a quick word of apology and she withdrew, closing the door again behind her.

Will hesitated. 'You know Mark McKusick?'

'Mark? Yes, of course I do. Why do you ask?'

'He and your brother, as I understand it, they broke up quite recently.'

'A month or so ago. Not long after I got back from New Zealand.'

'And they'd been together a long time.'

'The best part of three years, it must be.'

'He would have been pretty cut up, then? Mark? When it finished.'

'I suppose . . . No, wait. Wait. You don't think Mark . . . ?' Lesley looked at him in disbelief. 'You've met him? Talked to him?'

'Yes.'

'He loved Stephen. Really loved him.' A smile quickly crossed her face. 'He'd have had to, the way Stephen treated him sometimes.'

'How do you mean?'

'Oh, keeping him at arm's length. Not allowing Mark to move in, even after they'd been going together for ages and it was clearly what Mark wanted. It wasn't as if Stephen didn't have the room; the place he had in Leicester was big enough to have students lodging there, three or four of them, to help with the rent. But from what I could tell, if Mark was lucky enough to stay over more than two nights in a row, that was the best he could hope for. And even then, I think Stephen complained.'

'What about?'

'Oh, you know, he couldn't concentrate, couldn't get

on with his work. I was surprised Mark put up with it as long as he did.'

Perhaps he didn't, Will thought.

'Then when Stephen moved to Cambridge,' Lesley said, 'and Mark gave up his job to follow him, I think he imagined things would change. And when they didn't, he gave Stephen an ultimatum. And that was that. As far as Stephen was concerned, it was over.'

'That's what he told you?'

'Stephen? Yes.'

'And how about Mark? I don't imagine he just accepted it like that?'

'What else could he do? I presume he was angry and upset. He would be. So would anyone. But he'd been with Stephen for a long time, and I don't think he would have given up altogether. From what I know of Mark, I think he'd have been more likely to wait and bide his time. Hope that eventually Stephen would change his mind.'

'And you think he might have?'

'It's possible. It suited him somehow, the relationship, no matter how much he might have complained. It was almost as if when Mark was there that side of his life was settled and he didn't have to give it any more thought; didn't have to make too much of an effort.'

'You make it sound more like a convenience than anything else.'

'Maybe, for Stephen, it was in a way. Though that makes it seem as if he was deliberately taking advantage, and I don't think that's true. He was never less than honest with Mark. As far as I know, he never made promises he didn't keep.'

'And there wasn't anybody else, aside from Mark, your brother was involved with?'

'Not that I know of, no.'

'Okay.' Will looked pointedly at his watch.

'That's it?' Lesley said.

'I'm afraid so.'

Reluctantly, Lesley got to her feet. 'Here,' she said, fishing into her bag. 'Let me give you my card. If anything does materialise, perhaps you could let me know.'

'Of course,' Will said.

She couldn't help wondering if he would.

When Will got back from showing Lesley out, Helen was sitting in his chair, one foot resting on the edge of the desk.

'Who was that?'

'Bryan's sister.'

'Isn't she in New Zealand?'

'Clearly not. Not any more. Back here working for local radio.'

'In Cambridge?'

Will shook his head. 'Nottingham.'

'And did she have anything useful to say?'

'Not really.'

Helen got to her feet. 'You fancy lunch?'

'Can't. I've got a meeting over at HQ.'

'My heart bleeds.'

Will lifted his anorak down from the door; the forecast had been for rain. 'That list we got from McKusick, how're we doing with that?'

'Pretty well on to it, I think, but I can check.'

Helen walked with him as far as the stairs.

'Have fun in happy Huntingdon.'

'Do my best.'

Will hadn't reached his car before, sure enough, the rain started to fall.

6

The alarm shook Lesley from the ragged depths of a dream: the waves breaking, wild, against the rocks of the Coromandel, way up on the North Island of New Zealand, and a man's hand – her brother's? – rising and falling above the spray. The instant her feet touched the floor, all memories of that last trip north – Colville, Port Jackson, Waikawau Bay – were jolted from her mind. Through the gap in the curtains, the day, thankfully, looked promising: blue sky visible through a fenestration of flimsy cloud. The brick and stone of the old warehouse buildings of the Lace Market took their definition from the early light, the pale glimmerings of sun.

In her postage stamp-sized bathroom, Lesley splashed cold water on her face, cleaned her teeth and winced a little as a loose filling reminded her of a dental appointment she had still to make. Pulling on her cotton robe, she crossed towards the galley kitchen and filled the kettle, leafing through the previous day's paper as she waited for the water to boil; a few sips of tea and she carried the mug back into the bathroom, where it sat on the window shelf as she had her shower. Later, there would be a second cup to help wash down her regulation slice of toast. Time to read the paper in more detail, check her diary, give her mother a quick, re-assuring call; the studio flat she was renting, on the top floor of a converted factory, was just a short walk from where she worked.

Today she would be wearing her newsreader's hat, a nine-thirty start, five-minute bulletins throughout the day. The way it was structured was much as it had been before her year's sabbatical: Lesley and five others switched every few days between going out reporting – interviewing anyone and everyone from grief-stricken parents to the proud owners of prizewinning ferrets – and working in the newsroom, preparing bulletins and reading them on air. Somewhere in the midst of all this, the raw material had to be transferred from minidisc on to computer and then shaped, with the help of the new Radioman software and clips pulled from the Hub, into news packages which, with the appropriate cues, would be available to programme producers at the news editor's discretion.

Rarely a dull moment.

Rarely time to think outside the box.

Yet think she did. Partly about the future. The deal over her year away had been that she would remain at the station for a further twelve months before looking to move up, move on. But that didn't stop her consid-ering the possibilities. Maybe it was time to try London?

Mostly though, she thought about Stephen. His elation on the telephone, when he had called long distance to tell her about his appointment as full-time lecturer; the enthusiasm he had shown in his emails and letters – Lesley sometimes thought she and Stephen had been amongst the last people to write actual letters – for the new project he was beginning to work on, a biography of Stella Leonard, a British film star whose heyday had been back in the 1950s.

And then there was the last time she had seen him. When had it been? A little over three weeks before he had died. She stopped and caught her breath, held her hand to her chest, thinking she was about to cry.

They had arranged to meet in Ely. Lunch at the Old Fire Station. Good old-fashioned grub, well sourced and cooked, and the only restaurant Lesley knew where they came round and offered seconds of the main course. A little more of the pork loin, madam? Sir, another helping of the steak and kidney pie?

She had asked Stephen how he felt about breaking up with Mark, and had been assured that he was fine.

'No regrets then?'

Grinning, Stephen had treated the surrounding tables to a few appropriate lines from 'My Way'.

'Seriously, are you all right?'

'Seriously, I'm okay.'

'What about Mark?' Lesley had asked.

'Feeling lousy, probably. But what can you do? If I call and ask him how he is, make sympathetic noises, that only makes things worse.'

'Tough love,' Lesley said.

'Something like that.'

She should get in touch with Mark herself, Lesley thought now; it seemed only right.

Glancing at the clock, she saw that it was not so far off nine o'clock. Karl Cooper would soon be signing off and John Holmes starting the *Morning Show*. Time to fix her face and finish getting dressed, get herself moving. From Commerce Square, she would take the short cut down Long Stairs, before Canal Street and the London Road roundabout. Ten minutes tops, less if she hurried.

Newswise, it proved to be a busy day. Mid-morning, confirmation came through that a twenty-two-year-old Nottingham man, serving with the Sherwood Foresters, had been killed in Iraq. A roadside bomb had exploded as a vehicle, carrying five soldiers, had been going past. One dead, three seriously wounded, the fifth, thrown clear by the blast, had only minor scratches and abrasions. Clips of the parents' reactions were tearful, angry, difficult to listen to. 'Poor bastards,' Alan Pike, the news editor, said. 'Great radio.'

The judge sitting in the trial of three young men accused of trespassing with a firearm, aggravated burglary and unlawful wounding, had finished his summing-up and the jury had been closeted to consider its verdict. Relatives of the shopkeeper seriously injured in the incident were daily picketing the court. In excess of five thousand signatures had been collected to a petition demanding mandatory life sentences for anyone caught carrying guns during the commission of a crime.

Nottinghamshire Police had reported a marked increase in shed and garage burglaries in the suburban area south of the River Trent and, through the Area Commander for Rushcliffe North, had issued an appeal to residents to be watchful and increase their security. The commander would be appearing on the drive-time show that evening to outline simple preventative measures householders could take to secure their property, such as fitting metal grilles across shed windows and replacing the screws on exposed hinges with dome-head coach bolts.

Says it all, Lesley thought. In comfortable, middle-class Rushcliffe, the main concern was losing your electric lawnmower, whereas in St Ann's or the Meadows, it was getting shot.

And Natalie Prince, the twenty-six-year-old Nottingham-born model turned actor, on a return visit to the city of her birth, had been arrested in the early hours of the morning, after an altercation in the bar of the Lace Market Hotel, where she had been staying.

Lesley drank water, drank too much coffee, drank Coke, ate a sandwich at her desk without noticing the contents of the filling or the colour of the bread. At twenty minutes past three, the phone rang and, without taking her eyes from the screen, she picked it up.

'Someone here to see you,' the receptionist's voice sing-songed.

'I can't. I'm busy.'

'Scott Scarman?'

'Shit!'

'Shall I pass on that message?' Lesley could imagine the grin on the receptionist's face.

'Tell him . . . tell him I'll pop out in five minutes. Ten.'

'All righty.'

Lesley slammed the phone down hard. What the hell did he want now?

Scarman had been a successful print journalist when Lesley had first known him, one of the comparatively few who had made the leap from provincial newspapers to Canary Wharf. She had met him when she was doing her postgraduate diploma at Cardiff and Scarman had been invited to give a lecture to the students. In the bar afterwards, he had been showy, charming, charmingly indiscreet; somehow, as the party was breaking up, he had contrived to ask Lesley for the number of her mobile. The first time they had slept together had been in a second-floor room of a Travelodge off the A49 roundabout near Shrewsbury; Scarman not above smirking a little over his full English breakfast in the adjacent Little Chef afterwards, snazzy hire car shining outside.

He had driven her to the nearest station, walked with her as far as the ticket office.

'See you again some time.'

Kissing her cheek, he had slipped two twenty-pound notes into her hand.

'What's this meant to be?' Lesley had asked.

'For the ticket,' Scarman had said, grinning. 'What else?

'Fuck off!' she'd said, pushing it back at him.

'Hey!' he'd said, grin breaking into a laugh. 'No need to get your knickers in a twist. Not again.'

She'd swung at him then with the open palm of her free hand and he'd caught her by the wrist. Passengers around them were enjoying the show.

'Calm down, calm down. And take the money, for Christ's sake. I've read what it's like, getting by on a grant.'

'Bastard.'

'That's me,' Scarman had said, and winked. 'Till the next time, okay?'

'In your dreams.'

She had bumped into him again a year later in Derby, both crossing the broad pedestrian area alongside the Guildhall. Lesley had been not long into her first real job with BBC local radio and Scarman had been covering a court case that had already garnered a lot of publicity. A landowner from Crich was on trial for maliciously wounding a youth who had broken into his property, wounding him with a shotgun and then tying him up with baling wire and letting him bleed into the straw before calling for an ambulance. The paper for which Scarman then worked had offered to pay all the man's legal expenses and, should he be sentenced to anything more than community service, was preparing to mount a nationwide campaign for his release. An Englishman's home being his castle. Especially to readers of the *Daily Express,* the *Daily Mail.*

'Dinner?' Scarman asked.

'Fuck you!'

'Okay, but dinner first.'

Despite herself, Lesley had laughed.

At the restaurant, he had surprised her by being funny and self-deprecating about his own job, while taking an apparently genuine interest in hers, asking where she thought it might be leading and offering what seemed sensible advice about her future career. After the meal, he had dropped her back at the shared house she was renting on Chester Green, and, as she was worrying about how – or if – she was going to fend him off, he had given her a quick peck on the cheek and been on his way.

'See you again soon,' he said, and this time Lesley thought, well yes, she might. Maybe she'd misjudged him; maybe he wasn't such an arsehole as she'd thought.

We all make mistakes, as Lesley would tell herself later, and in this case it was a mistake that could be mended. She married him and within six years they were divorced. In retrospect, Lesley was surprised it had lasted as long as it did. At least they hadn't had any kids.

By that time, Lesley had moved east across the Erewash and was working for BBC Radio Nottingham, and Scarman had given up journalism altogether in favour of the increasingly lucrative field of public relations. Not another Max Clifford, not yet, but coming up fast.

After the divorce, Lesley had succeeded in talking the station manager into letting her have a couple of months' unpaid leave: Singapore, Tonga, Australia and, finally, her favourite, New Zealand. While she was there, she made contact with several radio producers and as soon as she was back in England, started working on a scheme for a year's exchange. NZ for UK. It took a while, but eventually there she was, on the Terrace in Wellington, co-presenting the mid-afternoon show from Radio New Zealand House. Once, when the redoubtable Kim Hill had called in sick, she even got to do the Saturday morning show and interview Peter Jackson, asking him about filming *Lord of the Rings* and *King Kong* between playing his choice of music.

She hadn't wanted to come back.

Not to this.

Scarman, resplendent in a suit Lesley was certain came from somewhere like Hugo Boss, was entertaining the receptionist and two couriers with a story from which he broke off the moment she appeared. His hair, which had scarcely started to thin, was cut just so and since she'd seen him last he'd affected a trim, greying beard.

He reached out, as if to give her a hug, and, bridling, she shied away.

'What the hell do you want?' Lesley said, stone faced.

'I've been out of the country,' Scarman said. 'Stephen, I only just heard. I'm so sorry.'

He took hold of her hand, but she pulled it away.

'Really?'

'Yes.'

'Sorry for whom, exactly?'

'For you, of course. And Stephen, naturally. A terrible thing to have happened. Barbaric.'

'You don't care a jot about Stephen. You never did.

You hated it when I as much as talked to him on the phone.'

'That's not true.'

'Isn't it? A pathetic little poof, that's what you called him. One of the kinder things.'

'Lesley . . .'

'And now, if you're being truthful, you probably think he got what was coming to him.' Her voice was loud and shrill and there were tears in her eyes.

'Lesley, come on. Calm down.'

'Don't tell me to fucking calm down!'

'Lesley . . .' He reached towards her again and she knocked his hand aside.

'And stop saying "Lesley, Lesley" all the time. Just fuck off and leave me alone. We've got nothing to say.'

There was a security guard hovering now at Scarman's shoulder, and the news editor had appeared in the doorway behind where Lesley was standing.

'Okay,' Scarman said, with the slightest shrug of his shoulders. 'Have it your way.' He smiled in the direction of the small audience by the reception desk. 'You always did.'

'Bastard!' Lesley spat the word across the distance between them.

'So you say, sweetheart.' Scarman winked and spun away, light on his feet. 'So you say.'

'Come on, Lesley,' Alan Pike said quietly. 'Let's go back inside.' He rested a hand on her shoulder and she shrugged it off, but, a moment later, turned and followed him back into the newsroom.

In Pike's office, she sat opposite his desk, still shaking, staring at the floor.

'What was that all about?'

'It doesn't matter.'

'If it happened here it does.'

Lesley sighed, sniffed, felt for a tissue she couldn't find. The news editor passed her a Kleenex from the packet on his desk.

'Look,' Pike said, 'why don't you finish up what you were doing and get off home? One way or another, we can manage.'

'No, it's all right, I'll be fine.'

'Maybe you should have taken more than a couple of days. After what happened to your brother, it can't be easy . . .'

Lesley stood up from the chair. 'Alan, I'm okay. Honestly.'

'If you're sure?'

'I'm sure.'

Back at her desk, she stared at the screen for several minutes before she could decipher a single word.

As soon as Lesley got home, she pulled off her clothes and stood in the warm water of the shower, allowing the tears to stream out of her, her body rocking back and forth in the steam and spray.

Dry, she dressed in a black roll neck and blue loose-fitting jeans, a pair of old gym shoes on her feet. Before phoning, she made herself eat a piece of toast and drink a cup of strong tea, unusually sweet.

McKusick answered on the fifth ring.

'Mark, it's Lesley.'

There was a long pause, in which she was conscious of McKusick's breathing. 'Stephen – I don't know what to say.'

'It's okay,' Lesley said. 'You don't have to say anything.'

'No, it's not that. I'd like to. It's just . . .'

'I know, I know,' Lesley said. And then, 'How are you holding up?'

'Not so badly, I suppose. You?'

'It comes and goes.'

'Yes.'

'Look, if you do want to talk, why don't we meet?'

'Okay, yes, I'd like that.'

'When's good for you?'

'Any time, really. The sooner the better.'

'I'm on a late tomorrow,' Lesley said. 'Not starting till two. No way we could meet up in the morning, I suppose?'

The hesitation was slight. 'I can wangle it, yes. You want me to come to you?'

'Either way, I don't mind.'

'I'll come over to you, then. Ten, ten-thirty?'

'Make it eleven. Give the traffic time to die down.'

'Suits me. Where d'you want to meet?'

'There's a place close to the car park on Fletcher Gate. Stones. I'll see you there. Upstairs.'

'Okay. Take care.'

'You too.'

Lesley put down the phone, feeling better for having made the call.

The rest of the evening stretched ahead.

There were friends, pals, mostly colleagues associated with work that she could call, but she realised company was not what she wanted just then.

She might have a drink, put her feet up, try to relax.

One of the positive things she'd taken from her relationship with Scott Scarman was an appreciation for a decent Scotch, single malt. Not long after she'd arrived back from New Zealand, the supermarket by Castle Marina had had an offer on Highland Park. There wasn't a great deal left, but there was enough. Pouring herself a good glass, she carried it over to the small two-seater settee and stretched out, feet over the edge, flicking through the TV channels with the remote. Sky News had the mother of the young Nottingham soldier killed in Iraq breaking down on camera; so did 5 and the rolling news on BBC News 24.

Too much grief.

Lesley switched off and fetched the DVD she'd bought for just a fiver in Fopp. *Bringing up Baby*. Katherine Hepburn and Cary Grant. One of Stephen's favourites, he'd given it to her once on video.

Fast and funny as it was, it couldn't totally dispel her mood and, finally, it couldn't keep her eyes from closing. When she woke a little after one, the film had long finished, the heating had switched itself off, and she took herself, cold, to bed.

7

There were friends, perhaps mostly colleagues associated with work that she could call, but she realised
company was not what she wanted just then.

The list of names Mark McKusick had provided for
the police was hardly extensive. A dozen in all. Whether
that marked Stephen Bryan out as gregarious or reclu-
sive, Helen wasn't sure. It depended, she thought, not
just on personality, but on the demands of whatever
job you did, the circles in which you mixed. She would
have found it difficult to come up with the names of
twelve friends herself she might describe as close. Shit,
she thought, make that six.

Of those McKusick had mentioned, three had
addresses in the Clarendon Park area of Leicester
where Bryan had previously lived, one in nearby
Stoneygate; four were fellow academics from the
years spent teaching at De Montfort University, just
one from his new post at Anglia Ruskin. Alongside
two of the names, one with an address in Warwick,
the other in Norwich, McKusick had added a note
describing them as film writers/historians. The last
name, also annotated, and the only woman, was

Siobhan Banham, an old school friend, apparently, who lived in London.

Helen had talked to most of these herself, either in person or on the telephone; detectives had interviewed all but three. None, so far, had provided anything to shake the image of Stephen Bryan as someone who was hard-working and enthusiastic, dedicated to his subject, generous to his friends, good-humoured and generally well liked. Nor had anyone, gay or straight, given support to the idea that Bryan had been sexually promiscuous. His relationship with Mark McKusick they had characterised as comfortable and relaxed; the occasional disagreement, naturally, but, all in all, they had seemed content in one another's company. A bit like an old married couple, someone had remarked. Helen's ears had pricked up at that: in her experience most happily married couples were less happily married than they seemed.

The lecturer from Anglia Ruskin had asked if she had spoken to Jack Rouse, who also taught there and was, apparently, someone who knew Bryan quite well.

Helen had not: his name had not been on the original list.

She had tried contacting Rouse several times in the last couple of days, but there had never been any reply on the number she'd been given and the university hadn't been able to track him down. Without any great hope, she dialled the number again and this time it was answered almost right away.

'Hello?'

'Jack Rouse? I'd like to speak to Jack Rouse.'

'This is he.' The voice was quite deep and smooth.

'This is DS Walker, Cambridgeshire Police.'

'I see. How can I be of help?' A hint of an accent. American?

'You knew Stephen Bryan, I believe?'

'Ah, yes.'

'You were friends?'

'I'd say so. At least, we were beginning to be. It was monstrous, what happened. I liked him a great deal.'

'I wonder, could we talk?'

'About Stephen?'

'Yes.'

'Certainly. Only it will have to be soon. The day after tomorrow I leave for Chicago.'

'When would be best? I could probably manage most times.'

'Today, then. How about today?'

'Fine.'

'You know the Fitzwilliam?'

'Of course.' The museum was no more than a ten-minute walk across Parker's Piece. If she cut through the grounds of Downing College, less than that.

'There's a music recital this lunch-time. Harpsichord. It finishes at around two. Why don't we meet after that?'

'How will I find you?'

'Well, the recital's on the first floor, in the long room that links the two parts of the building. On the north side you'll find some galleries devoted to French and

British painting. I'll be in number five, nineteenth and twentieth centuries. In the corner just behind the door, looking at the Vuillards.'

Lesley, slightly anxious without being sure why, was early for her meeting with Mark McKusick, whereas he was a good twenty minutes late. Seated near one of the upstairs windows, by the time he arrived Lesley had all but finished her first coffee, leafed through the *Guardian* and was starting on the *Independent*, both papers courtesy of the establishment.

She stood to greet him and they hugged briefly, McKusick apologising for his lateness: too many tractors either side of Melton Mowbray, driving via Grantham would have been the better option. The waitress allowed them to settle before approaching to take their order.

They made small talk until their coffees arrived, and then Lesley plunged in, unable to contain herself any longer. 'You saw Stephen, didn't you? After . . . The body, I mean . . . The other day . . .'

'Yes.'

'The police officer . . .'

'Irving.'

'Yes, him. He'd warned me, of course. Warned all three of us, Mum and Dad and me. But we never . . . I never . . .' Lesley stopped and gulped down air. 'I just wasn't prepared.'

'No.'

'If I hadn't have known . . . He was unrecognisable. At first.'

'I know.'

'His poor face . . . Whoever did that to him . . .'

'They're sick,' McKusick said. 'Whoever it was. I know it's a cliché, but it's true. It must be. Sick. Truly sick.'

Lesley turned her own face away. 'Do you think it had anything to do with the fact that he was gay?'

McKusick sighed. 'Maybe.'

'That seems to be what the police are thinking.'

McKusick nodded. 'When they're not thinking it was me.'

Lesley shook her head in disbelief.

'You know, spurned lover, hell hath no fury, that sort of thing.'

'Mark, that's ridiculous.'

'A little obvious, maybe. Convenient, though. For them, I mean. Not for me.' He tried for a smile that wasn't quite there.

Lesley was making patterns in the foam on top of her coffee with a spoon. 'What the police were suggesting to me, one possibility, is that Stephen went out and picked up the wrong man.'

'I know.'

'How likely is it, though? I mean, you knew Stephen far better than me. That aspect of his life, at least. I just don't know if Stephen . . . if that was the kind of thing he'd do. Meet someone casually and then invite them back.'

McKusick lingered a little over his coffee. 'It's hard to say. The whole gay scene, he hated it really – I can't see him going actively looking – but if he met someone he fancied, then yes, I suppose so. Why not? He was single, after all.'

'But surely there's a risk.'

'There's always a risk. Gay or straight, there's always risk.'

Lesley nodded, knowing it to be the truth. 'Had you seen Stephen?' she asked. 'Recently, I mean.'

'Not since we broke up.'

'I'm sorry.'

'Actually, that's not quite true. I did see him. Just the once. I was crossing Trinity Street, on my way to Heffers, and there was Stephen, some tome or other under his arm.'

'And he didn't see you?'

'No.'

'How did he seem?'

'Oh, you know Stephen. A little bit absent. Preoccupied.'

'With his teaching, you mean?'

'That and the book he was working on.'

'The Stella Leonard thing?'

'Yes. He was getting quite obsessed by it, it seemed to me.'

'I remember him writing to me about it when I was in Wellington. It must have been around the time he was starting his research. It was obviously a big deal to him, but I'd never heard of her, I'm afraid.'

'She was in some soap for a while, back in the eighties. Early eighties. I was vaguely aware of her from that, but that's all.'

'So why was Stephen so interested in her, do you know?'

McKusick smiled. 'He must have told me at length, but you know how it is when someone's carrying on about somebody and you don't have much of a clue who they are. It all tends to go in one ear, out the other.'

'I'd like to read what he'd written so far.'

'As far as I know the police have got all his papers. Boxed them up and carted them away. Just about everything. What's going to happen to them eventually, I've no idea. Go up to your parents, probably. Or to you.'

'I'll get in touch with the officer in charge.'

'Grayson?'

Lesley nodded.

'You've met him?'

'The other day.'

'Not a bad bloke, considering.' McKusick surprised her by grinning. 'Straight as a poker, sadly.'

Lesley laughed. When the waitress appeared and asked if they wanted any more coffee, both declined. Outside, the air seemed, if anything, a little colder, the sky more overcast. Perhaps they were due some more snow.

'You driving back right away?' Lesley asked.

McKusick shook his head. 'I thought I'd nose around for a bit while I'm here. Do a little shopping. Take a look at the new Paul Smith shop, maybe. In a Georgian town house or something?'

'Well, enjoy,' Lesley said. 'Just don't end up having to take out a second mortgage. And Mark . . .'

'Yes?'

'Keep in touch.'

'Of course.'

They waited as a tram made its stately way past and on down towards the station, then crossed towards the opposite pavement, said goodbye again and headed off in opposite directions.

The recital had just finished as Helen arrived, and she had to make her way through quite large numbers of people who were only slowly beginning to move away, others continuing to stand in small groups of three or four, talking about what they'd heard.

Some of the attendants were standing at the edges of the room, collecting donations, while others were starting to stack away the folding chairs. Helen asked where she could find room five, and was directed through a small, squarish space into a rectangular gallery that was largely empty of visitors. To her immediate right, a man stood with his back to her, looking at the paintings on the adjoining walls.

'Mr Rouse?'

'Jack.' He turned smartly, holding out his hand.

He was a light-toned black man, smart in a camel-coloured coat, dark loose-fitting trousers, tan leather shoes. His hand, Helen thought, was as smooth as his voice had been on the phone.

'How was your concert?' Helen asked.

'Oh, you know, pretty good. Some Handel. A piece or two by Lord Fitzwilliam himself. It's good to have an excuse to just sit for the best part of an hour, doing nothing. And I'm always happy for the chance to take another look at these.'

There were several paintings in the corner, hung at varying heights: portraits, interiors, still lives. The canvas immediately in front of Helen showed a woman sitting with her hands clasped in her lap, staring off into space. The heavy blue-grey dress she was wearing was difficult to pick out from the background, which was a not dissimilar muddy blue splotched with grey flowers. Just to the woman's left, a blue-and-white cup stood on a smudge of yellow tablecloth and, behind her, in the opposite corner, a door opened to what looked like the bathroom.

'Marvellous, isn't it?' Rouse said.

Helen was looking at the woman's almost feature-less face. Whoever the artist was who had painted this, he couldn't do faces to save his life.

'Look at it long enough, and that woman's life, it's all there. It's like a story. A really good short story. Someone like Alice Munro.'

Helen was sorry. She just didn't get it.

Edouard Vuillard. Seated Woman: Cup of Coffee. 1893.

On her feet, the woman seemed to be wearing trainers, but Helen was sure that couldn't be right.

'You wanted to talk about Stephen,' Rouse said.

'Yes, if we could.'

'Well, you have to understand, until he started here at the university, I'd only met him on a couple of occasions, through mutual friends. But once he was here, we saw a good deal more of one another.'

'You were in the same department?'

'No, not at all. Philosophy, that's my thing. But I teach a course on modern aesthetics and that's an area in which Stephen took quite an interest. Generally, though, it was more casual, social. We'd pass the time in the cafeteria, bump into one another in the town, meet at dinner from time to time with friends.'

'You liked him?'

'What was not to like? He was bright, outgoing – not like some of those film academics who seem to spend the best part of their time in the dark, the entire contents of their lives in an old carrier bag down between their feet.'

'And his partner, Mark? You knew him, too?'

Rouse nodded. 'I met him a few times. At Stephen's house, when we had supper there, and maybe one or two other occasions. I wouldn't claim to know him well.'

'Well enough to have some impression of them as a couple?'

Rouse smiled. 'I'll tell you a story. My maternal grandfather, back in the States, he was in vaudeville. Music hall, I guess you called it over here. He used to do magic tricks. Not very good magic tricks. And juggle.' Rouse raised his eyebrows towards the ceiling. 'Is it any wonder vaudeville died? Anyway, there he'd be onstage, all decked out in this black cloak, top hat, the whole works. The Great Whatever. He used to change his stage name every few years so as to keep getting bookings. But whatever he was called, there was always Maureen. She was the one standing off to the side of the stage in a little skirt and high heels, handing him things, clapping her hands in amazement whenever he pulled a pigeon out from beneath his cloak. The Great Whosit and Maureen. That's how they were billed. That's how they lived their lives. They were married for almost forty years. And she was always 'and Maureen'. An afterthought. An extra. All that time, she never got to keep four boxes in the air at once, or pull a rabbit out from a hat. And that's what I think they were like, Stephen and Mark. That's who they reminded me of.'

'And Mark was Maureen?'

'Absolutely.'

'Second fiddle.'

'You've got it.'

'How do you think he felt about that?'

Rouse fixed Helen with his gaze. 'How would you?'

'I wouldn't know.' It came out more sharply than she'd intended.

'I think most of the time,' Rouse said, 'it was fine. For both of them, it was fine. But I couldn't help thinking there were occasions when Stephen wished Mark was more, well, intellectual. That he could contribute to some discussion they were having about hegemonic structures or signs and signifiers or whatever. Instead of sitting there trying not to look bored.'

'Stephen looked down on him, is that what you're saying?'

'I suppose it is, in a way.'

'And Mark must have been aware of that?'

Rouse lifted his shoulders. 'I guess.'

'You think it led to any real animosity between them?'

Rouse's eyes widened a little. 'You're asking me if Mark might have had reason to kill him?'

'I'm asking you if you thought there was any real animosity between them.'

Rouse smiled. 'More than the average?'

'More than the average.'

Two Japanese tourists were hovering close, intent on examining the paintings in that particular corner, and Rouse motioned towards the opposite end of the gallery. 'They only allow themselves forty-seven seconds per painting; it's a shame to stand in their way.'

'Stephen and Mark,' Helen said, when they'd stopped walking.

'All right,' Rouse said, 'I'm going to tell you another story.'

'As long as the last one?'

'Quite possibly longer. But more to the point.'

Helen smiled and waited.

'This was only a few months ago, towards the end of November. Dinner at a friend's house in Waterbeach. Eight of us there would have been, mostly academics of one shade or another. It was a nice enough evening, the food was good, and as usual there was too much wine. Mark, it seemed, was the designated driver out of Stephen and himself, which was okay, except towards the end of the evening, having kept himself to a single glass earlier, he started in on the brandy like there was no tomorrow. Stephen said something to him, nothing too heavy, but Mark just seemed to ignore him.

'Well, they left a little before me, and I didn't know what they were going to do about the driving, whether Stephen was going to drive himself – something I'd hardly ever known him do – or maybe leave the car there and get a lift back with someone else. Anyway, the man whose house it was and I had some business to discuss, which we did for a while, and then, when I left – it must have been half an hour later – I heard all this shouting coming from the end of the drive. And there were Stephen and Mark, standing on either side of Mark's car, airing their dirty linen in public, as you Brits like to say, for all the world to hear.'

'All the world being you.'

'Exactly. And it was Mark that was doing most of the shouting.'

'Can you remember what he said?'

'I certainly do. "For years all I've been to you is something warm to take home and fuck and now you don't even do that" – that was one of the choicer bits. Stephen told him not to be so stupid, that he was acting like a spoiled kid, and, of course, that only made things worse.'

'They didn't know you were listening?'

'Not then. Stephen said something I didn't hear, turned around and started to walk away. Mark ran after him. Grabbed hold of Stephen and tried to pull him back. Stephen – I don't know, maybe he swung an arm

96

– tried to get Mark off him, anyway. Which was when Mark hit him.'

'He hit him?'

'Put two hands together and brought them down on the back of Stephen's neck. Stephen staggered, almost lost his footing, and then Mark hit him again. Next thing, Stephen was on his back, all sort of hunched up, and Mark was bending down and punching him and shouting, "If you ever do that again, I'll fucking kill you!"'

'What happened then?'

'I coughed and said something limp and ineffectual, like, "Excuse me, is everything all right?" and that acted like a bucket of ice water. Mark broke off and moved away and Stephen picked himself up from the ground and brushed himself down and said something like, just a little family squabble. Trying to make a joke out of it. But I could see he had a nasty cut over one eye, that at least. I offered to help him back inside and get it seen to, but he shrugged it off and said it would be fine, and that was about that. Stephen assured me they'd get home safely and everything would be okay. The next time I saw him he didn't mention it and neither did I.'

'And you don't know,' Helen said, 'if that incident was a one-off or part of a pattern?'

'I'm afraid I've no idea.'

'And there were no other witnesses to this?'

Rouse shook his head. 'The argument might have been heard from the house, but the end of the drive's quite a long way off.'

'There's nothing else you can tell me,' Helen said, 'that might be relevant?'

'Relevant, no. But come back and have a look at the Vuillards again some time. He's a great painter. You should give him another chance.'

From Will's office window, the car headlights progressing along Gonville Place towards the Newmarket Road were like slow-moving blips of yellow blistering through the glass. The snow had started to fall with the failing of the light, slow flakes meandering down.

'This Rouse character,' Will said, 'he wasn't on the list McKusick gave us at all?'

'Uh-uh.'

'You think he just forgot?'

'Selective amnesia, maybe,' Helen said.

'He knew if Rouse told his story . . .'

'We were going to look at him in a different light.'

'Another side of his character.'

'One he'd managed to keep hidden.'

'A violent temper.'

'When provoked.'

'The worm that turned,' Will said.

'Something along those lines.'

'What did Rouse quote him as saying?'

'"Do that again and I'll fucking kill you."'

The words had an uncomfortable echo in Will's mind.

'"Do that again",' he said, 'meaning what?'

Helen shrugged. 'Turn your back? Walk away?'

'Which is what Bryan did.'

'A mutual decision not to see each other for a while, that's how McKusick described it. Some kind of trial separation.'

'Do we believe that?'

'Not really.'

'So when shall we talk to McKusick again?'

'First thing tomorrow?'

'Let's bring him in here,' Will said. 'Sit him down for a while. Let him stew. Lean on him a little. See if we can't shake something from the tree.'

8

Lesley crossed Fletcher Gate towards a phalanx of tall hoardings, behind which yet another hotel or exciting mixed-use retail destination was doubtless under construction, cut down Bottle Lane and into Waterstone's.

Film books were on the third floor.

A quick riffle through the three histories of British cinema they had in stock came up with only two references to Stella Leonard, both brief. One listed her, along with Diana Dors, Jane Hylton, Susan Shaw and others, as a graduate of the J. Arthur Rank Charm School, which had been set up in the 1950s to mould and develop a new generation of British film actresses; the other briefly mentioned several films in which she'd appeared, notably the thriller, *Shattered Glass*, released in 1956.

Not a lot to go on there.

She scribbled a couple of things in her notebook and headed back up through Hockley towards London Road.

When she arrived, the news editor was mid-rant. 'Actresses, actors, whatever you're supposed to call them nowadays. Make a couple of movies no one bothers to go and see, spread their legs for the lads' magazines, make a name for themselves snorting cocaine off some Premiership player's backside, and they think they're God Almighty.'

At least he's got the gender right, Lesley thought.

'So here's Natalie Prince,' Alan Pike continued. 'Not so long ago, when all she could get were bit parts on the telly, more tarts in *The Bill* than in Gregg's front window, back then when she wanted all the publicity she could get, who gave her a hand up, more air time than David Blunkett in his prime? But now, ask for an interview and anyone'd think you were begging her for a shag in the middle of the Old Market Square.'

Pike slammed his office door, only to open it again moments later, waving a piece of paper in Lesley's direction. 'Here. Get yourself out to Langar. Talk to this James Crawford. Reckons he's seen a Yank plane coming in to land, local airport. One of those rendition jobs, he says.' Pike shook his head. 'Six months back, it'd likely been a UFO. Now every crank and crazy sees phantom CIA flights every time they buckle on their binoculars. But use your nous, see what he has to say. Might be something we can use, get another slow day.'

Lesley took a quick look at entries for CIA ghost flights on the Web before leaving: after skipping down

101

the first few pages, the sheer volume deterred her from going further. Too much detail for a piece that would probably never be aired. And besides, there were other things on her mind.

The room in which they'd finally put Mark McKusick was small and square, the air used and stale. Since the police had arrived on his doorstep early that morning – McKusick not even properly dressed, a mug of tea barely started, bowl of cereal scarcely touched – he had been moved from one part of the building to another, uniformed officers brushing past him as if he weren't really there, information as to what he was wanted for scant and unclear. Was he there to answer more questions, and, if so, why wasn't that happening? Was he about to be arrested, and, if so, what for? What charge? McKusick looked at his watch, looked at the walls, the ceiling, closed his eyes. No way he could have slept, but when the door opened suddenly, he jumped, as if jerking awake.

An officer he'd never seen before was standing in the doorway. 'Got everything you want?'

'Yes. I suppose so. But look . . .'

'Right, then.' The man stepped smartly back outside and the door was firmly closed.

McKusick waited. He sat, legs crossed, legs straight, arms folded, elbows resting on the table in front of him, arms down by his side. He got up and paced the room. Looked into the high corners for cameras through which he was being watched, and, even though he could see none, couldn't quite believe they weren't there.

After what seemed an eternity, he tried the handle of the door and, with little resistance, it opened. McKusick looked both ways along an empty corridor, seeing nothing, nobody. He stepped out of the room and, as he did, a uniformed officer appeared at the far end of the corridor and stood there, staring in his direction.

McKusick retreated back inside and closed the door.

It was another forty-five minutes before Will and Helen finally arrived and by then McKusick could smell his own sweat, acrid yet sweet, like the residue of the previous night's cheap curry.

'Hope you haven't been waiting long,' Will said, innocently. 'Bit of a mix-up. Nobody told us you were here.'

'I've been here bloody hours.'

'Oh, well. Can't be helped.'

'Here,' Helen said, passing across a polystyrene cup with a small hole torn from the lid. 'Have some tea.'

'I don't want any tea.'

Helen smiled sweetly. 'Suit yourself.'

They sat silently, looking at one another, a smile playing round the corners of Will's mouth.

'I don't see what's so funny.'

'Nothing,' Will said.

'Then what's the bloody joke?'

Both Will and Helen were smiling now, relaxed. 'There's no joke,' Will said.

'Then why have I been pissed around all morning? Why am I here?'

'We thought it needed,' Will said, 'a little chat. A little clarification.'

'About what? Clarification about what?' McKusick's face, naturally lean, was taut and flushed. 'I don't see what I'm doing here anyway. Stephen was robbed, wasn't he? A burglary. His laptop, for one. You think that was me? You think I know anything about that? Well, do you?'

Helen eased forward, one arm resting lightly on the table edge, waiting for him to calm down. 'You gave us a list,' she said.

'What list?'

'Friends of Stephen's.'

'What about it?'

'We wondered if you'd like to look at it again? Reconsider?' She took a sheet of paper from her bag, reversed it, and slid it across the table towards him.

'So?' McKusick said, glancing down, then away.

'We think you left someone off.'

McKusick shook his head.

'One of Stephen's friends,' Will said.

'I don't think so.'

'It's easy enough,' Helen said amiably. 'I leave stuff off lists all the time. Shopping lists. People to send Christmas cards to. Birthdays.'

'I'm sorry,' McKusick said. 'I don't . . .'

'Rouse,' Helen said. 'Jack Rouse. Not the kind of man to be forgotten easily, I'd have thought.'

McKusick shook his head again, more emphatically this time. 'He's no special friend of Stephen's.'

Helen noticed the slip of tense and let it go. 'It was no accident, then?' she asked.

'How d'you mean?'

'Not including him on the list.'

'No.'

'Funny,' Helen said. 'When I talked to him I got the impression he and Stephen knew one another rather well.'

'That's not true.'

Helen smiled and relaxed back against her chair.

'Not true?'

'No.'

'The fact his name wasn't there,' Will said, taking over, 'that wouldn't be anything to do with the fact you didn't want us to talk to him?'

'Of course not.' McKusick's throat was dry.

'Of course not?'

'Look, I don't know what you're implying . . .'

'You don't?'

'No.'

Will laughed. 'You didn't think if we talked to him, that conversation might leave us with a different impression?'

'Different to what? I don't understand.'

'Different to the one you've been trying so hard to cultivate. The long-suffering boyfriend, hard done by, certainly, but not one to complain. At least, not too loudly.'

'I'm sorry, this is . . .' McKusick was half out of his chair.

'This is what?' Will's voice was like steel.

McKusick lowered himself slowly back down.

'Aggrieved but accepting, that's you, isn't it?' Will said. 'At least, that's what you'd have us believe.'

McKusick was staring at the floor.

'Why don't you,' Helen said, 'tell us about it in your own words?'

'About what?'

Will's fist hit the table top with such force that even Helen, who had been half-expecting it, was jolted back with surprise, and McKusick cowered as if he'd been hit.

'You and Stephen Bryan were seen having a major argument in the early hours of the morning,' Will said. 'Seen and heard. An argument which rapidly became violent.'

'That's . . .'

'Yes?'

'That's an exaggeration.'

'You weren't violent?'

McKusick avoided Will's eyes.

'You hit him,' Will said. 'With both hands. From behind. You hit him with such force he fell to the ground. And then you carried on hitting him.'

'No.'

'You punched him in the face and the body. Hit him so hard he had a severe cut on his face.'

'No.'

'You lost it,' Will said. 'Lost it completely. If Jack Rouse hadn't been there, you could have killed him.'

106

'No!' McKusick's voice was raised in a virtual scream. His face, flushed before, was deathly white and his lips were pulled back, bloodless and thin, over his teeth.

'Is that what happened last week?' Helen said. 'When you went to visit Stephen? You lost your temper? Is that what happened then?'

McKusick slumped forward across the table, head in his hands, and started to sob. Short, inchoate sobs that shook his body.

Will and Helen looked at one another questioningly, both remembering what Helen had said before about McKusick's play-acting, both wondering if this were the same again.

After several minutes, in which the frequency of the sobbing lessened but did not stop, Helen reached forward and shook McKusick gently by the upper arm.

'Mark, come on. Snap out of it.'

Slowly, McKusick raised his head, took a crumpled tissue from his pocket and wiped his reddened eyes.

'Before I say anything else,' he said in a perfectly even voice, 'I want a lawyer.'

Will and Helen stood out on the edge of Parker's Piece, on the far side of the road from the police station. Will had his North Face anorak buttoned but not zipped; the collar of Helen's coat was turned up, a scarf knotted loosely at her neck. No snow now, but rain, soft-falling. The ends of Helen's hair were dark with it, almost black.

107

Helen lit one cigarette from the butt of another.

'What is this?' Will asked. 'A death wish?'

'You care?'

'Don't you ever read,' he said, 'the warning on the packet?'

Helen blew smoke from one side of her mouth. 'It never does,' she said, 'to believe everything you read. Especially on packaging. They taught us that. Fourth year social studies.'

'Aside from which,' Will said, 'the inside of your mouth must taste like an ashtray.'

Helen smiled. 'That need never bother you.'

'You know how close we came?' Will said. 'Back there?'

Helen held out her left hand, forefinger and thumb not quite touching. 'This close?'

'That close.'

'And now?'

'Now we wait.'

'Do we know who for?'

'Christine Costello, no less.'

Helen drew deeply on her cigarette. 'Why her?'

'Because the Good Lord didn't want it to be easy?'

Helen raised an eyebrow. 'Lorraine will have to watch out. Next thing you'll be sending Jake off to Sunday school. Getting him enrolled for confirmation class.'

'I think he needs to be baptised first. And besides, confirmation? That sounds more like your religion than mine.'

108

Helen shook her head. 'I became an agnostic the day the priest tried to get me to sit on his lap after mass.'

'He was just trying to be friendly. Make you feel at ease.'

'That wasn't what he was trying to make me feel at all.'

Will laughed and shook his head. 'You're a terrible woman.'

'I know. Now, shouldn't we get back inside?'

Christine Costello was wearing a well-weathered black leather jacket, a black dress in some shiny material or other, and black high-heeled boots. Anyone who didn't know her better might have assumed she'd left a Harley Davidson out in the car park and not a nearly new BMW saloon.

'Will,' she said, holding out her hand. 'Good to see you again.'

'Wish I could say the same.'

'Same old joker, eh, Helen?' the lawyer said. 'Always likes to kid around.'

Helen said nothing. Botox, she thought, was doing a reasonably good job at keeping Christine Costello's wrinkles at bay, a few hundred a year reasonably well spent. Helen wondered if, in Costello's line of work, it was tax deductible? Maybe that was only barristers.

'After listening to what my client has to say,' Costello said, 'you might almost consider the treatment meted out to him as harassment.'

'Not really,' Will said. 'All we did was lock him in

a darkened room. Whack him around the head a few times with a telephone directory. That kind of thing.'

'You see what I mean?' the lawyer said to Helen. 'Never takes anything seriously.'

'Shall we get on with it?' Helen said.

Sober-faced, McKusick told his version of the after-dinner argument with Stephen Bryan, less dramatic than that told by Jack Rouse, but basically the same. He admitted he had been drinking unusually heavily and blamed his behaviour on that. It had been, he claimed, entirely out of character.

Closely questioned, he resolutely denied having visited Bryan's house on the day of his death. He had not as much as spoken to him, never mind seen him, for weeks. The inspector was right, he had lost his temper on the night that he and Bryan had argued, back in November, but that had been the one and only time.

'Ask anyone else who knows me,' McKusick said. 'Anyone who knew Stephen and me at all well. They'll tell you the same.' He looked first at Will and then at Helen. 'I'm sure you have already.'

'I'd just like to confirm,' Christine Costello said, 'there is no evidence, physical or otherwise, which places my client at the deceased's premises at or around the time he died?'

'That's correct,' Will said, after a beat. Not joking now.

'Very well, then,' Costello said, rising to her feet. 'We're through here, I think.'

Helen looked for a sign of a smirk on McKusick's face as he walked past, but there was nothing, not even relief. Somehow, he'd regained control, not just of himself but of the situation.

'How close were we?' she asked, when they were alone.

'Don't ask,' Will said. 'Just don't ask.'

When Lesley had arrived in Langar, a small village east of the city, she had found Crawford's house without difficulty. A seventy-three-year old former pilot who was beginning to be troubled by osteoarthrosis, Crawford's mind was still sharp as a tack. And he was in no doubt as to what he'd seen: a Boeing 737 with the registration number N313P had come in to land in the early hours of the morning and taken off again ninety minutes later.

'Why here?' Lesley asked.

'Refuelling, most likely,' Crawford said.

He presented Lesley with photographic evidence to support his claims and pointed her to half a dozen websites where, he assured her, she would find conclusive proof that the CIA were using Britain as a landing stage in the process of flying prisoners to Eastern Europe and North Africa.

'Why would they do that?' Lesley asked, naive questions being sometimes the best.

Crawford screwed up his face. 'To get information about terrorism. Information they can only get through torture. And this way they can keep their hands clean, hold them up and swear by God Almighty they never took a step out of line, knowing there's them in Egypt or Romania with a lot less scruples.'

'And you believe this? You believe this is what's happening? And the government knows?'

'Sweetheart,' he said, covering her hand with his. 'If I know, an old bugger with no more resources than two good eyes and a decent camera, don't you think MI5 or the security services know what's going on, too? I should think the chap who wipes the Prime Minister's backside knows, wouldn't you?' He winked. 'Admitting it, of course, that's a different matter. Involves an old-fashioned strategy called telling the truth.'

Lesley left with forty minutes of material that she could probably whittle down to four, and which she thought Alan Pike might not even agree to use; and if he did, then Roger Hart, the station manager, might well find a reason for wielding his veto.

She had scarcely been back in the newsroom a couple of minutes, not time enough to shed her coat, than Pike appeared, brandishing a copy of the *Evening Post*.

'Look at this. Natalie Prince, too uptight to give us an interview, but here she is, splashed all over two pages of the bloody *Post*.' He dropped the paper, disparagingly, on Lesley's desk. 'How come they could get it and we couldn't?'

He didn't wait for an answer.

Lesley pushed her coat on to the back of her chair and started to read. The third paragraph stopped her cold:

Natalie Prince is here in the city to discuss star-ring in a remake of **Shattered Glass,** *a cult film from the 1950s that originally starred her great-aunt, Stella Leonard.*

19. EXT. HOUSE. NIGHT.

*Evening. A roadster pulls up in the driveway of a
substantial country house.* PHILIP *jumps out and hurries
round to open the car door for* ALMA.

Getting out of the car, ALMA *smiles and starts to walk
towards the door, taking her key from her bag as she
does so. Opening the door, she stands aside and smiles
at* PHILIP *again, letting him enter the house before her.*

20. INT. HALLWAY. NIGHT.

ALMA: *Hello? Is anyone home?*

*Moving further into the house, she pauses outside a
door before turning the handle and pushing it open.*

21. INT. DRAWING ROOM. NIGHT.

RUBY *is standing in front of the fireplace, her back to the door. Unlike* ALMA, *whose clothes are neat and utilitarian, the dress* RUBY *is wearing suggests worldliness and a degree of sophistication.*

As the door opens, RUBY *looks upwards into the mirror above the fireplace, so that, in its reflection, we see the upper part of her face and, from her POV,* ALMA *and* PHILIP *entering the room.*

ALMA (*to* PHILIP): *This is my sister, Ruby.*

RUBY *slowly turns to face them and we register the astonishment on* PHILIP'S *face as he sees the almost total resemblance between them, one a more sophisticated, highly made-up version of the other.*

ALMA: *Ruby, this is Philip.*

RUBY (*a smile playing round the corners of her mouth, as she sizes up* PHILIP *approvingly*): *Really?*

9

Natalie Prince had the distinction of being the only girl to have been expelled from the Nottingham High School for Girls twice. The first punishment – the culmination of many and diverse warnings – was for sneaking up onstage during assembly, while the head teacher was delivering a sombre lecture on responsibility, and mooning the entire student body. By dint of a large donation to the school fund, her father secured her re-instatement. On the second occasion, she was caught with a sixth former from the nearby High School for Boys on the bandstand of the adjacent arboretum, smoking dope and indulging in a degree of rather public sexual exploration. She was fifteen at the time and in – in and somewhat out of – her school uniform. There was nothing Daddy could do, aside from hiring a pride of private tutors for Natalie, who took, and passed, her GCSEs early, stormed through Clarendon College for the next two years and, at eighteen, was offered places at several universities, all of which she turned down.

By then, Natalie, a couple of inches short of six foot and skinny, had been spotted by a model agency and was quickly immersed in a world of photo shoots and fashion shows and yes, every female model's favourite slimming aid – aside, of course, from Diet Coke and Marlboro Lights – an elegant sufficiency of cocaine.

Kate Moss she was not.

Elle Macpherson she would not become.

But photographers liked her cheek-bones and they liked her attitude; when she worked she worked hard, didn't put on airs, let them get the shots they wanted with a minimum of fuss. Her face, sometimes framed by a raven wig, sometimes set off by her own spiky hair, became familiar to readers of the glossier weekend supplements and magazines such as *Heat* and *Red* and *Marie Claire*.

Television beckoned. Chat shows with the likes of Graham Norton and Lorraine Kelly. A notorious occasion on which, taking offence at an innocuous remark by Michael Parkinson, she shouted, 'Bollocks, granddad!', upended a water jug and pranced off.

She took a small part in *Casualty*, another in *The Bill*; for eight weeks she was a running character in *Coronation Street*, before an altercation with one of the featured actors necessitated her convenient demise, a dive from a twelfth-storey balcony on to concrete.

An all-too-public affair with the lead singer of an alt-country band called Sow's Ear ended when Natalie punched him out on stage at the Borderline in front of several hundred sweaty fans. Natalie was held overnight by the police and released with front-page pictures in the tabloids and a caution.

Which was when Orlando Rocca contacted her and offered her the lead in *Black Bullet*, a British-Portuguese-Romanian art-house thriller which tickled the critics' fancy and led to *Electric*, in which Rocca cast her as a low-level drug dealer and single mother who finds herself in debt to Albanian gangsters in East London. It was a role which won her a Best Actress award at Sundance and a couple of other nominations.

Since which time Natalie had been linked with numerous projects, ranging from a modern-dress version of *A Midsummer's Night's Dream* to *Slowdive*, a biopic based on Siouxsie Sioux of Siouxsie and the Banshees. And now, according to no less an authority than the *Nottingham Evening Post*, she was going to be starring in a retread of *Shattered Glass*, a film very few people had heard of, never mind seen.

All of the above Lesley pulled together from a variety of news reports and articles on the Web and a selection of interviews available through the BBC archives. Caught on microphone, Natalie at times sounded older if not necessarily wiser than her twenty-five years, at others she seemed gauche and startled; when she was comfortable enough with the interviewer to relax, her local Nottingham accent came through quite clearly, and it was then that Lesley found herself almost warming to her.

Now the thing to do was talk to her herself.

The piece in the *Post* was under Mel Mast's byline. 'Mel? Hi, it's Lesley, from BBC Radio Nottingham . . . Yes, fine thanks. Fine. . . . Listen, Mel, how the hell'd you manage to get to sit down with Natalie Prince? When we asked for an interview we were told she was only doing national and that was that. No exceptions.'

'Let's say I called in a couple of favours,' Mast said, and Lesley could almost visualise the smile crossing her face. 'It wasn't easy, even so. Her PR people insisted on seeing the final copy, vetting any photographs, real bullshit, you know? Anyone'd think she was Madonna, for God's sake.'

'The PR company, that's how you got to her?'

'How else?'

Lesley pitched a guess. 'Scott, he still looking after her?'

'Yes.' Mel laughed. 'Maybe there's a couple of favours of your own you could work on.'

Lesley thanked her and set down the phone. That explained what her ex had been doing in the city the other day, all spruced up. She wondered if he was still around.

Calls to Scott Scarman's mobile were being re-routed to his office. 'I'm sorry,' the woman said in her best estuary English, 'Mr Scarman's with a client and can't be disturbed.'

'When he comes up for air,' Lesley said, 'tell him his ex-wife wants to speak to him, okay?'

Scarman rang back just short of five, while Lesley was working on her plane-spotting interview; now that the Home Secretary had made a statement in the Commons assuring the House that no clandestine CIA flights had taken place, clearly lying to his back teeth, there was a chance her report might find its way into the news after all.

'Lesley,' Scarman said, his voice full of easy bonhomie, 'you didn't have to call and apologise.'

'I'm not.'

'Though if you'd care to meet for a drink, we can talk it through. A misunderstanding, you were emotional. After what you've just been through, not surprising.'

'Scott, shut the fuck up, okay? And as for apologising, there's nothing to apologise for. What I want is thirty minutes with Natalie Prince.'

Scarman's voice tightened. 'You know the drill on that. Just at the moment interviews with Natalie are very restricted, nothing local.'

'That was fine until you let her talk to the *Post*. Now it doesn't wash.'

'I'm sorry, sweetheart . . .'

She hated it when he called her that. 'Listen, Scott,' she lied, 'I just got through talking to Carl Peters, the guy from Sow's Ear, the one she used to date. We could run that instead.'

Scarman laughed. 'One, I don't believe you . . .'

'Try him, he's back home in Portland.'

'And two, that's blackmail.'

'Something you'd understand.'

This time Scarman's laugh sounded forced. 'I tell you what, meet me for that drink and I'll see if I can't talk Natalie into coming along. Six-thirty? Seven? The Poppy Club? We'll talk about it then.'

'Seven,' Lesley said.

'Fine.'

The line went dead.

'Bastard,' Lesley said quietly to herself.

The door to the news editor's room was open.

'I think I've got an interview with Natalie Prince.'

'How come?' Pike said.

Lesley set her face to one side and smiled. 'Natural charm?'

'Get me something for the afternoon show. We can start trailing it on drive-time.'

'Do what I can.'

The decor was upfront without being overwhelming: deep purple upholstery, large orange, red and yellow poppies on the walls. The background music, a sort of jazz-soul lite, was relatively subdued: Grover Washington, Kenny G. The usual types were lounging around looking cool, mobiles at the ready, drinks in hand.

Scarman, wearing a pale linen suit, was standing up against the bar, with Natalie Prince sitting on a high stool alongside him, heels of her black ankle boots hooked over the top rung of the stool. Lesley saw endless legs encased in silver tights and, above them, a red silk top; somewhere in between, she guessed, there was a wisp of skirt but from where she was standing it wasn't evident.

'Lesley! Great to see you,' Scarman said, swinging round.

She allowed her hand to be grasped, an air kiss to pass close to her face.

'So, Lesley, this is the wonderful Natalie. Nat, this is Lesley.' Then, with a grin, 'The former Mrs Scarman, no less.'

Lesley did her best not to scowl. Natalie's expression made it clear she couldn't care less.

'What'll you drink?' Scarman asked.

'Fruit juice.'

'Whisky chaser?'

'Just juice will be fine.'

'Which kind?'

'Any.'

Natalie was drinking lager from the bottle. Not, Lesley suspected, her first. Her lipstick was very dark, almost black, and there were careful gradations of brown above her eyes; her hair, cut shorter than Lesley's own, and spikier, was highlighted, here and there, with silver-grey.

'If you've got a recorder in there,' Scarman said, indicating the bag on Lesley's shoulder, 'and you're planning to use it, why don't we find somewhere quiet?'

The sofas were the kind you sink into, the lighting in that corner of the room designed for mood rather than illumination and Lesley was thankful she could work the controls on her recorder blindfold.

'A few ground rules,' Scarman said. 'Nothing about that nonsense the other night at the hotel . . .'

'I thought the police had agreed not to press charges?'

'Listen, will you, to what I'm saying. Nothing about . . .'

'Scott, Scott,' Lesley said, laughing. 'I'm winding you up, okay?'

Natalie giggled and took a swig from her beer.

'Okay, okay. Very fucking funny. But this is serious. Nothing about Natalie's personal life, relationships, past misdemeanours. Nothing about her family. Strictly out of bounds. She's happy to talk about her work with Orlando, future projects . . .'

'*Shattered Glass*?'

'*Shattered Glass*, maybe.'

'Maybe? I thought that was the reason for Natalie being here?'

Scarman essayed an elegant shrug of the shoulders. 'Let's say it's no longer as squared away as we thought.'

'Problems?'

'Nothing that can't be sorted. A glitch in the timing, that's all. But there are plenty of other things in the pipeline, a new theatre piece, for instance. Nat, why don't you tell Lesley something about that?'

Natalie held up her empty lager bottle with finger and thumb. 'I need another one of these before I can talk about anything.'

Scarman sighed but got to his feet all the same.

'Hate it when he calls me that,' Natalie said, as soon as Scarman had turned his back. 'Nat. As if I'm some stupid little buzzing thing he can swat.'

'At least it's a name,' Lesley said. 'With me it was sweetheart, sweetheart.'

Natalie made a face as though she was going to throw up.

'I think he called all his women sweetheart,' Lesley said. 'Saved any possible embarrassment.'

'While you were married, he screwed around?'

'Does the bear shit in the woods?'

Natalie laughed. It was a good sound, loud and untrammelled, and Lesley found herself joining in.

'You two seem to have found something amusing,' Scarman said, quickly back from the bar.

'What happened to my drink?' Natalie said.

'They're bringing it over.'

'I don't think,' Lesley said, 'he liked the idea of leaving us alone together for too long.'

'Really?' Natalie said, and fixed Scarman with her smile. 'Scott. Scottie. Now you've told us what we can talk about, really, you could just fuck off and leave us to it. Don't you think? Girls together?' The smile widened. 'There's a sweetheart.'

Scarman thought about standing his ground, but opted for yielding gracefully instead. 'An hour,' he said, summoning up a small degree of menace. 'Tops.'

'All right, sweetheart,' Natalie said, emphasising, with apparent innocence, the last word.

Lesley had to look away.

When the waiter arrived at their table a few minutes later, Natalie asked Lesley if she wouldn't like a real drink and with only a little hesitation, Lesley chose Oban from the list of single malts. 'Large one,' she said. 'No ice. Water on the side.' In for a penny, she thought, especially if the pennies were Scarman's and not her own.

For fifteen minutes or so girl talk was what it was, woman talk anyway; Lesley chose to be more than a little indiscreet about a brief fling she'd had when she was in New Zealand and Natalie responded with a tale, more or less blow by blow, of an affair she'd had with a screenwriter she'd met on the rebound from Carl Peters.

'Made love as if he'd just come back from a course on constructing a fucking story, yeah? Build up to a small climax, relax the tension, throw in something surprising around the end of act three, then hang on for dear life till the final credits.' Natalie laughed. 'There he'd be when it was over, 'stead of pulling his manky briefs back on, standing beside the bed like he was expecting a Golden Globe or something. A Bafta for bloody boffing.'

Lesley laughed along, then reached down and activated the recorder. Time to get down to business. 'It must have been difficult,' she said, 'after something as successful as *Electric*, to have known what to do next.'

'Not really.'

'But there would have been offers? Lots of them, I imagine. All the praise you got for that role, the award and everything, it gave you a level of recognition that as an actor you hadn't had before.'

'Look,' Natalie swung one of her long legs round from the settee. 'That award stuff, it's bollocks, right? Dog's bollocks, maybe, but bollocks all the same.' She smiled, remembering. 'There you are in a few grands' worth of borrowed dress, literally pissing yourself, and when they say your name, yeah, okay, it's amazing.'

The second leg followed the first and she stared at Lesley seriously.

'What I did though, what me and Orlando did, what ended up on screen, okay, it's there, some people like it, some people don't. But awards, Oscars, stuff like that. That's not down to me. That's Scarman, people like him. Marketing spend. Backhanders. Blow-jobs in stretch limos. That's where Oscars come from. Not what I do. Not really. It's what they do with it after. What they fuckin' make of it.'

She swallowed down the rest of her beer.

'Okay, end of lesson. Now let's have another drink.'

A young man in a too-shiny leather jacket, egged on by his mates, leaned between the two of them and said, 'S'cuse me, but you're Natalie Prince, right?'

'No, darlin', I'm Judi fuckin' Dench. Now why don't you go and play with yourself in the gents.'

Lesley was enjoying herself more and more.

'Doing a remake of *Shattered Glass*?' she said. 'Was that your idea, or . . . ?'

'Mine? God, no.'

'You didn't like the idea?'

'Liking didn't come into it. I didn't even know about it – the original, I mean – not till Orlando told me. Two years ago? Less. Made me sit down and watch it, one of them poky little viewing theatres in Soho. An old print, but even so. It's fantastic, right? Okay, some of it, it's a bit hokey, but, no, it's great, really great.'

'But she's what? Your great-aunt?'

'Yes.'

'On what? Your mother's side? Your father's?'

'My mother's.'

'I'm surprised you hadn't seen it before.'

'If it had been around – you know, on video or something – I suppose I would have. But there's nothing. I don't think it's even been on TV. Oh, TCM at four in the morning, maybe, but that's all. And besides . . .' Natalie threaded her fingers through her hair. 'What you have to realise, my aunt, Stella, okay, I knew about her when I was growing up, the soap stuff she did for telly, but that was about all. She made films, yeah. Back in the fifties. But that was history, right? All Trevor Howard and *Brief Encounter* and that was the last place I wanted to go.'

Natalie crossed her legs and the hearts of at least half a dozen men skipped a beat.

'Like I say, that was all a couple of years back. Ever since then, it's been a question of doing deals. Finance. Distribution. Orlando, not me. I wouldn't have a fucking clue.'

'And meantime you do what? Wait?'

'Meantime I sit around and get royally pissed.' Rising slightly unsteadily to her feet, Natalie put two fingers to her mouth and whistled. When the waiter looked in her direction, she signalled for more of the same.

'The problems Scott mentioned about doing the movie,' Lesley said, 'they're serious?'

'They were. One of the backers pulled out at the last

minute. Just when we were set to announce. Now it looks like my dad's going to step in and put up the money.' She crossed her fingers. 'Maybe.'

'He can do that?'

Natalie laughed. 'Howard? Ten times over. If he wants to. If he cares. Which usually he doesn't. If this happens, it'll be a first.'

'How come now?'

'God knows. He heard about what had happened – I mean, I told him, sort of begged, really. How it would be great for my career and that. Finally, he said he'd talk to his accountant, see what he could do. It's some dodge, bound to be, some way of writing it off as some kind of tax loss, but still, looks as if it's going to happen. Long as they can sort out a few things first.'

'What kind of things?'

'Oh, control. He'll want control, some anyway. Not over the movie, but other things. Budgets. Publicity. Publicity especially.'

'He doesn't want anyone to know he's investing the money?'

'That's part of it, yeah. But it's more than that. Reporters, press, media – where my father's concerned, they're dirty words.' Natalie paused while the drinks arrived, taking a good swallow at hers. 'My dad, he's made a lot of money, yeah? Shit loads. In fact, he's made a whole lot of money twice.'

'Most people find it hard enough once.'

Without asking, Natalie leaned down and switched off the recorder. 'First time he lost it, right? All of it.

Millions. Bad judgement, bad luck. Somebody screwed him, that's what he thinks. Got his confidence and then betrayed him. I don't know how exactly and he's certainly not saying. But now he's frightened, I guess, someone might do it again. It accounts for what you might call a degree of paranoia. And then, of course, there's Lily.' She lit another cigarette. 'My mother. She's what you might call fragile. I don't know. Clinically depressed? Bipolar? In Victorian times, they'd probably have shut her up in an attic.'

Seeing the look on Lesley's face, Natalie shook her head. 'I'm sorry. I shouldn't have said that. Not about my own mother. Too much *Jane Eyre* at an impressionable age. But my dad's right to be cautious. It doesn't take much to set her off.'

'She's in hospital?'

'Not right now. But she has been, off and on practically ever since I've known her. Since I've been able to understand what was going on.'

'I'm sorry.'

'Yeah, well. Shit happens. But it helps explain the way my dad feels about publicity.'

Lesley grinned. 'He must love you, then.'

'He loathes it, all the fuss and attention, course he does. But what can he do? And I think deep down, maybe he's proud. Not of all the bullshit, but of some of the things I've done. The work, you know? Least, I like to think so. And as long as I never go into print with anything about the family, I'm okay. Just so long as nothing spills over on to them.'

'It can't be that easy,' Lesley said. 'The media being what it is.'

'Bastards like you, you mean?'

'Exactly.'

Natalie sampled some more lager. 'It's not just reporters you have to be careful of, let me tell you.'

'What do you mean?'

Natalie leaned closer. 'Less than a year back, this guy gets in touch. This was before Scott was handling my PR, yeah, so he came straight to me. Talked my agent, the silly cow, into giving him my number. Says he's writing a book about Stella. You believe that? Reckons there's a big revival of interest and can he come and talk to me? So I tell him more or less what I told you, I hardly know anything about her at all, but he keeps at it and in the end I say okay. Fuck knows why.'

She paused to drink some more.

'He comes down to London, which is where I'm living. Primrose Hill. Bit of a geek, but there are worse things, right? Turns out what he really wants, as much as anything, is a way of getting to my mum and dad. Especially my dad. Seems he's written to him a score of times without getting as much as a reply. So, partly because, now I've met him, he is kind of nice – I mean, I don't fancy him or anything, which is as well 'cause he's queer as a clockwork mouse – and partly, if I'm honest, to get him off my back, I say, yes, sure, I'll do what I can. And so, next time I see him, my dad, I start mentioning it and he goes fucking ballistic. Bloody poof, sticking his nose where it's not wanted. Calm down, I told him. Chill. Poor guy's only trying to do his job. Just keep well away from him, my dad says, don't tell him a bloody thing.'

Natalie paused for a quick swallow from her beer.

'The geek,' Lesley said. 'I know him. He's my brother.'

'Your brother?' Natalie stared at her, amazed. 'You're kidding.'

'Correction,' Lesley said. 'He was my brother.'

'Was? What do you mean? He was? You mean . . . ?'

'He was murdered. Stephen was murdered. A week ago.'

'Murdered? How? I mean, Lesley . . . Jesus!'

'So?' Scarman was suddenly beside them, clapping his hands. 'We just about wrapped up here?'

'Fuck off, Scott,' Natalie said, scarcely throwing him a glance.

'Lesley, you must have enough now?'

'I said fuck off,' Natalie said, loud enough to divert a little attention. 'Or at least get me a fucking drink. Get us both a fucking drink.'

'I think you've already had quite enough, don't you?' Scarman stretched a proprietary hand towards her and she knocked it away.

'Who d'you think you are, my fucking father?'

'Natalie . . .'

She picked an empty bottle from the floor and slammed it down hard against the table edge. Glass shattered and people screamed and there were two suited

131

security guards shouldering their way towards them through the crowd.

'Look,' Scarman said, turning to face them. 'I can settle this. It's nothing. It's all in hand.'

The taller of the two guards went through him as if he weren't there. The other one lifted Natalie bodily into the air, blood running down from the hand she held to her mouth, and began to carry her, high through the crowd, towards the door.

'Fuck,' Lesley said quietly to herself. 'Oh, fuck.'

Grabbing both her recorder and her bag, she set off in Natalie's wake.

10

'You're supposed to report the news,' Alan Pike said, 'not be it.'

'Alan, come on . . .'

'Come on, nothing. Let you loose in the city with a bit of high-profile totty and the next minute it's like fucking Baghdad.'

'Oh, yes, exaggerate a little, why don't you?'

'All right, how's this? One of the customers, eighteen-year-old girl, took a piece of flying glass in her left eye. Could still lose her sight.'

'Well, I'm sorry.'

'She's threatening to sue your pal Natalie, the owners of the club and just about anybody else she can think of.'

'You mean her insurance company is.'

'No matter. Natalie, meantime, has spent the night in custody and, the last I heard, the police still haven't decided whether or not to bring charges.'

'Seems to me,' Lesley said, 'instead of complaining, you ought to be pleased I was there.'

Pike's face suggested otherwise.

Lesley moved towards the door. 'There's a voicer all cued up and ready for the next bulletin.'

'And where do you think you're going now?'

Lesley glanced at her watch. 'With any luck, I'll be in time to catch Natalie when they kick her out of the cells.'

Of course, it was a circus. Press, local television and radio: Lesley recognised Mel Mast and a couple of stringers for the nationals; photographers gazing lustfully along their long lenses, cameramen with cigarettes in cupped hands and featherweight equipment at the ready. Gawpers and hangers-on. Lesley didn't know exactly who Scarman's contacts inside Central Police Station were these days, but she knew there'd be someone. So when the tall, slim figure with the collar of her leather coat up high, heavy dark glasses, hat pulled low, emerged, escorted, at the top of the main steps, Lesley wasn't taken in. The action was elsewhere.

Leaving the bulk of her brethren breathlessly pursuing a decoy, she scooted round to the motor vehicle exit on South Sherwood Street in time to see Scarman's Audi easing through the gate. Natalie, she guessed, was hunkered down on the rear seat.

With an extra lick of speed, Lesley set herself on the pavement edge, blocking its progress. Not wanting to attract the wrong attention by sounding his horn, Scarman wound down his window instead.

'Lesley, for fuck's sake . . .'

'Ten minutes, that's all I want. Fifteen.'

'Jesus!'

'Come on. She's got to talk to someone. Let her talk to me first.'

With a scowl, Scarman reached across towards the passenger door and Lesley jumped in. The next moment they were away, even as the first of the media crew, realising they'd been had, hove into view at the bottom corner of the street.

Scarman had taken two rooms in a budget hotel out near the motorway. The kind Lesley imagined was patronised by low-level water board officials and sales reps trading in surgical appliances. Beyond six lanes of traffic, dark clouds rose ominously above Ratcliffe-on-Soar power station.

Cheerful, Lesley was examining the decor. 'The last time I saw so many plastic flowers was on a B&B holiday in Scotland when I was sixteen.'

'It's times like this,' Scarman said, 'when I remember how bloody irritating you were to live with.'

Natalie had still not said anything. She was sitting in the one easy chair, legs drawn up beneath her, hand bandaged, several items from the minibar in her lap. Without a scrap of make-up on her face, tired, fractious, her lip pushed out like a petulant child, she was, nevertheless, Lesley thought, beautiful. The beauty more striking, perhaps, for the lack of artifice.

A camera now and a picture of that face would find

its way on to most of the newspapers in the country and some beyond.

For Lesley, the wrong medium. She took out her Nagras recorder and moved one of the hard-backed chairs closer to where Natalie was, at that moment, twisting the top from a miniature of vodka.

'That's great,' Scarman said. 'Smart. Just what we need. You half-pissed and it's still morning.'

'Scott, for Christ's sake. Who's gonna know?'

'Who? That's a reporter sitting in front of you, in case you've forgotten.'

'That's my friend,' Natalie said, reaching out and squeezing Lesley's hand.

Scarman mumbled some obscenity and shook his head in disbelief.

Lesley, despite herself, was oddly moved. 'Why don't you tell me what happened yesterday evening?' she said. 'In your own words.'

Half an hour later, it was done. All through their conversation, Lesley could hear Scarman on his mobile phone in the adjacent room, not the actual words, but the tone; Scarman smoothing away rough edges, unruffling feathers, making promises he had little or no intention of keeping.

'What will you do now?' Lesley asked.

'Go back down to London, I suppose,' Natalie said. She gave Lesley a wan smile. 'It's easier there, somehow. Up here it's like being in a goldfish bowl. Fart in the wrong place and you're in the gossip column of the *Post*.'

'Maybe if you kept a lower profile . . .'

'Didn't get pilled up and pissed, that's what you mean.'
Lesley laughed. 'That might help, too.'

Natalie started to walk with her to the door. 'Your brother,' she said.

'Stephen.'

'Yesterday, I'd never have said what I said . . .'

'It's okay.'

'No, I didn't realise . . .'

'Look.' Lesley put her hand on Natalie's shoulder. 'I don't think he'd have much minded being called a geek. It's one up on being an anorak, after all.'

'How about queer as a clockwork mouse?'

Lesley grinned. 'Guilty as charged.'

'When did you . . . ?' Natalie blurted out the beginning of the question, then stopped.

'Go on. When did I what?'

'No, it doesn't matter.'

'When did I realise Stephen was gay?'

'Yes.'

A small sigh slipped from Lesley's mouth. 'It's funny, isn't it? Because Stephen was older than me, not by much, but when I was still at nursery, he was already at school, and then by the time I was at the juniors, he was moving into the seniors or just about, so I suppose I never really questioned what he did. He was just my big brother. And he was nice to me. He'd play with me, sometimes anyway, this farm I had – you know, cows and sheep and stuff – and, oh, God, dressing up.' Lesley laughed. 'I should have known then, shouldn't I? And he used to read to me, when I was a lot younger. All those stories about Little Grey Rabbit and Squirrel and Hare, I remember.' Lesley was smiling, but there were tears running down her face. '*Hare Joins the Home Guard*, that was our favourite. Hare getting it all wrong and hurling his ham and egg sandwiches at this army of weasels because he doesn't know what an ambush is.'

She was crying loudly now, taking in great gulps of air. Scarman looked round the door from the other room and quickly withdrew.

Natalie put an arm around her and led her back to the bed. 'Come on, sit down. Sit here.'

'I'm sorry, I . . .'

'Don't be stupid, it's fine.'

'I just haven't . . .'

'It's all right.'

'I haven't . . .'

'For fuck's sake, shut up and cry.'

Lesley laughed and cried and carried on crying until the tears had all gone.

The sleeve of Natalie's top, on which she'd been leaning, was soaked. What make-up she'd been wearing had smeared down her face.

'Jesus, I must look a sight!'

'Nothing half an hour in the bathroom won't cure.'

Lesley looked at her watch. 'I don't have half an hour.'

'Come on,' Natalie said, grabbing her hand. 'I'll help.'

After ten minutes, give or take, Lesley looked fit enough to return to work. 'I still didn't tell you,' she said, making the last adjustments in the mirror.

'Tell me what?'

'When I knew Stephen was gay.'

'It doesn't matter.'

'I don't think there was any one time,' Lesley said. 'No, you know, startling revelation, defining moment. I think I just realised – I suppose I was thirteen or fourteen, so Stephen must have already finished school, been going off to university – I just realised that's what he was. Gay.'

'You didn't mind? I mean, you weren't – I don't know – disgusted or anything? I'm trying to think back to when I was that age.'

Lesley smiled. 'No. It was just Stephen.'

Natalie gave her a quick kiss and a squeeze of the hand. 'Come on, let's get you out of here. Before you start up again.'

As the previous night's incident was reported, Natalie had been lifting an almost empty lager bottle from the table and it had slipped through her fingers, no more than that. There were press photographs of her turning up at the hospital with an array of flowers for the young woman with the injured eye. The injury itself had proved less serious than had been at first suspected; there would be some slight scarring but that, in time, would fade. In a brief interview for local television, the woman, holding the bouquet she'd been given up to her bandaged face, had absolved Natalie of any blame. 'Accident, weren't it? Could've happened to anyone.' Lesley wondered if anything other than promises had changed hands. Either way, Scarman had done his job well.

* * *

For the remainder of that day, Lesley was swept along on a slurry of news: police officers involved in Operation Kingdom had made 160 arrests for criminal and anti-social behaviour on the Bestwood estate; the trial began of the men accused of murdering three homeless women, two of the bodies having been discovered in a derelict warehouse, the third in a burnt-out flat; a man previously cautioned for downloading pornographic images of children had been discovered teaching in a school in East Anglia and local parent groups here in the city were demanding assurances that there were no such instances in their own schools. There might have been some good news somewhere, but if so, it passed Lesley by.

Scarman sent her a card, hand delivered. *Thanks. Let's keep in touch! Love, Scott.* The pieces floated like confetti in the toilet bowl and then they disappeared.

And despite everything else, odd thoughts about Stephen and what had happened kept drifting through.

Towards the end of the afternoon, finding five minutes to herself, Lesley phoned Cambridgeshire Police and asked to speak to either Detective Inspector Grayson or Detective Sergeant Walker. Neither, she was told, was available. To what was her call relating? The details were carefully, even laboriously noted and she was assured her message would be passed on and someone would call her back.

'Before the end of the afternoon?' Lesley asked.

'Before the end of the afternoon.'

Nobody did.

When the phone rang at last it was James Crawford.

He had received a visit from Special Branch, two officers who had questioned him politely but intensely for the best part of an hour, then left.

'So much for publicity,' Crawford said.

'I'm sorry.'

'Not to fret. Besides, you should be pleased. Shows there's someone out there listening to local radio. If it is only the so-called security services.'

A smile crossed Lesley's face. They'd have to soak up an awful lot of Abba and Neil Diamond before lighting on anything remotely subversive.

'Take care,' she said.

'You too.'

It was well past five. She considered ringing Will Grayson again, but thought better of it. There was a local residents' meeting out at Bestwood, with a police spokesperson and the local MP in attendance, and, even though one of the other reporters was covering it, she thought she might put in an appearance.

Back home, after a bath and a reheated bowl of Sainsbury's broccoli and stilton soup, she was having second thoughts. Let someone else report the meeting, she would go up to the estate the following morning and talk to some of the residents, those who'd perhaps not gone along for reasons of their own. She made a mug of coffee, switched on the television and switched it off again. The same with the radio. After half a dozen pages, a book she'd already made several attempts at reading failed to keep her attention. As did a magazine. Several magazines.

Lesley looked at her watch.

It was too late to go to the meeting now, little sense in getting there after the main speeches were over.

In her bag there was a comp someone at work had given her for a gig at Rock City. Beth Orton. Vaguely, she remembered a song about a woman coming home alone in the early hours of the morning after. What was it? Walking down somewhere in last night's dress, the smell of some man on her fingers, the taste of him on her breath. Been there, Lesley thought, done that. One-night stands. Though not for a while. Knickers either stuffed down into one of her pockets, or pushed down into the bottom of her bag.

There'd been a time, somewhere between leaving uni and coming to her senses, when if she'd been out with mates on a Saturday night and not pulled, she'd felt she'd failed. Life coming to an end. Now she didn't care. She didn't go out, not much, and when she did it was relatively sedate, most of her friends either married or with long-term partners. Tucked up in bed before the twelve o'clock news.

She looked again at the ticket, flicked it with her finger, then phoned the venue. Beth Orton would be onstage at nine-fifteen. Time enough to walk across town.

She hadn't been to Rock City in ages. The slightly scruffy entrance, just a few paces up from the back of the Royal Concert Hall, seemed scarcely to have changed; neither had the black-jacketed doormen who looked her over cursorily before nodding her through. The interior was dark, save for the bars at either end and the all-but-empty stage on which the ubiquitous roadie was going through the usual prolonged routine of testing mikes and tuning guitars, putting out set lists, towels and bottles of water. The place, Lesley judged, was a good two-thirds full, a real mix of people, some quite a bit younger than herself, students, but others in their thirties and even forties, couples many of them, women in twos and threes, the occasional intense man off on his own.

At first, she thought she'd go up on to the narrow gallery at the back, but decided instead to find a space for herself down front, six or seven uneven rows from the stage.

There wasn't long to wait.

Without preamble, the four male members of the band took their positions, and Orton, unannounced, walked on and took a seat at the piano. The first number was short and over almost before Lesley had got in tune with what was happening. The roadie handed Orton a guitar and she moved to the centre of the stage. A brief, jokey intro-duction and they were into song number two. The sound was loud without being deafening and mercifully clear; Orton's voice, high in places, occasionally wavering, almost shrill, rode over the insistent, drum-and bass-like rhythm with ease. Her manner between songs, as she grew more relaxed, was engagingly ditzy, taking on a vagueness Lesley thought was charming, even if, as she supposed, it was something of an affectation. However much she might pretend to uncertainty, it was clear that Orton was very much in control of what she was doing: the band, the audience, everything.

When she made fun of how awkward she felt to be wearing a dress – a rarity, apparently, in honour of the city that had nurtured Paul Smith – someone from the crowd yelled out, 'You look fit!' and followed this, in the next lull, with the number of his mobile phone.

A cliché, Lesley thought, but they were all in the palm of her hand.

When the band went off, leaving Orton to accompany herself on acoustic guitar, there was a new vulnerability in her voice that seemed to make the crowd draw closer.

Home is where the heartbreak
Wraps cold around my bones

Lesley felt something shiver inside.

The band came back and the tempo quickened, the volume increased, sweeping the crowd along with it. Then, all too soon, the set was over, save for the unison clapping, the stamping of feet and shouts for more, the obligatory encores.

Lesley was near the exit when Orton came out from the wings for one final time, singing the opening lines of 'It's Not the Spotlight', so softly over the ringing tones of her guitar, you had to strain to hear. Lesley listened, hanging on each fragile word, and then slipped outside before the song could end.

11

'Jesus!' Will said, kicking off his running shoes in the hall. 'That was hard.'

'Why do it then?' Lorraine asked. She was standing in the kitchen doorway in her towelling dressing gown, leaning sideways against the jamb. 'It's not as if you're putting on weight. Not too much, anyway.'

'Bloody cheek!' Will pulled his T-shirt over his head and flicked it towards her. 'And besides, you're in no position to talk.'

'I've got a reason.'

'An excuse.'

'I'm not like Madonna, you know. Pay a personal trainer and get my figure back in two weeks.'

Leaning forward, Will kissed Lorraine on the side of the face. 'Never fancied Madonna, anyway.'

'Get off, you're all sweaty.'

'Not for long. Quick shower and I'm yours.'

'Kids might have something to say about that.'

'Where are they anyway?'

'Jake's eating his breakfast, Susie's sleeping.'

'Making up for last night.'

'Something like that.'

On the landing, Will turned and called back down. 'Any chance of scrambled eggs?'

He wasn't sure if she'd heard, but there they were, twenty minutes later, soft and just slightly runny, the way he liked them, along with mushrooms, two rashers of bacon and toast.

'I'd forgotten,' Will said.

'What's that?'

'That it was my birthday.'

'You could have this every morning, if you weren't rushing out of the house as if the place were on fire.'

'And if you weren't busy feeding Susie.'

'You could do it yourself, you know.'

'Not until she's on to the bottle.'

'I meant make your own scrambled eggs.'

'Not half as well as you.'

'Bullshitter.'

'That's swearing,' Jake said from the door.

'I thought you were in the bathroom, young man. Cleaning your teeth.'

'I have.'

'Really?'

'Yes.'

'Come here then.'

'What for?'

'Let me smell your breath.'

Jake hesitated. 'I'll just go back upstairs. Do them again.'

'You do that.'

Will shook some brown sauce on to his plate. 'You're a hard taskmistress.'

'You want to be the one who takes him to the dentist?'

'Not particularly.'

'Well, then.'

There was frost on the car windows, a thin covering that scraped away cleanly, no need to use the spray. The sky was the same pale, opaque grey as the day before and the day before that. Though there was no sign of ice on the road, he felt the rear wheels sliding under him as he took the turn into the road along the fen.

Not so very long ago, a woman they knew from the village, not a friend exactly, but someone who would stop and chat with Lorraine if she met her rather than walking past, had driven off in her brand new Volvo, slid on a patch of black ice, lost control and ended up with the car wrapped around a tree. Safe herself, aside from being badly shaken, the car was a write-off – and it could have been so much worse.

Levelling out, Will moved up through the gears. He had to go to Police Headquarters in Huntingdon first thing; a meeting about information management systems for officers at the rank of detective inspector and above. Important, Will didn't doubt, but not the thing to whet his appetite for the rest of the day.

*   *   *

By the time he got to Parkside, a little after twelve, Will's head was heavy with a barely digested mix of common sense and poorly articulated mumbo-jumbo. What was it, he thought, that caused consultants and advisers and high-ranking individuals who should know better to adopt a language that, while it seemed to share a number of characteristics with normal everyday English, was as foreign as Serbo-Croat or Farsi?

He'd been back in his office barely ten minutes before Helen's face showed round the edge of his door, smiling.

'What's up?'

'You remember,' Helen said, 'the semen on the towel?'

'Great way to start a conversation.'

'You do remember?'

'From Stephen Bryan's laundry basket, yes.'

'We'd assumed it belonged to someone he'd met casually, but without any proof.'

'Something's happened to make us change our mind?'

'The opposite. It looks as though Nick Moyles has come up with the goods.'

'Go on.'

Helen perched herself on the edge of Will's desk. 'Moyles was in this bar, asking around, and this guy comes up to him, says he's got something he wants to say. Hadn't wanted to come forward at first, didn't want to get involved, but then he'd seen an appeal for information on TV. I suppose he thought we'd get to him sooner or later and figured sooner, under his own steam, would be better.'

'Nick's brought him in?'

148

'Downstairs now, waiting our pleasure.'

'Name?'

'Johnson. Russell Johnson.'

'What's he like?'

Helen shrugged. 'Nice, quiet, polite. A little earnest. Quite good-looking if you go for that fey kind of thing.' She swung her leg down from the desk. 'According to Nick, he's an ex-student, though not of Bryan's. Met when he was doing one of those charity muggings in the market square. "Excuse me, but have you got five minutes to discuss the famine in West Africa." You know what I mean.'

Will did. If ever anything was going to put him off donating to charity it was that: half a dozen healthy-looking specimens waiting to waylay him with tales of woe and misery, when all he wanted was to get into Pret A Manger before they ran out of cinnamon Danish.

'Anyway,' Helen said, 'it appears Bryan did. Have five minutes to spare for him. And more. Johnson ended up spending the night and Bryan sent him on his way next morning with a hot breakfast inside him and a standing order for famine relief.'

'When exactly was this?'

'Five days before the murder.'

Will whistled as he moved round from behind his desk. 'He's agreed to give a sample? DNA?'

'Apparently.'

'Let's go and see what he has to say.'

Russell Johnson was medium height, slight, fair hair falling forward a little over his forehead. When Will and Helen entered the room, he was standing, hands in pockets, close to the far wall, and without being asked, he went back to the table, pulled out a chair and sat down.

Will introduced Helen and himself. Chairs and table aside, there was no other furniture in the room. At the end of the table which butted against the wall was a twin-deck tape recorder; a video camera, not switched on, was bracketed to one of the upper corners of the room, behind where Will and Helen were now sitting.

Johnson fidgeted with his hands, brushed his hair away from his eyes, looked at Will and then Helen, looked away, fidgeting some more.

'You won't mind if we record this conversation, Russell?' Helen said.

'I'm not under arrest, am I?'

'Should you be?'

'No, of course not.' A nervous laugh.

'Well, then? We can go ahead?'

'Yes, I suppose so. Sure.'

He didn't look sure of very much at all.

Helen stripped the cellophane from around two new cassettes and slotted them into place.

'So how well did you know Stephen Bryan, Russell?' Will asked, once the preliminary rigmarole was over.

'I didn't really . . . I didn't know him . . . not very well at all.'

'As I understand it, you spent the night with him.'

'Yes.'

'Slept with him.'

'Yes.'

'Had sex. I assume you had sex?'

'Yes.' Johnson ran finger and thumb over his upper lip, covering his mouth. 'Look, there's nothing . . . there isn't any law. We're entitled . . .'

'Russell,' Helen said sweetly, 'within the bounds of reason, you're entitled to fuck who you want.'

Will shot her a warning glance.

'Stephen Bryan,' he said, 'how many times did you see him? In all?'

'I said, just the once.'

'Tell us about that. How you and Stephen met.'

Johnson repeated, more or less exactly, the story they'd already heard.

'And that was the only time you saw him? That night? The morning after?'

'Yes.'

'You're sure?'

'Of course I'm sure.'

'Why was that?'

'I don't understand.'

'Assuming, you know, you got on well, how come you saw him just the once?'

'He made that clear. Stephen. You know, before. Before I went with him.'

'And afterwards, he didn't change his mind?'

Johnson shook his head. 'A once-and-for-all-time thing. That's what he said.'

'You didn't try and get him to change his mind?' Helen asked.

Johnson nodded, not holding her gaze.

'Sorry?' Helen said.

'I . . . Yes, I did. I asked him . . .' Johnson shook his head.

'You liked him, then?'

'Yes.'

'What did you think when he was killed?'

'I didn't . . . I couldn't believe it . . . You don't, do you? Not someone you know. Someone you've known. It was horrible. Ghastly. What happened. What they said in the papers.'

Johnson closed his eyes.

'I want you to think carefully,' Will said. 'Was there anything that Stephen Bryan said when you were together that might have a bearing on what happened?'

Johnson looked up. 'What kind of thing?'

'Anything. Anything at all.'

'I can't think . . .'

'Take your time.'

After some moments, Johnson shook his head. 'I'm sorry.'

'Did he mention other people?' Helen asked. 'Other people he'd met, perhaps? Casually?'

'No. Not really. I did ask was he seeing anybody. You know, seriously, and he said no, not any more.' Johnson ran his tongue along his lips as if they were suddenly dry. 'There was this photograph beside the bed. Stephen with somebody else. I asked if that was the person he'd been involved with and he said yes. I don't know why I keep it there, he said, not any more. He . . . he turned it round before we . . . before we went to bed.'

152

'And did you get the impression,' Will said, 'since that relationship had finished, he'd been seeing other men?'

'I don't think so. I mean, I didn't ask him, not directly, and he didn't say, but no, that wasn't the impression I got. Although . . .'

He hesitated, uncertain.

'Although what?'

'When we got there, back to his place, there was a message on the answerphone. Stephen started to play it, almost automatically, I suppose, and then as soon as he heard the voice, he switched it off.'

'This message,' Will said, 'can you remember what it was?'

'Not really. I wasn't really paying much attention.'

'But you heard something?'

Johnson nodded. '"You better believe what I say." I think that's what it was. Something like that, anyway.'

'"You better believe what I say"?'

'Yes.'

'The exact words?'

'I don't know. I think so, yes.'

'And that's all you can remember?'

'Yes. Like I said, Stephen switched it off.'

'What kind of a voice was it?' Helen asked. 'Male, female?'

'Male, definitely.'

'How old?'

'I don't know. There wasn't enough to say.'

'Think. Your age? Older?'

'Definitely older.'

153

'Forties? Fifties? Older than that.'

Johnson shook his head. 'Forties, maybe. It's difficult to say.'

'Any kind of an accent?'

Johnson gave it some thought. 'A bit of one, yes. Not strong, though. But not – what's it called? – received pronunciation. Vaguely northern, I suppose. Yorkshire, maybe. South Yorkshire. Sheffield. I had a mate at uni, he was from Sheffield. It was a bit like that.'

'And this voice, was it angry? Calm? Matter of fact?'

'Not angry, not exactly, More firm. Positive. As though whoever it was wasn't going to take no for an answer.'

'Threatening, then?'

'Yes, I suppose so. Threatening. You could say that.'

'And how did Stephen respond? Aside from turning it off? Did he seem frightened?'

'No, not frightened. At least, I don't think so. More annoyed. Pissed off, you know? But not for long. It didn't get him in a mood or anything.'

'And did he say anything about it? Who it was? What it was about?'

'No, nothing.'

'And you didn't ask?'

'No.'

Will leaned back; he and Helen shared a quick glance.

'Do you think you'd be able to recognise the voice if you heard it again?' Will said.

'I'm not sure. I think I might.' He smiled, nervously. 'Not being a great deal of help, am I?'

'You're doing fine,' Helen said.

Johnson repeated the gesture of running finger and thumb over his lip, obscuring his mouth. 'I've thought about it a lot. Since, you know, what happened. It really upset me. He was nice. Genuine. And fun. He was fun.'

There was a quiver in his voice as he spoke.

'I wonder,' Helen said, 'why you didn't come forward sooner?'

Distress showed on Johnson's face. 'I should have done, I know. I feel really guilty about that. It's just . . . it was just . . . I didn't want to get involved, if I didn't have to. Be a witness, I suppose that's what I mean.' He squeezed his hands between his knees. 'My parents, they don't know. About me being gay. Well, they do. I'm sure they do. It's just that we've never talked about it, you know? And if it came out, into the open, like this . . . they wouldn't understand. Not properly. Me and Stephen . . .' He faltered into silence.

'If you think of anything else,' Will said, 'however trivial it might seem, you'll let us know?'

'Of course.'

'And if we want to get in touch with you, we've got your details?'

'Yes.'

Helen showed him from the building, stayed to light a cigarette, Will joining her moments later. The sky was a mottled grey, unbroken, no scrap or edge of blue. No glimmer of sun. Another drab winter's day, the temperature low.

'The tape from the answerphone . . .' Will began.

'Wiped.'

155

'You're sure?'

Helen nodded. 'Yes. We can get it checked, of course. But it's got one of those options, when you finish listening, press Delete.'

'And that's what Bryan must have done.'

'Unless somebody else did it for him.'

'Whoever killed him.'

'It's a possibility.' Helen drew deep on her cigarette. 'Especially if they knew their voice was on the tape.'

Will looked at her. 'That's a leap.'

'We haven't got a great deal else.'

'If it was the murderer, why not simply take the tape? Destroy it?'

She shrugged. 'This way it doesn't draw attention to itself. If Johnson hadn't told us about the call we'd have had no idea.'

She released a stream of smoke and Will wafted it away from his face.

'Whoever did this,' he said, 'he was careful. We know that. No prints anywhere. A few stray hairs which might or might not be his, and that's all. Almost no physical evidence at all. And that's at odds with the attack itself. Violence that extreme, it suggests real anger, doesn't it? Rage.'

'Maybe once that was spent,' Helen said, 'calm is what he was.'

'A bit like making love.'

Helen smiled. 'Poor Lorraine.'

'You know what I mean.'

'I think I can just about remember.'

'I'm pleased.'

'Our man climaxes, as it were, and then, in a spell of post-tumescent clarity, goes round wiping anything he might have touched.'

'Something like that.'

'There is one other possibility,' Helen said.

'What's that?'

'I was thinking – I'm not sure why – about the awful story McKusick told, the time Bryan was raped. You remember, two men. I just wondered, maybe, if something similar had happened here. Not in the same way, but two instead of one. One person who killed him and another who neutralised the scene.'

Will raised an eyebrow. 'Neutralised the scene? You're going to have to stop watching so much *CSI*. You're getting to sound like – what's her name? – that woman with the strange name. Marg something.'

'Helgenberger.'

'That's it. You're getting to sound more like her every day.'

Helen shook her head. 'I wasn't born on a ranch in Nebraska. Nor do I have an ex-rockstar boyfriend. And I certainly don't wear my T-shirts that tight. If I did, I'd probably be escorted from the building.'

Will grinned at the thought.

'The voice,' Helen said. 'On the tape. South Yorkshire, maybe. Close to middle age. Unless he's putting it on, that's not McKusick.' Dropping her cigarette to the ground, she squashed it beneath her shoe.

12

For Lesley, it had been another busy day. Several sets of background interviews made out at Bestwood had to be downloaded, edited and made available. Bulletins had to be prepared. And just when it was the last thing she wanted, there was another call from James Crawford. When he had returned from doing a little food shopping in Bingham, it was to find his house had been broken into; all the photographs of the suspected CIA plane were missing, prints as well as negatives; not only that, but his notebooks had been taken, along with the files he had been compiling and, almost more serious, his computer, together with assorted back-up disks and CDs.

'You've reported it to the police?' Lesley asked.

Crawford laughed. 'For all the good it will do me.'

At the end of the conversation, Lesley caught herself wondering, perhaps unfairly, whether some of the things Crawford had been telling her were happening in his imagination. What had Pike said? Every crank and crazy? Was that what Crawford was? Lesley hadn't thought so, but now . . .

There were two bulletins still to finish. Not to mention the scribbled Post-It notes which surrounded her computer screen like the petals of a demented sunflower and demanded her attention.

Neither Will Grayson nor Helen Walker had ever returned her call, and she thought she would give them one more try. This time, to her surprise, she was put through to Helen Walker without difficulty.

'Hello,' Lesley said, 'this is Lesley Scarman. I'm . . .'

'You're Stephen Bryan's sister.'

'That's right.'

'And a reporter.'

'Yes, but that's not why I'm phoning.'

There was a slight pause at the other end of the line. 'How can I help you, Ms Scarman?'

Lesley liked the Ms. 'My brother's papers. Things he was working on. I understand they're in your possession.'

'We needed to see if there was anything there that would help us with our investigation.'

'And was there?'

'Not as far as I know.'

'So you'll be releasing them.'

'Eventually, yes.'

'But if you've no further use . . .'

'You realise, the investigation is still ongoing.'

'Look,' Lesley said, 'I'd like a chance to see what's there. Apart from anything else, there's a book my brother was working on. I'd like to see how far he'd got. You never know, it might even be publishable.'

Helen hesitated.

'I could come over there,' Lesley said. 'You could shut me up with everything in a little room.'

Another pause. 'Let me get back to you.'

That hadn't happened by the time Lesley left work. She was standing at the London Road roundabout, waiting for the lights to change, when her mobile sounded and she had difficulty in hearing Helen Walker over the noise from four lanes of traffic.

'I'm sorry, could you . . .'

'I said, as long as you're prepared to come here and look at your brother's stuff under controlled conditions, there doesn't seem to be a problem.'

'Tomorrow?'

'Tomorrow would be fine.'

Closing the phone, Lesley smiled. She would persuade Alan Pike to let her go off diary, on the excuse maybe of following up Crawford's claim that he had been burgled. That would give her the time she needed.

Helen was waiting for Lesley on the second floor, just by the stairs, wearing black trousers and a loose cotton jacket over a pale green T-shirt, and looking younger somehow than Lesley had remembered.

Holding out her hand, Helen dismissed the uniformed constable who had escorted Lesley thus far with a nod. 'I'm sorry about your brother,' she said.

'Thank you.'

Helen turned and pushed through a door that led into a long corridor, Lesley following.

'We've put everything along here; everything we removed from the house. Papers, files. Some of it seems to be in order, but not all.'

Helen stopped and unlocked a door, standing aside to let Lesley through. There was a bare table and a single chair; storage boxes stacked three deep on the floor.

'Your bag,' Helen said.

'They checked it downstairs.'

'I'd like to check it again.'

Lesley swung the red and grey bag round from her shoulder on to the table and stood back.

'Open it for me, if you would.'

Lesley unclipped the two catches and pulled back the velcro. In one padded section was her laptop; in another were her mini disc recorder and microphone, notebook and pens. Her mobile phone was in a small pocket at the side.

Helen examined the contents briefly and then stepped away. 'Nice bag, by the way,' she said. 'Funky. Where'd you get it, if you don't mind me asking?'

Lesley smiled. 'Australia. Sydney. But I think you can get them here now. There's a shop in Nottingham stocks them, I think. Or, at least, it did. St James Street.'

'Thanks for the tip.' Helen moved back towards the door. 'I'll leave you alone. What? A couple of hours? You won't be disturbed.'

Lesley lifted the lid from the first of the boxes and sat down. Surrounded by four recently painted walls, she had only the one CCTV camera, high in the corner, for company.

It soon became clear that whereas some of her brother's papers were still more or less together, others had become seriously shuffled around, adjacent pages bearing little or no apparent relationship to one another. Lesley's first task was to sort through the miscellaneous material and impose, where she could, a sense of order.

By the end of the first hour, she had made significant progress – enough to realise she was never going to be able to read every word, not in the time available. She would have to prioritise as best she could.

There were lecture notes for the courses Stephen had been teaching, reading lists attached, plus drafts of articles he had written for a variety of journals, often several versions of each, printed out and then annotated and corrected by hand.

From Holiday Camp *to* Hollyoaks: *Representations of British Life, a Survey.*

Images of the Working Class: Ken Loach to Martin Parr.

Z Cars *and* The Wednesday Play *to* Lock, Stock and Two Smoking Barrels: *The British Crime Film and the Documentary Tradition.*

Victim of Life's Circumstances: Homosexuality in British Cinema.

Case Studies from the Rank Charm School and the

Company of Youth: From Diana Fluck to Diana Dors and Patsy Sloot to Susan Shaw.

Her brother wrote with a light, slightly caustic style, leavening what was clearly an encyclopedic knowledge with humour and anecdote, and keeping critical theory to a minimum.

There were also detailed notes on individual films, a large number of these, illustrated here and there with drawings in which the characters were rendered as little more than matchstick figures; some of those had been transcribed, others were still in the same scribbled hand Stephen had used while watching. *Dance Hall. Johnny Frenchman. The Singer Not the Song. The Pool of London. Peeping Tom.* When she first saw, and recognised, his quite distinctive writing, Lesley had to lean back and take a deep breath before continuing.

Apart from a few creased pages from what could have been an early draft, however, Lesley could find little direct reference to the promised biography of Stella Leonard. Bits and pieces, stops and starts, but no clear outline, no chapter by chapter breakdown, no detailed research notes, no plan. All of these, she presumed, had been kept on the hard drive of his computer, backed up, possibly, on disks which were also missing.

Checking back, she found Leonard herself mentioned in the articles on both the Rank Charm School and the British Crime Film, and in the latter there was a section devoted to *Shattered Glass*, comparing it favourably with various examples of American *film noir* from the 1940s, such as *The Dark Mirror* and *Double Indemnity*.

Lesley remembered seeing *Double Indemnity*, Barbara Stanwyck and Fred MacMurray plotting in the aisles of their local supermarket to murder Stanwyck's husband for his insurance money. So unlike Lesley's own experiences in Asda.

By now, her eyes were tired and she could feel a dull headache developing; according to her watch it was almost time. Just a few minutes later than she'd said, Helen Walker knocked on the door and pushed it open.

'How we doing?'

Lesley smiled. 'About to get an RSI from turning all these pages.'

'Let me help you box it all up again. Then I'll walk you out.'

As soon as they had stepped through into daylight, Helen started reaching for her cigarettes. 'You might have thought I was being overly polite, or making sure you didn't leave the building with a bit of police property in your pocket, but what this is really, is an excuse to smoke.'

She offered the pack to Lesley, who shook her head.

'You give it up?'

'Never started.'

'Never?'

'Never.'

Helen's thumb snapped down on her lighter. 'How could you not?'

'I just never fancied it. Something about the smell, I don't know. My mother, for one thing, was quite a

164

heavy smoker when she was younger. Around the house, you know. I think that helped to put me off.'

'But all your friends at school, weren't they sneaking out for fags, nicking them from their parents, lighting up on the way home?'

'Yes, of course.'

'Well,' Helen said, drawing smoke down into her lungs, 'you've saved yourself a small fortune, if nothing else.'

'Sweets,' Lesley said, with a shamefaced grin. 'Chocolate especially. That was what my pocket money went on. What I'd be lifting from the corner shop if I got the chance. Maltesers. Rolos. Twix. You know one of the saddest days of my life? When I heard this rumour there were going to be no more Terry's chocolate oranges.'

Helen laughed.

'I'm serious,' Lesley said.

Helen looked her up and down. 'Why aren't you about twelve stone?'

'I was.'

'You're kidding.'

'Only just.'

'So what happened?'

'Oh, acupuncture, hypnotism . . .'

'Really?'

Lesley smiled. 'No. Just plain old-fashioned will-power.'

'You gave up altogether?'

'One bar of dark chocolate a week. I keep it in the fridge. Two pieces a night.'

'Scary.'

'What?'

'That kind of self-discipline.' Helen tapped a funnel of grey ash towards the ground. 'Upstairs, you find what you were looking for?'

'Not really. A few stray pages, mixed in with all the rest. But no, as far as the book's concerned, there's nothing.'

'Maybe he kept it on his computer?'

'It's possible. But then why not make hard copies? He seems to have done that with almost everything else.'

Helen angled her head aside and released a small scurry of smoke. 'Bit of a wasted journey. I'm sorry.'

'You don't think it could have something to do with what happened? The fact that it's all missing?'

'I'm not sure what you mean.'

'Well, whoever killed Stephen, they were looking for something.'

'We're not sure of that.'

'The place was searched, you said so. At least, Grayson did.'

'Trashed rather than searched.'

'But things were missing. Taken.'

'Yes. Laptop, wallet, probably cash.'

'So why not the manuscript? However much he'd written so far?'

'But why? Who would do that? Why would it be so important?'

'I don't know. It just seems . . . it seems more than a coincidence, that's all.'

'Do you even know,' Helen asked, 'how much he'd written?'

'No.'

'Or if he'd written anything at all?'

'Not for certain, no. But I think so. He must have.'

'Couldn't he have been still – I don't know – putting it together? His research, whatever?'

'Then where is it? There's nothing.'

Helen sighed and shook her head. 'I don't know. I'm sorry.'

Lesley shifted the balance of her bag on her shoulder. 'I'd best go,' she said. 'Thanks for your help.'

Helen squeezed out a smile. 'There is one thing,' she said. 'Did Stephen ever say anything to you about McKusick losing his temper?'

'Mark? No.'

'You're sure?'

'Quite sure. Why?'

'Oh, just checking.'

Lesley took a step away. 'Thanks again.'

'Any time.'

Helen stood in the doorway, watching her go, taking one more drag on her cigarette.

Coincidence?

Coincidence or chance or nothing at all?

167

13

Helen looked out through Will's office window in the direction of the multi-storey car park and the YMCA. Ugly buildings both, fading now into the dusk. Maybe in Cambridge, you noticed their ugliness even more. 'I've been thinking about what Bryan's sister was suggesting . . .'

'The missing manuscript. So-called.'

'Yes.'

'What about it?'

'I got in touch with a couple of publishers Bryan had worked with before. One of them said Bryan had talked to him about the idea ages ago, come up with some kind of proposal, but they hadn't been able to come to terms. They're quite a small, specialist outfit, by the sound of it, and Bryan thought the book should have a wider audience. Wanted one of the bigger firms to take it on instead.'

'He hadn't seen it? This publisher? The book?'

Helen shook her head. 'Just an outline. A few notes, he said. Nothing more.'

'He have any idea who else Bryan might have talked to?'

'He made one or two suggestions, yes, gave me a couple of names. I spoke to this editor who'd had a few meetings with Bryan, a year or so ago. Basically, told Bryan his firm would be interested and that he should let him see the first dozen chapters or so when they were written.'

'And?'

'And nothing. Bryan never showed him anything.'

'He could have taken it elsewhere, couldn't he? Looking for a better deal?'

'I don't think so. I checked.'

'You've been busy.'

'Yes.'

'Getting nowhere.'

Helen smiled and made a small shrugging gesture with her shoulders. 'Police work.'

'Absolutely.'

'You're not convinced about all this, are you?' Helen said.

'Unless you can come up with something else, McKusick's still the best shot we've got.'

It was Helen's turn to look unconvinced.

'What we should do,' Will said, 'have another run at McKusick's friends. Bryan's, too. Go further back. If Rouse's account of McKusick losing his temper is accurate, it's hard to believe something like it hadn't happened before. Any luck we'll dig up something that'll give us some more purchase when we lean on McKusick again.'

*   *   *

It was not a good night. Susie had woken at one-thirty and a quarter to four; at a quarter past, Jake had come into their room, frightened by a dream, and refused to leave. All it needed was for the phone to ring and, just as both Will and Lorraine, Jake wedged awkwardly between them, had got back to sleep, that was what it did.

Lorraine picked it up first.

'Will,' she said, nudging him fully awake. 'It's for you. Helen.'

With a groan, Will pushed himself into a sitting position. 'What's up?'

'I remembered. In amongst Bryan's correspondence. An exchange of letters with a solicitor. Some kind of an injunction. To do with his research. Wait – I've got it here.'

'Where are you, anyway?'

'At the station.'

Will looked at the bedside clock. 'It's not even half past five.'

'I couldn't sleep.'

Join the club, Will thought.

'Listen,' Helen said. '"In the strongest possible terms we are requesting that you abjure . . ."'

'Abjure?'

'That's what it says. "Abjure from any further attempts to question or otherwise harass any members of the family."'

'Which family?'

'Not clear. Stella Leonard's, I assume.'

170

Will swung round so that his feet were touching the floor; now he was awake he needed to go and pee. 'Where's the letter from? Which solicitors?'

'Anstruther, Parks and Quince.'

'Local.'

'That's right.'

'Offices close to the Guildhall?'

'On Petty Cury, yes. You want to go and talk to them?'

'You think we should?'

'I think we should.'

'Okay. Why don't you give them a few hours, make an appointment?'

'Right. Give my love to Lorraine. Tell her I'm sorry I woke her.'

'Absolutely.'

But Lorraine was already in the bathroom, starting her day.

The student who nearly caromed off Will was wearing white tights under a strip of denim skirt scarcely as wide as the belt that supported it. The front wheel of her sit-up-and-beg bicycle had bumped against the kerb as she pedalled along King's Parade, the subsequent wobble unseating her and delivering her, almost, into Will's outstretched arms. Instead of catching her cleanly, however, he found, to his surprise, that he was clutching an outflung elbow and a significant piece of white-clad thigh.

'Oh, God! I'm sorry. I'm sorry,' the girl cried. The

171

fact that she was listening to her iPod beneath her knitted hat caused her to shout more than was necessary.

'Neat catch, Will,' Helen said, amused.

Disentangling himself, Will was careful not to pitch the student to the ground.

'I really am sorry,' the girl said again, pulling off her hat and slipping the small white headphones from her ears. 'I don't know what happened.'

'No harm done,' Will said.

She had startling blue eyes and a complexion like milk.

'Will,' Helen said, nudging him. 'Your tongue.'

'What about it?'

'It's hanging out.'

Helen helped the student retrieve her bike and held the handlebars for her while she readjusted the small rucksack, then climbed back on board. A quick wave and another shout of thanks and she was on her way, easing out into the unsteady stream of cyclists moving between one college and another.

'Okay,' Helen said, 'I'll never accuse you of fancying Nick Moyles again. It's young nubiles you lust over, pedalling their way to lectures with their head full of Coldcut and Kierkegaard.'

'Kierkegaard?'

'Just a name I picked up somewhere. *University Challenge*, probably.'

'Sometimes,' Will said, 'you're too clever for your own good.'

Not for the first time, Helen poked out her tongue,

a habit that had become ingrained in childhood and which she'd never quite been able to break. One day, as her mother was wont to say, someone will bite it off.

Well, Helen thought, just let them try.

The offices of Anstruther, Parks and Quince, as Helen had said, were on Petty Cury, at the far side of the Guildhall. Intimations of old-fashioned Tudor intermingled with turn-of-the-century modern, sleek lines and technological jurisprudence. Helen's request for an appointment had been successful: Mr Quentin Anstruther at ten forty-five.

Anstruther's eyrie was perched on the upper floor of the building, one wall lined with law books, mostly leather bound, another filled in the main with journals; the solicitor's desk was big enough for a decent game of ping-pong, a smart-looking silver laptop open at the centre, papers in some slight disarray to either side, a small bunch of purple tulips in a metal vase at one corner.

Despite his name, Anstruther was not in the least Dickensian, and Helen, who'd been hoping for at least a touch of Charles Dance's sexily repellent Tulkinghorn from the recent television adaptation of *Bleak House*, tried not to show her disappointment. This Anstruther, surely the third or fourth in line, was smooth jawed and whippet thin, a dark diagonally striped tie neatly knotted over a pink shirt that was turned back just once at the cuffs, a hint of dark hair curling out.

If the intended effect was to make both Will and

Helen seem slightly down at heel and out of place, to some extent it worked.

'It's good of you to see us at such short notice,' Will said. 'We won't take too much of your time.'

'A pleasure,' Anstruther said. 'After all, we do both . . .' A nod towards Helen. 'We do, all of us, uphold the law.'

'One way or another,' Helen said.

'Quite.'

Will took a copy of the solicitor's letter that had been sent to Stephen Bryan from the envelope in his pocket and passed it across the desk.

'You sent this?'

Anstruther gave it a cursory glance. 'On behalf of a client, yes. Mr Bryan, apparently, was being disturbingly insistent in his requests for information, telephoning my client at all hours, attempting to speak to other members of the family. It was an attempt to draw a line.'

'And this all related,' Helen said, 'to the book Stephen Bryan was proposing to write about Stella Leonard?'

Anstruther nodded imperiously. 'That is my understanding, yes.'

'Your client,' Will said, 'there's no problem about disclosing their name?'

The hesitation was slight. 'Howard Prince. Mr Prince is married to Stella Leonard's niece.'

'And acting on her behalf?'

'On the entire family's behalf, I believe.'

'Can you tell us,' Will said, 'how Mr Bryan responded to your letter?'

Anstruther smiled, showing teeth that were white at

the edges, yellower towards the roots. 'I expect you know that, Inspector. He called my bluff.'

'That's what it was?'

'At this stage, yes. From what I could ascertain, the only enquiries Mr Bryan had made in the course of his research, despite my client's complaints, had been unexceptional.'

'So, in your view, Mr Prince was overreacting?'

Anstruther smiled again. 'I can advise my clients, of course. Indeed, it would be negligent of me not to do so. But beyond a certain point, it is up to the client to decide how to proceed.'

'Once Mr Bryan had made it clear he was going to continue with his research, did you make any further efforts to dissuade him?'

'None at all.'

'You didn't, for instance, telephone him?'

'No. Certainly not.'

'Nor a member of your staff?'

'Nor a member of my staff.' Discreetly, but not so discreetly that neither Will nor Helen could fail to notice, Anstruther looked at his watch.

'Why do you think,' Helen said, 'Mr Prince proceeded as he did?'

'You're asking me to speculate.'

'I'm asking for your informed opinion.'

Anstruther smiled, a slight creasing of the skin around the eyes, a sideways twitch of the mouth. Perhaps in some respects, Helen thought, there was a little of Tulkinghorn in him after all.

'Mr Prince,' he said, 'did not discuss his reasons with me in any detail and had he done so, I would, of course, be obliged to keep them to myself.'

'So you can't tell us what he was afraid of?' Will said.

Anstruther smiled again and it was like cold light leaking out into the room. 'I very much doubt if Howard Prince is ever afraid at all.'

Back on the street, Helen adjusted her collar and refastened the scarf around her neck. 'I suppose it's too early for a drink?'

'Just a little.'

'Coffee, then?'

'Coffee it is.'

Within ten minutes they were settled into a pair of leather chairs, comfortable, if not quite as comfortable as they looked. Helen had opted for a double espresso, fresh orange juice and a blueberry muffin.

'Lunch?' Will asked.

'Breakfast.'

Will stirred a half-spoon of sugar into his regular latte. 'I don't know what we expected to learn, but whatever it was . . .' He made a vacant gesture with his hands.

'I know,' Helen said. 'Still, sometimes it's nice to have your prejudices confirmed.'

'Such as?'

'Upper-class Oxbridge lawyers with cut-glass accents and hairy wrists.' She shuddered. 'I bet he's got hair all over his back and shoulders, too.'

'Not a turn-on for you?'

Helen shuddered. Will remembered reading in some magazine or other of Lorraine's that the trend among certain young men was to have any excess body hair electronically removed. At the same time, presumably, as their girlfriends were being prematurely nipped and tucked and having their breasts surgically reduced or enhanced. A parallel world, Will thought, and one he was happy enough to keep at one remove.

'You think it's worth pushing this a little further?' Helen said.

'Talk to Prince himself, you mean?'

'Can't hurt.'

Will smiled. 'The man who knows no fear.'

'So they say.'

Helen drained her glass of juice and started to break the muffin into pieces with her fingers. When she offered some to Will, he declined.

'Let's just not get our hopes up, okay?'

14

Lesley took an early train from Nottingham down to London, the sun slanting low across the fields and so bright, at times, through the window, she had to shield her eyes. Cattle lazily grazing; two ponies standing side by side, close by a gap in the hedge; lapwings lifting off from the ground as a tractor churned past. The morning paper was full of Islam: riots in Somalia and Afghanistan; a radical cleric sentenced to seven years for soliciting murder and inciting racial hatred in his Finsbury Park mosque. In the sports sections there was a report on the vile chants some Spurs fans had unleashed at a former player, on the supposition that he was gay. Not just gay, but black and gay. Racist and homophobic both. Just reading them made Lesley sick to her stomach.

On the inside pages there was a review of a play being performed in Nottingham, *Saturday Night and Sunday Morning*, adapted for the stage. Arthur Seaton, Alan Sillitoe's working-class hero, crude and loud, on the lookout for a quick leg over and a pint of Shippo's.

Whatever people say I am, that's what I'm not. Then as now, Lesley thought, lads out on the town to get pissed, meet a lass by the left lion, throw up later in the Old Market Square. Only now it was lasses, too, and it was a phenomenon, had a name: binge drinking. Why was that? Maybe there are more of them now than back in 1958, she thought. Maybe we pay more attention.

She glanced down the carriage as a young Asian man got up and walked towards the automatic doors, leaving his rucksack on the seat next to where he'd been sitting. He was going to the toilet, most likely, or the buffet, maybe out to the space between the carriages to use his mobile phone. Of course he'd leave his rucksack behind. It didn't stop her replaying the CCTV images from the previous July in her mind: three young Asian men with rucksacks preparing to board the train to London. The bombings hours later. Bus and Tube. Flesh and bone. She would most likely take the Tube herself once she arrived, King's Cross to Chalk Farm, the easiest way.

The young Asian came back into the carriage and seeing Lesley looking at him, he smiled and she smiled back.

Whatever people say I am, that's what I'm not.

When she'd asked Alan Pike if, despite the short notice, she could take a few days' holiday that were still owing, he'd come out with something sarcastic about it being better than calling in sick and said fine. All else aside, she thought, he was pleased not to have her pestering him about Crawford.

'Special Branch doing break-ins? Intimidation? Where's your proof? That's an episode of *Spooks*, not news. No, a lad in Bulwell, robbed in his own flat, stripped stark naked and urinated on. That's news. That's a story. Or an eighty-five-year-old granny out in Netherfield, moved by social services into a care home fourteen miles away and her cat takes it into its head to follow her. That's a story.'

'Thanks, Alan,' she had said, 'for pointing it out.'

A break would do them both a bit of good.

Lesley turned right out of the Tube station and then left across the graffitied railway bridge; there was real warmth in the sun. Somewhere between finishing her post-grad diploma in Cardiff and getting established in the East Midlands, she'd gone out with a trainee print journalist who'd shared a flat in Ainger Road, not so far from where she was now. Saturday afternoons spent scouring the crowded stalls at Camden Lock and long, late Sunday lunches in the Engineer; sunbathing on Primrose Hill: it came back to her now through the haze of a remembered dream.

Natalie Prince was where she'd said she would be: sitting at a window table in the first of several cafés on Regent's Park Road.

Today she was wearing mostly yellow: a yellow tube top beneath a brown crocheted cardigan that hung loose from her shoulders, skintight yellow jeans; she had a paperback book propped up in front of her, a glass of orange juice close by, a pair of oversize sunglasses that seemed to cover half her face.

'Incognito?' Lesley said, at her shoulder.

'Too fucking bright.'

Lesley laughed and slid into the seat opposite.

'Stupid bloody weather,' Natalie said. 'Yesterday I was fucking freezing.'

'Me, too.'

'You read this?' Natalie said, holding up the book.

Lesley scanned the title – *Runaway* – and shook her head.

'Fuckin' brilliant.'

Lesley thought the last book she'd tried to read was *The Da Vinci Code*. Before she'd slung it across the room.

She ordered a latte and Natalie asked for another orange juice, even though the one she had was still unfinished. When she removed her glasses her face was so cleverly made up, she scarcely seemed to be wearing make-up at all. Perhaps she wasn't, Lesley thought. Frightening, that she could be that beautiful without assistance.

'You shouldn't drink too much of that, you know,' Natalie said. 'Coffee. Bad for you. Tea, either. Too much caffeine.' She reached for her glass of juice. 'Me, I've been on a real health kick this last week. Those little probiotic yoghurt things, you know. Broccoli, soya milk. Broccoli's got this stuff in it, yeah? I3C, helps stop you getting cancer. Some kinds, anyway. Omega-3 capsules, been eating those like Smarties. And all organic meat and veg. Eggs. What is it Alicia Silverstone says in that film? I never put anything in my mouth unless I know where it's been?' Natalie laughed. 'Didn't say anything about up her nose. Me, what I'm waiting for them to come out with is one hundred per cent organic cocaine.' She laughed again. 'Just see it, can't you, this guy on the bridge down by the Lock, trading these bags of coke out the back of his hand, got these little green stickers on, this bag must only be used for foods produced to the strictly controlled standards of the Soil Association.'

Now Natalie's laughter was almost out of control, so much so that it brought on a fit of coughing and she half-stumbled out of her chair, holding her side.

'You okay?' Lesley said, half out of her seat.

A smart young waiter was hovering anxiously nearby, an extra in a movie of his own making.

'Fine, yeah. Nearly pissed myself, that's all.' Pulling a tissue from one of the pockets of her cardigan, Natalie dabbed her eyes. 'God, that's better.'

Sitting back down, she practically drained her second glass of juice. 'So, what was it you wanted to talk about?'

'This business my brother came to see you about, the book he wanted to write about your aunt, Stella . . .'

'Great-aunt.'

'Great-aunt. I've been though all his stuff and there's hardly anything there.'

Natalie lightly shrugged her shoulders, a lazy gesture she somehow seemed to imbue with grace. 'Maybe he gave up on it? Never started? Just, you know, talked about it? People do that all the time.'

'Not Stephen.'

'Well . . . then I dunno.' Natalie sipped some orange juice and waited.

'I thought,' Lesley said, picking her words carefully, 'what I'd like to do, was try and find out some more about her, Stella. Maybe then I'd find out why it was so important to him.' She didn't want to say it might, just might, have some connection to his murder. Even to her, it didn't sound convincing.

'You're going to write the book yourself?' Natalie said.

'No, nothing like that.'

'Why not? You're a journalist, aren't you?'

Lesley shook her head. 'This is just for me.' She paused and looked directly at Natalie. 'I wondered if you might help?'

Natalie slipped her sunglasses back into place. 'Like I said before, I don't know much about her.'

'You must know somebody who does, though.'

'Not really.'

'Your father . . .'

'Stop. Don't even go there.'

'Somebody else in the family?'

Natalie shook her head. 'Not really. There's my mum – but, like I said, she's a little out of it most of the time. It's no use trying to talk to her. Even if my dad would allow it. Which he won't.'

'There's nobody else?'

Natalie grinned. 'There's crazy old Irene.'

'Who?'

'My gran. Irene. Lives up in Scotland somewhere. Some island. I haven't seen her in ages. Not since I was a kid. Twelve, thirteen. I was still at school.' Natalie laughed. 'Frightened the hell out of me. Like something out of Roald Dahl. *The Witches*, you know? All dressed in black from head to toe and paint all over her fingers. That's what she does. Paint. She's an artist. Least she was. No idea what she does now. If anything.'

'And she's Stella's sister?'

'Older sister, yes.'

'But she's still alive?'

'As far as I know.

'You think she might to talk to me?'

'I don't know. I don't think she talks to anyone.'

Lesley could see there was nothing to be gained from pushing it any further.

'Is there anyone else then you can think of?' she asked. 'Someone who might help to get me started, if nothing else.'

At the far side of the room, a toddler continued to wreak havoc between the tables, despite her mother's languid protests, while two slightly older children, who appeared to be called Tamsin and India, shrieked loudly as they played chase between the café entrance and the counter. It was enough to dispel any lingering thoughts Lesley might have had about children of her own. Even her mother had just about given up hope of that.

'There was this one guy,' Natalie said. 'He came round when I was having dinner with Orlando . . .'

'Orlando?'

'Orlando Rocca, the director. He's got this place in Ladbroke Grove, had it for years. In a real state when he got it, apparently. Been squatted in for ages, bailiffs came in with the police in the end and chucked them out. That's when Orlando stepped in. Must be worth a fucking fortune now.'

'You met someone there,' Lesley prompted.

'Yeah. Gordon something-or-other. Gordon ... Gordon ... Gordon Hedden. That's it. Orlando had invited him. We were going to talk about *Shattered Glass*. This was a couple of years ago.'

'Why him? Hedden? What was his connection?'

'He'd worked on it. The movie. He was the cameraman.'

'And that was when? 1955? '56?'

'I'm not sure. '55, I think.'

'He must be getting on by now, then?'

'Eighty or so? All his marbles about him, just the same. Walked with a stick, yeah, but he wore this really cool beret and could rattle on about lenses and exposures and process shots and fuck knows what else. After a while I just switched off, him and Orlando going at it like a couple of real techies, you know? Amazing.'

'What about Stella? Did he have a lot to say about her?'

'Not really. But then that wasn't what Orlando was interested in.'

'He might, though?'

Natalie angled her head to one side. 'He might.'

'I don't suppose you've any idea how I could get in touch with him?'

'No. But Orlando probably would.'

'You've got a number for him?'

Natalie was already fishing in her bag.

When they were out on the street, Lesley saw that Natalie's yellow jeans finished at mid-calf and that she was wearing what appeared to be pink ballet pumps on her feet. She found herself feeling frumpy and old.

'Come on,' Natalie said, moving away.

'Where to?'

'Just a bit of exercise.' She grinned. 'Goes with all that healthy eating.'

From the top of Primrose Hill they could see the steel-and-wire-mesh aviary and the reddish-brown terraces of London Zoo, the cylinder of the Post Office Tower at the far side of Regent's Park. More distant, away to the east, there were glimpses of the Shell building on the Embankment and the slow-moving wheel of the London Eye.

Natalie called Orlando Rocca herself on her mobile phone.

'No answer. I'll call him again. Don't worry, you can trust me. He'll see you if I ask him nicely.' A mischievous smile crossed her face. 'Just watch out, that's all.'

'What d'you mean?'

Natalie laughed. 'I read this biography once. Some Hollywood actress, I can't remember who. Movie directors, she said, they either want to fuck you out of your dress or take it off and wear it themselves.'

'Which is Orlando?'

'Given the chance, I'd say both.'

186

15

Anstruther got back to Will more speedily than he had expected. Howard Prince would be at the solicitor's office at eleven the following morning and any matters requiring clarification could be dealt with then.

Will decided to dress accordingly and asked Lorraine to iron one of his new blue cotton shirts, but, with one thing and another, time got away from her, and he ended up doing it himself; a quick run over the collar, front and sleeves – no one was going to see the back.

Then Jake clambered all over him in muddy trainers just as he was leaving and he had to use the clothes brush and a damp cloth to clean it off.

'Nice suit,' Helen said, when she saw him. 'Shame about the tie.'

'What's wrong with the tie?'

'Come here,' she said, 'let me fix it. Nobody has knots that size any more. Apart from second-division soccer players out on the pull.'

Will grinned. 'You'd know, I suppose.'

'I wish.'

Helen loosened the tie and refastened it in a smaller, smarter knot, adjusting the collar of his shirt and stepping back to judge the effect.

'There. Much better.'

'You tagging along this morning?'

Helen gave him an arch look. 'That what I do? Tag along?'

'When you aren't attending to my wardrobe.'

'In which case, O master, it will be my pleasure. Just in case one of your shoelaces needs retying or you're having trouble with your zip.'

'Actually, it's buttons.'

'You sweet old-fashioned thing.' Helen parted her lips and gave him a quick glimpse of tongue.

Anstruther made the introductions and then sat back, upright and alert. Howard Prince shook Will's hand and then Helen's, letting his eyes rest on Helen a fraction more than necessary, before relaxing back into the chair beside Anstruther's desk.

Prince was in his mid-fifties, Helen thought, possibly older, but could have passed for less. His hair was full and neatly, recently cut; it was greying a little at the temples but that only served to add a certain gravitas. His eyes were brown, chestnut almost, alive. She felt them pass across her body again, appraisingly. The light grey suit he was wearing sat easily on a body that suggested little weakness, no appreciable slack.

'Quentin says there are some questions you want to

ask,' Prince said. He was looking at Will now, nailing him with his stare.

'Stephen Bryan,' Will said, businesslike, 'I believe he contacted you a number of times about a book he was working on? A biography of Stella Leonard, your wife's aunt.'

'This is police business?'

'Since Mr Bryan died.'

'I heard about that. I'm sorry.' No change in his expression. 'It still doesn't explain why we're here.'

This is a man, Helen thought, who would throw anyone out of his own funeral for crying.

'You didn't comply with Mr Bryan's requests for an interview.'

'That's a crime now? An offence?'

'Certainly not.'

Prince angled his head towards Anstruther and smiled. 'The way they change the law so often these days, I'd not be surprised. Forbidden this, forbidden that. So desperate to be politically correct, bend over much further backwards they'd be looking up their own arses.'

'When Mr Bryan persevered,' Will said, persevering himself, 'you had Mr Anstruther here send him a solicitor's letter.'

'A shot across his bows,' Prince said.

'And when it didn't work?'

'Didn't it work?'

'It didn't appear to stop him from doing his research.'

'Researching my family, it did.'

189

'And that was the point?' Helen asked.

'What do you think? Some fag academic upsetting people, asking questions, foraging in your drawers. Who'd want that?'

There was no doubting the nature of his look, the lascivious ease of his eyes. Helen held his gaze a moment longer, before looking away.

'What makes you think,' Will asked, 'people would be upset?'

'What kind of a stupid question is that?'

'I don't know. Tell me.'

'Listen.' Prince jabbed his arm forward, finger pointing. 'You want to know what's wrong with this world? Our world? I don't mean drugs, I don't mean binge drinking, under-age sex. I mean privacy. The lack of fucking privacy. A man's right to the sanctity of his own life, his own home. Cameras everywhere. Newspaper exposés. CCTV. *Big Brother*.' He snorted. 'Big fucking Brother! Not that I've got any time for the bloke who thought that one up – Orwell – Sunday-afternoon kind of socialist who lived in poncey Hampstead and took his laundry home to his mum at weekends. Never did a day's real work in his life. But I tell you, if he was alive today and saw what had happened to this country he'd have a fucking fit.'

He threw back his head and laughed.

'There,' he said to Helen, 'I'm doing it again. Swearing like the proverbial. Too much time out on building sites. Getting stuck in. No offence meant.'

'None fucking taken,' Helen said, straight faced.

Prince laughed some more. 'What I like, a woman with some balls. What do the Yanks call it? Spunk. Not afraid to speak her mind.'

'I'd just like to be clear,' Will said, hauling back the conversation, 'when Bryan didn't respond positively to your warning letter, what other steps you took?'

'Steps? What steps? I don't get what you're driving at.'

'Maybe you phoned?'

'Like buggery!' Prince said, with a firm shake of the head. 'Last thing I'd want to do, that.'

'Had someone make contact for you, then? Phone on your behalf?'

'Look, look.' Prince spread his hands. 'He pestered me, letters, phone calls, faxes, emails, got up my arse and no mistake. So I blocked him out, shut him off. Which was all I ever wanted. Beginning and end. Since then, okay, the poor bastard's died. Been murdered. Nobody wants that, nobody applauds. But nothing's going to bring him back. None of this talk. Best that can happen, you know this better'n me, whoever did it gets caught. Your job, right? Not sitting here badgering me.'

With a nod towards Anstruther, Prince got to his feet.

'What is it about your family,' Will said, 'your wife's family, that you feel the need to protect it to this degree?'

Prince glared. 'I'll tell you. For one, that's what it is – my family. Old-fashioned, if you like, but that's the way I think. The way I was brought up. And for another – I don't know why I'm telling you this, but I will – my wife, Lily, she's not always as strong as she might be. Has what's called, layman's terms, a fragile personality.

191

Spent a lot of time under medical care. I don't want anything that might upset her, make her more disturbed. I don't want people writing about her either, her condition.' He had been leaning towards Will and now he straightened up. 'All right? Satisfied? Now, it's time I went. Time's money, eh?'

Sprightly for a man of middle years, he was already on his feet. A quick shake of Anstruther's hand, a nod towards Will and Helen, and he was gone.

'I don't imagine you'll be needing to talk to my client again,' Anstruther said pleasantly.

'If we do,' Will said, 'we'll let you know.'

The moment they got outside, Helen reached for her cigarettes. 'So, what did you think?' she said. 'You believe what he said?'

'About protecting his family, yes.'

'And the rest?'

'I'm happy to give him the benefit of the doubt. For now.'

'Where does that leave us?' Helen asked. 'Somewhere unpleasant without the proverbial paddle?'

'Not exactly. I'll see if we can't draft in a few uniforms, canvass Bryan's neighbours again. Might stir up a few memories, you never know.'

Together, they set off along Petty Cury, the sky above them a pale eggshell that augured neither good nor ill.

16

When uniformed constables Barrie Slater and Ashley Milne were shuffled out on to the streets surrounding the late Stephen Bryan's home, neither of them viewed the prospect of the coming hours with enthusiasm. Both men, after all, had taken part in the initial house-to-house inquiries and had little faith that knocking on the same doors and asking the same questions would result in much more than perplexed stares coupled with annoyance at being dragged away from that day's *Countdown*.

Added to which, Milne was nursing a bruised toe after turning out for his local pub team on the previous Sunday morning, his injury the result of a last-ditch blocking tackle in which he was adjudged to have missed the ball but not the man and promptly shown a red card for his pains.

Slater, for whom soccer was a game largely played by overpaid underachievers more interested in personal adornment than genuine physical effort or athleticism, was a coach for the East of England under-sixteen swimming team, and was often to be found pool side at some ungodly hour of the morning, urging one or other of his charges to even greater efforts at back-stroke or butterfly.

Both men, coincidentally, were engaged to members of the nursing staff at Addenbrooke's Hospital and, although any conversation about sport was bound to be short and adversarial, they could find common ground discussing starter mortgages and the best venues for the inevitable stag night, Milne currently favouring Dublin while Slater was torn between Tallin and Barcelona.

'You ever feel,' Milne said, stopping at the corner to rest his foot, 'all we're doing is going through the motions?'

'So someone can save face, you mean?'

'Will bloody Grayson, lost the plot on this one, no mistake.'

'Takin' a bit of hammer from above, bound to be. Got to show he's doing something.'

'What I reckon,' Milne said, easing off his shoe, 'blokes like him ought to be judged by results like bloody football managers. Lose too many and you're out. Like Souness at Newcastle, Megson at Forest. Saw it coming, mind, pair of 'em. Faces like a couple of sour oranges. Grayson's the same. Difference is, 'stead of gettin' the heave-ho, likely he'll get kicked upstairs out of harm's way.'

Slater disagreed. 'I don't reckon he's a bad bloke, Grayson. Give you the time of day, more than some. And far as results go, last couple he's worked – student's body in the river and that car park thing – two arrests, two convictions. Not a lot wrong there.'

'Yeah, maybe.' Milne's toe, not the littlest but the one alongside, was swollen to more than twice its normal size.

'Ought to get yourself off to A&E,' Slater said. 'Might be broken.'

Milne shook his head. 'Jennie took a look at it this morning. Bruising, she reckons, that's all. Keep taking the ibuprofen. Stick a bag of frozen peas on it when I get home.'

Slater looked at his watch. 'Let's get this next couple of streets done. Then we can take a break.'

Milne winced as he slowly manoeuvred his shoe back into place.

The first three they spoke to hadn't seen or heard a thing, regular three wise monkeys as Milne called them; two houses next with no one answering, and then a couple who'd moved in just a few days before and seemed to have a wardrobe wedged halfway up the stairs.

When the man suggested Milne and Slater might like to come in and give them a hand, they looked back at him in disbelief.

'Waste of time, this,' Milne grumbled, back on the pavement.

Without wanting to say so, Slater thought he was probably right.

The next house had fresh green paint around the windows and blue paint on the door, snowdrops and a few green shoots of daffodil coming up in the small front garden. 'No hawkers, no circulars, no free papers' clearly on display.

Slater rang the bell and knocked for good measure.

No reply.

No sounds of television or radio.

They were turning away when they heard footsteps on the stairs.

Two bolts and a chain: better safe than sorry.

The man in the doorway was wearing brown overalls with oil stains down one side; he was five eight or nine, late fifties at best, round faced with a thinning head of red hair. 'Didn't hear you at first, fixing the lagging on some pipes up in the loft. What can I do to help?'

Will, as to his regret seemed increasingly the case, was in a meeting. New Home Office directives with regard to clear-up rates and detection. More bum-fodder and folderol. Window dressing. Coffee but no biscuits.

Helen listened to Milne and Slater with interest.

'And why,' she said, 'hadn't he reported any of this before?'

'Been away,' Milne said. 'Since before it happened. Austrian Tyrol, Rhine Gorge and Bavaria. Train, apparently. Did everything but show us the timetable.'

'He's downstairs?'

Milne nodded.

'Fenwick? That's his name?'

'Richard Fenwick,' Slater said.

'Best bring him up. And listen, good work the pair of you.'

Both men had smiles on their faces as they walked away.

Helen had appropriated Will's empty office and Fenwick looked around with a mixture of curiosity and slight apprehension. 'It's the first time,' he said, 'I've ever been inside a police station.'

He had changed from his work-stained overalls into a pair of dark trousers and a grey tweed jacket that added another five years to his age.

Helen smiled. 'There are times when I wish I could say the same.'

Fenwick nodded wisely. 'It must be difficult, doing your job. Nowadays especially.'

'I think it's always been difficult,' Helen said defensively. 'It's the issues that change.'

Fenwick would not be put off. 'You go to other countries, and I do, especially since . . . well, especially since I've been on my own . . . and they don't seem to have the problems we do. All this binge drinking. Drugs. Muggings.'

'I don't know,' Helen said. 'Take the average group of tourists who come here. From Japan, say. Germany. What do they see? Buildings going back to the twelfth century. Dreaming spires. They don't see down-at-heel housing estates or kids copping ten-pound deals outside shopping centres. They see what they want to see.'

'I suppose that's true. But even so . . .'

Helen decided to head the remainder of the all-too-familiar diatribe off at the pass. 'You told the officers,

Mr Fenwick, that you saw someone hanging around close to Stephen Bryan's house. Acting suspiciously.'

'Yes, that's right. On the Tuesday. Tuesday afternoon.'

'What time?'

'Oh, four o'clock, it must have been. No later than four-thirty, certainly.'

'And Stephen Bryan – you knew him well?'

'Not well. I wouldn't say that. First-name terms, just about. Neighbours, you know? His house, it more or less backs on to mine. The gardens. We'd exchange the occasional few words if we were both out there at the same time.' Fenwick leaned in towards the desk. 'Once or twice recently I couldn't help but notice him paying a lot of attention to the drain, at the rear of his place, so I asked him one day what was wrong. Thinking I might be able to help, you know? It seemed there was a blockage further back. In the main drain. All this sewage had backed up and was close to over-flowing. There was a smell, I can tell you. Quite oppressive.'

Why am I hearing this? Helen asked herself.

'Apparently,' Fenwick continued, oblivious, 'he'd been on to the water company, and although they'd accepted responsibility, getting them to actually come and deal with it, well, you can imagine. They keep you on hold the best part of an hour, listening to a very bad recording of *The Four Seasons* and then, when you do get through, you're speaking to someone in Bombay or Mumbai, who, with the best will in the world, hasn't got a clue how to help.'

Helen screwed up her face into a quick, sympathetic smile. Get on with it, man.

'A couple of days after we spoke,' Fenwick said, 'Stephen came round. Said the water people had promised to send someone that morning, but he had to go out and could he leave the key with me? He'd put a note on the door telling them where to call. So, naturally, I said, yes, that would be fine.'

'And someone did call?'

'No. Not at all. What happened was, in the end I had to nip out myself. It was well into the afternoon by then, and I thought whoever's meant to come they're not going to now. But then as I was going past the end of Stephen's road I happened to glance down and saw this man just going in through his gate. So naturally I went along and asked him if he was from the water company? And he said no, in no uncertain terms. Quite belligerent, in fact. I won't repeat the exact words he used, but it was to the effect that I should mind my own business and what he was doing there was no concern of mine.'

'And then what happened?'

Fenwick shifted awkwardly in his chair. 'I said there was no need for him to speak in that way and he told me – well, you can imagine what he told me, the kind of language that he used – so I went back up the street and carried on with what I had to do.'

'And the man?'

'I looked back several times. Just quickly. These days you can never tell. People take offence so easily, road rage and everything, and I didn't want to provoke him any further.'

Provocation? Helen thought. Give me patience. 'What did you see?' she asked.

'He stayed in the garden for a short while after I'd gone. Just looking up at the house. And then he went and stood across the street, still looking. Stood there for a few moments, no more, and then he started to walk away.'

'In which direction?'

'The opposite way, thank heavens. I watched him go round the corner and out of sight and that was that. I assumed he was going back to his car, I suppose.'

'But you didn't see a car?'

'Not that day, no.'

Helen took a deep breath. 'Go on.'

'It was two days later,' Fenwick said, 'the day before I went off on holiday, in fact. I'd been into town to buy a new thermos for the journey and just as I was crossing the road – the junction where Stephen's and my streets join – this vehicle came out of Stephen's road right at me. Far too fast for a built-up area. One of those huge things so many people drive nowadays. Quite unsuitable for town.'

'An SUV?'

'Is that what they're called?'

'A big, four-wheel drive?'

'Yes. Range Rover, that sort of thing. And there he was, behind the wheel.'

'You're sure it was the same man?'

'Positive.'

'And did he recognise you?'

'I don't know. It's impossible to say. If he did, he gave no sign. Just braked and swerved. I jumped back and then he was gone.'

'And you can't remember anything more about the vehicle?'

Fenwick shook his head. 'I'm afraid not. Never been very interested in cars. Trains, they're more my thing.'

'How about the colour? Can you remember the colour?'

Fenwick considered. 'Dark, certainly. Sort of khaki, perhaps? Muddy green?' He smiled. 'I'm not being a great deal of use, am I?'

Helen smiled back, reassuringly. 'Not at all. Why don't we concentrate on the man?'

'A description, you mean?'

Helen nodded.

'Well, he was quite a big man, as I say. Not six foot, exactly, but not so far short. And well built. Easily, I would have thought, twelve or thirteen stone. I'm afraid I don't know what that is in kilograms.'

'Never mind.'

Fenwick hesitated. 'I'm finding it difficult to put an age on him. Late forties? Fifty?'

'Was he white, black, Asian?'

'Oh, white. Definitely.'

'And his hair?'

Fenwick hesitated again, not wishing to give the wrong information. 'No, it's no good. I can't remember.'

'Never mind,' Helen said, not letting her frustration show. 'How about what was he wearing, can you remember that?'

Fenwick could. 'Some kind of overcoat, I think. But short. You know, just down to the hips. And grey. What else, I don't know. Trousers of some kind, obviously. They could have been grey, too.'

'How about on the second occasion?'

'In the car? It was all too quick to see.'

'And since that time, when he came close to running you down, you haven't seen him again?'

'As I told you, the next day I went away.'

Helen rose smartly to her feet. 'Mr Fenwick, you've been a great help. We may want you to look at some photographs. Help a sketch artist, even. You wouldn't have any objection?'

'Of course not.'

'Good. I'm sure we'll be in touch.'

With less alacrity than Helen, Fenwick eased himself out of the chair. 'This man, you don't think . . . . Stephen's murder, you think he could have been involved?'

Helen brushed him off with a quick smile. 'It's really impossible to say. But it might be someone we'd like to talk to.' She held open the door and Fenwick hesitated, as if wanting her to go through first. Chivalry dies hard.

'We're grateful for your help,' Helen said. 'I'll go down with you, see if we can't arrange for someone to give you a lift home. No sirens, mind. No flashing blue lights.'

He had to look at her twice to see if she were joking.

*   *   *

After three and a half hours sitting in a stuffy meeting room, while the arguments ebbed and flowed around him, Will was in sore need of fresh air. The chance to stretch his legs. The way he strode on to the slice of open land directly across from the police station, Helen was having to hurry to keep up with him. Off the paths, the ground was even but slippery and her low heels failed to grip on the grass.

'Slow down, for God's sake.'

'I thought you were fit?'

'Don't start.'

'If you didn't . . .'

'And don't say anything about me smoking.'

'If you didn't clog up your lungs with all that gunk . . .'

'I said don't.'

'Okay. Okay.' Will stopped and looked at her and grinned. 'Stubborn,' he said, 'is that the word?'

Helen made a face and reached into her bag for her cigarettes.

'How about contrary?' she said. 'Wilful? That'd suit.' Snapping her lighter with her thumb, she inclined her head towards the flame. 'Self-destructive, even?'

'That's two words.'

'Joined at the hip.' Arching her neck she released a coil of smoke that mixed with her breath in the air. It was perhaps a degree or two warmer than the previous day but no more.

'This stranger outside Bryan's house,' Will said, 'he could have been there for half a hundred reasons.

Anything from persuading him to change his gas supplier to talking him into having his drive tarmacked or his roof retiled.'

'There isn't a drive.'

'You know what I mean.'

Helen tapped ash towards the ground. 'If he's got legitimate reasons for being there, why react to Fenwick so aggressively?'

'I don't know. Maybe he thought he was an interfering old busybody. Perhaps he was just having a bad day.'

'And you don't think it's a bit of an odd coincidence he's driving around the same area just a couple of days later?'

'Not if he's canvassing or touting for work – it's what you'd expect.'

'That shouldn't be too difficult to check.'

'There is always the possibility,' Will said, 'he was casing the street. Seeing who was home and who wasn't.'

'Looking for somewhere to break into?'

'It's been known.'

'In which case, we might have him on our books.'

'We might.'

'I could get Fenwick back in to look at some pictures.'

'Can't do any harm.' Will pushed up his coat sleeve to look at his watch. 'We ought to be getting back.'

'It's tempting to want to join up the dots, isn't it?' Helen said, as they started walking.

'How d'you mean?'

'You know, Bryan gets a threatening phone call to

204

which he doesn't respond. So what does our caller do?
He goes round, intent on seeing Bryan in person. The
harder it is to get to talk to him, the angrier he becomes.'
She shook her head. 'It's too simple, isn't it? Too
straightforward?'

'That's the problem with dots,' Will said. 'But it's
something. A break of a kind. And we've not had many.'

They were back at the road, facing the ugly cement-
and-brick building where they spent so much of their
lives.

'Let's find the man first, if we can,' Will said. 'Then
take it from there.'

'And we keep digging at McKusick just the same?'

'Just the same.'

17

The house was flat-fronted, three storeys tall, paint beginning to flake here and there from the facing wall. Iron railings and a high hedge separated it from the street. It was a part of London Lesley scarcely knew, Notting Hill, save through some conglomeration of old images culled from television: affluent upper classes side by side with slum landlords – Rachmanism, is that what it had been called? – West Indians tramping from door to door with cardboard suitcases, looking for lodgings; Mick Jagger wearing make-up, doing drugs, luxuriating naked with beautiful women – a movie that had been, she couldn't remember the name.

A black-and-white cat with a stubby tail peered at Lesley from the low window ledge alongside the door, jumped down and ran off in the direction of the adjoining garden. Lesley set her thumb against the ivory lozenge of a bell.

The woman who answered the door was olive-skinned with a swathe of fair hair in artful disarray, strands dangling haphazardly across her perfect face and neck. Seventeen, Lesley wondered? Eighteen?

'Lesley Scarman. I'm here to see Orlando Rocca. Three o'clock?'

The young woman spun away and walked back into the house, leaving Lesley to follow or not as she pleased.

Stepping inside, Lesley closed the heavy door behind herself and moved in along the high-ceilinged hallway, past framed posters for what she presumed were some of Rocca's films. *Last Target*, *Nick's Blues*, *Truth* and *Black Bullet*, this last featuring an airbrushed Natalie leaning back against a rough-hewn wall in torn top and short skirt, legs spread, smoking a cigarette.

Classy, Lesley thought.

She set the flat of her hand against a partly opened door at the end of the hall and entered a vast room – two rooms, long since knocked into one – with virulent abstract paintings hanging on green walls and little furniture save for two low settees and a large mahogany table at which a man in a black T-shirt and black jeans was making notes in a small sketch-book. He was completely bald.

'Orlando Rocca?'

He looked up in his own time, sliding his spectacles forward on his nose. His eyes were a darker green than that of the walls, shading towards black. His teeth when he smiled were even and white and, Lesley guessed, expensively capped. If she hadn't already known him to be forty-nine, she would have found it near impossible to tell his age.

'You are a friend of Natalie.' He took her hand in both of his. 'You wish to talk about Stella Leonard.' His voice was low, quite heavily accented. Italian, Lesley thought, without being sure that was correct.

'Come,' he said. 'First we will have a drink.'

'I'm fine, thanks,' Lesley said, with a shake of her head.

Rocca took a step back and looked her up and down. 'You are pregnant, perhaps?'

Lesley blushed and shook her head.

'You do not have to drive?'

'No.'

'Then join me, please, in a glass of wine. Vermentino. From Sicily. It helps the long hours of the afternoon.' He gestured towards the paired settees. 'Please sit.'

The creased leather of the cushions gave beneath her weight and she felt herself sinking further back than was comfortable. By the time Rocca returned with two tulip-shaped glasses, she had repositioned herself on the front edge of the settee, legs angled to one side.

He touched his glass to hers. 'You are a journalist, Natalie said.'

'Yes. For radio.'

'And you are wanting to make what? A feature about Stella?'

'No, not exactly. My brother, he was writing her biography when he died.'

'I am sorry about your brother.' With quick, economical movements, Rocca crossed himself. 'But you will finish his work? In his memory?'

Lesley half-smiled. 'Perhaps. Something like that, yes.'

'That is good.'

Music started playing somewhere in the house. Loudly at first, and then more restrained. Samba? Bossa nova? Lesley wasn't sure.

'My daughter, Savia. She is living with me until the summer. While she learns English.' Rocca raised his eyes towards the ceiling, as if to signal the implausibility. 'All she does is sit in her room and play this music. Text her friends back home.' He shook his head in dismay. 'I ask her the other night, come with me to this movie premiere, Leicester Square. Brad Pitt. Angelina. Many stars. But no. She does not want to go. I ask her why and she says it is boring. The only word aside from "Fuck you" and "Big Brother" she has learned in English. "Boring".' He shook his head again. 'She does not know she is born.'

Leaning back, one arm thrust out along the top of the settee, he enjoyed a few moments of despair.

Lesley sipped some wine and set down the glass.

'I met her only once,' Rocca said, 'Stella Leonard. A festival in Dinard. They were making a retrospective of her work. Most of it . . .' he gestured with his hands outspread, '. . . was poor, without distinction, without . . .' he shrugged, '. . . fire in the belly. Po-faced, you understand? Uptight. When they kiss, these people on the screen, they kiss with their mouths closed. When they fuck, they fuck with their clothes on. Except, of course, they do not fuck. This is this country, what? 1955. The actors, characters, they are like Barbie and Ken. They have nothing here.' He cupped himself generously between his legs. 'No cock, no balls, no cunt. Only Stella. In *Shattered Glass* especially. She was a woman, you know? A real woman. You can smell her from the screen. She sweats, she bleeds. You believe this. She makes you believe. You can see it in her face, her eyes.'

Rocca's own eyes were so bright, so wide, Lesley had to look away. Leaning forward, he touched her leg just above the knee, and, involuntarily, she jumped.

Rocca laughed.

'I was only young,' he said. 'Twenty-something. A boy. I had made one or two short films. Written screen-plays that had not been produced. There was one about a woman of a certain age who knows she is dying, but is still beautiful. She becomes obsessed with a young man who lives nearby, a pianist. With his hands, she loves his hands. She wants to make love to him before she dies. Wants him to make love to her. Wants to feel those hands on her body. I ask Stella if she will read it, this script, as a favour to me. So, she takes pity on me, I think. Or perhaps she, too, is bored. That word again. Either way, she tells me to bring the script to her room at the hotel. When I arrive she is sitting there, dressed very properly, demure, no longer young. She is sitting on the chaise longue with a blanket over her knees because somehow, despite the heat in the room, she feels the cold. And so she begins to read. As if I am no longer in the room.

'After a while, she looks up and says, "Come sit with me," and pats the upholstery beside her, so I go and sit there – a little nervously, but I sit there and her eyes go back to the script and she reads some more and then she says, "Is this me?" And I say, "What do you mean?" and she says, "Is this me? This woman here?" and I say, "'I think you can play her, yes. I think it is a wonderful part for you." So she looks at me, into my face, and says, "Is this you? This boy?" And when I shake my head, she laughs and says, "Show me your hands."'

Rocca paused and looked at Lesley over the rim of his glass.

'Someone said, the lovers you regret are the ones you could have had but never did. Opportunities that were there, but never seized. Those are the ones that haunt you, he said, and that is true. "Show me your hands," she said, Stella Leonard, and I could have placed them in her own, reached out and touched her cheek, her hair. Then, who knows? Instead I sat there like a fool and she laughed and said, "All right, I will be in your film," and a year later, less, before we could start shooting, she was dead.' Rocca sighed. 'She died in a car accident, you know?'

Lesley nodded.

'Her father was with her in the car. Just the two of them. Stella was driving. For some reason, they went off the road. Both were killed.'

He fixed her with his eyes.

'You've seen it, *Shattered Glass*? You know how she dies? Her character in the movie?'

'No,' Lesley said, and a chill ran through her as she spoke.

'Ah, then you must see it. But not only for that. All

211

other things aside, it is an extraordinary film. To have been made here in England at that time. And Stella – she is wonderful. She plays two sisters, you know. Twins. One is the good little patient wife who goes to church and does all the right things and the other – well, you will see.'

'What's happening,' Lesley asked, 'to your plans for the remake?'

Rocca shook his head as if in pain. 'Please, do not ask.'

'I thought Natalie's father had agreed to put up the money?'

'What Natalie's father agreed was to make a loan against the profits from the movie. Not the same thing at all. And, even then, he demands to know how every penny will be spent before giving us as much as a sniff at his money. Meantime, we have a script, we have actors, we have a crew, we have nothing.' Rocca sighed elaborately. 'If he had wanted to prevent us from filming, he could not have done better.'

He drained his glass. 'A little more?'

'Thank you, no.'

'You're sure?'

'Quite sure.'

Rocca smiled, merriment in his eyes. 'You should remember what I said, about opportunities that are missed.'

'And that's what this is?'

Rocca shrugged easily and Lesley shook her head. 'According to Natalie,' she said, 'you know the cameraman who worked on *Shattered Glass*?'

'Gordon Hedden, yes.'

'If you have a number for him, I'd like to get in touch.'

'Of course.'

For a moment, Lesley wondered if she were going to have to rebuff another advance, but Rocca levered himself up from the settee and returned several minutes later with a battered-looking Filofax and a silver pen. 'Here we are. The coast. Broadstairs. Not the best time of year to visit the English seaside, but never mind.' He handed Lesley the piece of paper on which he'd written the details. 'Please give Gordon my regards.'

His daughter's music was still drifting down the stairs. Trombone. Organ. A woman's voice. A burst of shrill, almost psychedelic guitar, as if, instead of dying, Jimi Hendrix had emigrated to Brazil.

18

There was a Springsteen song Will used to listen to a lot, back when he had listened to Springsteen. When he had listened seriously to anything.

'One Step Up'.

One step up and two steps back.

In Will's experience, this was how investigations progressed, if progress was the word: like the slow dripping of a tap. Occasionally, if rarely, they could be jump-started by a sudden, previously unsuspected clue, a moment of inspiration, a bolt from the blue; at other times, and all too regrettably, the way forward was found to have been staring them in the face all the while; but most often what progress was made came through a process of accretion, check and cross-check, dull routine, dribs and drabs.

The lab had confirmed that the stray semen found on one of Stephen Bryan's towels had, as assumed, belonged to Russell Johnson, and since Johnson was in no real sense a suspect, that simply proved to be another dead end.

Inquiries into McKusick's background had, so far, proved equally fruitless, the testimony of friends and colleagues suggesting the outburst Jake Rouse had witnessed was very much the exception rather than the rule. The picture that came across was of someone who held quite strong opinions and would express them forcefully where necessary, but without any loss of temper; there were times, it was agreed, especially where more than a few academics were involved, when McKusick seemed to feel shut out of the conversation, and then he might adopt a sullen, almost surly pose, but nothing more demonstrative than that.

'Maybe we're barking up the wrong tree entirely,' Helen said. 'The wrong trees. You ever think of that?'

They were standing in the market square close to the Guildhall, Will biting his way into a bacon-and-tomato roll, Helen sipping a take-away coffee through a hole in the lid. Fifteen minutes stolen from the middle of the day.

'Only all the time,' Will replied.

Ever since the Yorkshire Ripper investigation back in the seventies and early eighties, it was something close to every police officer's mind: falling foul of tunnel vision and allowing one particular line of inquiry – in the Ripper case, the belief, fuelled by hoax letters and tapes, that the murderer came from a particular area of the north-east – to steer them away from the truth. And both Will and Helen knew the same could happen here; and that if following the wrong trail allowed their true suspect to remain free, then he could kill again.

Will screwed up the paper in which his roll had been wrapped and tossed it towards the nearest bin.

They arrived back at Parkside in time to see Christine Costello's BMW gliding into view.

'Great!' Will said.

'She doesn't have to be coming to see us.'

'Don't hold your breath.'

Not so many moments later, the solicitor was bearing down on them, leather jacket, leather trousers, spiked-up hair.

'Ms Costello,' Will said, forcing out a smile. 'To what do we owe the pleasure?'

'I've just come to warn you.'

'What about?'

'Harassing my client.'

'Which client is this?'

Costello's face tightened. 'Don't play silly buggers, Grayson.'

'You mean McKusick?'

'You know bloody well . . .'

'I don't think we're aware of any harassment, are we, Will?' Helen said sweetly.

'How about parking a police car outside his house for all the neighbours to see? Driving past every few hours?'

'Not necessarily anything to do with us,' Will said. 'Neighbourhood security.'

'Don't bullshit me.'

'Bullshit?' Will said innocently.

'How about knocking on doors, stopping neighbours

in the street? Contacting friends, people he's worked with previously, digging for dirt?'

'Seeking out relevant information,' Helen said. 'It's called police work.'

'When you're actively encouraging people to support unsubstantiated allegations, it's called something else.'

'If you've any evidence,' Will said, 'of officers overstepping the mark, I trust you'll complain through the usual channels.'

'Putting my client in a compromising position by publicly questioning his manager and colleagues at his place of work, not once but several times, how's that for overstepping?' Costello jabbed a finger in Will's direction. 'And I'm complaining now. To you. Understood?'

'This is a murder investigation,' Will said, stony faced.

'And one in which I understood my client was no longer a suspect.'

'Your understanding. Not necessarily mine.'

Costello laughed in his face. 'This is a witch-hunt, and you know it. Ease back on the heavy stuff or you'll get your official complaint soon enough.' Stepping back, she winked. 'Nice talking to you both, as usual.'

'Don't say it,' Helen whispered, as they watched her walk away. Will thought it instead.

When he arrived home there was still some vestige of light in the sky and Lorraine and Jake were playing football in the garden, Jake scampering after the white ball and kicking it as hard as he could, regardless of direction. Snug in her padded all-in-one, Susie was strapped into her Rock-a-Tot, swinging her legs back and forth and gurgling happily.

'Dad! Dad! I scored nine goals and Mum's only got one.'

'Well done!' Will hoisted his son off the ground and planted a kiss on the top of his head, then held him closer in a hug.

'If you'd like to take over,' Lorraine said, 'I could do something about the tea.'

'I think it's time to pack it in, don't you?'

'No!' Jake shouted, defiant. 'Not yet.'

'It's too dark to see what you're doing.'

'No!' Without warning, Jake took a wild kick at the ball and it went sailing too close to Susie for comfort.

'For Christ's sake!' Will shouted, seizing his son by the arm. 'Look what you're doing.'

'Ow!' Jake yelled. 'That hurts.'

'Will,' Lorraine said, hurrying towards them. 'There's no need.'

'He only nearly took Susie's head off, that's all.'

Head down, Jake retreated, rubbing his arm. Susie, aware of something untoward going on around her, had started to cry.

'It's all right, sweetheart,' Lorraine said, unbuckling her straps. 'It's all okay now.'

Susie shook her little fists and cried all the more.

Will went over to Jake and rested a hand on his shoulder. 'Give me five minutes to get changed, and then we'll play a quick game. Best of five. What d'you say?'

Petulant, Jake said nothing.

'Suit yourself,' Will said, rebuffed, and turned away.

In the kitchen, Lorraine was somehow managing to fill the kettle, while still holding the baby to her chest. 'You're rough with him sometimes, you know.'

'I don't mean to be.'

'He's only little.'

'I know.'

Through the window they could see Jake continuing to stand with his back towards them, letting them see his hurt and indignation.

Will leaned across and kissed both of Susie's hands and then kissed Lorraine on the cheek. 'I'll go and get out of these things.'

'So you keep saying,' Lorraine said, smiling.

After Susie had been fed and the rest of them had eaten, Lorraine chivvied Jake through his various bathroom tasks while Will washed up; later, he dozed over the paper while Lorraine watched a programme in which several dowdy middle-aged women were encouraged to dress like Joan Collins.

Watching Lorraine get undressed, ready for bed, Will wondered if they might make love, but almost as soon as his head touched the pillow he was asleep, leaving his wife with the new Joanna Trollope she'd got that morning when the travelling library had come to the village.

Unusually, Will slept through the small hours, a deep dreamless sleep from which he was woken by his wife's voice, urgent, from below. 'Will! Will! Switch on the radio.'

He fumbled with the small portable on the bedside table.

'. . . has been taken to the intensive care unit of Addenbrooke's Hospital after undergoing emergency surgery. The officer, who was off duty at the time, is said to be in a serious but stable condition.'

Pushing back the covers, Will turned up the volume.

'Detective Sergeant Helen Walker was on her way home in the early hours of this morning, after a night out with friends, when she attempted to intervene in a fight that had broken out between a number of men close to the Magdalene Street Bridge.

'In the course of the fracas, Sergeant Walker was beaten about the head and received stab wounds to the body, one at least of which is said to be serious, but not life-threatening. Since she was off duty, Detective Sergeant Walker was not wearing body armour at the time of the incident.'

Will was tucking his shirt awkwardly into his trousers, buckling his belt. His face was white. When Lorraine, from the doorway, started to ask another question, he shushed her angrily and put a finger to his lips.

'One man who was injured in the incident,' the news-reader continued, 'is being treated for serious head injuries. A second man was kept in hospital overnight for observation. Both are believed to be students. Police have cordoned off the area where the attack took place for forensic examinations. Traffic is being diverted.'

Will pulled on his shoes.

'Detective Superintendent Malcolm Rastrick, who is leading the investigation into the incident, urged anyone who was in the area at the time, or has any information, to come forward without delay. "This was a cowardly attack on an unarmed female officer," the superintendent said, "and we are determined to apprehend those responsible as soon as possible."'

'You got time for a cup of tea?' Lorraine asked. 'Anything?'

'Best not.' He kissed her quickly as he went past and continued on down the stairs.

'I hope she's okay.'

Will nodded.

'Give her my love. And drive safely.'

He called the hospital from the car.

Will hated hospitals. The smell, the poverty, the lack of hope. He had watched his father slowly dying, had sat hour after hour beside his bed. Only when he had turned away, walked outside for a change of air, had his father ceased the struggle for breath, as if Will's absence had somehow given him permission.

The intensive care ward was divided, for the most part, into bays of four beds, with individual side rooms at the furthest end. Helen lay in one of these, an IV line attached to a vein at the side of her neck, the clear plastic tube opening into a blue triple pigtail through which blood and fluids were being pumped systematically into her body.

Will had stayed with her for almost an hour, during which time he held her hand and told her repeatedly that she was going to be okay. Whether or not she heard him, he didn't know.

'She'll be woozy for a while,' the nurse had said, 'while the anaesthetic wears off.'

Will had nodded and continued to sit, watching for each small sign of movement, the flicker of an eyelid, anything. Once she did open her eyes and speak – a sound, at least, a garbled word such as his son might utter from the midst of sleep – before relapsing back into silence.

When Helen's parents arrived – rushed, nervous, panicking with concern – followed closely by her sister, he gave up his chair and moved away, standing behind the glass wall at the end of the room and looking in. Helen's face so pale against the white pillow it almost disappeared.

As if underwater, nurses moved methodically, almost silently, behind him, going from patient to patient, bed to bed, checking, recording.

Helen's father gently lifted one of her hands and held it to his lips, and, embarrassed, Will looked away.

When a doctor came out from one of the side rooms opposite, walking fast, white coat flapping, Will tried to intercept him, but he swept on past.

'Excuse me . . .' His words left hanging on the sterile air.

Controlling his impatience, he waited for the doctor to return. His own heart, racing earlier, seemed to have slowed to the point where he could scarcely feel it beating. Aside from wanting to know about Helen, he wanted to know more about what had happened and how close they were to finding those who were responsible; he wanted to talk to Malcolm Rastrick in the incident room that had doubtless been set up at the station, but overwhelmingly he felt the need for reassurance first. Five minutes, ten, fifteen. How in fuck's name could the time move so slowly?

At last, he saw the doctor heading back down the ward, the same earnest stride as before, and went to meet him, setting himself squarely in his path. Sandy haired, glasses, the equal of Will's height if not more, he fully expected Will to step aside.

'Helen Walker,' Will said.

'Would you mind moving out of my way?'

'Helen Walker,' Will said again. 'She's a police officer. She was brought in last night after being attacked.'

'You're her husband? Partner?'

Will shook his head.

'Family?'

'No.'

'Then I'm afraid . . .'

'We work together,' Will said.

'I see.' The doctor looked into Will's face for the first time. 'I'll tell you what I can. She was brought in having received a single stab wound to the abdomen, some eight or nine centimetres deep. Fortunately, no vital organs were damaged. Nevertheless, your colleague had lost a

223

great deal of blood. We had to operate to stop any further bleeding and repair the damaged tissue.'

'And she'll be okay?'

'Oh, yes,' the doctor said. 'She's fit. She's strong. She did sustain other injuries, but these were comparatively minor, certainly not life-threatening, and I would say, yes, there's every indication she'll make a full recovery, given time.'

'Other injuries?' Will said. 'What other injuries?'

'Not surprisingly, there was some bruising at the entrance to the wound, caused, most probably, by the hilt of the knife or the assailant's fist or both. There's also quite severe bruising to other areas, as a result of blows she received, in addition cuts on her forearms and the palms of both hands.'

Defence wounds, Will thought, Helen trying to protect herself from the blade.

'As I say, no need to concern yourself unduly,' the doctor said. There was a faint smell of eucalyptus on his breath.

Will thanked him and stepped aside and the doctor hurried on his way.

Malcolm Rastrick was in his early fifties, a thin, near-cadaverous man with a sallow complexion and sucked-in cheeks. He had transferred down from North Yorkshire fifteen or more years previously and the accent still clung to him like burrs on a dog's coat. A stickler, that was the word. Slow to take offence, slower to forgive. No lover of fools. Will had worked closely with him a time or two before, and held him in respect.

He greeted Will now with a quick handshake and a nod of sympathy. 'You've been to the hospital?'

'Yes.'

'How's she bearing up?'

'Okay, apparently. Still not come round properly after the operation. Doctor says she'll be fine.'

'She's a strong lass,' Rastrick said, and then, 'you'll want to know what's what.'

Will nodded.

'Some of this you'll likely know already, some you might not. She'd been out with friends, Helen, girl-friends, four altogether. A few drinks, something to eat – that Turkish place on King Street – a couple more jars before calling it a night. Walked one of her pals as far as Market Street, saw her into a taxi and set off to walk the rest of the way home alone.'

'She should have got a cab herself.'

'Ten minutes from there to where she lives. Fifteen tops. Wanted the fresh air, I dare say. Clear her head.'

'She should have got a cab,' Will said again.

'Best as we can tell, and this is conjecture, so far, nothing more – we're taking witness statements now – Helen saw a fight going off down on the quayside, to the right of the bridge, Magdalene Bridge. A bunch of blokes, a dozen or so, maybe more, kicking all tomorrow out of two men on the ground. Not just kicking. Clubs, baseball bats, you name it. Seems like Helen waded in, tried to put a stop to it, haul 'em off.'

'She didn't call it in? Ask for help?'

Rastrick shook his head. 'Likely thought if she didn't act then, someone might get killed. What happened, of course, they turned on her. Some of them, anyway. You've seen the result. Stabbed her and ran off, cowardly bastards that they are. Left her bleeding out on to the pavement. Luckily someone coming across the bridge saw her and stopped, called emergency services, did what he could to halt the bleeding. The ambulance was there inside seven minutes.'

'Any idea who they were? These blokes?'

'Early days.'

'Christ!'

'Come on, Will. We'll get there.'

'You said witnesses . . .'

'Not so many this far. There'll be some, heard the disturbance, decided they didn't want to know. Besides, it was dark. Taxi-driver, though, saw two groups of men coming off the other side of the bridge, running fast, sprinting. One lot got into a white van. They're arguing the toss over the details now. The others he lost sight of.'

'Two groups, you said?'

'Apparently. One lot – four of them, he thinks, could be five – went off in the van. We're bringing in all the CCTV footage we can. It'll take a while, but we'll have a sighting, with any luck.'

'And the two who were attacked?'

'One's still not regained consciousness. Maybe never will, poor sod. Officers talking to the other one now.' Rastrick checked his watch. 'Back any time.'

'They're gay? The pair who were set upon?'

'Who's to say?' A smile flickered across Rastrick's face. 'Used to be, I was a youth, ring in your ear and a few dangly bits, dead give-away. Not any more. We'll have to bide our time, see what laddie's had to say for 'isself. But if I were a betting man . . .'

The two detectives were back from the hospital within the next half-hour. The victim they had been able to speak to was a twenty-two-year-old student from Hong Kong, currently in his second year at the Department of Architecture, following a special interest in environmental design. His companion was a twenty-six-year-old Roman Catholic from Honduras, studying theology.

They had been drinking with friends in a pub in the city with a large, but not exclusively, gay clientele, and, a clear night, not too cold, had chosen to stroll down to the river. They were within sight of the bridge when several men started shouting abuse at them from across the street. At first the students ignored them, merely quickening their pace, but the abuse had got louder and more strident and then, when a half-brick was thrown in their direction, they decided to cut and run.

Fifty metres along, several more men jumped out of a doorway in front of them. They tried to make their escape along the quayside, but the architecture student slipped and lost his footing, his friend hesitated, and once that had happened, the men were all over them, punching and kicking, yelling more abuse, and then, once they were down, hitting them with clubs or sticks or whatever weapons they had with them.

The student said he was certain they were both going to be killed. Would have been killed, had not a woman tried to intervene, only to have several of the gang set about her as well. One man in particular, the student said, had attacked her with some kind of club, a baseball bat perhaps, and knocked her off her feet. Somehow, she had managed to get up, but then another man grabbed hold of her from behind and swung her round and then seemed to punch her in the stomach. At which point the student himself had been hit on the head – kicked, he thinks – and must have lost consciousness for quite a while, because the next thing he could remember there were ambulances and flashing lights and he was told his friend was being taken off to hospital. When he asked about the woman, he was told that she was already on her way.

'Bastards,' Will said softly. 'Bastards.'

'Don't fret,' Rastrick said, a hand to Will's shoulder. 'We'll get them. We'll see they pay.'

19

Lesley had some vague idea of having been there before, Broadstairs, without remembering clearly when or why. Most of her early life, her childhood certainly, she had lived with her family in Derbyshire, and holidays, following her parents' inclinations, had been spent camping in the Lakes. Midges and mint cake and endless trudges up this or that mountain, most often in search of a view that, when they eventually arrived, was lost in mist. Damp visits to the Pencil Museum in Keswick.

But Broadstairs? The south-east? That nub of land that jutted bluntly out into the Strait of Dover, the watery point where the English Channel and the North Sea met.

Ramsgate, Margate, Broadstairs.

Stephen and herself playing cricket with their father on the sand, building castles that collapsed into the tide. An ice-cream parlour, Italian, on the far side of the promenade and reached by a set of steps. Her mother reading Dickens – was it *David Copperfield*? – and taking them to look at the house where the writer had lived.

She couldn't be making all that up. But how had it happened?

She had a vague recollection of going with her parents to visit some family friends who'd moved somewhere south of London. Had it been when they'd stayed with them?

Until recently, she would have called Stephen or sent him an email. Am I going crazy, Steve, or . . . ? Something squeezed tight, high in her chest, rose in her throat. She could never now do that again.

Seeing a lay-by ahead, she pulled off the road and sat there for fully fifteen minutes, her face in her hands, sobbing, tears trickling through her fingers and running down her neck.

Gordon Hedden's house was one of several medium-sized villas on the road that rose slowly upwards from the centre of the town in the direction of Ramsgate and Pegwell Bay. Like the others, it was neat and unobtrusive, quintessentially English – a certain kind of English – with its low painted gate and privet hedge and window boxes green with daffodils that were yet to flower.

A chill wind rose off the sea as Lesley got out of the car and, despite the sun, shivered and fastened the buttons of her coat.

Hedden had seemed less than enthusiastic when she had first phoned, but in the end she had won him round. His voice had sounded a little tremulous and uncertain, but the man who opened the front door now and came down the path to meet her was spry enough, despite his years. No more than medium height, small-featured, silver-haired, he was wearing a beige cardigan over a broad-check Viyella shirt which, like his cavalry twill trousers, had almost certainly been in his wardrobe for years. Decades, even.

There was a faint tremor in his hand when he shook hers, but otherwise his grip was firm.

'You found it all right, then?' he said pleasantly.

Lesley assured him the journey had been no problem and, after a brief exchange about the weather and some moments spent admiring the view out to where a container ship laboured along the horizon, they went inside.

The interior was as neat and spruce as Hedden himself, and Lesley was reminded of her parents' home in Kirkby Stephen: a place for everything, as her mother liked to say, and everything in its place.

Hedden ushered her into a room that smelt of furniture polish and bade her sit down. There was a three-piece suite, an upright piano against one wall, a circular table by the window. On a tray at the centre of the table, there was a rectangle of fruit cake on a white plate, several slices ready cut, cups and saucers close at hand.

'I take it you'd like tea?' Hedden said.

'Please. That would be nice.'

'Nothing too fancy, I'm afraid. PG Tips.'

'That's fine,' Lesley said, and smiled.

The cake was rich and crumbled against her fingers when she picked it up. He asked her more about her interest in Stella Leonard and *Shattered Glass*, and she told him about Stephen, coming close again to tears when she spoke of his death. Was it some kind of delayed reaction that it was affecting her more now than it had closer to the event itself?

To change the subject, she asked, looking across the room, if he played the piano himself and Hedden shook his head.

'I used to, an hour or more a day. Nothing too difficult. Mozart. Brahms. Just the shorter pieces. Nothing fancy. But now, with these hands . . .' arm angled outwards, he raised his right hand to shoulder height, '. . . even the gentlest lullaby comes out sounding like something from *The Sting*.'

Lesley shook her head. She could remember the film from television – Robert Redford and Robert Shaw – but not the music.

'Ragtime,' Hedden said. 'Always makes me think of Winifred Atwell. You're far too young to remember her, of course. But she was a trained concert pianist. A big woman, too. West Indian. A lovely smile. She came over here hoping to perform Rachmaninov at the Royal Albert Hall and ended up playing these tinkly little numbers on the radio and round the music halls. "Coronation Rag", that's one I remember. "Black and White Rag". That would have been the time we were working on *Shattered Glass*, of course, her heyday. Not that it's the kind of music I associate with that film.' Hedden laughed. 'Too cheerful by half. No, slow jazz in a smoky cellar bar, that's *Shattered Glass*.'

He paused to sip some tea.

'There was this nightclub sequence, a few musicians

on a small stage in one corner, piano, bass and drums. Someone from Ted Heath's band on saxophone. Bob somebody? Bobby? I can't remember. Perhaps a dozen tables on the set, lots of extras. Stella's character, one of them – I suppose you know she plays twins – gets up to sing with the band. "I Must Have That Man". One of those songs Billie Holiday used to sing. I think she even had a carnation pinned to the dress she was wearing. The same as Holiday used to. I thought they'd get someone else to do the vocals for her, dub it in later, but, no, she did it all herself. Not a great voice, small, but she could carry a tune.

'Shooting it, though, that was a nightmare. Smoke everywhere. Gauze across the lens at one point. Curtis, the director, he'd been making us watch all these movies from America. *Out of the Past*. *The Dark Mirror*. A couple he'd made himself. *Death by Night*, one of them, I can't remember the other. Real Poverty Row stuff. Most of the set in shadow because there is no set to speak of, and precious little scenery. All shot in ten days, too. Cheap and quick. "Just light the faces," he'd say. "That's what I want, just let me see the faces." Black and white, you know, but a lot more black than white.'

With a slight rattle, Hedden set his cup back in its saucer.

'Considering it was all done pretty much on a shoe-string, I don't think it looks too bad.' He leaned forward. 'You've seen the film, of course.'

'No, I'm afraid not. There's a DVD available now in

the States, apparently, I checked on Amazon, but because it's a different system, you can't play it here.'

'Well,' Hedden said, 'if you don't mind helping me set up the screen, I've got an old 16 mil. print. We can watch that.' He was already on his feet. 'You might have to help me lace the film through the projector, as well.'

The plot, despite devious twists and turns and a succession of betrayals, was relatively simple. Good sister, Alma, meets the man of her dreams, a clean-living and heroic surgeon named Philip, who is dedicated to furthering medical understanding of the human brain, and accepts his proposal of marriage, while bad sister, Ruby, no better than she should be, sneers from the sidelines. There is a sub-plot, involving Ruby, a crooked nightclub owner and some stolen jewels, but the main concern of the story is with Ruby's jealousy of her sister and her intention to steal Philip away at all costs. Which, for a time, of course she does.

In the build-up to the final scene – borrowed, Hedden told Lesley, from an earlier film called *Angel Face* – Philip, having finally succumbed to Ruby's seductive wiles, comes to his senses after being confronted by a distraught Alma, and goes to Ruby to tell her their affair is over and he is going to marry Alma after all. Putting on her best false face, Ruby pretends to understand, even to be pleased, and says she will drive Philip to where Alma is waiting. Once behind the wheel, however, she accelerates faster and faster and finally drives the car off the edge of a cliff and into the sea, where they both drown.

The last shot is a close-up of Alma, black veil across her face, at the funeral of both her betrothed and her sister, where they are being buried side by side.

'Not exactly,' Lesley said, 'what you'd call a happy ending.'

Hedden reached up and switched off the projector, stopping the end frames of celluloid from flapping in loose circles. Lesley pulled back the curtains, letting natural light back into the room.

'So,' Hedden said, 'what did you think?'

'I liked it. The camera work, especially. And I'm not saying that just because you're standing there. It was really atmospheric.'

'Ah, that was down to Jack, the director of photography, more than me. I just pointed the camera through the gloom and hoped for the best.'

'I'm sure that's not true. But anyway, that was what I liked. And Stella, of course. She's extraordinary, isn't she?'

'She was very good,' Hedden agreed.

'First she's this nice young girl, butter wouldn't melt in her mouth, and then, the next minute, she's changed into this – I don't know what you'd call it? Tart? Harlot? Slapper, I suppose that's what we'd say today. Except that she's evil with it. And sexy, my God! Talk about sex on a stick.'

'Exactly,' Hedden said. 'And this, remember, was Britain in the fifties, when everything that wasn't buttoned down was buttoned up.'

235

'You know the scene that threw me most?' Lesley said. 'When Alma's sitting at her dressing-table mirror, dabbing a little powder on her face, running a comb through her hair, all very demure, and then she stands up and turns around and suddenly she's face to face with Ruby and it's as if she's still looking in a mirror, except that Ruby's got all this heavy make-up on, the whole works, and even though it's black and white you can feel how red the lipstick is on her mouth. Extraordinary.'

Hedden smiled, almost apologetically. 'We stole that, too. From *Black Narcissus*. Powell and Pressburger. Except it's in reverse. In Michael Powell's film, Deborah Kerr walks in on Kathleen Byron inside the convent where they're both nuns, and surprises Byron secretly putting on make-up. But then, nothing's new.' He looked across at the clock on the mantelpiece. 'I have to take a tablet. Three, actually. Then perhaps we can have another cup of tea. And talk about Stella.'

By now the light outside was beginning to fade. Hedden's hand shook noticeably less, Lesley noticed, when he lifted the teapot. There was a wedge of Lancashire cheese to accompany the cake.

'Which one was she most like in real life?' Lesley asked. 'Stella? The good twin or the bad?'

Hedden didn't answer immediately. 'It's hard to say. When you're filming, it's a bit like – I suppose it's a bit like being on holiday. Except you're working twelve, thirteen hours a day. What I mean is, you're thrown together with people who, for the most part, you don't know and suddenly you're in their company all the time. You might think that's a way of getting to know someone really well, and so it can be, except the way people often behave in those kinds of situations – stars, especially, and that's what Stella was – it isn't natural.' He shook his head. 'Hedging my bets, aren't I?'

'That's okay.'

'I suppose if I had to come down one way or another, I'd say she was both. I know that sounds as if I'm avoiding the issue altogether, but I think it's true. She was one inside the other: the bad Stella hiding inside the good. You'd meet her and she'd be very polite and proper – she'd been through the Rank Charm School after all. Deportment and elocution and all the rest. But there was something in her eyes. At the back of her eyes. Meet her under normal circumstances and you could miss it. But looking at her through the lens, it was there. Waiting to be let loose. So that when the storyline gave her the chance . . . well, some of those scenes, you said yourself, her sexuality, it's tangible.'

'And you put it on the screen.'

'I did my best.'

'What I don't understand, if she could do that, act like that, why wasn't she a bigger star than she was?'

Hedden cut off another corner of cheese.

'That's a difficult one. But I think what she had to offer, what made her stand out from all the Jills and Belindas, wasn't what was wanted just then. The occasional sex symbol was allowed, but they had to be more like Diana Dors, busty and blonde and a bit exaggerated. Just this side of a seaside postcard. The sexiness Stella had wasn't just in her body, it was in here too.' Hedden touched his fingers to the side of his head. 'The British film industry didn't want to know. Oh, if *Shattered Glass* had made a fortune at the box office, it might have been different, but I doubt if it did much more than break even. If that. To the best of my knowledge, Stella didn't work for well over a year after we wrapped. And when she did, it was back to playing the Almas of this world. Where Ruby was concerned, no one wanted to know.'

'What was she like to work with?'

'Professional. On the set on time, knew her lines. However many takes Curtis asked for, she didn't complain.'

'And she got on with everyone?'

'I'd say so. Some more than others, that's inevitable. But she never came over all grand, like some, and as far as the grips and lighting technicians and so on were concerned, she went out of her way to be pleasant.'

'You said some more than others?'

'I did, didn't I?' He smiled ruefully. 'In those days, if you didn't have an American star, there was no chance of getting US distribution. Not that Dennis Wade was any kind of a star. But he was an American. And he'd had so-so parts in a couple of decent Hollywood movies. Curtis had worked with him before on a couple of occasions. Just when Dennis was getting started. He'd played Dane Clark's younger brother, got shot by Dan Duryea

238

in the first reel, that kind of thing. What he did have in his favour, nationality aside, he was handsome and he was cheap.'

Lesley could agree with the handsome part. Dark curly hair, even features, a strong jaw. 'He and Stella, they were an item?'

'Supposedly. They spent quite a lot of time in one another's company certainly. Around the set, at least. And the publicity department made the most of it. Photographs of them together in *Picturegoer* and *Picture Show*. You can imagine the kind of thing, I'm sure.'

'And you think that's what it all was? A publicity stunt?'

'I honestly don't know.' Levering himself forward, he refreshed their cups with more tea. 'There were rumours even – I heard this later, of course, after we'd finished editing – that she'd become pregnant.'

'By Wade?'

'So the story went.'

'When I looked up her biography, there was no mention of a child.'

Hedden gestured with his hands as if to say, who knows?

'She could have had an abortion,' Lesley said. 'Or had the baby and then put it up for adoption. That could account for the time she didn't work.'

'I don't know. I think the reason for not working was simply, for her, the work wasn't there.'

Lesley could hear the tiredness in his voice. 'I've kept you too long,' she said.

'No, not at all. It's been most enjoyable. It's not that often nowadays I get the chance to talk about old times.'

At the doorway, they shook hands.

'Safe journey,' Hedden said.

The sky overhead was several shades of grey and, out to sea, the horizon had been swallowed up in a darkening blur of what could be snow.

35. INT. NIGHTCLUB. NIGHT.

The interior of the club is small, intimate, hazed in smoke. RUBY *stands at the microphone on a small, circular stage, a white baby grand at her back. At slow to medium tempo, she is singing 'I Must Have That Man', accompanied by piano, bass, drums and saxophone. Hair up, she is wearing a long, close-fitting dress, a spray of gardenias pinned to her shoulder.*

As the camera pulls back, we see RUBY'*s twin sister,* ALMA, *sitting at one of the tables with* PHILIP. *Their hands are close together on the table's surface, fingers slightly overlapping.*

From what we understand to be PHILIP'*s POV, we cut to a close shot of* RUBY *as she sings, moving in on her mouth and then pulling back to show first the fingers of one hand caressing the microphone, then her other hand stroking her thigh.*

We cut back to PHILIP'*s face, fascinated, watching,*

241

before seeing a smile in RUBY's *eyes as she realises all of his attention is focused on her, and then* ALMA's *expression as she watches him watching* RUBY.

We pull back to a full shot of the stage as RUBY *finishes her song to applause, which fades and takes us into . . .*

36. INT. DRESSING ROOM. NIGHT.

RUBY *is sitting at the dressing table, looking at herself in the mirror. Perhaps she has started to remove some of her make-up. She takes a cigarette from a silver case and is just putting it in her mouth as someone knocks at the door.*

RUBY: *Who is it?*

ALMA *(from outside the door): It's me, Alma.*

RUBY *reaches for her lighter, clicks it to life, lights her cigarette, inhales and then releases a slow plume of smoke towards the mirror before answering.*

RUBY: *Come in.*

RUBY *swivels round in her chair as* ALMA *enters,* PHILIP *just behind her.*

ALMA: *You remember Philip?*

It is clear that RUBY *does. She looks at him in a half-amused, half-admiring kind of way.*

242

Moving forward, PHILIP *holds out his hand and, with the same look still on her face,* RUBY *takes it.*

PHILIP: *You were marvellous.*

She has not let go of his hand. ALMA *notices this.*

RUBY: *Yes, I was, wasn't I?*

20

CCTV cameras on a pedestrian bridge near Craft's Hill, on the A14 Cambridge – Huntingdon road, had recorded a white 15 cwt Ford van travelling fast in the outside lane, no more than ten minutes after the incident. The number-plate seemed to have been deliberately dirtied over, only one number and two letters visible. Further footage, this time from a camera close to a motel on the outskirts of Huntingdon, showed the van still heading west, but moving more steadily now in the inside lane.

Without any details from the taxi-driver who had seen the men running across the bridge after the attack, it was not yet possible to ascertain what vehicle the second group had used to make their getaway – or if they had used a vehicle at all. If they were local, as seemed possible, they could simply have split up and disappeared back into the city on foot. Witnesses were being asked to come forward, and those few that had so far done so were being interviewed and the value of their information assessed.

The two young men who had been attacked were still in Addenbrooke's Hospital, where the condition of one of them, the theology student, was a matter of grave concern; he had not yet fully regained consciousness, and members of his family had flown in from Honduras to be by his bedside. The architecture student from Hong Kong, meanwhile, despite two broken ribs and extensive bruising, had been able to sit up in bed and talk to detectives. Any descriptions he had so far been able to give them of his attackers, however, had been disappointingly vague and sketchy. One thing he had told them was that he thought several members of the gang had been using their mobile phones to photograph the attack.

Helen Walker, while not exactly sitting up, had recovered sufficiently to be lying on the bed with her head raised, propped up by pillows; the IV line was still attached to the vein at the side of her neck and she was somewhat hazy from the painkillers she had taken.

Her sister had left at the end of the previous afternoon, promising to return; her parents had stayed until late into the evening and returned at first light. When Will arrived later that morning, they hesitantly took the opportunity to go down to the cafeteria for some breakfast.

'Flowers, Will?' Helen said, her face breaking into a weak grin.

Will glanced down at the mixed bouquet in his hand. 'Lorraine's idea. She sends her love.'

'You'd never have thought of it otherwise.'

'Unlikely.'

'Too unmanly.'

'By half.' He set the flowers down and pulled a chair closer to the bed. Her hand struck him as surprisingly cold.

'How you feeling?'

'Other than like shit?'

'Other than that.'

She tried for a smile. 'Let's say I'm a way off spring training.'

'No ten K this year, then?'

'I doubt I could manage ten metres on my hands and knees.' With an effort, she pushed herself almost into a sitting position, then collapsed back down. 'I can't even sit up in bed.'

'Take it easy,' Will said. 'Don't force things.'

'All right for you to say.'

'Push it too hard and you'll end up being here all the longer.'

'Yes, doctor.'

Will grinned.

'I just feel so bloody useless,' Helen said.

'You probably saved someone's life. Maybe two. Your picture's in all the papers, you know. And on TV. *Look East*, anyway. Regular heroine. Sorry, hero.'

'That's all bollocks and you know it.'

'Course it is. Be some kind of commendation, though, I'd not be surprised. Chance to shake the Chief Constable's hand. Won't hurt those chances of promotion.'

'Fuck off, Will.'

He looked at his watch. 'Any minute.'

'Don't you start,' Helen said.

'What do you mean?'

'My dad, he sits there pretending not to be bored, sneaking glances at his watch when he thinks I'm not looking. Mum witters on endlessly, like she thinks if I haven't got her to listen to I'll keel over and die.'

'Family, eh?' Will lightly squeezed her hand. 'These blokes who attacked you, if you'd remembered anything useful, you'd have said?'

Helen moved her head slowly from side to side. 'Like I told Rastrick, it all happened so fast. And it was dark, besides. The two who came at me, they were both white. Youngish. The one with the knife, he could have still been in his teens.'

'And the other?'

'Older than that, but not by much. Late twenties, maybe?'

'Size?'

'The older one? Your kind of height. Sort of skinny. One of those wool caps on his head.'

Will nodded and checked his watch a second time. 'Look, I really do have to go.' He gave her hand another squeeze. 'I'll pop in and see you this evening, okay?'

Helen smiled weakly. 'Okay.'

'The student from Hong Kong,' Will said at the door, 'he thinks a couple of the gang might have been taking pictures with their mobile phones.'

Helen felt sick inside. 'I didn't notice. That doesn't mean it didn't happen.'

'I know.'

'Thank Lorraine for the flowers.'

'Sure.' When he switched his own mobile back on outside the hospital, there was a message from the station: Malcolm Rastrick wanted to see him ASAP.

Rastrick was looking inordinately cheerful – for Rastrick. A suggestion of brightness in his grey eyes, pale cheeks still sunken in.

'Ford Escort, wrapped round a lamp post on the Newmarket Road. Not so far from the retail park. Three youths seen running from the scene.'

'Descriptions?'

A curt shake of the head. 'Still working on it.'

'How about the vehicle?'

'Stolen earlier the same day. Park-and-ride out past the cemetery.'

'Anything to tie it in with the attack?'

'Only the time so far. Near as we can pin it down, fifteen, twenty minutes after they scarpered.'

'And if they took off on foot after crashing the car . . . ?'

'Could live local, Barnwell, out by the airport. Alternatively, they could've been heading out somewhere on the Newmarket Road. Newmarket itself.'

'Or making for the A14 east.'

'Or that.'

'No other vehicles reported stolen? Around that time?'

'Not as yet. We're checking.'

Will's face set in a frown. 'How about the van?'

'One more sighting. A1 North. Just below Grantham. We're pulling in everything else we can get our hands on now.'

'Could have been heading practically bloody any-where,' Will said. 'Leeds to Scotch bloody Corner. Sheffield. Nottingham.'

'No point guessing,' Rastrick said. 'Let's wait and see.'

Back in his office, Will started sifting through paper-work, reading emails, prioritising as best he could. The Stephen Bryan murder was not the only investigation he was nominally responsible for, and now there was the attack on Helen and the two students, which he could have left entirely to Rastrick, though both men knew he never would.

In Helen's absence, Paul Irving, the family liaison officer, had stepped up, and with Nick Moyles pitching in, was doing his best to keep the Bryan inquiry on track. So far, however, they'd had no joy in tracing the man who'd been seen hanging around Bryan's house, nor identifying whoever had left a message on his answerphone. A backtrack into Russell Johnson's past had yielded nothing that led them to believe either that he had been lying in his account of his one-night stand, or had been involved in any way with Bryan's murder. And still no murder weapon had been found.

Will was still working at his desk when Rastrick appeared in the open doorway, sometime after seven.

'No home to go to?' Rastrick said.

Will looked up wearily. 'Not if I don't get back to it soon.'

'Women, wives, whatever, you can warn them beforehand what it'll be like, and they'll nod their heads and say they understand, but they don't, not really.' He coughed drily into the back of his hand. 'None of mine ever did.'

'Lorraine's okay,' Will said.

'You been married how long? Five year?'

'Somewhere round there.'

Rastrick chuckled, a dry rattle in the back of his throat. 'Give it time.'

'Thanks,' Will said. 'Thanks a lot.'

'Okay,' Rastrick said, standing. 'I'm off to the pub for a pint or two, likely pick up an Indian on the way home, watch the box till I can't keep my eyes open any longer and then fall into bed. I don't recommend it till you've run out of alternatives.'

21

The burnt-out van was found early the following morning, close to the dismantled railway between Eastwood and Brinsley, ten miles or so from Nottingham city centre. A teacher, out on her morning run, had seen the van from the track leading towards Coneygrey Farm, and remembering the appeal on the previous night's news, phoned the local police on her mobile. That close to the Nottinghamshire–Derbyshire border, early liaison with both forces would be essential.

Officers in protective clothing would conduct a fingertip search of the immediate area, hoping that whoever set light to the van had left some physical evidence behind – a thread of trouser material caught on a tuft of rough grass, a button that had become detached. The recent wet weather made the recovery of any shoe prints relatively easy to photograph, without having recourse to the gelatine or electrostatic lifters used on drier surfaces. Tyre tracks would be treated in the same way. Samples of soil and dirt would also be taken, as this could potentially place suspects at the scene.

Only when this process was over would heavy lifting equipment be brought in and the van be taken away for thorough forensic examination. Whoever had been responsible for torching it had done the job well – the interior was little more than a charred shell – and it was doubtful if any prints or marks would have survived.

But they were due a break: they could hope.

Nick Moyles caught Will in his office that afternoon, Will doing his best to pull together details of half a dozen other cases he was still nominally supervising.

'You've heard about the van?' Moyles said.

Will nodded.

'Where it was found,' Moyles said. 'Could be something in that.'

'How so?'

'Year or so back, there was a spate of homophobic attacks in the same area. Eastwood, Kimberley, Heanor. All inside a twelve-month. All serious. One bloke especially, got himself badly beaten in a gents toilet. This lad set him up, sounds like, pretending to be gay. Trousers round the guy's ankles when six or seven of them came barging in. Knives and baseball bats. Near killed him.'

'And this was when, you say?'

'Good year back, maybe more. Notts and Derbyshire set up a joint task force, managed to infiltrate the group responsible for a while. Pretty successful, by all accounts.

Half a dozen arrests, two or three convictions. Since then, no more attacks as we've heard of.'

'Till now, maybe.'

'Maybe.'

'This task force,' Will asked, 'it's still operational?'

'I'm not sure. I can talk to Chris Parsons, Notts Hate Crimes, he'd likely know.'

'Okay, see if you can't set up a meeting. And be sure to keep Rastrick in the loop, okay?'

'Right,' Moyles said. 'Understood.'

Checking through his messages, Will saw that Lesley Scarman had rung twice since noon. He called her work number and she picked up the phone on the second ring, the buzz of voices audible around her, the sound of a radio presenter deeper into the background.

'Thanks for getting back to me,' Lesley said.

'No problem.'

'I was ringing about Helen,' Lesley said. 'Helen Walker. I was wondering how she was?'

'As well as can be expected.'

'The last bulletin I heard, she was still in intensive care.'

'Not any more, thank heavens. Out of the woods, by all accounts.'

'It sounds as if she was lucky.'

'I suppose so,' Will said. 'In a way.' He wondered how being stabbed within an inch or two of your life counted as lucky? But then, if you were comparing it to what had happened to Lesley's brother, lucky is what she was.

'While you're on the phone,' Will said, 'Howard

Prince, we met him. Asked him about the solicitor's letter he had sent to your brother.'

'What did he say?'

'Said it was a matter of privacy. Family privacy. His wife, apparently, she's – how did he put it? – fragile. Mentally unstable, I suppose that means. Seems it was her he was trying to protect more than anyone.'

'More than himself,' Lesley said with a certain scorn.

'What d'you mean?'

A pause. 'I don't know.'

Will made no response.

'But what he said, you believed him?'

'Yes. Yes, I think we did. No reason not to.'

Lesley started to say something, then changed her mind. 'Your colleague,' she said. 'Helen. Give her my best wishes.'

'Of course.'

Lesley broke the connection before Will could do so himself and, almost immediately, the phone rang again. It was Rastrick.

'Moyles has just been on to me – this meeting out at Notts, all yours and welcome. What with following up that business on the Newmarket Road, never mind witness reports to wade through and the forensics on the van, I've got more than enough to handle. Just keep me informed.'

Will assured him that he would.

Earlier that day, even as a flurry of rain had blown fiercely against the police station windows, the sun had

254

come out from behind dark clouds and a rainbow had appeared above the city. Now, as Will stepped out into the early evening, the sun had long gone and the rain had slackened to a drizzle. The hospital was so close that taking the car was a nonsense: besides which, there was never anywhere to park.

He called Lorraine on his mobile as he walked. 'Hi. Everything okay?'

'Fine.'

'I thought I'd just nip in and see Helen before coming home.'

'You should. How was she this morning?'

'Not too bad,' Will said. 'Is Jake there?'

'Yes. Why?'

'I thought he might be in bed by the time I get back.'

'You want to talk to him?'

'Yes, please.'

He could hear a brief exchange of voices and then, 'Here he is now.'

'Hey, Jake,' Will said.

'Daddy,' his son said, cheerfully.

'What you been up to?'

Walking, collar up, Will listened to a wandering tale of marble paintings and playtime and friends, both real and imaginary.

'Listen, Jake, I'm going to have to go now. Okay?'

Silence.

'You'll probably be in bed by the time I'm home.'

Nothing.

'If you're asleep, I'll come in and give you a kiss.'

'Give Puppy a kiss.'

'All right, I'll give Puppy a kiss as well.'

'And Brian.' Brian, for some reason, was the name Jake had given to his toy lion.

'Okay, and Brian,' Will said. 'If Mummy's still there, can you give her back the phone?'

After a few more words with Lorraine, Will slipped his mobile back into his pocket and quickened his stride. The rain was slackening off and the wind was dropping. Driving home later might not be as unpleasant as he'd feared.

Neither of Helen's parents was at her bedside. In their place was a man Will had never seen before. Mid- to late-thirties, brown leather jacket, jeans, a full head of fairish hair that rose to a V at the front and fell away a little to one side. His hand was close to Helen's on top of the sheet, not touching. Helen's eyes were closed and it was impossible to tell if she were sleeping or not.

Will stood, watching through the glass screen, until the man at the bedside turned his head towards him.

No, Will thought, he didn't recognise the face at all.

For some seconds they stared at one another, before the man half-rose from the chair and, leaning towards Helen, kissed her softly on the cheek.

As he left, he looked Will directly in the eye and, without speaking, walked off down the ward. Will watched him go, then stepped into the room. Not wanting to wake Helen, he sat down as quietly as he could.

When she spoke, it was without opening her eyes, and her voice startled him.

'Will?'

'Yes?'

'I don't want him to come here again.'

'Who is he?'

'It doesn't matter. I just don't want him here again, that's all.'

'I don't see how . . .'

'Tell him. Please, Will. Tell him not to come.'

Will caught up with the man as he was leaving the main entrance, dropped back several paces and followed him to his car. As he was about to get in, Will increased his pace and set a hand on the door, keeping it closed.

'What?' the man said. His face showed little concern, but his hands were clenched into fists.

'She doesn't want to see you again.'

'Who says?'

'She does. Helen. Okay? Don't come back. We understood?' Will stepped back from the car.

The man smiled with his eyes; his eyes were blue. 'And if I do?'

'Don't,' Will said. 'Just don't.'

The smile flickered and faded and with an almost nonchalant shake of the head, the man got into his car, turned the key in the ignition and, without a further glance towards Will, reversed out of his space and drove slowly away.

One of the nurses was raising Helen up a little on her pillows when he got back to the ward.

257

'Who was that?' Will asked.

'I said, it doesn't matter.'

'It mattered enough for me to warn him off.'

'Just leave it, okay?'

'Okay.'

For twenty minutes or so they talked haltingly about the progress the inquiry was making and then, when her parents returned from wherever they'd been, he said goodbye and promised to come back the next day.

Jake was indeed in bed when he arrived home, though Susie was still awake and fretful. Will kissed his wife and daughter and then his son, though he broke his promise about both the puppy and the lion. After supper, he and Lorraine watched an hour or so of mindless TV, before settling for an early night. This time it was Lorraine who fell asleep first, leaving Will staring at the ceiling, the mocking smile of Helen's anonymous visitor imprinted above him.

22

News bulletins cued up and ready, Lesley pulled what the station had on Howard Prince. Surprisingly little. He was a member of the Rotary Club and the Chamber of Commerce and had associations with the East Midlands Development Agency but, a few passing references to his wilder past aside, there was little, if anything, about his private life. And nothing about his wife.

In the last eighteen months, Prince's name had been linked to a consortium with plans to build on reclaimed railway land out towards the racecourse, and with a scheme for a new leisure centre and adjacent high-end accommodation, overlooking the Trent.

He had a house out in Cambridgeshire, north of the county, the Fens; mention of a second home in the south of France. Frontignan.

Lesley checked the phone book. There was a Prince Holdings listed on Friar Lane.

The receptionist, sounding bored out of her skull and not yet mid-morning, asked Lesley to hold. A snatch of the inevitable Vivaldi and then, 'Raymond James here. How can I help?' The voice was cultured, supercilious.

Lesley repeated her request to speak to Howard Prince.

'I'm sorry, who did you say you were?'

'Lesley Scarman, BBC Radio Nottingham.'

The man's sniffy tone suggested he was not a regular listener. 'And this was in relation to . . . ?'

'A film Mr Prince is funding.'

There was a pause.

'It's due to be made here in the city. Partly, at least.'

'Please wait a moment. I'm just going to put you on hold.'

Polite, if disdainful. The line went temporarily dead. Lesley tapped at the computer keyboard, accessing her emails.

He was swiftly back. 'I'm sorry, we have no record of any such project.'

'My information is that Mr Prince is providing substantial financing. The film features his daughter, Natalie.'

'As I say, we have no knowledge of this. I'm sorry.'

'Is it possible, then, that Mr Prince could be funding the production personally?'

'I couldn't possibly comment.'

'But it is a possibility?'

'I'm sorry, Miss Scarman, but there's nothing I can do to help.'

'Perhaps if I could speak to Mr Prince directly . . . ?'

The line went dead, this time for good.

* * *

There were boards all around the Old Market Square, behind which a major makeover was in process. Water terraces, trees and coloured lights were set to transform fifteen acres of concrete wasteland, long a meeting place for Goths, skateboarders, down-at-heel boozers and raggedy-arsed pigeons, into what some bright spark from the council's marketing department had called the beating heart of our vibrant city.

Lesley might not have couched it in such grandiose terms herself.

It was true, though, that the centre of the city was changing. Everywhere you looked whole blocks were being pulled down, new buildings rising in their place. Hotels, apartments, new retail opportunities. Build, build, build.

Someone, Lesley reasoned, was making a bushel of money, square metre by square metre, brick by brick.

As she waited on the edge of Maid Marian Way, an inner-city ring road of almost unsurpassed ugliness, and a testament to the last splurge of urban renewal back in the 1970s, Lesley wondered what weasel words some marketing whizz-kid had thought up back then to acclaim its particular beauties. A vital artery pumping lifeblood into the city's burnished heart? A gash of viral reconstruction ripping the guts out of the city centre?

The lights changed and she crossed on to the upper half of Friar Lane.

The sign alongside the door was small and discreet, dark lettering engraved into polished gold. Prince

Holdings. Lesley pressed the buzzer and inclined her head towards the intercom.

'Lesley Scarman, BBC Radio Nottingham. I was speaking to someone here earlier.'

After several seconds, the buzzer sounded and she pushed back the door. Carpeted hallway, tasteful prints on the walls, stairs at the far end leading temptingly upwards. To her right there was a panelled door marked Reception. Lesley knocked and went in.

More carpet, but with a deeper pile and in a different shade. Paintings and not prints on the walls. An idealised version of the castle; a couple of idyllic views of the River Trent, as seen from the southern bank: rowers, swans, couples gently strolling past an avenue of trees. The site, Lesley wondered, of Prince's prospective chunk of new development?

The woman behind the desk blinked twice, then sighed with the effort.

'I'm here to see Mr Prince,' Lesley said, even as she heard the footsteps behind her.

'Miss Scarman?'

He was in his forties, a lean face that looked to have been chiselled from wood, with rimless glasses shielding his pale blue eyes. Thin lips. His dark suit was almost the same colour as his tie; his shirt could have been ironed five minutes before. Spruce might be the word. One word.

'Raymond James, Miss Scarman, Mr Prince's assistant. If you're hoping for more information than I was able to give you earlier, I'm afraid you've wasted your time.'

'More,' Lesley said, 'is a bit of an overstatement, don't you think? Mr James?'

It earned her a small condescending smile.

'Howard Prince,' Lesley said, 'this is his business? Still, I mean.'

'I'm not quite sure I understand.'

'He hasn't retired, sold up, taken himself off into the sun?'

'Not at all.'

'He takes an active interest, then?'

'Of course.'

'Hands on?'

'Very much so.'

Lesley glanced round towards the door. 'He's here now then, I imagine?'

'I'm afraid I can't say.'

'It would only take a moment . . .'

'Miss Scarman . . .'

'A minute of his time.'

'Miss Scarman, I'm afraid I must ask you to leave.'

Lesley assumed the receptionist had summoned up the energy to press a button beneath her desk. In less time than it took her to formulate another question, two young men appeared, slender and smiling, behind James. Hair short but neat, shirtsleeves turned back at the cuff. If they'd turned up on her doorstep, she would have taken them for Mormons, intent on spreading the word.

James favoured her with a superior, you-should-have-listened-to-me look. Any moment, Lesley thought, he's going to say, 'Miss Scarman was just leaving.'

He did.

One of the young men gently touched her arm below the elbow and she shrugged him off. She took a business card from her bag and held it out towards James, leaving him little alternative other than to take it.

'Please tell Mr Prince I was here. Tell him if he'd like to talk to me about his daughter's film, I can be reached on either of these numbers. And thank you for your time.'

No smile.

She stepped between the two young men, out along the short stretch of hallway and through the door, which sprang open on her approach. Perhaps, she thought, Natalie Prince's penchant for newsworthy misbehaviour had made her father's firm more than usually cautious about media intrusion – or maybe there were other reasons altogether.

The air outside was cold and fresh and Lesley thought she might take a stroll round the Castle grounds before returning to work.

She bought a coffee in the cafeteria and sat thinking, none too coherently, random ideas and images shuffling through her brain without ever really connecting. When she'd finished her coffee, she went outside on to the terrace and leaned on the stone balustrade, looking out over the new office buildings at the far side of the canal to the bright green roofs of the county council offices alongside the Trent. Beyond those, she could see the darker green of the fields either side of Sharphill Wood. Fields and trees that would soon, if the council's decision was upheld, be bulldozed by developers with plans to build a thousand new homes.

The last time she'd stood on that spot, Lesley remembered, it had been with Stephen, who had told her it was where Albert Finney had stood with Rachel Roberts in the film of *Saturday Night and Sunday Morning*, the smoky landscape of the city etched in behind them in hazy black and white.

At the memory of Stephen, she pressed her hands harder against the pitted surface of the stone.

After her visit to Prince Holdings and the Castle, Lesley was busy for the remainder of the day, headphones in place, fingers to the keyboard, eyes on the screen. By the time she finished there was an ache across her shoulders, a dull pain in the small of her back and she'd put in at least forty-five minutes overtime she'd never see.

She thought Alan Pike had already left, but as she was putting on her coat, he stepped out of his office.

'Howard Prince, Lesley, there's nothing to interest us there.'

Lesley flushed. 'I thought I might do a follow-up on that stuff about Natalie, you know, the movie.'

'I don't think so.'

'Come on, Alan. As long as I can do it in my own time . . .'

'Lesley, you're not listening. Leave it alone. Okay?' He was a little dishevelled, tie at half-mast, but his voice was firm and unwavering.

'Okay.'

'It's not just me,' Pike said.

'Roger?'

Pike nodded.

Why, Lesley thought, was the station manager getting involved?

'Someone's been leaning on him,' she said.

'It's possible. I don't know.'

'Prince.'

'Lesley, go home. It's late.' Pike turned back towards his office.

No other option open, Lesley picked up her bag and left.

The reception desk had closed down for the evening. One of the cleaning staff was manoeuvring a rotund vacuum cleaner around the stands in the far corner, and Lesley called out goodnight and let herself out on to the street.

London Road was busy as usual, the traffic not exactly stalled, but barely moving. A slow drizzle was falling and the pavements were slick with rain.

She was almost at the top of the steps leading up towards Commerce Square, her usual cut-through, when she heard a sound behind her, a footfall other than her own, but when she turned there was no one there. Just the rough bare brick walls to either side and the worn steps themselves funnelling down into the dark.

23

Will drove over to Nottingham under lowering skies, the car radio releasing a stream of background conversation and anodyne music, neither of which connected with what was going on inside his head. The news about Helen was good: if things continued to progress as expected, she could be discharged within days.

The theology student, however, having rallied, had slipped backward during the night and was now unconscious and breathing with the help of a respirator, his condition giving grave cause for concern.

No sign of the knife with which Helen had been stabbed, nor of any other weapon that had been used; bins and back alleys and bits of wasteland close to the attack were still being searched; divers were going down again, Will guessed, even now.

When he arrived in Nottingham, he found that, thanks to demolition and rebuilding in the city centre, there were diversions on the roads leading to the Central Police Station, and it took him several attempts before finding his way into the parking area at the rear.

Nick Moyles had driven over separately and was waiting for him in the foyer, well turned out as usual. Moyles's clothes, he had once told Will, were from White Stuff or, occasionally, Diesel, and tended towards the casually fashionable, without ever overstepping some recognised but invisible mark.

Chris Parsons was waiting for them in a room on the second floor with views out towards several acres of rubble and a large crane.

Parsons himself was around the same height as Will, five or six years older. He was clean-shaven, sandy hair trimmed fairly short, wearing dark trousers and a pale green shirt, the sleeves rolled back above the wrist. His jacket hung neatly from the back of his chair.

'What happened to your DS,' Parsons said, as he shook Will's hand, 'I'm sorry.' His accent was local, without being too pronounced.

'Thanks,' Will said.

'She's on the mend?'

'Seems that way.'

'That's good.'

There was a stainless-steel flask of coffee on the table, milk in a jug, sachets of sugar in a bowl.

'This task force,' Will said, once they were all seated. 'Perhaps you could fill me in on the background?'

Parsons nodded and took a quick sip of coffee. 'Where we operated, in the main, was between here and Derby, to the east. The Erewash Valley. Ex-mining towns, for the most part. Eastwood. Kimberley. Heanor. Used to be, lads went down the pit as soon as they were of an age, girls into the hosiery factories. That's how it was. No question. Then, twenty years or so back, the miners' strike – before that really – everything changed. Pits closed, factories as well, most of them. Lots of folk out of a job and little prospect of anything new. Kids leave school with scarcely a qualification to their name and what do they do? Hang round street corners, sign on. Bored rigid, most of the time.'

'How about BNP activity?' Moyles asked. 'Is there much of that?'

'You bet. Just the sort of thing the BNP thrive on. They've got a lot of support in that area and it's not hard to see why. They give people a focus for all that frustration. Or seem to. Some people, at any rate. And it doesn't take much for it to roll over into violence. Looking for someone to blame. Anyone other than themselves. Blacks, Asians, gays, asylum seekers.'

Parsons paused for a mouthful of coffee.

'The task force managed to get someone inside. Undercover. Till they had him sussed. Gave us names, places, dates, enabled us to make arrests. After that it all calmed down. Or so it seemed.' He shook his head. 'Homophobic incidents reported in the county last year were up again by nearly thirty per cent. Not in the city, but outside. Assault, harassment, criminal damage. Okay, some of that's down to more people having the confidence to come forward, but not all.'

'Any chance of the task force being made operational again?' Will asked.

Parsons shrugged. 'It's been talked about. But, you know, it's finance as much as anything. Manpower. Resources.'

Will knew the problems only too well.

'The people you were talking about,' Moyles said, 'the ones the task force was investigating, you think they could have been behind the attack in Cambridge the other night?'

Parsons took his time. 'The van being found where it was, that's what it points to. I'm just not sure about that degree of organisation. Cambridge, it's a way off. Our of their normal territory. And most of the incidents – not all, but most – they tend to be more casual, no real plan at all. Whatever triggers them off, it's usually something small, local. A couple of gay guys holding hands at a bus-stop, quick kiss goodnight, that kind of thing. But then again, there were instances where things were clearly well organised beforehand, a pub or a club would be targeted, some particular toilet used for cottaging. So, yes, it's possible. And they'll have contact with other groups, I don't doubt.'

Will nodded and helped himself to more coffee from the flask.

'Aside from where the van was found,' Parsons asked, 'is there any other evidence that points in this direction?'

'Not so far.'

'And there were others involved, I think Nick said.'

'Yes. Could be local. Could be from further afield. Newmarket, possibly. We're chasing it down now.'

'What's the likelihood,' Parsons asked, 'of any of the victims being able to identify their attackers?'

Will shook his head. 'Doubtful.'

'Because we've got names and faces on file, some at least. That'd be somewhere to start.'

'Thanks,' Will said. 'We can give it a try.'

'How about hauling a few in?' Moyles suggested. 'Rattling some cages?'

'We've got to be careful,' Parsons said. 'Jump in willy-nilly, make a bunch of arrests, likely see them all released forty-eight hours later. Doesn't help any of us.' He paused. 'Reported hate-crime incidents are up, like I said before, but the number of successful prosecutions is lagging behind. Talk to the local CPS, and they'll say it's because we're not always giving them all the ammunition they need.'

'They would,' Moyles said.

'Agreed. But I'd rather have something definite to bite on, before we show our hand.'

'Message taken,' Will said and Moyles nodded agreement.

Parsons got to his feet and they followed suit.

'There is one thing might prove useful,' Will said. 'Seems as if some of the gang were using their mobiles to take pictures of what was happening.'

'In which case,' Parsons said, 'sooner or later they'll turn up on the Internet. One right-wing site or another. Takes time, but we could do a trawl. See what we can come up with.'

He walked them downstairs and they shook hands.

'Thanks for your time,' Will said.

'Any time,' Parsons said. 'Nick, see you again.'

'Sure.'

Burly men in Day-glo jackets and yellow hats were standing around the entrance to the building site opposite, cigarettes cupped in their hands. The noise from behind them was such that neither Will nor Nick Moyles could hear themselves speak.

Driving back to Cambridge, Will was mindful of what awaited him at his office. The fact that he got out from behind his desk as often as he did drew down a lot of flak from on high, his bosses forever pointing out his job now was managing, not detecting. If I'd wanted to manage, Will stopped short of saying, I'd have signed up for an MBA, gone to work for someone like Shell or Unilever, not joined the bloody police force.

Thinking of work was enough to remind him of a conversation he was due to have with Lorraine, one he was conscious of avoiding. Her work and not his. She'd been pushing him about it again that morning, not wanting to let the chance go begging, assuring him it was all for the best. One of her friends from the antenatal group was back doing three days a week already, insurance company where she'd worked before, short days mind, finishing at three. Baby off with a childminder, happy as anything. Did them both a power of good, this woman reckoned, a break from one another that way. A bit of adult company, that was what made the difference. Someone your own age to talk to.

'You can talk to me,' Will had said.

Lorraine had looked at him. 'While you read the paper, while you eat your breakfast, while you clean your shoes.'

'What's wrong with that?'

'Nothing, as long as you listen.'

'I do listen.'

'Listen and respond.'

Will craned his neck towards the clock on the kitchen wall. 'Time I wasn't here.'

In the car, he checked his rear-view mirror, indicated, and accelerated smoothly into the fast lane.

Helen was sitting up in bed when he got to the hospital that evening, thumbing through a copy of *Marie Claire*. *Vogue* and *Harper's* and several other magazines were scattered across her bed. She'd been feeling well enough, Will noticed, to apply a little make-up and her hair looked recently brushed, if not washed.

'You know the trouble with magazines like this?' she asked Will, as he pulled over a chair.

'Aside from the distractions of beautiful young women in their underwear?'

'Aside from that.'

'I can't imagine.'

'It's almost impossible to work out where the adverts end and the articles begin.'

'Synergy,' Will suggested. 'Synthesis. Something.'

'Will, you're going to have to stop doing the *Police Gazette* crossword. Or is it Scrabble? You and Lorraine, these long winter evenings?'

'She's been offered a job,' Will said.

'Lorraine?'

'Yes.'

'Will, that's great.'

The expression on his face told her he didn't necessarily agree.

'Don't tell me. That new pole-dancing club. Will, you should be proud.'

'Very funny.'

'What is it, then? What's the problem?'

'It's at one of the colleges. King's. Something in the admissions office. Overseas students in particular. Three days a week.'

'And you're worried about what? The kids?'

'She says she's got it covered, a childminder for Susie, someone to pick up Jake after school.'

'Then that's perfect, surely?'

'I don't know.'

'Will, for heaven's sake.'

'By the time all the childcare's paid for, travel, national insurance, God knows what else, I can't see us being a great deal better off.'

'Come on, Will. That's not the point.'

'Isn't it?'

'It's for her, surely? Something to get her out of the house and doing something useful. Somewhere she can use her brain, instead of just hanging round the house all day reading nursery rhymes.'

'In a few more years, once Susie's at school too, maybe.'

'A few more years, she might have forgotten she's got a brain at all.'

'That's crap.'

'Is it? What would you be like without a job to go to? The kind of job you do?'

'That's different.'

'The principle's the same. Self-respect, Will, that's what it comes down to.'

'And you don't get that from being a mum? Bringing up a kid? Two kids?'

'Not on its own, no. I don't think so. Oh, some people, maybe. And if it works, then fine. But where Lorraine's concerned, she clearly wants more. Who's going to lose from that? You?'

Will shook his head; he didn't know. Neither did he like the way the conversation was going. He usually avoided talking about Lorraine with Helen, problems between them especially, something about it making him feel uneasy, and now it felt as if, somehow, they were both ganging up on him.

'My sister,' Helen said, 'she stayed home, two kids, just like you and Lorraine. Afternoons pushing a buggy round the park, mother-and-toddler groups, the whole bit. By the time the oldest started school, the inside of her head was like mashed swede. Valium, beta blockers, she ended up close to walking away from the whole shoot, husband, kids, everything.'

'That's not Lorraine.'

Helen looked at him squarely. 'Not now. Let's hope it never is.'

Above the blackened silhouette of the cathedral, the moon was a faint lozenge, fading behind cloud. Closer to, the fields were touched, here and there, with tracings of white. A few stray flakes brushed against Will's face as he approached the house, his feet soft and quiet on the pebbled surface leading to the porch.

Closing the front door behind him, he stood for several moments in the half-darkness, before removing his coat and shoes.

Lorraine was leaning back against the sofa, arms spread, eyes closed. The sound of her breathing was surprisingly loud in the room, a faint whistling whenever she breathed in. Will reached down and touched her hand and her fingers moved inwards a little, as if to enclose his.

She did not wake.

The children, Will assumed, were both upstairs in bed.

At the sink, he let the tap run until the water was cold, then drank from a glass.

When he opened the door to Jake's room, the boy stirred and Will waited for him to settle before going over and standing beside the bed, looking down.

In his and Lorraine's bedroom, Susie lay on her back, thumb in her mouth, pressed up against one side of the cot.

Will slid a blanket from one of the drawers beneath their bed and carried it downstairs.

Lorraine had not moved.

Will spoke her name, once and then again.

Bending, he lifted her legs round on to the settee, so that she was lying more or less flat and then placed the blanket over her. Carefully, he kissed her on the forehead and she murmured something from inside her dream.

He waited, then went back into the kitchen, refilled his water glass, and carried it up to bed.

24

Spluttering, gasping for breath, Lesley flailed her arms and it was only when her outflung hand struck the digital alarm and knocked it to the floor, that she realised she'd been dreaming. Not drowning, but dreaming. What was it? 'Not waving, but drowning'? One of the only two lines she remembered from two years of sixth form English Literature. Stevie Smith and Larkin. What was his? 'They fuck you up, your mum and dad'?

Lesley disentangled herself from the bedclothes and swung her feet towards the floor. One way or another, she thought Larkin was probably right.

In the shower, radio playing at a level below which the words could actually be heard, water bouncing off her head and shoulders, she thought again about her dream. Her nightmare. It came from the film, of course, from *Shattered Glass*. Stella Leonard's Ruby benignly smiling at the man who has chosen virtue over what? Evil? Experience? Adventure? Sexuality? A life of the body instead of a life of the mind? 'I'll take you to her,' she says, 'my sister.' And then, just for a moment, a split second which only the camera sees, something in her eyes changes as she slips the car into gear before driving, headlong, towards the precipice, the cliff, the sea.

You know how she died? Orlando Rocca had asked her. *In real life? She drowned. Trapped in her car. Her father was with her at the time. Just the two of them. Stella was driving. For some reason, they went off the road. Neither survived.*

Turning, Lesley switched off the shower and stepped away, reaching for a towel.

What did they call it? Coincidence? Life imitating Art?

Dry, she applied moisturiser, put a comb through her hair and found clean underwear, pulled on a V-neck jumper and jeans. She made instant coffee and took it across to the computer. What was the year? 1985? The Internet, she thought, and not for the first time, can be a wonderful thing. Since her conversation with Rocca, she had been putting together all she could find about the accident.

Both national and regional press had carried the story, running it alongside pictures of Stella in her later, soap-star days. Several accounts alluded to her earlier film career, singling out *Shattered Glass* for special mention, but, amazingly, only one drew attention to the film's ending.

Maybe not so amazing, Lesley thought, on reflection, more a testimony to the fact that the film was little known and rarely seen.

Stella's father, Adam, was referred to as a retired businessman, who had made his money from property and manufacturing. The pair, the reports agreed, had been visiting Stella's niece, Lily Prince, who lived with her husband, Howard, in the Cambridgeshire fens. For reasons that were still unclear, the car in which they had been travelling had gone off the road crossing the Great Fen and plunged into a drainage ditch running close alongside. The water level was such that the car had become quickly submerged and, possibly rendered unconscious in their fall, both Stella and Adam had drowned.

At a later date, the coroner returned a verdict of death by misadventure.

Not being able to sign out a radio car meant using the old Peugeot Lesley kept parked on a piece of waste-land facing the bricked-up remnants of the old city wall, just a few minutes' walk from where she lived. Nothing inside worth stealing, the radio long gone, it had only been broken into twice in recent months, the last occasion damaging the offside handle beyond repair. She was half-hoping someone would take it for a joyride and leave it somewhere smashed and abandoned, so that she could claim what little it was worth back on the insurance, but of course nobody did.

At the garage off the roundabout she checked the air in the tyres and filled up with petrol. In that vehicle, any journey much further than a trip to the supermarket had a certain element of risk attached. She didn't exactly keep spare blankets and a thermos of coffee on the back seat, but maybe she should.

Beyond Grantham, the land levelled out into that flat terrain of marsh and fen where Lincolnshire and Cambridgeshire merged and hills were a thing of the imagination only. She'd printed out directions from Multimap.com on her computer and still it took her three attempts before she found the road, a narrow, raised strip that carried her between two slabs of dark earth, a deep drainage ditch running all the way along on the left-hand side. Lesley kept her hands steady on the wheel. It would only need a moment's lack of concentration for her to be off and down.

She passed the low buildings of a farm and then a small collection of ramshackle caravans marooned in a half-acre of mud, before the road veered right towards a sketchy line of poplar trees through which she could just see the house she was looking for.

Behind the trees, there was a low wall with tiled coping and a thick, spiny hedge; windows but no obvious door.

Lesley pulled her car off the road and parked.

Around the corner of the hedge, a gravelled path turned inwards towards a five-bar gate which gave access to the rear of the house. Attached to the post at the side of the gate was a metal plate with the word 'Press'. Lesley did so and after a few seconds' pause, the gate swung slowly open and she walked through.

The path took her between two sets of barns and into a courtyard, in which several vehicles were parked: a mud-spattered Range Rover, a rather elderly but well-groomed Jaguar and a small Vauxhall saloon. A blackbird paused from tugging at something in the earth as she walked past.

The house itself was L-shaped and far larger than it appeared from the road; ivy trailed across two sides of its cream walls. The windows on one side were square, on the other, long and narrow. There was a choice of doors, three in total, all painted a dark brownish-red. Close to one of them a bicycle with a wicker basket hanging from its handlebars leaned against the wall, and that was the one she chose.

There was no bell that she could see, so she knocked instead.

Looking up, she saw she was staring into the lens of a small camera, positioned just above the top corner of the door.

Automatically, she pushed a hand up through her hair.

Nothing happened.

She put her ear against the door and listened. A sound came faintly from inside, the low electric whine of a vacuum cleaner.

She knocked again, louder.

The woman who eventually opened the door was in her middle years, grey hair pinned close to her head and caught up at the back in a bun; a floral pinafore tied over her loose dark trousers and pale top.

'Mr Prince,' Lesley said. 'Is he at home?'

'You are selling something?' the woman asked. 'We

do not buy at the door.' Lesley had expected an accent that was local, but this was Eastern European. Polish? Czech? Hungarian?

'No, I just wanted a word with Mr Prince.'

'Not selling?'

Lesley showed her card. 'I'm from the BBC. Radio. I wanted to speak to Mr Prince.'

'Radio?'

'Yes.'

'Mr Prince not here.' Already, the woman's hand was firm against the door, pushing it closed.

'You don't know when he might be home?'

A quick shake of the head.

'Mrs Prince, then? Is she here? Perhaps I could talk to her?'

'Mrs Prince not home either.'

The door closed further. Lesley pushed the card into the woman's hand. 'Please take that. Tell Mr Prince I called. Ask him would he be good enough to phone me.'

The door shut with a satisfying thunk. Solid wood. No space for draughts. Halfway back across the courtyard, Lesley swung her head around and saw, at one of the upstairs windows, the head and shoulders of a woman staring down. Not the same woman at all. Dark hair framing a pale, narrow face. A hand pressed against the glass. Lesley looked away and when she turned again, the woman had gone.

Back in the car, she sat for several moments, uncertain what to do; then she started the engine, drove a short way back along the narrow road, switched off the engine, and sat watching the house. For the first time in a while, she wished her car radio had not been stolen, or that she had brought a book, perhaps, to read. Time passed slowly, fifteen minutes, thirty, forty-five. No one approached the house or left. Nothing moved on the horizon or changed in the sky.

By the time Lesley got home that night it was late: with some reluctance she'd responded to a text message from some colleagues and agreed to meet them for a quick drink after work and, not unpleasantly, one glass had become another, till finally four of them had bundled into the Pizza Express on Goose Gate for supper and had shared another bottle of wine. Feeling the slightest of headaches coming on, Lesley reminded herself to drink plenty of water before going to bed. At her front door, the key fumbled from her hand and bending too quickly was not a good idea at all. For a moment, she steadied herself against the wall.

The overhead light inside the flat was so bright it made her flinch and quickly she turned it back off, crossing the room and switching on the lamp at her desk instead. Instantly, a chill claimed her arms and the backs of her legs.

Her breath stopped.

Someone had been in the room, the flat. She didn't know how, but she sensed it. She knew. Every part of her, right to her finger ends, seemed to be alive and yet numb. For what was little more than seconds but seemed far longer, she was unable to move.

Then, when she could, she checked the other rooms.

Nothing was out of place; nothing, seemingly, had been moved.

Back in the main room she checked her desk, the filing cabinet, the drawers. There was no sign of the lock being forced; the windows were still fastened firm. You're imagining it, she told herself. Too long spent listening to James Crawford's tales of being turned over by Special Branch.

Relax.

But she couldn't relax.

She heated milk in the small saucepan and made a cup of Milo, which she drank while she was getting undressed and ready for bed.

Though now she felt sober as a nun, she nevertheless drank a full glass of cold water after cleaning her teeth. In bed she tried to read, but couldn't concentrate. Even when the sounds of traffic had died down and the numbers on their way back from the Pitcher and Piano and the Hoop and Toy and the other pubs and clubs along High Pavement had slowed to the occasional one or two, she lay there, eyes open, staring at the ceiling, unable to sleep.

52. EXT. SWIMMING POOL. NIGHT.

Small floodlights illuminate the pool at the rear of the house. PHILIP *turns at the far end of the pool and swims towards us vigorously.*

   As he pulls himself from the water, RUBY, *wearing a white towelling robe, steps forward and hands him a towel.*

   PHILIP's *body glistens.*

PHILIP: *Where's Alma?*

RUBY: *Do you care?*

Taking another step towards him, his arms go round her and they kiss passionately.

   RUBY's *towelling robe slides to the tiled floor at her feet.*

25

Bits and pieces. Dribs and drabs. One step up, two steps back. Nothing was coming together the way it should. Will was tetchy. He snapped at Lorraine, barked at Jake, the house pitched on tenterhooks, waiting for him to explode. The business of Lorraine's going back to work hung between them, unresolved.

Last thing at night, Will stood alone by the blackened glass, staring out; morning, he was up before first light, a splash of cold water in his face, before pulling on his running shoes as he stepped out into the dark.

Despite renewed efforts, still no weapon from the attack on the two Cambridge students had been found; not only that, no mobile phone-generated images had yet appeared on the Web. Neither Helen, nor the architecture student, had been able to make a positive identification from the photographs Chris Parsons had provided. Young faces with short-cropped hair, tattoos, and a taunting, impoverished stare.

And when Milne and Slater had gone back around

Stephen Bryan's neighbourhood, there were enough vague recollections of being canvassed by someone from one of the energy companies to suggest that was the identity of the man Fenwick had confronted outside Bryan's house. Both Eastern Electricity and British Gas confirmed that they had representatives in the area at and around the dates concerned.

Home from his run, Will hammered the heel of his bunched-up hand against the wall. Dark with sweat, his running vest stuck clammily to his back. There was a pain behind his left knee, deep in the joint.

Lorraine was just coming out of the bathroom as he climbed the stairs, her hair tied back, rubbing moisturiser into her hands. 'Will, I know this isn't a good time . . .'

'No, it's not.'

'This job, we do need to talk.'

'Not now.'

'Will . . .'

'Not fucking now!'

Pushing past her, he went into the bathroom and slammed the door shut. In the bedroom, Susie started to cry. Will closed his eyes, ran water from the tap.

When he went back downstairs, less than twenty minutes later, dressed, Lorraine was sitting at the table with a mug of tea, the baby at her breast. Jake ducked his head when his father entered the room and shovelled Rice Krispies up towards his mouth.

'I'm sorry,' Will said. Leaning down towards Lorraine, he kissed her on the neck.

'It's okay,' she said, reaching up a hand towards his.

'I understand.' More sympathy, Will knew, than he deserved.

He kissed her again, on the top of her head, leaving his face there for a moment against the smell and silk of her hair.

'Dad,' Jake said, uncertain. 'After school, can we play football?'

'Absolutely.'

'You promise?'

'Soon as I get home.'

'What if it's dark?'

'We'll switch on all the lights. Floodlit. Just like Old Trafford. Highbury. Man U versus the Arsenal.'

'I wanna be Man U.'

'It's a deal. Now finish those up, there's a good lad.'

Lorraine followed him to the door. 'This job,' she said, 'I can't keep them hanging on much longer.'

'I know. We'll talk about it tonight, okay? After the big match. I promise.'

A kiss and he was gone.

The radio was full of riot and dissent: riots in Sri Lanka, riots in Nepal. Terrorist bombs at an Egyptian resort. Closer to home, the Health Minister had been booed off the platform at a conference of nurses, and the Deputy Prime Minister had been caught with his nose in the sexual trough; a fourteen-year-old kid had been stabbed to death in a racially motivated attack in Kent; high-ranking police officers were expressing their discontent at the fact that due to a series of administrative cock-ups, hundreds of convicted foreign prisoners, instead of being deported, had been allowed to drift anonymously back into the community instead. Catch the bastards once, Will thought, then catch them again.

He switched to Radio 2 in time to hear some callow-voiced girl singer bleed the guts out of 'Just One of Those Things'. Cole Porter, for God's sake! Will's father had loved Cole Porter, Jerome Kern, Gershwin. His LPs were in the attic somewhere now, unplayed. Sinatra. Ella. Peggy Lee. 'The Folks Who Live on the Hill'.

All nonsense, of course. Love and marriage yoked together like a horse and carriage. Old-fashioned, romantic nonsense. At the next junction, he swung the car around and headed back in the opposite direction. Lorraine was just leaving the house, Susie in the buggy, Jake kicking pebbles out into the road.

'What have you forgotten?' Lorraine asked, as he got out of the car.

'Nothing.'

'Then what . . . ?'

'The job. You should take it.'

'But you said . . .'

'Call them today, this morning. Take it.'

'You're sure?'

'Go on. I'll look after the kids a minute. Do it now.'

'All right, I will.' No disguising the brightness in her eyes.

Amongst all the spam that had made its way, unfiltered, on to Will's office computer, there was an email Chris Parsons had sent to both Rastrick and himself. Parsons had finally succeeded in tracking down a site showing images that could well have come from the Cambridge attack.

When Will finally managed to open the attachment he found getting on for two dozen photographs, mostly in short sequences of three or four, as if taken in quick succession. A hooded figure close to the camera, his face distorted; a blur of flailing arms and fists; some kind of bat or club raised high, then swinging down towards a figure crouching low, arms raised protectively overhead.

There was just enough in the background to suggest, yes, this was on the riverside, close to the Magdalene Street Bridge, but, other than that, the focus was variable and the images unclear. Individual identification would be difficult, nigh on impossible.

Will scanned the images again for someone who might be Helen, but she was nowhere to be seen. More than likely, he thought, all the shots had been taken before she had intervened.

Less than an hour later, a second email arrived from the same source. Parsons had successfully followed a trail from the initial site to another and come up with four short video sequences, each little more than a minute in length and with its own muffled soundtrack of chants and shouts and screams.

In one sequence, a man wearing sweatshirt and jeans – one of the injured students, Will was sure – was seen running away before being tripped and sent sprawling; in another, filmed, presumably, soon after, the same person was being kicked savagely as he curled on the ground, making himself as small as possible; the third video was little more than a kaleidoscope of indistinguishable movement, a mass of bodies surging across the frame. In the fourth, a figure lurched forwards, thrusting a hand towards the lens, middle finger raised. Even here, the focus was less than perfect, never as sharp as Will would have liked, the light over-bright at the centre and fading into black around the edges.

The lower half of the person's face was covered by a scarf, wrapped round twice, a dark tight-fitting hat, wool or some synthetic material, pulled low towards his eyes. Enough to see that he was white, youngish – somewhere, most probably, between seventeen and twenty-four – but little more. Until just before the sequence ended, when the scarf slipped away.

Will called Rastrick's extension. 'You had a chance to look at what Parsons sent across?'

'Looking at it now.'

'What do you think?' Will asked.

'Magdalene Street, has to be.'

'The youth in the scarf, giving the finger, you think tech services can freeze those last few frames? Get them cleaned up somehow?'

'Worth a try.'

'Should we handle that ourselves, or get Parsons to do it at his end?'

'On to it already, more than likely. Why don't you give him a bell and see? Meantime, I'll talk to our people here. Show them what we've got.'

'Right away,' Will said, reading the number off the screen.

Parsons answered almost immediately. 'Everything download okay?'

'No problem.'

'Whoever shot this stuff, not exactly Steven Spielberg.'

'The last piece of video, the youth with the scarf . . .'

'Cocky little sod, isn't he? Thinks it's all some great fucking joke.'

'Think we can get an ID?'

'I don't know. I'll run a visual check as soon as I can, but I'd say the chances weren't brilliant.'

Will swore beneath his breath.

'You'll let me know either way?'

'Of course.'

'How about the site where this stuff was posted?' Will asked. 'Do we know whose it is? Who maintains it, anything like that?'

'Not really. Small sites like this, they're all over the Net. Difficult to track down. Start up one day, close down the next. People posting things on them without leaving any obvious trail. You could spend an eternity trying to get to the bottom of it and end up back where you started. But I'll get our IT boys on to that video, see what they come up with. Any luck, I'll get back to you tomorrow.'

An hour later, the news came through that the theology student from Honduras had died.

*   *   *

293

Lorraine had put candles on the table, readied a bottle of wine, Australian Shiraz. While Will and Jake played out their floodlit cup final, she peeled potatoes, sliced carrots, pork and rabbit casserole already in the oven, one of Will's favourites.

When Jake was in the bath under Will's supervision and the vegetables were simmering, she went upstairs to fix her face and change.

'You look nice,' Will said, when she put her head round the bathroom door.

'Dinner's in twenty minutes.'

'No chance of a quick one first, then?'

'Sshh,' she said, with an eye towards Jake, and laughed.

The casserole was as tasty as usual, the wine went down easily, both Jake and Susie seemed to be sleeping. When Lorraine walked past the table on her way to the kitchen, Will reached for her hand and brought it, palm first, to his mouth. The palm and then the fingers, one by one.

'Only teenagers do this,' Lorraine said later, raising herself up on to one elbow.

'Have sex?'

'Have sex on the living-room carpet.'

'While their parents are out.'

'Or upstairs in bed.'

'We are the parents,' Will said.

'And the children are upstairs in bed.'

'That's because they're not teenagers.'

'Not yet.'

'Not for a long time.' He moved his face towards hers and kissed her again.

'Did you talk to Helen?' she asked, when the kiss was over.

'About the job?'

'Uh-huh.'

Will looked into her face, considering his answer. 'I suppose so. Just a bit, you know. In passing.'

'And that's why you changed your mind. Because of what she said.'

'Not entirely, no.'

'You'd have done it anyway?'

'I expect so.'

'Come around.'

'Don't I usually?'

'No,' Lorraine said, laughing. 'No, you don't. You're a stubborn bastard, and you know it.'

'Shame you married me, then, isn't it?'

'Is it?'

'You tell me.'

For an answer, Lorraine reached her hand out towards his ribs, and ran her nails down towards the dark hair curling up from between his legs.

'Do you ever think,' she said, resting her head on his chest, 'you should have married her instead of me?'

'Her?'

She bit lightly into his skin. 'Helen.'

'No,' he said, bringing her face up towards his. 'No, I never do.'

26

Lesley woke early, uncertain why, and then realised it was because she was cold. Hugging herself, knees to her chest, she tried to get back to sleep and, when that didn't work, decided on a slow, warm bath. Weetabix she ate with hot milk, a banana sliced on top. Tea in her large Cornish-ware mug. When she checked on the local weather site, it showed heavy cloud throughout the day and a maximum temperature of nought degrees Celsius, thirty-two degrees Fahrenheit, winds from the north-west. Just a short while ago, on the south coast, despite a chilly wind, there had been definite warmth in the sun. And travelling down to London by train, not so many days before that, she had been certain spring had arrived.

Now this. A day for her thermal vest if ever there was one. Except she couldn't find it in the drawer. Any of the drawers.

Stephen had once given her a yellow Notts County T-shirt as some kind of joke, and she put that on instead.

Several layers over the top of that. She had almost finished buttoning and zipping herself up when the phone rang, not her mobile, but the regular land line. Her mother. Earnest cold callers from the Indian subcontinent aside, intent on persuading her to change her gas supplier, subscribe to Sky, sign up for Broadband or switch her bank account, it had to be her mother. At first, Lesley decided to let it ring, and then, smitten by guilt, lifted the receiver.

'Ah, Lesley, I was hoping I'd just catch you before you left for work.'

Thirty minutes later, in the course of which her mother had broken down several times into tears, Lesley managed to say goodbye, send love to her father, grab her hat and bag and let herself out of the door.

You're a hard-hearted bitch, she said to herself, walking out into the cold: her son's been killed, murdered, your brother. Shame you couldn't shed a few more tears yourself. But she had cried enough.

Outside, Lesley tightened her scarf. The steps down from Commerce Square were treacherous, with a covering of frost and near-ice that threatened to upend her more than once.

It was the second item on the local news: at a meeting of the City Council Development Control Committee, plans registered by a local consortium led by Prince Holdings, to build an apartment complex on open ground adjacent to the Victoria Embankment, had yesterday been given the go-ahead. The complex, which would incorporate a leisure centre and multi-purpose gym, would comprise forty-four one-and two-bedroom flats and ten penthouse apartments in a premium position overlooking the River Trent.

Lesley clicked on to the City Council website and found the appropriate page. In his report, the case officer for Planning Services outlined the objections to the scheme. The Ward Councillor had protested in the strongest possible terms against the loss of open space that was regularly used by local people and a nearby primary school for sports and recreation, claiming, in addition, that the extra traffic that would ensue would serve to create a bottleneck at the Trent Bridge end of the Embankment, especially on match days, because of its proximity to both the Nottingham Forest and Notts County grounds. The local residents' committee had also objected on the grounds of increased vehicular and pedestrian traffic and the loss of recreational space.

While acknowledging these objections, the case officer commented that only a small percentage of land between the Embankment and the Meadows would be given over to the project, and that this would be more than made up for by the specialised facilities that would be provided as part of the scheme, in compliance with section R7 of the Nottingham Local Plan, agreed 28 November 2005. Nottinghamshire Police, moreover, had raised no objection to the scheme on the grounds of any potential increased traffic congestion.

Taking all of these matters into consideration, the

committee granted the scheme approval, with a three-year limit for implementation.

Well, why not, thought Lesley, clicking the council page into oblivion. What was a little open space, after all? Somewhere for kids to kick a ball, people to walk their dogs, ride bikes, fly kites. What was that compared to another bevy of upscale apartments? As if the city didn't have enough of those already. And these, with their views along the river, would doubtless fetch premium prices, premium rents.

Was she being overly cynical, Lesley wondered, to imagine the well-oiled turning of wheels within wheels, the slick and silent greasing of palms?

She dialled the number for Prince Holdings and instantly recognised the supercilious tones of Raymond James.

'Hello,' Lesley said, 'this is BBC Radio Nottingham. We were wondering if you had any comment to make about the council's approval of your scheme for the Embankment?'

James cleared his throat discreetly. 'Naturally, we are delighted on behalf of ourselves and the other members of the consortium. We see this as a really forward-looking development and one that can only serve to enhance the reputation of the city.'

If he recognised her voice, he gave no sign.

'You don't think, then,' Lesley said, 'there was any merit to the many objections that were raised?'

James coughed. 'I'm afraid I can't possibly go into such matters on the telephone. A press conference has been called for this afternoon and there will be an opportunity for asking questions then.'

Alan Pike was in his office, sleeves rolled back, tie discarded, a look of puzzlement on his face; the coming week's rotas were spread across his desk.

'Alan,' Lesley said, poking her head round the door. 'You got a minute?'

'No.'

'This press conference, Prince Holdings, have we got somebody covering that?'

'Jerry.'

'Let me go instead.'

'No.'

'Alan . . .'

'No. No way.'

'Jerry hates that stuff. Suits. Business. Let me swap.'

Pike looked at her for the first time. 'How many ways do I have to say this? Absolutely and categorically, no.'

'You're weakening, Alan, I can tell.'

'Okay.' Pike made his way round his desk towards her. 'Okay, here it is. That press conference, words of one syllable. You do not go anywhere near.'

'Anywhere, that's . . .'

'Not even close. Is that understood?'

Lesley raised a hand and smiled. 'Absolutely. Couldn't be clearer. Nowhere near.'

Half an hour later, she waylaid Jerry Walton as he emerged from the gents, still fastening his flies.

'Jerry . . .'

'Damn buttons! What the hell was wrong with zips?'

'You're going to that Prince Holdings thing?'

'For my sins.'

'Thought I might tag along. Just out of interest. Long as you don't mind, that is?'

'No. Why should I? Help yourself.'

'Thanks, Jerry. I'll be quiet as a mouse. Won't say a word. Oh, and Jerry, no need to mention it to Alan, okay?'

The oak table that normally dominated the Prince Holdings boardroom had been cleared away, and in its place a pale plywood model of the Trent River Project stood on a perspex plinth, awaiting inspection. Behind and to one side, a shimmer of green cloth suggested lawns reaching towards an avenue of matching trees, while in front, plastic couples strolled comfortably pushing plastic buggies, and miniature oarsmen sculled along a winding strip of blue.

Lesley glanced at the glossy press pack she'd been handed by an eager young PR woman at the door, and accepted a glass of white wine from a tanned waiter in a short white jacket, moonlighting from Hart's or Merchant's or somewhere else discreetly flash.

Jerry was already helping himself to a small selection of canapés from a side table, beyond which Mel Mast and Mark Patterson from the *Post* were chatting to a jolly broadcast journalist from Saga, whose name Lesley could never remember. A number of middle-aged men in suits, whom she assumed to be councillors or fellow developers, were standing at the far end of the room, where a small platform had been placed in readiness. A small clutch of student types, meanwhile, who were probably from *Left Lion* or one of the proliferation of lifestyle magazines, were keeping within arm's reach of the wine.

Of Howard Prince, there was as yet no sign.

Lesley took a closer look at the model, which on further inspection, with its curved edges, was not unlike a ship, then moved across the room and helped herself to the world's smallest sausage roll and a prawn thingumajig on sesame toast.

'Ms Scarman.'

She heard Raymond James's voice before she saw him.

'Mr James.' She held out her hand, which he studiously ignored.

'You're not planning to make any kind of a fuss?'

Lesley treated him to her best smile. 'Perish the thought.'

'Perish, indeed.'

He stared at her a moment longer, then moved away.

'Who was that?' Jerry asked, appearing at her side.

'The Devil, probably. Or his assistant.'

Before Jerry could ask for clarification, James had called the assembly to attention and introduced Howard Prince, who had entered without Lesley noticing, and, at his side, the project's architect, Carl Richter.

In the flesh, Prince looked, if anything, younger than his photographs suggested; more stylish, too, Lesley thought, though to her eyes, the suit he was wearing, which had cost however many hundred pounds, did little to disguise the rough and ready man underneath.

'There are people,' Prince began, 'maybe some of you here, who think men like me and my colleagues here are only interested in one thing above all else. And that's money.' He held his pause, surveying the room. 'Well, let me tell you, that's too fucking right.'

Laughter all round; broad grins from amongst the suits.

'But let me say this too, that's not all we're interested in. What we are interested in, what we care about – what I care about – is this city. And the people who live in it. And when I die – oh, yes, I know it's a long way off, it bloody better be – but when I die I don't want people to say, he knocked down shit and he put shit up in its place. A selfish, greedy bastard to boot. I want them to say, he built places to last, places with style where people liked to live. I want them to say, while he was here, he did this city proud.'

Murmurs of affirmation and a smattering of applause. Only one muffled comment of dissent from behind where Lesley was standing.

'And this building,' Prince went on, 'which Carl has designed, is one that should make us all very proud indeed.'

Richter came forward and, after acknowledging the applause with a small bow, spoke in an over-precise Swiss-German accent of his ambition to create something which was sympathetic to the building's riverside setting, echoing its fluidity with a sense of space and light.

303

He lost Lesley for a while when he talked about the plasticity of materials and the aesthetic context of landscape, but she rallied when he concluded by drawing a comparison between his design and that of an ocean liner.

'Let's hope it's not the *Titanic*,' Jerry whispered in her ear.

Rounding off the speeches, the leader of the City Council's urban design team congratulated everyone involved in the project, hailing it as a fine example of the kind of high-quality, exemplary development that was making the city's regeneration the envy not just of the rest of the country, but of the whole of Europe.

'Why not the world while he's about it?' Jerry hissed.

But Lesley had become aware of Raymond James leaning towards Howard Prince and the pair of them looking in her direction. After which James stepped on to the platform and fielded questions, most of which were positive and friendly, save for one young man at the rear of the room, who wanted to know, in the light of similar unkept promises in the past, what assurances there were that the promised leisure centre would remain part of the project.

James began to answer this urbanely himself, but Prince pushed him aside, fixing the questioner with an outstretched finger and a glare.

'You want to know what assurances? I'll tell you what assurances. My fuckin' word.'

'And I think,' James said, composure regained, 'we can safely leave things there. Thank you all for your time.'

'Well,' Jerry said, 'back to the grind.'

'You go ahead,' Lesley replied. 'Someone I want to see.'

'Suit yourself.'

She could see Prince speaking to Richter, patting him on the shoulder, shaking his hand. When he turned and began to walk away, she moved to intercept him.

'Mr Prince. I wonder if I could have a word?'

'About what?'

'My brother.'

Prince's eyes narrowed. 'Your brother died, Miss Scarman, and I'm sorry. Did they catch whoever did it?'

'Not yet.'

'Well, I'm sorry about that too. Now if you'll excuse me . . .'

Instead of moving, Lesley stood her ground. 'There were questions Stephen wanted to ask you, about a book he was writing. Background, really.'

'I told him. I've got nothing to say.'

'I know. I thought perhaps you might talk to me instead.'

Prince's hand reached out and enclosed her wrist. 'Don't make the mistake your brother made.'

His breath, a mixture of wine and tobacco, was warm on her face.

'What was that?' Lesley said.

'I expect there were several. Not taking no for an answer was one.'

He snatched his hand away, pushed through a knot of lingering visitors and was gone. Lesley waited until her own breathing had steadied and, under Raymond James's interested gaze, headed for the door. The impressions left by Prince's fingers and thumb were clear on her wrist, and by the time she arrived back at work, the bruises had started to show through the skin.

27

Earlier that morning, careful and slow, Helen had had her second unassisted shower since the operation, the nurse checking halfway through that she was still okay, and that afternoon there was another session with the physio.

Back at work before you know it, the young doctor had joked.

Before she knew it, Helen realised, she could have died. All it took: a single second, the flicker of an eye. Another twist of the knife.

After her shower, she had rested on her bed and then, bored, she had managed to walk the length of the ward and out into the broad corridor by the lifts, which was where she now stood, leaning up against the wall and staring down through smudged glass towards the car park below. People scurrying to and fro, some bearing gifts, others glancing at their watches and then quickening their pace, already late. Still leading normal hurried lives. The quick and the dead? Was that the phrase? Some left, some stayed behind. Slid, unknowing, into a sleep, natural or drug induced, anaesthetised, from which they didn't wake up.

No clamour, nothing dramatic, no fuss.

One moment you were there and then you were not.

That, Helen thought, was what frightened her most. That you could take a breath and then disappear.

And who would know or care? Her parents, certainly, her sister, a handful of colleagues, possibly a few friends from school. And Will.

Some burial that would be, she thought. Some fucking funeral there. The only people she cared for or who cared for her?

Angry, Helen shook her head. Angry with herself. Snap out of it, for fuck's sake, you maudlin cow! Feeling sorry for yourself for being alive. How pathetic, how stupid is that?

When she made her way back to the bed, she was surprised to see Lesley there, waiting. Some grapes, a box of chocolates, a bunch of daffodils. 'I didn't know what to bring.'

'So you thought you'd bring a bit of everything.'

'Something like that.'

For a few awkward moments, neither spoke.

'The nurse wasn't sure where you were. She thought you might be in the loo.'

'No, I was . . .' Helen glanced back over her shoulder. 'It gets you down, stuck here all the time. I go for a little wander when I can.'

'I wanted to come before. When I heard what had happened. It's just, you know, work and . . .'

'I understand.'

'I spoke to Inspector Grayson. On the phone. Asked him how you were.'

'Yes. I think he said.'

'Everything's okay?'

Helen smiled. 'Good as new.'

'Good.'

'There'll be a scar.'

'You look great.'

'Not really.'

'Yes. Yes, you do.'

Seeing Lesley, the same age as herself, more or less, standing there fresh in her blue cotton jacket, cream top, and black tapered trousers, Helen felt like shit.

'There was something I wanted to talk to you about,' Lesley said. 'But only if you feel up to it. I . . .'

'About your brother?'

'Yes. Sort of.'

'Something's happened?'

'Not exactly.'

Helen pulled open the narrow drawer at the top of the bedside cabinet and reached towards the back. 'I have to keep hiding these.' She eased a packet of cigarettes and a lighter down into the pocket of her dressing gown. 'If you don't mind giving me a bit of help, we could go outside, pollute the fresh air.'

Down below, Helen found a bench out of sight of the No Smoking sign before lighting up. 'You should've nipped into the shop,' she suggested. 'Bought yourself a Twix.'

Lesley smiled and shook her head.

'Whatever it is,' Helen said, 'You can tell me now.'

As succinctly as she could, Lesley told her about her attempts to question Howard Prince, including the visit to his house in the Fens; about the manner in which she'd been warned off at work, and her fears about being followed, her certainty that her flat had been searched.

'Looking for what?' Helen asked.

'I don't know.'

'But whatever it was, you think, in some way, Howard Prince was behind it?'

'Yes. Yes, I do.'

Helen leaned forward. 'Tell me again what he said. The other day.'

'He said, "Don't make the mistake your brother made."'

'What did you think he meant by that?'

'That's what I asked him.'

'And?'

'And he said, "I expect there were several." And then, "Not taking no for an answer was one."'

'And you thought he was referring to the book your brother wanted to write.'

'What else? What else is there?'

Helen released a coil of smoke out on to the air. 'Prince – what sort of an accent would you say he has?'

'I don't know. Local, I suppose.'

'Local to where? Here or . . .'

'No. Nottingham.'

310

'East Midlands, then?'

'Yes, why?'

Helen tapped ash from the end of her cigarette. 'There was a message on your brother's answerphone.'

'When?'

'A few days before he died.'

Lesley's face went pale. 'How do you know?'

'Someone your brother knew, someone he'd met, he heard the message and reported it to us. Part of it, anyway. The part he heard.'

'Someone? What do you mean, someone? Who?'

'It doesn't matter.'

'Of course it does.'

'No, really. Believe me, it doesn't matter.'

'The message, then, what was it?'

'"You better believe what I say."'

'That's it? That's all?'

'That's all he heard.'

Lesley looked across to where an elderly woman with wisps of thinning grey hair was being lifted from an ambulance car by a paramedic and lowered into a wheelchair. 'You think it might have been Prince,' she said. 'The message.'

'I don't know.'

'But that's why you asked? About the accent?'

'Yes.'

'And that's what it was? East Midlands? Nottingham?'

'As far as we know. But we've only one person's word.'

Lesley arched her back and closed her eyes. For a moment she saw Stephen's body, the technician slowly folding back the sheet.

'Can't you question Prince about it?' she said. 'He'd have to speak to you.'

Helen stubbed the remnant of her cigarette out against the underside of the bench and dropped it to the ground. 'If we confront him with what he said to you, all he needs to do is deny it, and then we've got nowhere to go.'

A flash of anger showed on Lesley's face. 'So that's it? You're just going to leave it at that?'

'No. Not at all. I'll talk to Will, as soon as I can.'

'But then, if as you say . . . .'

'When we asked Prince his reasons for trying to stop your brother writing his book, refusing to give him access for his research, the only one he gave was wanting to protect his wife and prevent her from getting upset.'

'And now you think it might be more than that?'

Cautiously, Helen started to get to her feet. 'Skeletons in the cupboard? Who knows? Nothing to stop us digging around.'

'I can send you a few bits and pieces I've put together. Just background, mostly downloaded from the Net.'

'All right, thanks. That would help.'

Lesley held out her hand. 'Take care.'

'You, too.'

'You want me to walk you back to the ward?'

'No, it's okay. I'll be fine.'

Lesley smiled and turned and Helen watched her

walk away. One more cigarette, she thought, before I go inside.

How long the letter had been there, Helen didn't know. But there it was on her bedside table, propped up between the things Lesley had brought. Stamped, addressed: she didn't have to open it to know who it was from.

When she'd first known him, the first months, before anything had really happened between them, he had written all the time. Sometimes just a note, a card; sometimes a long ambling account of somewhere he'd been, something he'd seen. Only two weeks after they'd met, he had gone off on a trip to the States – Washington DC, Chicago, Ann Arbor, Minneapolis–St Paul.

He. Andrew. She didn't even like to say his name.

She had met him at the airport on his return and less than a month later they had moved in together. Rather, she had moved in with him. A flat in Camden, sublet to Andrew by a friend of a friend. Not that he was there all the time: his line of work, a lot of travelling.

She was twenty-five and still in uniform. Old enough to have known better. It was a while before she acknowledged his drinking was a problem, still longer before she challenged him about all the pills he was taking. When she fell pregnant, he persuaded her it was the wrong time; she was pushing for promotion to CID, wasn't she, and this next year or so he was likely to be busy, busier than ever. Plenty of time for kids later on.

It was less than a month after the abortion, the woman

came to the door. Pale, thin-faced, a sketch of prettiness with most of the lines erased; at first glance Helen had thought she was just a girl, but then realised she was wrong. When the sides of the fawn raincoat she was wearing fell aside, Helen could clearly see the child she was carrying. Six months or seven.

'I'm sorry,' she said. 'I'm sorry. I didn't know if I should come. Andrew would kill me if he knew.'

But Andrew was in Amsterdam.

Helen invited her in.

Her name was Brenda and she was twenty-two. She had a one-room flat in Shepherd's Bush, but Andrew had promised he'd find something larger when the baby came. No, she hadn't seen so much of him lately, but he was extra busy at work, she knew that. And she knew about Helen too. Andrew had told her in a drunken outburst – trying to make her jealous, she supposed.

Now she was frightened, she said, that Andrew might change his mind about the baby once it was born, although he'd promised he wouldn't. She'd even said, early on, when first she'd known she was pregnant, that she'd, you know, have something done, but Andrew had said no, that would be wrong.

Tears stung Helen's eyes.

She made Brenda tea and held her hand. She shouldn't worry, everything would be fine. Andrew and herself, it was nothing too serious, just a fling. You know what men are like. Once the baby comes it would all be all right, she'd see.

Helen had walked with her as far as the Tube, then

noted down the numbers of several white-van men from a newsagent's window and phoned them from her mobile as she packed. Unable to face her parents, she rang her sister in Stevenage.

'You're a bloody fool,' her sister had said, when she'd heard Helen out. Cold comfort and strong gin and tonic; a bed in the spare room for as long as she wanted, as long as Gary didn't kick up a fuss. She could do a bit of babysitting maybe, earn her keep.

She had moved to Cambridge by the time Andrew tracked her down. His face, smiling, at her door. 'Hel, come on, let me in. It's freezing out here and I've driven bloody miles. One cup of coffee and I'll be on my way.'

He waited until she was at the sink, rinsing the mugs, before standing close behind her, his body pressing against hers, his breath on her neck.

'Andrew, don't . . .' But she shuddered and shook and her voice caught in her throat.

He took her on the kitchen floor and then, later, in her bed, and by the morning he was gone, leaving her feeling hollow and raw.

Never again.

But when she should have been playing Gloria Gaynor's 'I Will Survive', she was listening to Emmylou Harris's 'Lovin' You Again'. And when he phoned three months later, two in the morning, and swore that he loved her and had nowhere to go, she told him to go to hell. But when he knocked on the door and she saw his face, she let him in, lying to herself that he could sleep on the settee.

She went into therapy. Talked about her dreams, about issues of self-esteem. She grew up. By this time she was working with Will and something of a corner had been turned. She liked her job, she even liked herself. Could it really be that simple?

The next time Andrew called, she put down the phone. And then the next. And the next. Till he stopped phoning.

It wasn't until she was in the hospital that she saw him again.

Tell him. Please, Will. Tell him not to come.

She took the letter in her hand. Opening it would be like opening a door. She tore the envelope and the pages it contained into shreds and dropped them down into the pocket of her dressing gown; the next time she went to the toilet, she would flush them away.

Right now, she had to phone Will and pass on what Lesley had told her about Howard Prince.

28

Rastrick's team were working the Cambridge–Newmarket connection, cross-referencing available records and compiling a list of offenders between the ages of sixteen and twenty-five who showed a propensity for street violence or taking and driving away.

Of the thirty-four names, eleven were currently serving sentences ranging from six months to five years; one had left the country; and two others had died in the same road accident, when a nearly-new Mercedes they had stolen had gone headlong into a lorry laden with aggregate on the A11, ten miles short of Thetford. The lorry driver had escaped with cuts and bruises and was still suffering from shock. Both of the youths, cousins, seventeen and eighteen, had been pronounced dead at the scene.

Which left twenty at large, all told, fourteen of whom were subject to ASBOs or on probation.

Adam.

Daryl.

Brian.

Matt.

Liam.

Stuart.

Kyle.

Stuart again.

Shane.

Eddie.

Jason.

Another Adam.

Alex.

Jon.

Rob.

Daniel.

Darren.

John.

Mark.

Jamie.

The next task was locating them and bringing them in for questioning. Some of the addresses on file were still current, but by no means all; the probation service were able to provide some, social services others. Telephone call after telephone call. Officers driving round back doubles, climbing stairs, knocking on doors. Their inquiries being met with surprise, confusion, sudden bouts of amnesia, circumlocution, barefaced lies.

After three days of diligent searching, fifteen had been found.

Adam Priestley was number fifteen.

Number fifteen in a long day.

Priestley was eighteen, but looked younger. Skinny, with a pitted face, his mouth was small and his eyes too wide. Five foot six at best. The number one crop he'd paid for at the barber's was doing him no favours whatsoever. The kind who, as a kid, was forever being bullied at school, the last to be chosen, the butt of jokes. There was a small silver ring in his left ear; dragon tattoos at the side of his neck and on the back of his right wrist.

Faced with two plain-clothes officers, by then tired themselves, Priestley blinked, scratched and fidgeted incessantly on his chair. Questioned, he denied everything. Didn't know what they were talking about. Didn't know anything about any car. He was home. He was out. He was watching a video with his mates. He wasn't there. Looking almost pleased with himself, Priestley sniffed loudly and then chewed at a broken piece of nail.

Fuck this for a game of soldiers, Rastrick thought, watching on video; I've had kids like him for dinner before now, dinner, breakfast and tea.

'Okay,' he said, stepping into the room. 'Why don't we all take a break? A breather? Go on, bugger off, get yourselves down the canteen. I'll keep Adam here amused.'

The recording equipment switched off, Rastrick eased himself into a chair.

'Right. Adam. Time to stop pissing about. I ask you questions and you give me answers. Only this time, the truth, okay?' He stared at Priestley hard. 'Okay? We understood?'

'Yes.' Almost too faint to hear.

'Understood?'

'Yes.'

'Good. That's better. Now, whose idea was it to take the car?'

Priestley blinked. 'Wh-which car?'

'The Escort.'

Priestley blinked. 'Which Escort? I don't know 'bout any Escort.'

'The one you left wrapped round a lamp post on the Newmarket Road.'

'I never . . .'

'You weren't the driver?'

'No. I don't . . .'

'They wouldn't let you drive.'

'No, that's not . . .'

'Lucky to let you sit in the back, I shouldn't wonder.'

'That's not right.'

'They did let you sit up front. They let you drive. Is that it? Too fast round that bend, doing your best to straighten out. Bang!' Rastrick slammed the flat of his hand down in front of Priestley and Priestley jumped. 'Into the fucking post. Happen to anyone. Total write-off. Lucky to get out of there alive, all three of you. You and who was it? Stuart and Kyle? Eddie and Shane? Your mates? Mates of yours?'

Priestley shivered and shook his head as Rastrick leaned forward.

'Names, you arsehole, that's what I want. Alex and Liam? Daryl and Mark? That who it was? With you in the car? Running away? Running away from what you did?'

Rastrick's face was inches away now, almost touching.

'What you did? You and these pals of yours? Big men. Hard. Is that how it felt? Couple of students you all thought it'd be fun to beat the holy shit out of. Couple of gays. Teach them a lesson? That what you were doing? Teaching them a lesson? You and Daniel? You and Darren? Well, you taught him a lesson right enough, one of them. Died, didn't he? You know that? You know one of them died. Killed the poor bastard, that's what you did. You, Adam. You. How's that make you feel? Make you feel more like a man?'

Rastrick pulled his face away, not far, his voice a whisper now, a caress.

'They'll put you up for it, you know that, don't you? These mates of yours. That's what they're doing out there now. In rooms like this. Just like always. Giving you up. Letting you take the blame. Adam put the boot. Adam had the iron bar. The knife. Adam whose idea it was in the first place. Adam who drove the car. You're dead meat, son. Hung out to dry. Rest of your life inside, and you know what that'll mean? Kid like you. Small. Small bones. Small like a girl. They'll put lipstick on your mouth and buy you a dress. A pretty little dress.'

As Priestley jerked back, the chair he was sitting on slipped away under him and he fell to the floor, legs thrashing, feet drumming the ground.

'Jesus Christ!' Rastrick said, throwing open the door and shouting at the officers waiting in the corridor. 'He's shat himself and now he's throwing a bloody fit. Get

in here and stop him swallowing his tongue, then take
him off and hose him down.'

Will was having a slightly better day. When the first of
Richard Fenwick's calls had come in, it had been routed
to Will, who had failed to grasp the significance of the
name. Only on the second occasion did he remember
who Fenwick was and return the call. Inside five minutes
a car had been dispatched to bring Fenwick to the station.

When he arrived, Will ushered him into his office,
shook his hand, sat him down and offered him a drink
of tea or coffee, which he refused.

Fenwick fiddled nervously with the knot of his tie,
shuffled his well-shined shoes, fidgeted with his tie again.
'I only hope I'm not wasting your time,' he said.

'Best let me be the judge of that,' Will said.

'Only when I spoke to one of your colleagues . . .'

'Detective Sergeant Walker.'

'Yes. She wanted me to describe the person I saw
outside Stephen's house – Stephen Bryan – and, well,
I didn't make a very good job of it, I'm afraid. It was
difficult, you see, remembering, and I didn't want to say
the wrong thing, send you off on a wild goose chase.
Only you hear about that, don't you? The police, going
after the wrong person – all in good faith, I realise –
but because the information they have is incorrect.'

He paused and coughed, lightly, into the back of his
hand.

Will leaned back and crossed his legs. Traffic droned
by outside.

'Do you have some new information, then, Mr Fenwick? Is that it? Something's jogged your memory?'

'Yes. Yes, sort of. At least . . .' He broke off, uncertainly, cleared his throat and started again. 'Last night, no, sorry, two nights ago now – before I first phoned – there was this item on the television news. The local news, that is, it comes on after the main bulletin, just ten minutes, five or ten. It was about this new development beside the River Trent, in Nottingham. Fancy flats and all that kind of thing. At first I couldn't understand why it was on at all. I mean, it's not exactly local, Nottingham. But then I realised, the man who was responsible – not the architect, but the man behind it all – he lived locally, local to here, so it was about him. How he'd made one fortune, lost it all, and then made another. Howard Prince, that was his name. I wrote it down, so that I wouldn't forget.'

Will was sitting forward now, forearms resting on his desk. 'What about him?' he asked.

'He was the one,' Fenwick said. 'It was him that I saw, outside Stephen's house. As soon as I saw him, I said to myself, That's him.'

Will could feel the adrenalin running through his body.

'You're sure.'

'Yes. Yes, I think so.'

'You think so or you're certain?'

'I think I'm certain.'

'Certain enough to swear in a court of law?'

Fenwick took a handkerchief from his jacket pocket and wiped the palms of his hands. 'I don't know.'

Will leaned back and for an instant closed his eyes.

'You said, when you saw him on the television you recognised Prince as being the same man that you saw in front of Stephen Bryan's house a few days before he was murdered?'

'Yes, but . . .'

'The same man you saw a day later driving past the end of the road?'

'Yes.'

'Then you are sure?'

'Yes. I mean, I thought so at the time. I just don't know if I could stand up in court, under oath, and swear they were one and the same person. I'm sorry. I thought if I told you . . .' He pulled out his handkerchief again. 'I shouldn't have come. I'm sorry. If I wasn't more certain, I should never have said anything at all. I realise that now.'

Will pushed back his chair. 'Mr Fenwick, you did absolutely the right thing. There's no question of that. Now just hang on here while I get you a glass of water. And then we'll go through everything again. Slowly. In your own time.' He rested a hand on Fenwick's shoulder as he went past. 'There's nothing to worry about, nothing at all. You're doing fine.'

The Lord giveth, Will thought, as he stepped out into the corridor, the Lord giveth and he taketh away. Another of those bits of flimflam from Sunday school that come back to haunt you when you need them least.

29

The Assistant Chief Constable had summoned both Rastrick and Will Grayson and then kept them waiting the obligatory twenty minutes or so, cooling their heels in the outer office; both men feigning indifference under the watchful eye of the ACC's secretary, a redoubtable woman of indeterminate years, who fingered the keyboard of her computer with the deftness and concentration of a concert pianist.

'What's he up to in there, Enid?' Rastrick said around the ten-minute mark. 'Sorting out his golf date for Saturday? Short of a four? Wants someone to caddy, does he?'

Enid, if indeed that was her name, shot Rastrick a scornful glance and kept her counsel.

'Anyone'd think we didn't have better things to bloody do,' Rastrick grumbled.

Will said nothing: if they'd been doing things better, they would neither of them have been there.

When finally they were ushered in, the ACC shook

Rastrick's hand, greeted Will with a nod, and told the pair of them to sit.

A heavy-chested man in his fifties, greying hair brushed neatly into place, were it not for his uniform, Will thought, he could have been the CEO of some company quoted on the Stock Exchange, anything from biscuits to ball bearings.

'I've read these reports I asked for,' the ACC said, indicating the files on his desk, 'and it's difficult to tell which of you's got your head jammed further up your own arse.'

Rastrick coughed; Will examined the floor close to his feet.

'Straightforward enough case, this, Malcolm, I'd have thought. High-profile. One student dead and another injured, one of our own in hospital, sort of thing that has the media blowing a gasket. What it needs, tact, organisation, a pair of safe hands, which is supposed to be you, and suddenly you turn into something out of the bloody *Sweeney*. Too much time watching reruns on *Men and* sodding *Motors*. That kid, that youth, what in God's name did you think you were playing at? A wonder you didn't hit him round the head with a couple of telephone directories while you were at it. Just for old times' sake. Threaten to wire up his sweaty little bollocks.'

Rastrick seemed to have given himself over to a careful examination of the cracks in the ceiling.

'Jesus, Malcolm,' the ACC continued, 'this is the twenty-first fucking century, or haven't you heard? The age of accountability. I can't take a piss while I'm wearing this uniform, without measuring the content and the duration to ensure they're in line with some Home Office directive. Can't drop a fart with the wind in the wrong direction, for fear of abusing someone's Human fucking Rights. And if we want to squeeze the truth out of some miserable scrote, we don't have the wherewithal to ship him off to Egypt or fucking Albania and get someone else to do our dirty work for us. No. We're responsible. I'm responsible. You get some kid in a room on his own, no witnesses, no legal fucking representation, and come on like it's Guantanamo fucking Bay and it's okay for you to be a law unto yourself, leaving me carrying the fucking can and trying to excuse the fucking inexcusable. Do I make myself clear?'

'Yes, sir.' Rastrick's normally dolorous face looked more so than usual, his complexion more ashen.

'Yes? Just yes? No smart comebacks, no pithy one-liners, no excuses?'

'No, sir.'

'Good. Because if you ever put me in that position again, I will personally hang you out to dry. Am I understood?'

'Yes, sir.'

With a grunt, the ACC slid Will's file across the desk and glanced at the notes he'd written on the first page of the report; only then did he look at Will carefully for the first time.

'Now, Grayson – bit of a cowboy, we know that, least you like to think you are. Out on the streets, knocking on doors, anything rather than do what I'm doing, sitting behind a desk and taking some fucking responsibility.' He jabbed a finger in Will's direction. 'Just as well, son, because carry on the way you are now, the nearest you're going to get to a desk like this is where you are now, waiting for a reprimand. Fuck this up, this inquiry, and you'll be on the streets, all right, you'll be back in uniform; you'll be going into schools giving little kids lectures on road fucking safety, that's what you'll be doing.'

Will said nothing.

The ACC flipped open the file. 'Howard Prince, you think there's a link between him and Bryan's murder?'

'I think it's a possibility, yes, sir.'

'Because he was apparently seen hanging around outside Bryan's house? God, man, what does that prove?'

'In itself, nothing, sir. And I certainly wouldn't want to rely on that witness in court. But he does seem to be almost paranoid about anyone looking into his affairs. And we know he warned Bryan off . . .'

'Long step between there and having him murdered.'

'Yes, sir, I know, but there's also evidence that suggests he's not above using force when he feels it necessary. Making threats. Various kinds of intimidation. Not Prince directly, but a lot of it pointing in his direction. I'm going back through the files now.'

'And this McCormick . . .'

'McKusick, sir.'

'This McKusick you wasted several hundred police

hours investigating, the boyfriend, he's all squeaky clean, you've decided?'

'It looks that way, sir.'

'Bit of a waste of time, then. Time and resources.'

'McKusick was a viable suspect . . .'

'But not to the exclusion of all others.'

'Sir?'

'Prince, why wasn't he investigated sooner?'

'We did speak to him, sir. Quite early on.'

'And he pulled the wool over your eyes.'

A denial formed in Will's mind, but he choked it off.

'The thing about doing your own legwork,' the ACC said, 'conducting your own interrogations, there's no one else to point a finger at when you come a fucking cropper.' He tapped his fingers briskly down on top of the file. 'Now you've got your feet wet, you'd best follow this through. Notts force, they're giving you all the cooperation you need?'

'Yes, sir.'

'Good. Keep in contact with Malcolm here about this other business. You and Moyles, you're in touch with this fellow from Hate Crimes?'

'Parsons. Yes, sir.'

'Right.' The ACC leaned back in his executive chair. 'Bugger off, the pair of you. Just heed what I've said. And Grayson, I'd step carefully with Prince if I were you – a few friends in high places, I'd not be surprised.'

Both men got to their feet.

'Your DS,' the ACC said. 'Walker. She's out of any danger, I take it? Making a good recovery?'

'Discharged from hospital any day, sir,' Will said.

'Excellent.'

Enid barely glanced up as they entered the outer office, a three-colour spreadsheet filling the screen of her computer. Rastrick blew her a kiss in passing, but if she noticed she gave no sign.

30

'Got a minute?' Rastrick said.

Will looked up from his desk and read the grin of satisfaction writ large on the detective superintendent's sallow face.

'Take a look at this.'

This was a length of wood, enclosed in a plastic evidence bag, enclosed and tagged.

'One of the divers,' Rastrick said, 'pulled it out of the Cam. Couple of hundred metres or so along from the bridge. Best bet, one of the gang running off that way took it so far and then chucked it in.'

The wood was almost as long as a man's arm and splintered across the top, where a section had broken off; the width, tapering slightly, was such that it could be held firmly in a man's hand. Tape, fraying and discoloured, was attached to one end.

'What do you reckon?' Will said. 'Hockey stick?'

Rastrick shrugged. 'Lacking the business end? Could be.'

'Or that Irish game.'

'Hurley?'

'Hurley, hurling, something like that.'

'Hurled into the river, that's for sure.'

'Could have been in there a while,' Will said.

'That it could. Then again, it could be what fitted out that poor bastard with a requiem mass.'

Will lifted it with one hand, feeling the weight, the heft; he imagined the impact it would have had if swung, full force, against someone's ribs; brought down from a height against someone's head.

'Any chance of prints from this?' Will asked, doubtfully.

'Some.'

'They'll not have been washed away?'

'Sending it along to the Fingerprint Office first thing. Have to wait and see.' Rastrick perched his angular frame on the edge of Will's desk. 'Time the tide turned our way, don't you think?'

Less than an hour later, Will was heading for alien turf. Well, perhaps alien was putting it a bit strong. But Nottingham was where the bulk of Howard Prince's activities were centred, so that was where he needed to be. Earlier that morning, he'd had a meeting with Lynn Kellogg, from the Force Crime Directorate, the Notts equivalent of the Major Investigation Team to which he himself belonged.

Neat and businesslike in a black roll-neck jumper and matching skirt, Kellogg had listened as Will outlined his reasons for looking into Prince's background.

'A lot of supposition and not much substance,' she said when he'd finished.

Will nodded. 'At the moment, it's all we have. But I'm confident we'll find more.'

'And the reason you're here to see me – it's Prince's business dealings, primarily?'

'For now, yes.'

'You think that's what he's protecting, not his family?'

Will smiled. 'It has to be a possibility.'

'It's scrabbling in the dark, you know that, don't you?'

'I know.'

Kellogg wrote a name and contact details in the leather-bound notebook on her desk, tore out the page and handed it across. 'Terry Challoner, that's who you should talk to. Till he took retirement six months ago, he was number two in the Fraud Squad. If there was anything other than squeaky clean about Prince's dealings, chances are he'd have known about it. I'll give him a call, tell him you'll be in touch.'

'Thanks.' Folding the sheet of paper, Will slipped it down into his inside pocket.

'Need anything else, let me know. I'll see what I can do. And good luck.'

Terry Challoner was cheery and precise in his instructions. 'Notts Police HQ, you know where that is, I dare say? Take the main road from there north towards Mansfield. Carry on till you come to a big roundabout and fork right on to the A614, the Doncaster road. About four miles along there you'll see a sign that says burial ground, pointing off to the right. That'll take you on to Salterford Lane. Go along there just above half a mile – you'll have gone past the burial ground itself, Tithe Green, that's what it's called – and just after a rise, you'll see a track leading off to the left. Quite a sharp turn. Couple of hundred yards along there you'll see a couple of old farm workers' cottages on the right-hand side. We're in the first one of those. Black-and-white collie comes running out and tries to have your balls for breakfast, you know you're in the right place.'

The wind was blowing quite strongly as Will drove, and clouds, varying in shade from off-white to battlefield grey, scudded fast across the open sky. Fields to either side showed the first signs of early growth, hedgerows thickening to green. A Range Rover accelerated on to his shoulder, anxious to pass. When last he'd spoken to Lorraine, she'd told him of her appointment with the manager at the university admissions office, and he'd felt bad at not being able to share her excitement.

He saw the sign for the burial ground with plenty of time, slowed to a standstill so that a tractor travelling in the opposite direction could pass, and turned into the lane. Classic FM was playing low on his car radio, some tinkly piano music or other. Handel, he thought the presenter might have said.

There were several cars in the parking area along-side the burial ground, small knots of people standing between them, some waiting silently, others turned inwards in conversation; behind them a path led towards what Will assumed were the graves, marked by small splashes of flower. A tall woman in a black cape stood amongst them, bareheaded, staring at the sky.

He missed the turning into the farm track and had to continue along the lane for a good half-mile before finding space enough to reverse and try again. When he was in sight of the cottages, the collie came running towards him and crouched, splay-footed, in his path, head back, barking. Having stopped, Will released the handbrake and continued slowly forward, the dog now running from one side of the car to the other, jumping up at the windows and showing its teeth.

No chance, Will thought, of anyone taking Terry Challoner by surprise.

Challoner himself was standing in the front garden of the cottage as Will drew up: dark green waxed jacket, open-neck check shirt, muddied brown cords, wellington boots. A word to the dog to be quiet all that was needed.

He took Will's hand in a hearty grip. 'Found your way, then?'

'More or less.'

'Long as you don't turn off too soon, down to Tithe Green.' Challoner laughed. 'Worse places to fetch up, mind you, when the time comes. Crematorium some-where, soulless bloody places, like something on one of these industrial estates, most of 'em. Pumping out more smoke into the bloody ozone. Down there, a few years on and you're just so much mulch.' He laughed again. 'Pushing up daisies, isn't that what they used to say? Well, down there it's true. Fertiliser, that's what you become. And none of this religious hocuspocus, neither. Just a wicker coffin, that or cardboard, someone says a few words and then them as wants sling down a bit of earth. I've got mine booked, I tell you. Booked and paid for.'

'Bit premature?' Will said.

Challoner shook his head. 'Get it settled. Then it's done. Two hundred and fifty quid for a prepaid plot; another hundred or so to have the grave dug and then filled in again. I've even splashed out another seventy to have a tree planted up on the hill there . . .' He turned towards the dog. 'Something for him to piss against when I'm gone.'

Will was looking back at the cottage with its white walls and faded green trim, its neighbour almost identical, the line between the gardens marked with a low fence of looped iron.

'You live here alone?' Will asked.

'Aside from the dog? Aye. Wife died just over a year back. Bastard cancer. Ate her away from the inside in less time'n it took one of her grandkids to grow inside the bloody womb.'

'I'm sorry.'

'Yes, well . . .' Challoner shook his head. 'We'd had our eye on this place for a few years, somewhere to retire when I jacked it all in. Never thought I'd be up here on me own. You don't. Not when you've been together as long as we had. But there you are . . .'

He started to walk back towards the cottage and Will walked with him. 'You like it here, though?' Will said. 'You'd not sooner be back in the city?'

Challoner stopped short of the door. 'You know what I did? The day I retired? Took all my suits, shirts, ties, all the stuff I'd worn every day of my working life, built a bonfire out back and burned the bloody lot. Ashes. This is what I wear now, this and an old jumper full of holes. I doubt I've set foot back in Nottingham more than once since the turn of the year.'

'And you're not lonely?'

'Course I'm bloody lonely. But I've got the dog and a bottle of good Scotch. Couple next door, old as Methuselah, but not above telling me what's wrong with the way I've set my runner beans, or offering to lend a hand when the septic tank wants some attention. Outlive me, the pair of them.'

The inside was cosy, if a little cramped: a couple of armchairs and a two-seater settee that had seen service, Will thought, wherever Challoner had lived before; photographs of a young man and woman in robes on the day they had received their degrees; grand-children, three of them, beaming out from between simple wooden frames. Knick-knacks, a few books, wild flowers in a vase, a small TV; everything clean and in its place, much as it would have been, Will imagined, when Challoner's wife was still alive. Just a few scrapings of mud on the rug and the telltale black-and-white hairs on the settee to suggest a little slackening off.

'Tea or whisky? Take your pick.'

'Whisky sounds good, but I'd best stick to tea.'

'Suit yourself.'

One of the armchairs had a footstool in front of it and Will chose the other and sat, thumbing through a week-old edition of the *Radio Times*, while the dog watched him carefully from the doorway, and Challoner, whistling tunelessly, busied himself in the kitchen.

'Now then,' Challoner said, when they were both settled. 'Tell me what you want to know.'

'Howard Prince.'

'What about him?'

'Anything. Any dealings you might have had with him; anything he might be concerned to keep quiet, out of the public eye.'

A smile came to Challoner's face. 'How long have you got?'

'As long as it takes.'

Challoner lifted his mug of tea and held it in both hands and, as if this were some kind of sign, the dog jumped on to the settee, curled up in one corner and feigned sleep.

'First time he came to our attention, that would have been, oh, arse-end of the seventies, early eighties, maybe. This builder who'd been working for Prince, fair-sized little firm, doing work on some houses Prince had bought from the Coal Board, came to us with a story about how Prince had got hold of them on the cheap. Sour grapes, of course, often is, that kind of accusation. Someone out for revenge over money, jealousy maybe, some sexual shenanigans. Prince had thrown a lot of work the builder's way, and then, after some row or other, dropped him in favour of somebody else.'

'You investigated it all the same?' Will asked.

'What he said, fitted in with one or two other things we'd heard, whispers, you know. And this wasn't just some penny ante deal, there was serious money involved. At least two hundred houses, north of the county, one way or another they'd fallen into disrepair. Get worse after the miners' strike, of course, but that's a different story. What Prince was doing, renovating some places, then selling them for four or five times the paltry price he'd paid for them; others he was just bulldozing, whole streets of them, building new ones in their stead. Making a small fortune.'

'So what was the allegation? Prince had been doling out backhanders?'

'Backhanders, fancy dinners, weekends in some country house hotel, the odd holiday. Usual malarkey.'

'What did he say when you put it to him?'

Challoner laughed. 'Never worked in the Fraud Squad, did you?'

Will shook his head.

'Way we investigate, whoever's affairs we're looking into, he's the last one we talk to. Accumulate the evidence first and then, if it looks like there's a case to answer, that's when we'll go after the offender.'

'What if he gets wind of it and does a bunk?'

'It can happen. But if it does, well, not exactly tanta-mount to admitting guilt, but near as. And anyhow, in this case, whatever whispers came back to him down the track, Prince stayed put. We started taking state-ments from witnesses and found, yes, there'd been hospitality, lavish some of it, but as to where or when that becomes bribery, it's a fine line. Especially when, down the road, there's a jury to convince. Then this one official came forward, prepared to swear he'd seen Prince and one of his bosses in a nice little tête-à-tête, money changing hands. Later, we discovered the boss had been rimming this bloke's wife for a twelvemonth and he'd have said bloody anything to get back at him. But by then we'd got a warrant to examine Prince's books – bank accounts, contracts, VAT returns, the whole works. Prince thought he'd been clever, kept them lodged with his solicitor, as if somehow that made them sacrosanct.'

Challoner shook his head. 'I'll never forget the look on that solicitor's face when we went marching into his office. Up on his high horse like he was three-day bloody evening. Soon cut him down to size. Took away every scrap of paper with Prince's name to it. Box after bloody box.'

'It proved your case?'

'In the end it was all we had. Jury threw the rest out of court. Defence barrister had pretty much pulled us to bits. Hearsay, uncorroborated allegations, petty jeal-ousy. All we could convict Prince on, failure to submit statutory records for the purposes of Company House.'

'He walked away with a fine.'

'Banned from running a company or being a director for five years. Judge saw our side of it, didn't want to see him getting off scot-free.'

'And you think he was guilty?'

'Bloody sure of it.'

Will sighed and looked away. The collie whimpered as if he were now really asleep and something had disturbed his dreams.

'Here,' Challoner said, reaching for Will's mug. 'Let me top that up with some hot.'

'No, it's okay.'

'Come on, give it here.'

While Challoner was in the kitchen, Will went to the door and looked out, the view not so different from his own at home – hillier certainly, more trees, but almost devoid of houses, habitation. He tried to imagine what it would be like to be there all the time, no other adult company. What it was like for Lorraine.

'Old times that,' Challoner said at his shoulder. 'Not what you were wanting.'

'Maybe not.'

'Best come back inside, then. There's more.'

31

'You know it's going to piss down with rain, don't you?'

Helen cast a glance up at the sky, which was an almost uniform steely grey, if anything darker towards the east. 'A shower,' she said, with a small shrug of her shoulders. 'This time of the year, it's what you expect.'

They were making a slow circuit of the hospital grounds, Will with his waterproof partly fastened, Helen with a scarf tucked down inside the collar of her dressing gown and a pair of borrowed tennis shoes on her feet.

'Besides,' Helen said, 'you've got your anorak, what do you care?'

'Just as long as you're not expecting me to take it off and give it to you once the heavens open.'

'Chivalry, Will? I don't think so.'

'Absolutely. All that standing back and opening doors, laying down cloaks over puddles, that all went out with Walter Raleigh, right?'

'Germaine Greer, at least.'

'Who?'

'Come on, Will, even you know who Germaine Greer is.'

'She's the one who walked off *Celebrity Island*. Or was it *Big Brother?*'

'One thing I've always admired about you, Will. The way you keep abreast of ideas. Don't keep your head stuck in lads' mags or the Police and Criminal Evidence Act, like some.'

'Just because you saw me reading the *Guardian* once, don't let that fool you.'

Helen paused long enough to light a cigarette. 'Lorraine, how's it going with that job she was after?'

'Seems to have got through the interview. Just waiting for her CRB clearance, and that's it.'

'Not holding her breath, then.'

'I don't know. It should be pretty quick.'

Helen drew smoke down deep into her lungs. 'Let's hope there's not another Lorraine Grayson out in Wisbech or somewhere, with a string of convictions for drugs offences or molesting small boys.'

'There's a lot of that in Wisbech?'

'Probably no more than anywhere else.'

Will took another look up at the sky. 'Are you sure you don't want to go back inside? Or at least find somewhere to sit down? This is making me giddy.'

Helen pointed. 'There's a bench over there.'

She winced slightly as she sat down and Will's face asked the question.

'I'm fine,' Helen said. 'Now tell me again about Prince. After the court case. Just to make sure I've got it clear in my head.'

According to Terry Challoner, Howard Prince had pretty much gone off the radar during the five years he'd been banned from running a company. There were stories that he'd gone abroad; others that he was living the life of a recluse somewhere in the Fens. On one occasion, police were called to a disturbance at a hotel in Ely – Will would be able to check this easily enough – at which Prince and his wife had been having dinner. Shouting, screaming, smashing of plates. That apart, Challoner didn't hear anything about him until '92: there were grumblings about a bid he'd made on behalf of a firm called Shotton Properties, for whom he was working as a consultant. Usual kind of thing, obtaining preferential treatment by unfair methods. Fraud Squad officers had poked around, asked a few questions, the whole thing seemed to die a death of its own accord. That was that.

'Then, a few years later,' Challoner had told Will, 'in '94 or '95, there were more rumblings, louder this time, and with a sight more involved. Major development project out at Worksop: new shopping centre, flats, the whole works, you might say.'

Will had smiled to acknowledge Challoner's joke and let him continue.

'This feller came to us, former councillor – Allen, that's the name, I think, Michael Allen. Self-righteous

344

son of a bitch, but straight, or so it seemed. According to him, Prince had been up there greasing palms, making promises like they were going out of style. Claimed to have evidence, time and place, so, fair enough, we started asking around. Sour grapes, some said, lost his seat on the council, Allen, and been stirring up trouble ever since. But by then there seemed to be enough truth in it to persevere. And there were signs, you know, someone driving round in a new car, brand new extension going up on somebody's house, that kind of thing. But this councillor, ex-councillor, his evidence was holding it all together. So there we are, thinking we've got enough to go to a judge, ask for a warrant, and wham, in walks Allen and claims it was all a mistake. Withdraws his evidence, very sorry, got carried away, didn't know what I was doing, none of it was true.'

'He'd been got at,' Will said.

'Course he had. We did everything we could to get him to change his mind, up to and including threatening to prosecute him for wasting police time. Nothing doing. Six months later, the whole thing fell apart of its own accord, something to do with the land they were intending to build on not being structurally viable. After that we didn't feel too bad. If Prince had been handing out freebies, then he was out of pocket for nothing.'

'And there's nothing else?' Will had asked. 'More recent?'

Challoner had shaken his head. 'Not of the same order, no. The occasional rumour, but that's par for the course, keep your ear to the ground, it happens all the time.'

345

'But there was something?'

'Something, aye.' Challoner had fetched a pipe from a sideboard drawer, sniffed at the bowl and set it between his teeth. 'Don't fill it with tobacco any more, just the habit, I suppose. That and the smell. Something good about the smell. Anyhow, Prince. He'd been back in business on his own account a good while and doing well. Big projects, too – hotels, student apartments, a new estate out on the edge of town.

'Then – this was no more than a few years back – a whole raft of houses, ex-council, came up for sale in Forest Fields. Local housing association made a bid for them, thought they were pretty much home and dried, till Prince came in over the top of them. Only problem he had then, sitting tenants, some of them, weren't of a mind to move. Refused point-blank, despite all of Prince's offers to rehouse them, cash bonuses, whatever. Lo and behold, just a few months later, they'd changed their mind. Couldn't get out fast enough.'

'Intimidation?'

Challoner nodded. 'So it seemed. Little things at first, wheelie bins turned upside down, rubbish spilled all over house fronts, graffiti on walls. After that it got worse: shit through the letter-box, an elderly couple mugged on their way home, pensions stolen. Top it all, one house set ablaze, no one hurt, thank God, but it could've been a lot nastier than it was. Place burned almost to the ground.'

'And this was down to Prince?'

'Not in a way that we could ever prove.'

'Too much of a coincidence, surely?'

'His firm put out a press release, deploring the general lawlessness in the area and the lack of respect for private property. Promised that things would improve after the rebuilding they were planning had taken place. Even had the gall to suggest the police sent out more foot patrols.'

'And you couldn't touch him?'

'The local lads pulled in a few kids, made some arrests. One youth charged with arson, as I remember, not sure if it ever got to court. But no one would admit as much as having heard Prince's name.' Challoner tapped his pipe. 'What do they say about the Devil? Something about supping with a long spoon? If Prince was behind what happened, he was so far behind as to not leave a trace.'

While Will was recounting the story, Helen had listened carefully, blanking out the people walking close to where they were sitting, the sounds of traffic, the fact that the first drops of rain were beginning to fall.

'The time Prince was up in court – '82, was it?'

'Thereabouts.'

'He didn't exactly walk away scot-free, but if the Fraud Squad case was as strong as Challoner said, it sounds as if the jury did him a real favour.'

'You think they might have been got at?'

'It happens. And Prince – if what Challoner told you was right, bribery for him seems pretty much a way of life.'

347

'Or intimidation.'

'You're thinking about the witness in that business out at Worksop?'

Will nodded. 'Something made him change his mind sharpish and I doubt it was a change of heart.'

The rain was falling more steadily now and Will got to his feet. 'We should be heading back inside.'

'If even half of this is true,' Helen said, 'if this is the way Prince operates, the way he's made his money, it's no wonder he doesn't welcome anyone coming sniffing round, asking questions.'

'Like Stephen Bryan?'

'Yes.'

'Surely, the kind of questions he would have been asking, they wouldn't have been anything to do with Prince's business?'

'You wouldn't have thought so. But maybe Prince reckons it's safer to keep everyone at arm's length as a matter of principle. Or maybe he's afraid if too many people start digging around, sooner or later, they're going to find out where the bodies are buried.'

'You're speaking metaphorically?'

Helen smiled. 'For now.'

Will unzipped his waterproof jacket and placed it around Helen's shoulders and they hurried out of the rain.

64. EXT. COAST ROAD. DAY.

RUBY *and* PHILIP *are driving along the coast road,* RUBY *at the wheel.*

This is the same stretch of road that we have seen in the opening scenes, but now everything is sunlit, the car windows are wound down and RUBY's *hair is blowing in the wind, and both she and* PHILIP *look happy.*

At the approach to a bend in the road, RUBY *slows the car to a halt and pulls over on to the grass verge. They get out and walk hand in hand to the edge of the cliff and stand there, looking down at the waves churning against the rocks below.*

PHILIP: *It's beautiful. (Turning to face her.) Wild but beautiful.*

RUBY *seizes hold of him and kisses him, and, as they embrace, the camera cranes up and then angles down beyond them to the crashing waves.*

32

Lesley, who for most of her adult life had been untroubled by dreams, woke again in the small hours, her skin clammy with sweat. When she tried to ease the T-shirt she'd been wearing up over her head, it stuck to her skin and she had to wriggle and then tug it free. Sodden, she dumped it in the washing basket and, running barely warm water into the sink, washed herself with the aid of a flannel. Dry, she pulled on a pair of sweat pants and a long-sleeved cotton top before setting the kettle to boil.

Just one or two of the apartment windows she could see had lights showing behind their blinds, the remainder shrouded in darkness. Through a gap between the buildings, she could just see the southern end of St Mary's Church outlined against the dull orange-yellow light of the city beyond.

Tea made, she picked up a book and switched on the radio.

Through the Night on Radio 3.

She was reading one of the No.1 Ladies' Detective Agency stories she'd picked up in the Oxfam shop. *In the Company of Cheerful Ladies*. Several people at work had recommended them and she'd thought she'd give them a try. Somehow, buying a book set in Botswana in an Oxfam shop, amongst all the Fair Trade this and that, had seemed particularly appropriate.

And it was pleasant, quietly amusing: reading about these two African ladies who spent their time, between eating doughnuts and drinking copious cups of tea, solving small mysteries and generally smoothing over the lives of those around them. Charming, Lesley thought. Soothing.

If only life were like that. Maybe it had been once.

Well, here she was drinking tea after all. And in those hours before the day had really started, couldn't she imagine that with the dawn everything would fall back into place, questions answered, mysteries solved?

In the place of tinkly piano from the radio – or had it been harpsichord? – there was something she recognised. Those short jittery phrases from the strings before they were answered by the horns, the music rising in volume as it swirled towards the end of that first short section, when the orchestra fell away and the soloist entered, sure-footed yet just so slightly ponderous – Mozart's Concerto for Bassoon and Orchestra in B flat major, K. 191.

When Stephen had been sixteen, his O-level year, he had suddenly befriended a boy in the year above him, the lower sixth. A crush, Lesley realised later. And this boy had played in the school orchestra, the woodwind section, bassoon. Not just the school orchestra, the county one as well. Hadn't he had an audition for the National Youth Orchestra, too? She couldn't recall. But what she did remember was going with Stephen to hear him play the Mozart concerto in a church somewhere in Leicester. She remembered the absolute concentration on Stephen's face, the way his hands had gripped his legs at the knee. She remembered his breathing; she could hear it now, below the music, as she had heard it then, the Allegro coming to an end.

Jumping up, she snapped off the radio.

She was sweating again, but this was something different. Her throat was dry and her skin prickled. She could listen to that music again and again, buy a CD of it and play it endlessly, just as Stephen had done when the boy had transferred to the Northern College of Music in Manchester and Stephen had never heard from him or seen him again.

But, other than in her imagination, she could not hear Stephen breathe. Stephen was dead and she still didn't know how or why. And though Helen Walker had promised she would alert her colleagues, do what she could, neither did the police.

Outside, the first light was slowly steeping into the sky.

The further she drove into the Fens that afternoon, the more distance between herself and the horizon there seemed to be, as if the earth were curving away from

352

her grasp. At intervals, the sun broke through the otherwise omnipresent grey and spun the fields silver at a touch.

Having been there before didn't prevent her from getting lost and twice she pulled in at the side of the road and struggled to compare her map with the expanse around her, barely broken by house or tree.

Somehow, she found herself approaching from the opposite direction and, surprised, she slowed to a halt and tried again to get her bearings. Ahead of her, on the narrow strip of road, a crow was pecking at something on the surface, tearing at it with its beak. Only when she was a car's length away did it rise with a brusque squawk and an easy flap of wings.

Lesley parked on the rough triangle of grass in front of the gate and, after only a moment's hesitation, activated the mechanism that would allow her through on to the path. There was a tiny remote camera that she hadn't noticed previously, attached to a post further back along the fence.

Only the Jaguar was present this time in the yard, shining and buffed; no other vehicles, no bicycle leaning against the wall. A few tea towels on a washing line aside, there were no signs of life at all.

She knocked at the same door as before and waited: nothing happened. For a moment, she looked up into the lens of the camera angling down. She knocked again and listened, her ear close to the wooden panel. Nothing stirred.

When she called out her voice came back strangely

flat. Everything around her was silent, except for the distant mithering of the birds. Through the kitchen window she could see cups and plates left to drain beside the sink. Fruit in a bowl. The same washing-up liquid she used herself.

Stepping back, she looked up towards the upstairs windows, but this time there was no one, no face peering down. Through the slats of the first barn she could see tools and boxes, logs stacked against one wall; in the second, larger barn a small boat rested on a trailer, partly covered by tarpaulin. More logs were stacked against the back wall of the house itself, wood chips on the ground.

She walked down through the orchard, between apple trees that were yet to come into blossom. Two taller pear trees stood over towards the hedge dividing the garden from the adjacent field. How far could you walk, Lesley wondered, without coming across another house, another person?

And then she saw her, just a shape and little more. Sitting low down against the field edge, some distance away. Lesley called a greeting and for a moment the face turned towards her, before looking away. It could be anyone, she thought, a traveller perhaps, someone out for a walk, taking a rest.

She squeezed through the hedge and began to walk around the curve of grass that marked the field end, the grass itself slippery and the ground damp beneath her feet.

When she was little more than twenty metres off, the

woman slowly turned her head towards her and Lesley could see the face was the same one she had seen up at the window, the same lank, dark hair, the same pale, narrow features.

Lesley raised a hand in greeting and the face turned away.

In the distance, Lesley could hear now the rough chatter of a tractor and, following the sound, could see it moving across a field to the west.

The woman, she saw now, was resting on her haunches, the folds of the dress she was wearing trailing on the ground and flecked quite liberally with mud. The dress had once been green, dark green, and was decked out here and there with lace. Below the capped sleeves, her arms were bare, the flesh loose and the skin, save from a garland of soft brown blotches, was paler than that of her face. She had a pair of oversize men's shoes, unlaced, on her feet. Her hair, Lesley could now see, was knotted and unkempt.

Lesley bent down towards her. 'Hello,' she said. 'I'm Lesley.'

A slight movement of the head, but nothing more.

'I think you must be Lily. Is that right?'

Lily began to cry.

'It's all right,' Lesley said. 'Nothing's going to happen. I just saw you sitting here, from the garden. I thought you might like some company.'

Lily picked a small grey stone from the soil, examined it in the palm of her hand, then let it fall. 'Are you the nurse?' she said. 'The new nurse?'

'No.' Easing herself down, Lesley sat beside her, their arms just touching.

'The last one,' Lily said, 'she stole from me, you know. From my purse. All the money I'd saved.' She stole a quick glance across her shoulder, past Lesley and back towards the house. 'The money for my ticket. All I had. I told them and that's why they fired her. That Mrs Thingumajig.' A glimmer of amusement played in Lily's eyes. 'Threw her out on her arse, that's what they did. Out on her bony arse.'

'Mrs Thingumajig,' said Lesley, 'that's the housekeeper?'

Lily looked at her. 'She's the witch.'

'You don't like her.'

'Oh . . .' Head to one side, Lily wafted her hand through the air. 'She's not as bad as some. She doesn't hurt me, not like some. They used to beat me, you know? Pull out my hair.'

'Surely not.'

'In those other places, not here. Howard wouldn't let them. He took me away. I told him what they were doing and he took me away. Brought me home, here.' Her hand rested for a moment on Lesley's arm. 'He loves me, you know? Looks after me.'

The hand fell away and she leaned backwards, mouth partly open, looking up at the sky.

'Do you want to go back?' Lesley asked. 'To the house? I'll walk with you, if you like.'

'I've seen you before,' Lily said. 'You were here, once before.'

'That's right. I came to see you.'

'No.' Lily shook her head. 'No one ever comes to see me. Howard says it's not good for me. And the witch, she sends them away.'

'My brother,' Lesley said. 'Stephen. It's possible he might have come to see you. A little while ago. He wanted to talk to you.'

'Howard says . . .'

'He was writing a book and he wanted to ask you some questions.'

'A book?'

'Yes. About Stella.'

'About my mother?'

'No, your aunt. Stella's your aunt.'

'Oh, yes, of course. I know. Irene, that's my mother. I should know my own mother.' Lily reached out and patted her hand. 'You'll have to excuse me, I get confused. Everyone says so.' She tapped the side of her head and smiled. 'Confused.'

'Perhaps you'd like to talk to me?' Lesley said. 'About your aunt?'

'She died,' Lily said.

'Yes, I know.'

'She died.'

Lesley could see the housekeeper, still wearing her topcoat, stepping through the gap in the hedge and hurrying towards them.

'Why don't you let me help you up?' Lesley said, taking hold of Lily's hand. 'It's probably not good for you, sitting here all this time.'

Lily looked at her doubtfully, then at the house-keeper, closing on them fast.

'Don't let her . . .' Lily said.

'It's all right.'

'Don't let her hit me.'

'Mrs Prince,' the housekeeper called.

'I'm sure she won't hit you,' Lesley said.

'Mrs Prince. What do you think you are doing? You must come inside. And you,' she said to Lesley, 'you are the person from the radio. A reporter. What are you doing here?'

'I saw Lily out here,' Lesley said. 'And there didn't seem to be anybody at the house. I just came to make sure she was all right.'

'She is fine,' the woman said, edging Lesley aside. 'Come along, Mrs Prince. You will come with me.' Reaching down, she lifted Lily to her feet as if she were made from paper and straw. 'Look at your lovely dress, the state it is in. We will have to wash it carefully, by hand. You can help me if you wish.'

'Yes,' Lily said. 'Yes.' She seemed to have forgotten anyone else was there.

'You must go now,' the housekeeper said to Lesley. 'It is not good for you to be here. Please go.'

'Mrs Prince and I, I thought we might have a little talk.'

The housekeeper's voice was firm. 'Mr Prince, he will be home soon.' She glanced back at Lily. 'For her sake, you should not be here when he comes.'

* * *

358

The rain that had threatened on and off all day began to fall when Lesley was still twenty miles from home. Small drops at first, spotted here and there across the windscreen, gradually accelerating into long slanting lines which swerved across the front of the car and left the surface of the road awash within moments.

Lesley slowed her speed, set the wipers to double speed, and peered through the gloom.

Only ten minutes later, the rain had ceased, the vast bulwark of black cloud diminished, and, ahead of her, a rainbow rose over the city, bathing it in light.

Switching on her radio, she listened to the local news: yet another survey had been published, asserting that Nottingham – taking into account murder, rape, robbery, gun crime, assault – was the most dangerous city in England and Wales in which to live. Lies, damned lies and statistics, the leader of the city council had retorted.

Well, he would, Lesley thought.

And yet was it true, in her experience, that the city was a dangerous place? Did she hesitate to walk alone at night? Compared to other cities she'd lived in, or knew – Derby, Cardiff, Manchester, Leeds – did she feel less safe?

The answer, in general, was no, she did not.

Turning right in front of County Hall and crossing the Trent, she continued along London Road, past the building where she worked, around the roundabout and left on to the road leading to High Pavement and Weekday Cross. Miracle of miracles, there was a parking place on the wasteground at the corner of Hollowstone

Hill, and she swung the Peugeot into the space – tight, but just room enough – grabbed her bag, locked the car and set off up the short hill on foot.

As she turned into Commerce Square, her foot slipped on the damp cobbles and her legs went from under her, but before she could hit the ground a hand reached out and grabbed her arm, hauling her upright.

'Thanks,' she mumbled, turning, surprised, and as the grip on her elbow fastened, she was slapped hard across the face by an open hand. She screamed and a fist drove into her chest and as she doubled forward, too winded to cry out, the hand that had held her tugged at her bag, struggling to free it from her arm.

'Bitch! Leggo, you fucking bitch!'

Blindly, Lesley clung to the strap of her bag all the harder and her attacker kneed her in the shoulder, kicked her in the ribs.

'Let fucking go!'

Two fortyish couples turned in from the street at the same time as a younger man exited from one of the buildings across the square.

'Hey!' one of the men shouted. 'Hey!' And the younger man started to run to Lesley's aid.

The attacker swung one more blow in her direction and set off diagonally across the square, fending off the man trying to intercept him, and disappearing down the narrow slope of Malin Hill, the sound of his boots on the cobblestones echoing back into the dark.

'Here,' one of the women said, leaning over Lesley. 'Let me help you up.'

'Leave her, Margaret,' said her friend. 'Let her sit awhile. Come to.'

'Could've been a sight worse,' one of the husbands said. 'Didn't get away with anything, at least.'

Lesley thanked them for coming to her assistance and assured them a taxi to take her to Accident and Emergency was unnecessary. Between them they helped her to her feet and two of the men insisted on walking her to her door.

'Sure you'll be all right?'

'Just a few cuts and bruises, I'll be fine. And thanks again.'

She had only been indoors a few minutes, and was gingerly removing her clothes to inspect the damage, when the telephone rang.

'Hello?'

Silence at the other end, save for the sound of someone breathing; someone breathing quite heavily as if perhaps he or she had just been running fast.

33

The police officer who took Lesley's statement was meticulous, polite and young enough to make Lesley aware of every line in her face, every ache of her already aching body. He should be wearing, Lesley thought, as she watched him make another careful entry in his notebook, one of those signs some drivers have nowadays when they've just passed their test. Probationer: beware.

Having taken her through it all once, he did so again, in brief; just checking the salient points. Yes, her attacker had been white, tall, clean-shaven; yes, he had certainly been young, twenty-three, twenty-four at most. At this point she had given the officer a look and smiled and, catching her meaning, he had blushed.

Sweet, Lesley thought.

Would she recognise him again? Well, it had been getting dark, and she wasn't sure. But she thought she might. The officer checked the details, as far as Lesley had been able to remember, of what the man had been wearing. Jeans, boots, dark tracksuit top.

And his voice? She'd heard his voice?

'He called me a fucking bitch,' Lesley said, and the officer blushed again. Where do they get them from, she thought?

'Was there anything distinctive about it?' the officer asked. 'The way he spoke?'

'Not really. He sounded local, that's all. But not broad. You know, not strong.'

'And you're positive you didn't know him? You hadn't seen him before? Hanging round?'

'Positive.'

'This call, then. To your flat. Just after the incident, I think you said?'

'Yes, a couple of minutes, no more.'

'And you thought it was the same person who'd attacked you?'

'Yes. That was what I thought then.'

'But not now?'

'It's possible. I don't know.'

'And you thought it was the same man because . . .'

'Because he was breathing heavily, as if he'd just been running. Running away, that's what I thought.'

'Those kind of phone calls,' the officer said, 'men who don't identify themselves, there are other reasons for them breathing heavily.'

And a blush came to his cheeks yet again.

* * *

Though it had taken her twice as long as usual to get there, and despite one side of her face looking like celeriac, Lesley had presented herself for work on time, ready for the late shift starting at two.

Alan Pike's immediate response was to tell her for heaven's sake to get back home.

Stubborn, Lesley had refused. 'There's no need.'

'Look at yourself.'

'Alan, it's radio. Not television. It doesn't matter how I look.'

'You've been beaten up. You've been mugged.'

'If everyone in this city who was mugged refused to turn in for work next day, the whole place would come to a standstill.'

Pike had sighed and shaken his head and allowed her to stay. 'Just as long as you're here, a personal response to the new crime figures, that wouldn't be a bad idea.'

Lesley had phoned Helen at the hospital that morning to tell her what had happened – Helen's last day there, she was being discharged that afternoon – and Helen had called Will, who had driven over to Nottingham as soon as he could get away.

When he arrived, asking for her, Lesley decided it was time to take a break and they sat outside on the steps, making the best of the weak sunshine, Lesley breaking her own rules and treating herself to a bar of chocolate and a can of Coke, Will with a cup of tea from the machine.

He listened attentively as she described her visit to Prince's house in the Fens the day before.

'This housekeeper,' Will said, when she was through. 'She seemed genuinely concerned Prince didn't find you there?'

'Yes.'

'Frightened, even?'

'Maybe not frightened exactly, but worried, apprehensive. More for Lily's sake, though, than for mine.'

'You have any sense of why that was?'

Lesley broke off another piece of Fruit & Nut. 'Because he wouldn't have wanted her talking to me? Answering questions? Because he was afraid of what she might say? I don't know.' She popped the square of chocolate into her mouth. 'It's as if he doesn't want her talking to anyone.'

Will nodded. *Maybe he's afraid if too many people start digging around, sooner or later, they're going to find out where the bodies are buried.* Helen's words came back to him, clear as day.

'If she was that concerned about Lily,' Will said, 'the housekeeper probably wouldn't have told him you'd been there.'

'Agreed. But Lily could have said something herself. I got the impression she just came out with whatever crossed her mind, irrespective of the consequences. Besides which, there are the cameras.'

'Cameras?'

'One behind the gate at the side, where people drive in, and another over the main door at the rear. There may even be more.'

'They were switched on when you were there?'

'I suppose so, I really don't know.'

Will leaned back and tried some more tea. Maybe he'd pressed the wrong button by mistake.

'You think there's a connection, then,' Lesley said, 'between me going there and what happened later?'

Will set the tea aside. 'You go to this meeting, press conference, whatever, and Prince threatens you. What was it? Don't make the mistake your brother made? You try and track him down at his house, and afterwards someone's broken into your flat and been through your things.'

'I've got no proof of that. It could just have been my imagination.'

'I know. But let's say for the moment, your intuition was right. You've been asking questions, after all. And not taking no for an answer. Isn't that what Prince said about Stephen, where he went wrong?'

'Yes.'

'So he wants to find out what, if anything, you know, what you've learned, and gets someone to search your flat – I doubt very much if he would have done it himself. Whoever it is goes through any papers, files, whatever's on your computer.'

'He wouldn't have found anything.'

'Which is maybe why he left you alone. Until yesterday.'

Lesley was shaking her head. 'I don't know.'

Will smiled. 'You were the one who thought Prince was behind everything.'

'Yes, it's just . . .'

'How long was there between you leaving the house and returning home? A couple of hours?'

'At least.'

'Plenty of time to set something up, assuming he knows the right people. Teach you a lesson.'

'And Prince does? Know those kind of people?'

'Everything I've learned about him these last few days suggests that he does. Bribery, threats, intimidation, that seems to be how he works. When he feels he has to.'

'He's been in trouble, then? With the law?'

'Not as much as he should have been.'

Will levered himself to his feet and Lesley followed suit. 'I owe you an apology,' he said. 'When you first came to us, I should have taken this more seriously. I should have had someone look at Prince right away.'

Lesley held out her hand. 'You'll let me know what's happening?'

'As much as I can. Only promise me one thing.'

Lesley knew what he was going to say.

'Keep away from Prince and that place of his. Okay?'

Lesley smiled. 'Okay.'

Will went down to where he'd parked his car and Lesley watched him drive away. She considered eating the last two pieces of chocolate before going back to work, but folded the paper back round them instead and dropped them down into her bag, pleased to have restored her self-control.

Michael Allen had moved from Worksop, but not far. Mansfield he was now, working three days a week in a charity shop just off the market square, volunteering two evenings at a homeless shelter. The rest of the time got filled in somehow, books from the library, occasionally something worth seeing at the Palace Theatre, nieces and nephews he liked to keep in touch with, holidays in Devon – the same spot, Paignton, he'd been going to now for years, a self-catering apartment overlooking the beach.

When first he'd relocated to Mansfield, one or two had approached him about standing for the local council, but he'd declined. All that behind me now. Done my bit. Retired.

When Will had phoned him, Allen had not been inclined to talk to him at all. But Will had persevered, and finally, his interest piqued, Allen had agreed. There was a room at the back of the shop where they could talk. Somewhere between half-past three and four?

Will crossed the square, weaving his way between stalls selling everything from fruit and vegetables to electrical goods and clothing that paid little or no heed to fashion.

Allen was repositioning some boxes of children's board games in the window when Will arrived, extricating himself carefully and, once Will had introduced himself, shaking his hand.

Mid-sixties, Will thought, certainly no more: a trim man, medium height, with thinning hair; grey trousers with a vestige of a crease, check shirt, a neat brown woollen slipover, polished brogues on his feet.

'If you'll just give me a few minutes,' Allen said, 'then we can talk.'

Will browsed through several shelves of books, videos nobody wanted any more, audio tapes of *Just William* and *Hancock's Half Hour*, a rack of men's shirts, striped most of them, each one more impossible than the last.

'Would you like something?' Allen asked when he reappeared. 'I can make coffee? Tea?'

Will said thanks, but he was fine.

The room they sat in was a storeroom with just space enough for the two folding chairs on which they sat, knees almost touching. Up close, Will thought he might have been wrong about Allen's age and that he was older than he'd thought. Sixty-nine? Seventy?

'All that business,' Allen began uncomfortably, 'it was a long time ago. I don't . . . well, I don't think about it, it's all in the past.' He was rubbing his hands along his thighs. 'We move on, don't we? We move on.'

'The last thing I want to do,' Will said carefully, 'is to bring up stuff that's going to make you feel uncomfortable. All I'm looking for really is a bit of clarification. Whatever went on in Worksop, the shopping centre business, the detail, that's immaterial.'

He paused and Allen looked at him, apprehensive, concerned.

'Like you say,' Will went on, 'it's all in the past.'

'Yes.'

'It's just that, coming at things from something of a tangent, there are issues I'd like to feel clear about. Clearer than I am now.'

'Issues?' Allen had ceased to rub his legs and was

pressing his hands together at the same time as moving them round, finger over finger, thumb to palm.

'You put yourself forward to the Fraud Squad, claimed to have information about wrongdoing. Whistle-blower, I suppose we'd call it now.'

'Yes, but . . .'

'I'm not sure how much evidence you actually produced, enough to persuade the Fraud Squad to investigate, certainly.'

'Look . . .'

'And then you changed your mind, withdrew whatever accusations you'd made . . .'

'I never accused . . .'

'Accusations, suggestions, whatever. You took it all back. And all absolutely fine, within your rights to do so.'

'I'd made a mistake.'

'So, I believe, you said at the time.'

'Let myself get carried away. Stupid, really. Wasting police time, last thing I wanted to do. The man in charge, Challoner, he was angry and I couldn't blame him, but what else was I to do?'

Allen's hands were pressed tightly now between his knees. His breathing loud in the closeness of the room.

'Howard Prince,' Will said, 'did he approach you directly, or was it somebody else? Someone acting on his instructions?'

'I don't know what you mean.' But everything about him told Will that he did.

'Look,' Will said quietly, the voice of reason, 'whatever you tell me now, there's no way you're going to be called to testify, you won't have to sign anything, make a sworn statement. I meant what I said, all that is in the past, been and gone, but just to corroborate what I'm thinking, I'd like to know what happened to make you change your mind.'

'But if that's right, what you just said, then why, why does it matter?'

'An investigation I'm working on now, concerning Howard Prince, I'm just trying to build a picture.'

'This investigation,' Allen said hesitantly, 'it's similar?'

'I think so. Yes. Except this time someone died.'

'Died? How?'

'They were murdered.'

'And you think . . . ?' Allen began, then faltered.

'Mr Allen,' Will said evenly, 'just tell me what you can. Please.'

For several moments, Allen closed his eyes.

'The first time he spoke to me, anything more than just passing the time of day, it was a dinner. Big council affair. Annual dinner. He must have been a guest of someone or other. Someone on the planning committee, I'd not be surprised. After the speeches and all that, everything winding down, he got me in a corner. "I hear you've been telling tales, Michael," he says. "Tales out of school. Porkies. You don't want to do that, do you?" And he got hold of me here . . .'

Allen indicated the place between his legs.

'Got hold of me there and squeezed. It hurt terribly,

I don't mind telling you, and fetched tears to my eyes, I'm not ashamed to admit it, but I said to him, "You needn't think you're going to frighten me, because you're not." And he let go and laughed and slapped me on the shoulder and said, "You're a good bloke, Michael, I've always said that. More than some of them round here."'

'And that was that?' Will said.

'That was that. Until a while later, I thought some of my post was being tampered with. Not just at the office, but at home, too. There would be nothing delivered for several days – that was unusual – and then there'd be this great pile and some of it had been opened and resealed, you could see.

'Of course, I reported it to the post office and the police and nothing happened and then, just a little while after that, the house was burgled, twice in quick succession. Nothing too much was taken, not a lot of damage, kids, I thought at first. They'd helped themselves to stuff from the fridge, scribbled rubbish on the walls.'

'What kind of rubbish?'

'Oh, it doesn't matter. The Fraud Squad investigation was continuing and other members of the council had been questioned. I knew that because some of them came to me and accused me of creating mischief, telling lies, and I told them if they'd done nothing wrong, well, they had nothing to worry about.'

Allen's mouth was dry and he ran his tongue quickly around his lips.

'Then I had a phone call, late one evening. He didn't

372

identify himself, but it was Prince. I knew. He said . . .
He asked me when I'd last seen . . .' Allen looked away.
'He named a boy, a boy I'd . . . befriended. A church
youth club I used to go along to sometimes. I was on
the committee there. I used to go along and see things
were, lend a . . . lend a hand.'

A sob caught in Allen's throat.

'Nothing . . . You have to believe me . . . Nothing ever
happened. But he said, Prince said . . .'

Leaning forward, Will took hold of Allen's arms.
'It's okay,' he said. 'It's okay.'

Allen sniffed and found a handkerchief. 'I'm sorry.'
'It's fine.'

Allen wiped his face again. 'I went to see Challoner
the next morning and withdrew what I'd said. It was a
cowardly thing to do, I know, and I've been ashamed
of it ever since.'

'You're not the coward,' Will said. 'And what you
did, it's understandable. I don't think you've any need
to feel ashamed.'

Tears sprang again to Allen's eyes and he grasped
Will's hand.

34

Two days passed. Three. Efforts to clean up and clarify the mobile phone images downloaded from the Internet had so far failed to provide any clear identification. The prints that had been lifted from the length of wood recovered from the river had come back coded NUM. No useful marks. The contrast between the developed prints and the background had been too indistinct. Now the local fingerprint office was going to ask for assistance from the Home Office lab at Sandridge.

Threats of legal action from Adam Priestley's family rumbled on. Officers questioning Liam Ibbotson discovered that he had a cousin, Evan, who lived in Cambridge and had been banned from attending Cambridge United home games on account of antisocial behaviour: to whit, making monkey chants and shouting out racist and homophobic remarks, punching one of the club's stewards, throwing coins at the visiting team's goalkeeper and hitting one of the opposition fans with a half-brick.

Evan was duly hauled in.

Liam, yeah, he saw Liam once in a while, family, right? But not for a couple of months. Not since the bastard nicked a brand new fucking X-Box from round ours and sold it down the pub. And all that crap about racist chanting, that's all bollocks. One of my best mates he's black, yeah? Old man comes from fucking Mali and you don't get much blacker than that. What it is, we got this banner, right? Fucking great flag of St George. Took it with us, away games, everything. Not like these half-arsed twats stick a couple of flags on their car every four years on account of the fuckin' World Cup. No, this was Sat'day after Sat'day, rain an' all. And what it is, there you are, this banner hung out behind you so's everyone can see, and maybe there's a bit of chanting going on, not us, could be anyone, and some dickhead with his brains where his arse ought to be thinks, right that lot up there, got to be them. Makes you fuckin' sick. Stand proud by the flag of St George, your own country's flag, and they think that means you got to be racist, got to be in BNP, niggers out, out, out, know what I mean? And, like I say, that's all bollocks, right? I mean, okay, I might vote BNP if I could be arsed, but that's not what we're talking about, what we're talking about, there's cunts who are ashamed to stand up for their club and stand up for their country and we're not and that shouldn't be no fucking crime.

The officer questioning him thought perhaps he had a point there, several in fact, but he kept his opinions to himself.

Will, meanwhile, wanting to check what he'd read

in the file, spoke to the detective sergeant who'd investigated the house fire in Forest Fields for which Challoner had assumed Prince bore responsibility.

No doubt it was arson, the sergeant said, petrol bombs, three of them, two through the upstairs windows, one down. Couple as was in there, lucky to get out alive. They'd pulled in a brace of likely suspects, one of them with a record of setting fires – burned this temporary classroom down when he was still at primary school, no more than nine – but the forensics had never matched up and, one of them besides, he couldn't remember which, he'd had an alibi, off with an aunt in Sheffield, or some such. As to whether they'd been put up to it, the place targeted, there'd never been any proof.

Back on his own patch, Will tracked down one of the two officers who'd been called to the Ely hotel where Howard and Lily Prince had been causing a disturbance, retired now and working three nights a week as a security guard on an industrial estate to the east of Cambridge. Bored shitless with staring at half a dozen CCTV screens and only too glad for an opportunity to talk.

'By the time we arrived,' he told Will, 'things had pretty much calmed down. She, the wife that is, was sitting in the middle of the dining room, not moving, not saying a thing, while the staff cleared up around her. Plates, glasses, all broken, food everywhere, you never saw such a mess. Prince, he was pacing up and down outside, furious at the manager for having called us in the first place, making assurances everything would be paid for. Did his best to talk us into getting back in the car and driving away again. But, of course, we couldn't do that.

'"My wife's been under a lot of strain," he said. "She's not been well for some time." And there was something about medication, that's it, she'd not been taking her medication.

'We talked to the manager of the hotel, took statements from the staff, some of the people who'd been eating in the restaurant. Family who'd been sitting near them, said they'd been sniping at each other all evening. Got to the point, he'd had enough, raised his voice, told her to shut her mouth. Then suddenly she was on her feet and throwing things, yelling at him, calling him names. Fornicator, that was one. I remember it striking me at the time. Not the kind of word you ever hear someone use, not unless it's in one of them period things on the telly. Most of her language, it was a good deal fruitier than that, apparently. Shocked one or two.'

'How did it all resolve itself?' Will asked.

'Oh, the doctor came eventually, her doctor, spoke to her for quite a little while and gave her some kind of pills, tranquillisers, I suppose. Prince himself, he'd calmed down by then, thanked us for the tactful way we'd handled everything. Promised to write a letter to the Chief Constable, though we never heard no more about it if he ever did. The hotel, of course, they didn't want to press charges, best for them if the whole business was swept under the carpet.'

'There wasn't any report of him hitting her,' Will

asked, 'when they were arguing, Prince and his wife? Striking out in anger?'

'Nothing like that, no. More the opposite, I'd say. Once she'd really lost it, gone into overdrive, his main concern, witnesses thought, had been with her, that she wouldn't hurt herself somehow, do herself an injury.'

Will thanked him and let him get back to his desk.

'When you've got your years in . . .' the former officer said.

'Yes?'

'Make sure you've got something better lined up than this.'

Helen's pleasure at being discharged from hospital soon evaporated amidst the boredom of her own company and daytime TV. She wasn't ready to go along and see her colleagues at Parkside, and the few friends she had outside the force were working nine to five or longer. As long as she took the occasional painkiller, she could walk without discomfort, if slowly, but the local park soon outlived its interest. On day two she went to see some drab comedy with that woman from *Friends* and left midway through. She was hesitant about phoning Lorraine, but when she did, Lorraine said, without a second's thought, 'God, yes, come over, it would be great to see you.'

Jake was at nursery and Susie was playing content-edly with five brightly coloured cups of different sizes, banging them against one another and, just occasion-ally, more by accident than design, fitting one inside another.

'It isn't always like this you know,' Lorraine said, smiling. 'Sometimes it's like World War Three.'

'I'm sure.'

Lorraine had slid back the glass window and they were sitting on folding chairs on the patio with mugs of coffee – 'The real thing, not instant. I can't be bothered to do it for myself, but with two of you it's different' – and slices of fruit cake.

The sky was opaque and still, with just the occasional hint of sun, little wind to speak of, just a slight breeze. A couple of blackbirds busied themselves at the field end, in and out of the hedge. In the distance, the cathedral pressed up from the horizon like something from a fairy tale, another world.

'I should have come to see you in the hospital,' Lorraine said. 'I kept meaning to, but somehow . . .'

'Nonsense. You've got other things to do, the children and everything. And besides, Will was there often enough for the pair of you. Come round any more often, the nurses would have been mistaking him for one of the consultants.'

Lorraine laughed. 'He was worried about you.'

'I know.'

'But you're okay now. I mean, you seem . . .'

'I'm fine. Fine.'

'How about work? Can you go back . . .'

'A couple of weeks, they say. Light duties. Whatever that means.'

'I suppose it doesn't do to rush it.'

'No.'

They sat for a while and drank their coffee, looking out. Lorraine took Susie off to the bathroom and changed her nappy, then put her back down on the rug with a rag book and an assortment of soft toys.

'She's a sweetheart,' Helen said.

'I think she's showing off. If it's just me here and I'm trying to do something – I don't know, hoovering, or getting something ready for the oven – she just wants to be picked up and then the minute I put her down she starts crying.'

'I couldn't do it,' Helen said. 'I used to think, yes, you know, it would be great. But now . . . I just wouldn't have the patience, I know I wouldn't.'

'I used to think that. I'd be round at my brother's – they've got two kids, boys, eighteen months between them – and watch his wife practically tearing her hair out sometimes, and think, no thanks, not for me, not in a million years. But then . . .' She smiled. 'It's different when they're your own.'

'I'm sure it must be. It's the level of dependence, though, that's what gets me. Not when they're babies so much, I don't think, even though I suppose that's when they're most dependent of all. But later – tomorrow and the day after and the day after that. On and on. Not just months, but years. I couldn't do it, I know I couldn't. I wouldn't want to.'

Lorraine looked at her indulgently. 'You'll change your mind.'

Helen smiled. 'I don't think so. Not now.'

They lapsed into an easy silence.

'Are you seeing anyone?' Lorraine asked.

Helen laughed. 'Following a train of thought.'

'Sorry, it's none of my business.'

'No, it's okay. And, no. No, I'm not.' Helen broke off a piece of cake with her fingers. 'I was. A while ago now.'

'It didn't work out?'

'Something like that.'

'You want some more coffee?'

'I'm still fine.'

'Cake?'

'No, thanks. Really.'

'It's not as fresh as it could be. It'd probably be better with some butter.'

'Did you ever have that thing,' Helen said suddenly, 'when you just can't say no to someone? Someone you were involved with. No matter how much you wanted to.'

'You mean . . . sexually?'

'Yes, partly. Partly that.' Helen smiled. 'Mostly.'

Lorraine hesitated before answering. 'Once or twice, I suppose, when I was a lot younger . . .' She blushed, remembering. 'Fifteen or sixteen, hanging out with boys a lot older.' She laughed. 'Round the back of the bus station. But that's not what you mean, is it?'

Automatically, Helen reached for her cigarettes, but then dropped them back in her bag. Since leaving hospital she'd kept herself down to two, maybe three a day. 'There's this bloke,' she said, 'I went out with him, off and on, the best part of a year. Lived with him for a bit. He was in the music business. Still is, I suppose. Concerts, stuff like that. Promoting, you know? Used to manage a couple of bands as well. Quite big names. I hadn't seen him for ages, and then when I was in the hospital, he turned up. Flowers, sympathy. I couldn't handle it – I was half out of my head on painkillers, anyway – and I asked Will – I never should have done this – I asked Will to tell him to stay away.'

'He never mentioned it.'

'No, well, anyway, after that he sent me a letter. Andrew. That's his name. I tore it up. Never read it. And then he phoned. A couple of times he phoned and as soon as I knew it was him I hung up. But now I'm worried he's going to come round, one evening, you know, out of the blue. He's done it before. Knock on the door, late, and when I open it he's standing there . . .' She took out a cigarette, and this time lit it quickly and drew the smoke down deep into her lungs. 'There's this song. Emmylou Harris. 'Lovin' You Again', something like that. This man she used to know, he calls her from a phone booth, two in the morning, says he's got nowhere to go. When he gets round there, where she lives, she pays for the taxi, tells him, okay, he can sleep on the couch or the floor, I can't remember which, but even as she's saying it she knows that's not how it's going to be, you know? As soon as he steps inside and shuts the door that's it, she knows she's going to sleep with him, she can't stop herself, even though next day he's going to be gone.'

'And that's what it's like with him?' Lorraine said. 'This man? Andrew?'

Helen fanned smoke away. 'It was. For a while. He'd be on his way back from some gig, three or four in the morning, and he'd ring or, more than likely, just turn up at the door, and I'd tell myself, when I was unlocking the door, tell myself that it was because I was feeling sorry for him, stuck out in the cold or whatever, but I knew it was a lie, I knew it was because I wanted him. Sometimes we'd be pulling off our clothes almost before he got inside and we'd fuck on the floor. And then, just like the fucking song, in the morning he'd be gone.'

She glanced back into the room. 'I'm sorry, I shouldn't swear in front of the baby.'

'That's okay. She'll hear it all soon enough.'

Helen stubbed out her cigarette, half-smoked. 'Anyway, that's my problem.'

'And there's no way you could ever – I don't know – sort things out? You know, go out with him properly?'

'Get back together?'

'Yes.'

Helen shook her head emphatically. 'No way at all.'

Lorraine was thoughtful. 'If you really feel that bad about it,' she said, 'him coming round, perhaps you should move?'

'I did that once. He found me.'

'What about getting one of those restraining orders?'

Helen laughed. 'On what grounds? Man gives great sex?'

'But if you don't want him . . . ?'

'It's not rape, he's not forcing me. I'm the one who's saying yes, remember? And the sex is great. When it's happening, it's unbelievable. Almost every time. But afterwards . . .' She shook her head. 'I feel dirty. Like something he's used. And I hate myself.'

'I don't know,' Lorraine said. 'I don't know what to say.'

Helen smiled. 'There's nothing, is there?'

'I'm going to heat up some more coffee, you sure you don't want some?'

'Sure.'

Lorraine squeezed Helen's shoulder as she passed.

Helen watched Susie pulling at the pages of her rag book and had to resist the impulse to go over and pick her up. If she hadn't had the abortion, her own child would be how old?

She didn't want to go there.

Quickly she got to her feet and followed Lorraine into the kitchen. 'That coffee – is it too late to change my mind?'

Later, they put Susie in the buggy and went for a walk to the small recreation ground at the centre of the village.

'So,' Helen said, 'when d'you start the new job?'

'I never thanked you for that,' Lorraine said. 'Talking Will into changing his mind.'

'He just needs a kick up the arse once in a while, that's all.'

Lorraine smiled. 'He's not so bad.'

'I know.'

Susie stirred in her buggy.

'I used to be jealous of you sometimes,' Lorraine said.

'You'd no need.'

'Some weeks I'd scarcely see him and the two of you, you'd be together all the time. Early in the morning till God knows when.'

Helen took hold of her hand. 'Will's a lovely man. He's a good boss and good to work with and I enjoy his company, I like it a lot, but I don't fancy him, okay?'

'Okay.'

Helen smiled. Most of the time it was true.

35

The trouble started two nights later, a little before ten o'clock. Two groups of teenagers, as many as fifteen all told, mostly boys, became involved in an argument between themselves in the market place at the centre of Heanor, the next small town along from Eastwood, across the river and up the hill through Langley Mill.

Pushing and shoving, name calling, swearing, threats of violence and retribution, a few random punches thrown. A lot of noise. Fair to say that most if not all had been drinking – cider and cans of cheap-label lager in the main, though an empty bottle of vodka was found, smashed against the kerb – and more than a few would have been pilled up.

After a while – who knows how? – some kind of reconciliation was reached and, en masse, the group ran off down one the residential streets leading from the square. Wheelie bins were turned over, windows broken, wooden staves broken from a fence and brandished as weapons. At this juncture three separate calls were made to the police.

After terrorising an elderly couple on their way back from bingo, snatching the woman's handbag and then tossing it into a garden further down, the youths turned round upon themselves and headed back towards the square.

As they arrived, Quadeer Ali and his girlfriend, Kylie Lewis, were emerging from the Golden Fish and Kebab Bar with two doner kebabs, which they intended to take home to Lewis's flat, where Ali was staying. The pair immediately became the focus for racist taunts and jeers, the three girls in the group calling Lewis a slapper and a slag for going with someone of a different race and colour. One of the girls grabbed Lewis's wrapped kebab from her hand and threw it across the square, while another spat in her face; when Ali moved to defend her, half a dozen of the gang set upon him, the rest cheering them on.

Eventually, the pair managed to get to Ali's car, an ageing Ford Escort, and lock themselves inside, whereupon the gang started attacking the doors and windows with lengths of fence post, boots and fists.

By this time several more calls had been made to the police, and three units had been dispatched.

Inside the car Kylie Lewis crouched low, sobbing and shaking. Ali, bleeding from a cut to the side of the head and one corner of his mouth, tried and failed to start the engine. From somewhere, one of the attackers found a piece of broken paving stone and hurled this from close quarters against the front windscreen, splintering it across.

Lewis screamed.

Ali turned the key in the ignition, pressed his foot down hard, and put the car into reverse; it skidded through a half-circle, scattering the crowd, struck the rear of the vehicle parked nearby, bounced forward and stalled.

The offside window had been smashed by the impact, glass lacerating Ali's face.

Sirens blaring, police cars were approaching fast. A riot van, carrying nine officers, was speeding past the hospital on its way from Ilkeston. Two ambulances were on their way. Within five more minutes, the gang scattering as best they could, a police helicopter was hovering overhead.

Both Quadeer Ali and Kylie Lewis were treated by paramedics at the scene.

Twelve arrests were made, three girls and nine boys aged between fourteen and eighteen.

Gary Maitland was sixteen years and eleven months old and unemployed. He'd left school with minimal qualifications and some kind of a record for truancy, tried college for barely six weeks before chucking it in in favour of hanging out with his mates, a little mild shoplifting, playing video games and sponging off his mum.

Slumped back in his chair in the interview room, one leg of Gary's trackie bottoms was ripped and there was blood on the sleeve of the knock-off England replica shirt he was wearing. His dark hair, unlike that of most of his friends, was quite long, falling across his face in two strands. There were two small studs in the lobe of his left ear and a silver ring, which he fiddled with constantly, in the right. A cut, partly healed, continued the line of his mouth across his cheek, and, when he wasn't toying with the silver ring, Gary picked at the edges where it was starting to scab over.

He looked, Chris Parsons thought – the comparison provoked as much by the name as the shirt – a bit like a young Gary Neville, but one who'd have neither the nous nor the skill to pick out Beckham, free on the wing.

His mother, Christine, sitting alongside him in fake leather jacket and baggy jeans, wore the long-suffering expression of the perpetually disappointed, exhausted from having been up half the night, and desperate for a cigarette, that at least.

Almost the only time she'd looked at her son directly in the past twenty minutes had been when he had sniffed loudly and wiped his nose with the back of his hand; the used tissue she'd pushed towards him he had ignored and it had slipped to the floor between them where it still lay.

Three sons, of whom Gary was the youngest, their father long gone; she worked shifts at the local super-market, occasional afternoons at the newsagent's. Saturday nights, if she wasn't working, she got dressed up and went for a drink with her mates. Once in a while, not often, she talked some man or other into coming back home with her, instead of just a quick fumble in the alley alongside the working men's club or the back seat of his car. Two weeks in Skegness every summer.

Parsons wondered if he felt sorry for her and thought most probably he did. Not that that was going to help here.

'Nasty cut, Gary,' Parsons observed.

Maitland said nothing.

'Get that last night, did you?'

No reply.

'Last night, Gary? When you and your mates were having a bit of fun?'

A quick shake of the head.

'The confrontation with Quadeer Ali and his girl-friend? Is that when it was? Catch you one, did he? Smacked you in the mouth?'

Maitland sneered. 'Never fuckin' touched me.'

'Watch your mouth,' his mother said.

'Someone did,' Parsons said. 'Caught you fair and square.'

'Well, it weren't no fuckin' Paki.'

'I told you,' his mother said, aiming a blow at his head, 'to watch your fucking mouth.'

Maitland ducked and glared.

'You were there, though, Gary?' Parsons said. 'When it was all happening.'

'I'm not saying nothing.'

'Your version of what happened, that's all we need.'

Maitland shook his head again, more emphatically this time.

'We know you were there, Gary.'

'So?'

'So it's not the first time, is it?'

His chin jutted forward. 'What d'you mean?'

'It's not the first time you've been involved in that sort of situation.'

'What sort of situation?'

'Harassing someone because of the colour of their skin.'

Christine Maitland murmured something beneath her breath.

'Last year some time, wasn't it?' Parsons looked at the computer printout in front of him. 'Nottingham city centre. The Old Market Square.'

Maitland shifted a little uneasily on his chair.

'And then there was this other incident, a little over twelve months ago. When you and three others assaulted a man in Shipley Country Park.'

Maitland bristled. 'He come on to me, that's why. Fuckin' pervert. Got what he fuckin' deserved.'

'Gary's right,' his mother said. 'Bloke was a pervert. A bloody paedophile.'

'Perhaps fortunately for Gary,' Parsons said, 'the man concerned declined to bring charges.'

'He should have been locked up, not out there preying on young boys.'

'Gary was fifteen, nearly sixteen. And the man claimed one of Gary's friends led him on, then asked for money.'

'Well, he would, wouldn't he? And anyway, what's all that got to do with keeping my Gary here now?'

'We're treating last night's incident, Mrs Maitland, with the utmost seriousness. And Gary's behaviour forms part of a pattern.'

'It wasn't just him though, was it? There was a whole bunch of them. Why you pickin' on him?'

'We're not, I can assure you.'

'It don't look like it.'

'Mrs Maitland . . .'

'No.' She scraped back her chair. 'I've had enough of this. We're getting out of here. You come round the house, knock me up in the middle of the bloody night, tell me Gary's in trouble, drag me down here and then keep us waiting for soddin' hours and all because of what? Nothing. There was a bit of a fight – so what? Anybody get hurt serious? Anyone get killed? No.' Getting to her feet, she caught hold of her son by the arm. 'Come on, Gary, you're not under arrest, we're getting out of here.'

'Mrs Maitland, you're making a mistake.'

'Gary, come on.'

They got almost to the door before the uniformed officer moved to intercept them.

Parsons was swiftly out of his chair. 'Gary Maitland,' he said, placing a hand on his shoulder, 'I am arresting you under the Offences Against the Person Act of 1861 . . .'

Amongst the personal belongings Maitland handed over to the custody sergeant was his mobile phone. And amongst the images stored therein, were a number which matched those Parsons had previously seen on a right-wing website, similar, if not identical, to those established as having been taken in Cambridge, close to Magdalene Bridge.

Some days, Parsons had learned from an old hippy song his father had liked to play, you got the bear and some days the bear got you.

Well, this was shaping up to be one of those days you got the bear.

36

'Will,' Lorraine called down. 'Keep your eye on the toast a minute.'

'Okay,' Will called back. He was cleaning his shoes.

Jake was crying over a plastic toy that had failed to emerge from a packet of Rice Krispies. Susie was upstairs with Lorraine, presumably having her nappy changed. Why was it that, unless you stood over it every second, the moment your head turned away was the moment toast started to burn?

'Will!'

'I've got it. It's fine.'

If they could find some way of getting the toaster mended, or, more simply, buy another one, there would be no need to make toast under the grill. The thing was, Will preferred toast made that way: he could cut slices as thick as he liked.

He was still scraping away at the charred edges when Lorraine came back down, Susie on her hip.

'I hope that's your piece, not mine.'

'There's another piece on for you,' Will said.

The tea in the pot was stewed and Lorraine poured it away and set the kettle to boil anew.

'Helen came round yesterday.'

Will set the butter knife aside. 'You never said.'

'I'm telling you now. She was bored, I think. Wanted someone to talk to.'

'What about?'

Lorraine fastened the last of the straps, securing Susie in her Rock-a-tot. 'Oh, nothing special.'

'It's a long way to come for nothing special.'

'Like I say, she was bored. Can't wait to get back to work.'

'You want marmalade on this toast or jam?'

'Jam. As long as you don't burn it like you did the last piece.'

Reaching round, Will slid the grill pan to safety. Lorraine took Jake's bowl and plastic mug and, with a warning that she'd check to make sure he'd done them properly, sent him off to clean his teeth and wash his face and hands. She poured boiling water into the pot, swirled it round several times and emptied it into the sink, then dropped two tea bags down inside and covered them with more water.

'How did she seem?' Will asked when they were sitting down. 'Helen?'

'Okay, I think. Pretty well, considering what happened.'

'She talk about it at all?'

Lorraine shook her head.

'What did you talk about then?'

'I told you, nothing special. Just this and that, you know?' Lorraine laughed. 'We didn't waste our time talking about you, if that's what you're thinking.'

Will felt himself blushing slightly.

'Far better things to do.'

Will reached around for the pot and poured the tea.

'Jake,' Lorraine called up the stairs. 'Have you done your teeth yet?'

'Just about to,' came the reply.

Will kept turning it over in his mind while he was driving to work, something he quite liked by the Pet Shop Boys, but couldn't name, playing quietly on Radio 2.

Quite why the thought of Lorraine and Helen spending time together unsettled him he wasn't sure, but unsettle him it did. Something about keeping work and home separate? He wasn't sure.

One thing he was sure of: the sooner Helen was back in harness the better.

The temperature must have risen five degrees. Chris Parsons had dispensed with his jacket and then his tie, undone the first three buttons of his denim shirt. Mr Casual in pale grey slacks, cuffs of his shirt rolled back. Opposite him, Gary Maitland was squirming in his seat and starting to sweat. The scab alongside his mouth had been almost picked clean.

Parsons's questioning was consistent and level-toned, probing at the same small points over and over again.

Little or nothing so far about which either Gary's mother or the assigned duty solicitor could complain.

As the questioning continued, however, the assault on Quadeer Ali and his girlfriend slipped more and more to one side, in favour of the homophobic attack in Cambridge.

'May I remind you,' the solicitor pointed out, 'this incident, regrettable as it is, is not the one for which my client has been charged.'

Parsons looked pointedly at the images which had been downloaded from Maitland's phone and printed on to sheets of eight by ten. 'If that's what concerns you, we could probably arrange it any time now.'

The solicitor sat back in his chair.

Christine Maitland closed her eyes; the lines around her mouth seemed more deeply etched than ever.

'Tell me about these photos, Gary,' Parsons said again. 'Tell me how they came to be on your phone.'

The denials were evasive and contradictory. Gary didn't know. It wasn't his phone. He'd borrowed it to call one of his mates, call his mum. Nicked it from one of his brothers. Someone must have stuck it in his pocket when they were running away. Or okay, it was his, he'd bought it just a few days ago. In the park, the pub, from someone he didn't know. Never seen them before or since. He'd swapped the SIM card, hadn't he? Swiped it from one of his mates. Never knew them pictures were there, never seen them before. And that evening, the evening Parsons kept on about, he'd been home, hadn't he? Home with his mum. Watching telly, most likely. What else was there to do?

Yes, Christine Maitland confirmed, Gary had been in all that evening. The two of them. Maybe Dennis, one of his brothers, had looked in, she couldn't be sure. But they'd been there. Watching telly, like Gary'd said, she couldn't remember what.

She didn't sound as if she believed it herself.

Time ticked on.

Parsons was far from sure that the charge of assaulting Quadeer Ali with intention to cause actual bodily harm would stand up; passed on to the CPS, it might not get past first glance. And was the presence of those images on the mobile found in his possession sufficient to tie him into the Cambridge incident conclusively?

Maybe a bit more leverage would help.

Another voice, another point of view.

He had alerted both Rastrick and Grayson earlier and now he called Will Grayson again. The line busy, he left a message and twenty minutes later Will phoned him back.

Maitland? Maitland?

It rang a bell, Will thought, but he couldn't be sure which one.

It would come to him, he was certain of that.

When it did, he rang Parsons again. 'I'll be there as soon as I can.'

Three brothers, Gary, Dennis and Lee, ten years between them. Lee was the eldest. Lee Maitland. When

Will had remembered the name, he'd checked back in the file to make sure. Two young men who had been arrested for the arson attack on a terraced house in Forest Fields, November 2002: Lee Maitland and Mark Knight. Knight it was who had set fire to a building at his primary school; Maitland had come to the attention of both police and social services on a number of occasions but without ever ending up in court. Due to a lack of sufficient evidence both arson charges had been dropped.

Parsons let Maitland have a meal break while he and Will talked, Will filling him in on the investigation into Howard Prince and its possible connections to the Bryan murder.

'This Lee,' Parsons said, 'you think he's still around?'

'We can find out.'

'Still doing favours for Prince?'

'It's a possibility.'

No expenses spared, Parsons had sent one of the PCs out for deep-fried chicken and chips and a can of Coke; before Maitland had finished the last of the chips, tech services had come up with an audit trail for the mobile phone.

Looking over the printout, Parsons whistled.

There were three calls listed to the Newmarket area in the days immediately preceding the attack in which Helen had been injured, one early that evening and another, to the same mobile number but now in Cambridge itself, no more than an hour before the actual attack took place.

'This and the photographs, doesn't leave poor Gary an awful lot of room for manoeuvre,' Will said.

Parsons grinned. 'Short-and-curlies time.'

'You think he'll start talking?'

'Unless he's made out of stronger stuff than I've got him marked down for, I don't see he's got a lot of alternatives.'

Back in the interview room, there were greasy spots down Maitland's front and a flake of something orangey brown adhering to the pinkish scab alongside his mouth.

'Liam Ibbotson,' Parsons said. 'A good friend of yours, is he?'

'Never heard of him,' Maitland said.

'How about his cousin, Evan?'

Maitland shook his head.

'You don't know Evan?'

'No.'

'Funny. You spoke to him the same evening you and your pals stalked those two students in Cambridge; not so long before you beat the holy shit out of them.'

'I don't know what you're talking about.' Maitland's voice now close to a whine.

'And those other calls, earlier. To Newmarket. Setting things up. Where to meet and when. Bit of an organiser, Gary, I can see that. Bit of a shaker and mover.'

'Shut up!'

'Sorry?'

'I said, shut up!'

The solicitor gave Parsons a warning look. Christine

Maitland reached for her son's hand, but he pulled it away.

'Let me tell you a story, Gary,' Parsons said, leaning forward. 'About a couple of men I've had dealings with. They didn't like gays. Didn't like homosexuals. Thought they were vermin. Weak. Contemptible. Hated them. Hate, Gary, you know what that means?'

There were tears welling up behind Maitland's eyes.

'They went out, these two men, on to the common, in London, looking for a gay man to beat up. And this man they found, they didn't even know if he was gay, but they thought he was and that was enough. They called him every hateful name they could think of and started hitting him and by the time they'd finished punching him and kicking him he had over thirty different injuries and he was dead. They killed him. Because he was gay. Because they thought he was gay.'

Maitland was biting the inside of his lower lip, raising blood.

'Under a new tariff for hate crimes against homosexuals, they were sentenced to a minimum of twenty-eight years in prison. Twenty-eight years before they'll be eligible for parole.'

A sob broke from Maitland's throat.

'I don't know how many favours you can do yourself here, Gary – your solicitor will inform you as best he can – but unless you want to take all the blame for what happened, if there were others involved in the attack on those two students, more involved possibly than you, I should start naming names.'

401

Maitland pitched abruptly forward, slamming his face against the table, causing his nose to bleed.

'You and your client,' Parsons said to the solicitor. 'You might want time to consult.'

It was late enough in the afternoon for the sun – what there was of it – to have dropped below the rooftops, leaving a pale smear of colour in its wake. Will leaned against the wall and watched Christine Maitland light a fresh cigarette from the embers of the last.

'It's not gonna make a scrap of difference, is it? No matter what he tells them now.'

Gary had claimed that all the calls to Evan and Liam Ibbotson had been made by someone else using his phone. He had given that person's name. He admitted being present when the two students were attacked, but said he had struck no blows himself. Instead, he had pleaded with the others to stop. He gave Chris Parsons the names of six others who had been present and had taken part in the assault, including the one youth barely identifiable from the photographs posted on the Web.

Already, arrests had been made; others would follow.

'You never know,' Will said. 'It might help when it comes to sentencing, always assuming it gets that far. The judge might look at him more leniently.'

She cast him a scornful glance. 'Pigs might fuckin' fly.'

Will fingered a mint from his pocket and slipped it into his mouth.

'Gary's elder brother, Lee – he doesn't still live at home?'

Christine Maitland blew smoke down her nose. 'Never comes near the place unless he wants summat. On the soddin' scrounge.'

'You don't know where I might find him?' Will said.

'Lee? Scarcely ever see him.'

'But you're in touch?'

A quick shake of the head. 'Not really.'

'But if it were important?'

She swivelled her body so that she was looking directly at him. 'He's not involved in this, is he?'

'Not as far as I know.'

'Thank Christ for that.' She drew hard on her cigarette and then exhaled. 'Last I knew he was working on this building site. Nottingham. Near the ice stadium. Some new hotel?'

Will thanked her and crumbled the mint between his teeth, anxious now to get back inside, anxious to go.

37

Lee Maitland didn't show up for work the following morning and neither the site foreman nor any of his mates had any idea why. His Meadows flat was empty; recently occupied, but empty. Most of his belongings were still there. A call from his mother, Will thought, the night before. Not really in touch. Not much.

'Think he'll go far?' Will said.

Parsons shook his head. 'I don't think we'll be putting out a call to ports and airports, if that's what you mean. Couple of weeks in Ibiza aside, his sort, they don't tend to stray.'

'Watch on the mother's place, then? Another here?'

'I'd say.'

The hoarding on the fence around the site where Maitland was employed had 'Prince Holdings' stencilled neatly in the bottom right-hand corner. White paint on to blue. 'Prince Holdings – Principal Contractor'.

Will found the offices without difficulty.

His warrant card was sufficient to fetch Raymond James hurrying from his office. 'Detective Inspector, is there some way in which I might help?'

'A few words with Mr Prince,' Will said. 'It needn't take long.'

'Ah.' James fingered the lapel of his jacket. 'That might be a little difficult to arrange. Mr Prince has a meeting with the Development Agency a short while from now. I could look at his diary for this afternoon and see . . .'

'Now then, Raymond. What's up?' Prince strode forward purposefully from the end of the corridor. 'Grayson – it is Grayson, isn't it? What are you doing here?'

He was either wearing the same grey suit Will had seen him in last time, or he had had several made to fit in the same style.

'The detective inspector wanted to speak with you,' James said, 'but I've told him you've a meeting already scheduled.'

'Give 'em a call,' Prince said. 'Tell 'em I'll get there as soon as I can.'

'Of course,' James said, unruffled, and went off to do his master's bidding.

'Man's a bloody marvel,' Prince said. 'Runs this place like clockwork. Run me like clockwork if I'd let him.'

Will followed him up a double flight of stairs towards the first floor and they sat in easy chairs in a sort of anteroom to what Will assumed was Prince's own office.

Prince didn't waste any time. 'I thought it was the Fraud Squad,' he said. 'Sniffing round. But it's you, isn't it? Backtracking. Asking questions. Seeing who you can get to dish the dirt.'

Will said nothing.

Prince pointed a finger. 'Let me tell you something. This business. Any business. There's always someone with a knife ready to stick in your back. Some petty grievance. Some contract they thought should have gone their way, went to you instead. Jealousy, that's what it is, more often than not. Shouldn't give it too much credence, if I were you.'

'I'll bear that in mind,' Will said.

'So, anyway,' Prince said, 'let's get to the point.'

'Lee Maitland,' Will said.

Prince stared back at him blankly.

'One of your employees. That hotel going up in the Lace Market.'

Prince laughed. 'If I knew the name of everyone working on our construction sites, I'd be on fucking *Mastermind*.'

'This particular employee, there's a reason to remember.'

'How's that?'

'He was arrested under suspicion of setting fire to a property in Forest Fields that you'd recently acquired. One in which the sitting tenants were otherwise proving difficult to shift.'

Prince jutted out his chin. 'Arrested and then released. Without charge.'

'So you do know who he is?'

'Yes, I know who he is.'

'When the incident took place, the fire, he was working for you then?'

'No. No, he was not. But he came to me afterwards and asked for a job. Enterprising of him, I thought.'

'And you didn't have any qualms about taking him on?'

'Why should I? Been cleared, hadn't he? And besides, he was a strong-looking lad. Looked as if he might be useful. Good with his hands.' Prince held Will's gaze, letting him make from that what he would.

Whatever Will thought, he kept it to himself. 'He's worked for you ever since?' he said.

'Off and on. I don't keep close track.'

'He's gone missing.'

'Since when?'

'Last night. Some time early this morning.'

'Out on the piss. Crashed on someone else's floor.' Prince gestured carelessly with his hands. 'It happens.' He looked at his watch. 'You want to talk to him about anything special?'

'A number of things.'

The silence was broken only by the hushed sounds from other parts of the building, the opening and closing of other doors.

'That murder you were investigating,' Prince said. 'The writer who kept pestering me. Bryan. You get anyone for that?'

'Not yet.'

407

Prince looked at his watch. 'This meeting . . .'

'Last time we spoke,' Will said, 'I asked you if you'd ever made a phone call to Stephen Bryan.'

'And I told you then . . .'

'This would have been a couple of days before he died.'

'And my answer's still the same.'

'You never phoned him at his home.'

'Correct.' Prince was halfway out of his chair.

'How about calling round?'

'What?'

'Calling at his house to talk to him. Have it out with him, maybe. Explain your reasons face to face.'

'I'm leaving,' Prince said. 'I'm already late.'

'You did go round to see him, Mr Prince, didn't you?' Will said. 'And he wasn't in. The first time, he wasn't in.'

Prince turned angrily, the colour high in his cheeks. 'The two of us here, you can make all the insinuations you like. But any time you want to make them in public, make sure you've got evidence, make sure you've got witnesses, because I'll have you broken down to constable if you don't.'

He took the stairs two at a time and Will waited until he heard the slamming of the front door before making his own way out.

'What on earth did you think?' Helen said. 'That he was going to break down and confess?'

They were in a pub near where Helen lived, early

408

evening – early doors, as the saying went – Helen nursing a gin and tonic, Will making his way slowly through a pint of Greene King.

'Without a better witness than we've got, I thought it might be a good idea to force the issue a little. Provoke some kind of reaction, at least.'

'And was it?'

'A good idea?'

'Yes.'

Will smiled. 'Not especially. Although – I don't know – that remark he made about Maitland . . .'

'About him being strong?'

Will nodded. 'Good with his hands. As if he was deliberately pointing me in his direction.'

'And away from himself.'

'Why do that, though? If Maitland were responsible for Bryan's death, the only way it makes sense is if he's doing it on Prince's say-so. He's only bringing it all back on himself.'

'Maybe he sent him round to put the frighteners on, and things got out of hand?'

'It's possible.' Will picked up his glass. 'Then again, it could be Prince is just playing mind games, messing me around.'

They sat for a while, comfortable in one another's company, chatting, drinking, talking about other things.

'Those prints,' Helen said, 'from that piece of wood – any news?'

Will shook his head. 'Still waiting.'

'Taking their bloody time.'

Will shrugged.

Helen finished her gin. 'Get you another?' she said, pointing at Will's glass.

'Best not.'

'Time for home and family?'

'Something like that.' Looking at her, he smiled. 'Sooner you're back at work, the better.'

'For whom?'

'Both of us?'

Lee Maitland showed up for work the next day. Mid-morning, he saw the two police cars approaching along the broad swath of road that led up towards the ice stadium, turning off then towards the site. No sirens, no flashing lights. Low-key.

The two uniformed officers who came through the entrance were young, younger than Maitland himself, early to mid-twenties, talking first to the site foreman, a degree of nervousness about them, wondering, with all the other workmen looking on, how it was going to play.

There were a couple more, Maitland knew, waiting in the other car. He took a couple of paces towards them and stopped, took off his green hard hat and held it before him. Both his jeans and his T-shirt were covered in dust and grit. Dust in his dark hair. A blue tattoo on his neck, beginning to fade; another, in the shape of a dragon, along his left arm.

'Lee Maitland?' the taller of the policemen said, moving a step closer.

'So?'

'We'd like you to come with us.'

'Party, is it, then? Fancy dress.'

One of the workmen laughed, loud and raw.

'Come with us to the station, sir, if you don't mind.'

As the officer took another pace forward, Maitland dropped his helmet to the ground, and, ducking, feinted to swerve to the right.

'Hey!' the officer shouted, reaching out a hand, and, grinning, Maitland rocked back on to his heels and straightened, then relaxed.

'Just fooling,' he said.

More laughter; a few whistles of approval.

A smile on his face, Lee Maitland was led away.

They left him cooling his heels for the best part of an hour, before a uniform showed him into one of the interview rooms and told him to wait. Another fucking age, Maitland thought, but then, after just a few minutes, Chris Parsons walked in, taking off his jacket and draping it carefully over the back of a chair, smoothing his hands along the shoulders as he did so.

'Where's the other one?' Maitland said. He'd taken the opportunity earlier to wipe most of the dirt from his face, but there was still a streak of something white up by his left eye.

'Which other one's this?' Parsons said.

'I thought there were always two of you. You know, good cop, bad cop. Pinky and Perky.'

Parsons remembered Pinky and Perky from when he

was a kid: two chubby pink piglets with high squeaky voices singing 'How Much is that Doggie in the Window?', 'Who's Afraid of the Big Bad Wolf?' How Lee Maitland had heard of them, he had no idea.

'Stuck in traffic somewhere,' Maitland suggested.

Parsons hoped not; he hoped Will was on the A52 and making good progress, somewhere the right side of Grantham.

'Something of a comedian, I hear,' Parsons said, affably.

'How d'you mean?'

'Earlier. Putting on a bit of a show for your mates.'

'Just a laugh, yeah?'

'You weren't at work yesterday.'

'No crime.'

'Where were you?'

'Nowhere special. Just didn't fancy it. Threw a sickie.'

'Weren't at your flat last night, either.'

'Stayed round a mate's.'

'Which mate's this?'

Maitland gave him a name.

'Address?'

Maitland gave him an address.

'We thought you might have done a runner.'

Maitland looked at him. 'Why should I do that?'

'You tell me.'

He told him nothing.

There was a knock at the door and Will Grayson entered. A quick nod at Parsons and he took the seat alongside him. Maitland looked as if he was about to make some crack about small pink pigs but, perhaps wisely, held his tongue.

Parsons asked him about his younger brother, Gary, who Gary's friends and associates were, who he spent time with; Will content to listen, biding his time.

As far as Gary went, it seemed Lee knew little and cared less.

'For one,' he said, 'he's ten years younger than me. We never hung out much together when he was a kid and we don't now. And for another, he's stupid. Want someone to play chicken on a level crossing, wait till the train's almost there and jump out in front of it, ask Gary. Want someone to play dob, chasin' across the fuckin' motorway, ask Gary. Whatever you reckon he's done, it was never his idea, I can tell you that.'

'Not like you, then,' Will said quietly, speaking for the first time.

'Sorry?'

'I said, not like you.'

'That's right.'

'Your own man.'

'There a point to all this?' Maitland asked. 'I'm losing money, sitting here.'

The muscles in his arms were well defined, Will thought. If he struck someone, struck them full force, serious damage could be done.

'Howard Prince,' Will said, 'you've known him a long time?'

'Known him?'

'You work for him.'

413

Maitland shrugged. 'Don't mean anything.'

'He did you a favour, taking you on. Paying you back for a favour you did him.'

Maitland narrowed his eyes, as if taking Will in for the first time.

'That fire you and your pal set in Forest Fields.'

'I never set no fire,' Maitland said.

'What I heard,' Will said, 'the only reason you and – what was his name? Knight? Mark Knight – the only reason you and Knight walked free was some kind of technicality.'

'Yeah, well,' Maitland said, leaning back, 'what you hear's bollocks.'

Will smiled. 'Depends who I'm talking to.'

Maitland sneered. It was a good sneer, Will thought, just the right mixture of cockiness and disdain. Practised in front of the mirror, he didn't doubt, starting around the age his youngest brother was now. And it worked. It made Will want to give him a good hard slap round the face and tell him to stop pissing him around.

Instead, he said calmly, 'Knight, he was the one into fires, wasn't he? You probably just went along for the ride, the crack. Add a bit of muscle if it were needed.'

'I keep telling you, I wasn't there.'

'And I imagine Prince liked that,' Will went on, as if Maitland hadn't spoken. 'Found it useful. Kept you around, on tap. Handy. Should any other little jobs come up requiring a bit of muscle.' Will winked. 'Cash in hand. No questions asked.'

414

'Fuck this,' Maitland said, for a big man quick and easy to his feet.

'Sit down,' Will said. 'We're not through.'

'I'm through.'

'Cambridge, first,' Will said. 'Tell me about Cambridge.'

'What about Cambridge?'

'A man named Stephen Bryan.'

'Never heard of him.'

'Lived there. Cambridge. Worked there, too. A lecturer. Liked his movies. Someone beat him so badly around the head, even his own parents couldn't recognise him.'

'What's that got to do with me?'

'Your boss. He might have said, go over there. Have a word with him. Get him to see reason.'

'I don't know what . . .'

'Use a little force if you have to.'

'Bollocks! This is all bollocks! I haven't got a fuckin' clue what you're talking about. This bloke, this bloke you said was murdered, I never heard of him. Never seen him. All right? Never fuckin' seen him.'

The pupils of his eyes were dark with anger; the muscles on his upper arms were like tightly coiled rope beneath the skin.

'How about Lesley Scarman?' Will said, much as if he'd been asking about the weather.

'Who?'

'Lesley Scarman. She was attacked a few days ago. Nottingham. Knocked to the ground.'

'Too bad.'

'A young man, she said. Fit and strong.'

'Oh, right. Must be me, then.'

'She thinks she could recognise him if she saw him again.'

'Yeah? Bring her in here, then. Bring her in here now. Let's see what she says then.'

'How about an identity parade?' Will said. 'You up for that?'

Cockily, Maitland threw back his head. 'Yeah, why not?'

'What do you think?' Parsons said.

They were in his office on the third floor, posters about Hate Crime on the walls, a view out over the car park, the sky milky blue, hazed here and there with thinnish cloud.

Will was leaning on a filing cabinet by the side wall, Parsons sitting on a corner of his desk.

'I don't know,' Will said.

'He's sure of himself, that's one thing,' Parsons said. 'Him and his brother, chalk and cheese.'

'Could be it's all front.'

'Could be.'

'Got away with it before – the arson – reckons he's going to get away with it again. Yesterday – if he is doing stuff for Prince on the side – maybe he got in touch with him and Prince told him to brazen it out, said if it came to it he'd get him a good brief, see he was all right.'

'As long as he kept his mouth shut.'

'As long as that.'

'It's a long stretch,' Parsons said. 'The one you're making. Prince and Bryan. Prince and this lad, Maitland.' He walked to the window and looked out. 'This bloody weather. I keep wanting to take my kids camping. You know, Derbyshire. Miller's Dale, Monsal, somewhere round there. Keep thinking, okay, it's going to change, get better. Next weekend, maybe. Then just when it should be getting warmer, the temperature drops another five degrees or you get one of those days you're driving round with sidelights on all the time like you're in mist.'

'It's England, Chris.'

'You mean it's always like this?'

'Pretty much.'

'Then why is it always a surprise?'

Will stood away from the cabinet. 'Because we're optimists? Always hoping for the best.'

'This identity parade, what d'you think?'

'What've we got to lose?'

'The woman, the journalist, you can get in touch with her?'

Will nodded.

Parsons reached for his phone. 'I'll get someone to set it up.'

The left side of Lesley's face was still bruised and her hip was sore when she walked. The identification officer explained the procedure clearly but in such a way that Lesley felt this was a test she was being set and the pressure was on her to pass and not fail. The screen, he assured her, would allow her to see the eight men clearly without them seeing her. Eight young men of similar height, wearing a mixture of tracksuits and jeans.

Before Lesley had entered, Lee Maitland had glanced cursorily at a written notice of the Code of Practice before scribbling his signature. If the solicitor with him – a bored thirty-year-old in a shabby suit that hung off him like washing off a line – had been arranged by Howard Prince, then he hadn't dipped far into his pocket.

Maitland objected to the presence of one of the others in the line and a young PC was quickly told to put on appropriate clothes and substituted. Maitland chose his place in the line, then changed his mind, and chose again.

Only then was Lesley brought into the room, the nerves of her stomach tense and taut. She walked slowly, looking at each face; stopped, turned and walked back. That one standing fourth in line, was that the beginnings of a smile in his eyes? She struggled to match his face to that of the young man who had appeared in front of her suddenly in the square. His face in front of her before he swung his hand, his fist.

She moved on. Back at the beginning she turned and walked along beside the screen again.

'Take as much time as you need,' the identification officer said.

'Can you have them say something?' Lesley asked.

'You can, certainly. But I have to point out those taking part in the parade were chosen on the basis of their physical appearance only, not their voice.'

Lesley told him she understood.

'What you like them to say?'

'I'd like them to say, "Leggo, you fucking bitch!" And I'd like them to shout it out loud.'

It took several minutes to set up, and then shout it they did, some with relish, some more diffidently, afraid of letting themselves go.

Those eyes, did they smile this time?

Not really, no. There was nothing else she could do.

'Is the person who attacked you in Commerce Square and tried to steal your bag present in the parade?' the officer asked.

'I'm not sure,' Lesley said. 'I'm sorry, but I'm not sure.'

On his way out of the police station, Lee Maitland passed Will on the stairs, and, as the two men brushed shoulders, Maitland swung his head towards him and winked broadly.

38

The call from Natalie came from out of the blue. Lesley was still low after the identity parade, feeling that in some way she'd let both Will Grayson and herself down, and it was good to hear Natalie's voice, full on and lively.

'So, how's it going? How you feeling?'

'I've been better.'

'How come?'

'I was mugged, wasn't I?'

'You're kidding!'

'I wish.'

'Where was this?'

'Right outside where I live.'

'Oh, Jesus!'

'Yes, well, it's okay. It could have been worse.'

'You're all right, though? You're not badly hurt or anything?'

'I'll survive.'

'Good. Cause I thought you might like to take a little trip.'

'What kind of a trip?'

'My great-aunt, Stella? All that stuff your brother was into. You're still interested in that, right?'

'Yes. Yes, I am. Why?'

'Stella's sister, Irene. My gran. The painter, you know?'

'The recluse.'

'Yeah. Well, it seems she's not such a recluse any more. She's going to have an exhibition. In London. Not as though she'd think to tell me or anything. Had to read about it in some magazine. "Eighty-year-old artist's first show in thirty years."' Natalie laughed. 'Far as I know, she's seventy-nine, but who's counting?'

'So you're going to go? To the show?'

'No. I mean, yes, yes, I will, but that's not for ages. A couple of months at least. No, I'm going up to see her. And I want you to come with me.'

Lesley breathed out slowly. 'And up is where, exactly?'

'Orkney.'

'Orkney? She couldn't live anywhere nearer?'

'Not a problem. You can fly up from Glasgow. Edinburgh, even. It's a piece of piss.'

Lesley hesitated. Prince had warned her off meddling in his affairs clearly enough; and the attack outside her flat, though it need not necessarily have been connected, gave her further cause for thought.

'Come on,' Natalie said. 'You want to do this or not?'

'You think she might talk to me about her sister?'

Natalie's turn to hesitate. 'She might.'

'Then, yes,' Lesley said. 'Yes, I'll come.'

What kind of a reporter was she, if she said anything else?

Irene Bast – she had taken her husband's name when she married and retained it after his death – had trained, Lesley learned, after Googling her name on the Internet, at the Byam Shaw School of Art and then at the Slade. She lived and worked for several years as one of a group of artists based at Lamorna in south-west Cornwall, and then, briefly, at Staithes in north Yorkshire, before moving to Scotland. Her favoured subjects were gardens and domestic interiors, and comparisons, which meant little or nothing to Lesley, were made with Angela Burfoot and Winifred Nicholson.

The only reproduction of her work that Lesley could find, and which she printed out, was of a quite delicate painting of pink and blue flowers – carnations? – in a slim-necked glass vase, with an empty water glass close by. Vase and glass stood on a pale yellow cloth, which hung, with an even fold, over the table edge at the front of the picture. In the background, a length of dark, patterned material – predominantly green and red – was draped with apparent casualness over the back of a chair, and, behind that, the wall was a wash of muted orange-brown and grey.

Somehow, even with all those colours, none of them clashed; everything was in its place. Lesley thought she could live with that painting for a long time and find it calming, even beautiful.

They met at Glasgow airport, Natalie having flown up from Heathrow, Lesley from Nottingham East Midlands. Lesley was travelling sensibly in a lightweight crease-resistant suit, carrying a change of clothes and a few extras in an overnight bag; Natalie had opted for a kingfisher-blue dress over black tights that cut off at mid-calf, with silver shoes on her feet. A chunky gold chain, bracelets that jingled when she walked. A red canvas bag with broad green straps. She gave a little shriek of delight when she saw Lesley and hugged her close, kissing the air beside her cheeks.

'You all set?'

'I think so.'

'An adventure, right?'

'Right.'

'I can't wait to see my gran's face.'

'She does know we're coming?'

For a moment, Natalie hesitated. 'Sort of.'

'And you saw her last when?'

Natalie grinned. 'When I was twelve. Thirteen.'

'And now you're just going to drop in?'

'I sent a postcard.'

'Terrific.'

Natalie laughed. 'Relax. It'll be fine.'

'How about your father?'

'What about him?'

'Does he know you're going up there? More to the point, that I'm going with you?'

'Why should he care? I doubt if he and Irene have exchanged a dozen words in more than twenty years.'

'He cared enough to warn Stephen off writing anything about the family. Me too, and in no uncertain terms.'

'That's because of Lily. The way it might affect her. Irene's a different kettle of fish, believe me. Besides . . .' Natalie giggled, '. . . how's he going to know?'

How did he know a lot of things? Lesley decided it was best not to ask any more.

The flight was two-thirds full, a mixture of holiday-makers – young climbers or Arran-sweatered couples in their mid-sixties – and men returning to work at the oil terminal on Flotta.

'You went to see Orlando,' Natalie said, once the plane had levelled out.

'Yes.'

'How long did he take before he tried to talk his way into your pants?'

'Long enough to open another bottle of wine.'

Natalie laughed.

'Actually,' Lesley said, 'I don't think he was inter-ested at all. Not really. It was more of an act than anything. As if, somehow, he thought it was expected of him.'

'Maybe you should've taken him up on it. Seen what he'd done. Prob'ly come in his knickers.'

They both laughed, Natalie in danger of getting the giggles.

Lesley took out the paper she'd bought at the airport and Natalie started thumbing through the in-flight magazine.

'So what's happening with the film?' Lesley asked.

'*Shattered Glass*?' Natalie shook her head. 'It's not going to happen.'

'How come?'

'A million reasons. Most of them down to money. Push came to shove, we just couldn't get the money.'

'I thought your father . . .'

'Orlando was right about my father. If he'd wanted to find a way of stopping us making the movie, he couldn't have done it any better. Once he'd come in and brought all these conditions with him, it was like putting a strangle-hold on the whole project. Other people started dropping out, the distributor who was interested had second thoughts. In the end Orlando just couldn't be arsed. He's gone off to make some vampire movie in Spain.'

'And you? You must be disappointed.'

'You get used to it. And anyway it might be for the best. There's a part in the new Woody Allen that's being shot in London. I'm supposed to go and meet him next week. It'll probably be crap, but, fuck, it's still Woody Allen, right?'

The last Woody Allen film Lesley had seen had been on TV and she'd loved it, but that must have been made almost thirty years before. His most recent stuff had been so slightingly reviewed, she'd steered clear. And he had to be what? Seventy, if he was a day.

That was the thing with people in the arts, though, Lesley thought. Writers, directors, painters, musicians: the ones that didn't die young seemed to live for ever. Carried on working till they dropped, most of them, too. Well, Lesley thought, what else were they going to do? And some of them seemed to take on a new lease of life, find new directions, actually get better, while others just kept repeating themselves, unable or unwilling to see they'd lost what they once had.

She wondered which Irene Bast would prove to be.

'Here,' Natalie said, taking a folded piece of paper from her bag. 'This is what I meant to show you.'

It was the announcement of Irene's forthcoming show, tied in to a mention of her fiery film-star granddaughter. Above it was a head-and-shoulders shot of Natalie, taken, by the look of it, at a premiere somewhere, and below, a reproduction of one of Irene's new paintings.

The image was small and the definition uncertain, but clear enough, nevertheless, to show Irene's ideas of domestic interiors had changed. A girl with long black hair that twisted forward over one shoulder sat on a white kitchen chair, naked, legs spread. Less a girl than a child. On the table behind her, instead of chrysanthemums, were what could best be described as instruments of torture, and in the background, half-hidden in shadow beside a partly open door, stood a figure that was half-man, half-bear.

Uneasy, a queasy feeling in her stomach, Lesley refolded the sheet of glossy paper and handed it back to Natalie, who took it without comment.

New directions, indeed.

The taxi took them south from Kirkwall along a narrow causeway between the vast sea barriers that Churchill had ordered built to protect the fleet sheltering at Scapa Flow during the Second World War. Lesley was surprised at how flat the land was after the Highland peaks they had flown over, and by the brightness of the light, which gave both the blue of the water and the green of the fields an almost unnatural glow.

Irene Bast lived in a pair of old crofters' cottages outside the village of St Margaret's Hope, rugged single-storey buildings with sloping walls and slate roofs.

When the taxi drew up, she was in her front garden, stooping to weed out some stranger from the profusion of flowers. She straightened at the sound of the car doors closing and stood, a severe figure in black, arms folded low across her chest, as Natalie stepped towards her, Lesley following several paces behind.

Natalie stopped at the wooden gate, tried a smile that was not returned, slipped the latch and went through.

'You look like her, well enough,' Irene said. 'I always thought you would.'

Her eyes were bright but dark, reminding Lesley of the jet she had seen on holidays to Whitby; cheek-bones threatened to pierce the parchment of her skin; her jaw was strong and full, her mouth a line drawn hard across her face. Mrs Danvers, Lesley thought, in the film of *Rebecca*, but with paint at her finger ends.

'You'd best to come inside,' she said.

The cottages had been knocked into one: one half was where she lived, the other her studio.

Natalie introduced Lesley; her grandmother looked

at the journalist for several seconds, nodded, and then busied herself with a kettle, making tea.

'Lesley's brother was writing a book about Stella,' Natalie said. 'Before he died.'

Irene said nothing in reply. From an old circular tin, she took oatcakes, and from the larder, butter, cheese and jam. Lesley and Natalie sat in high-sided armchairs, the patterns of the upholstery faded, the edges worn and frayed. The tea was black and strong and the yellow-looking milk turned it the colour of brown buttery cream.

Natalie gestured towards the mantelpiece. 'I see you got my card.'

'I'm surprised to see you all the same.'

'I said I would come.'

Irene sliced her knife through a wedge of cheese. 'What's said is not always what's done. Besides, if it was me you wanted to see, you could have done that any time in this past dozen years. How old were you when I saw you last? Thirteen?'

'Around there.'

'And already a little wildness in your eyes.'

Natalie started to say something but thought better of it. There was little sound save for the older woman's slightly laboured breathing and the distant breaking of the sea back in the bay. Conversation, Lesley thought, did not come to her easily at all.

'I was wondering,' Lesley said, 'why, after not exhibiting for such a long time, you've decided to do so now.'

'Because I've got something to show,' Irene said. She

428

lifted her cup from its saucer and then put it back down. 'You'd better come and see. After travelling all that way.'

Standing, Irene pulled aside the curtain separating the studio from the remainder of the building. Skylights had been let into the roof to give extra light. Numerous canvases stood against the walls in twos and threes, some of them already wrapped and covered, ready for shipment. More paintings hung above them, filling almost every available space.

At the centre of the room a large canvas rested on an easel, unframed and unfinished. An adolescent girl lies on a stone floor that is scattered here and there with mud and straw; her ribs are clearly visible through her pallid skin and blood sprays dark across her unformed breasts. Behind her, on the walls, hang an assortment of old farming tools, bridles and whips, the curved edge of a scythe catching the light. The girl's mouth is open in a scream, a cry for help: her eyes, open, dark, imploring.

'Margaret,' Irene said. 'The Maid of Norway. She was on her way to marry Prince Edward, Edward II, and be Queen of Scotland. This is where she died. The village is named after her. St Margaret's Hope.'

'What happened to her?' Natalie asked. 'I mean, how did she die?'

'There are stories,' Irene said. 'Something she said or did to offend the villagers. A jealous rival. Nobody knows for sure. It is left to us to imagine.'

'Is this her, here?' Lesley said, moving towards one of the paintings on the left-hand wall.

'Yes. Her coronation.'

Surrounded by a raggle-taggle mixture of soldiers and villagers, Margaret stands at the head of an open grave, a trickle of blood running down the inside of her leg, naked save for a crown of thorns.

Only when they had stepped clear of the unfinished work on its easel, did they see fully the painting that, spotlit, dominated the end wall.

Natalie alongside her, Lesley took half a dozen paces towards it and stopped, open-mouthed.

A young girl, slender, no more than eight or nine – a younger version of the girl in the reproduction Lesley had seen on the plane – was kneeling on the sagging mattress of an iron bed, while the figure of the half-man, half-bear penetrated her from behind. At the head of the bed, another girl stood weeping, looking on. The face of the girl on the bed, even though her body was tensed with pain, showed only pleasure, a kind of joy lighting up the face, which so closely resembled Natalie's as to be her double.

'Oh, Jesus!' Lesley whispered as beside her Natalie turned aside and, head bent, vomited on the floor.

Irene made more tea and from somewhere produced a bottle of brandy. Natalie sat with a borrowed shawl around her shoulders, shaking as if from a fever. She had not seen the rest of the paintings, but Lesley had. More than a dozen of them reworked the same theme: the two young girls, one forced to watch the other's pleasure and pain; the humanised bear.

430

In some ways she was reminded of a film she'd seen about Robert Crumb, an American artist whose comic strips were full of salacious schoolgirls and salivating older men, but those were comic grotesques, absurd; these paintings, for all their elements of fantasy, were real. Undeniably real.

Leaning forward, Irene straightened the shawl around Natalie's shoulders, then, easing back a little, took hold of both her hands.

'I should have warned you.'

There was a tenderness in her voice that had not been there before.

'It's okay,' Natalie said, little more than a whisper.

Irene held her hands tighter. 'It started after my seventh birthday. He came to me when everyone else was in bed and said he had this special present for me.'

For a moment, Lesley looked away. Bile caught at the back of Natalie's throat.

'After that, he came to my room two or three times a week. And when he didn't come, I thought I had done something wrong. Something to make him mad at me. Then when he came back again, it was all right. But then, one year, after Christmas – I was nearly nine – he stopped coming for a long, long time and that was when I realised he was going into Stella's room instead. And I could see it in her face, at breakfast the next morning, after she'd been with him, that look of triumph in her eyes.'

Natalie pulled her hands free and grabbed hold of Lesley's arm instead.

'When we grew up, went off to grammar school, I

431

thought it had stopped, Stella and our father, but it hadn't. It didn't even stop when she was old enough to have boyfriends of her own. And sometimes they would scarcely try to hide it, what was happening, as if they were taunting us, the rest of us. As if they didn't care.

'And then Stella got pregnant. She tried to pretend it was that actor she was working with, but that was never the truth. In the end she came to me and told me, asked me to take the child when it was born and bring it up as my own. Keep it in the family, that's what she said. Keep it in the family.'

'How could you?' Natalie shrieked. 'How the fuck could you?'

Irene sighed. 'If I hadn't agreed, Stella would have had an abortion. The child would have died.'

Tears began to roll down Natalie's cheeks.

'All those years,' Irene said, 'I'd been jealous. Whatever else I'd been – disgusted, ashamed – I'd been jealous that what they'd had had lasted for so long. And I loved him. I still loved him, in a way. No matter how much I hated him too. And this was his child. I would be having his child.'

'Oh, God!' Natalie said.

'That child was Lily. Your mother.'

A sound broke, harsh, from Natalie's mouth and she covered her face with her hands. Lesley tried to put an arm around her, but Natalie pushed her away.

'Let her cry,' Irene said. 'Leave her be.' She got up slowly and went back into the studio, leaving the two younger women together.

When Natalie had stopped crying, she wiped her face on the sleeve of her dress and went outside. After several moments, Lesley followed and together they walked, not speaking, down to the bay and stood looking out across the sound towards Burray and the Cairn Head.

By the time they got back to the cottage, the light had started to fade.

Irene was in her garden once more, staring at the reddening sky. She seemed older than she had an hour before; older and, somehow, calmer too.

'Why now?' Natalie said. 'Why now, after all this time?'

Irene looked at her for some moments before she replied. 'Because it was stifling me. More and more. I couldn't breathe. I'd kept it all here for so long.' She struck her breast. 'I had to let it go before I die.'

'No matter what? No matter who it hurt?'

'Yes, no matter what.'

There were tears again in Natalie's eyes. 'And my mother, Lily, does she know?'

'I don't think she did for a long time. But then, when Stella and our father went to see her together, I think they told her then.'

'The time their car went off the road?'

'Yes.'

It was becoming difficult to see the features of Irene's face in the fading light.

71. INT. DRAWING ROOM. NIGHT.

The two sisters alone in the room. At the centre, ALMA *is pale, distraught, her make-up is smeared and she has clearly been crying.* RUBY *stands near the fireplace, haughty, distanced, smoking a cigarette.*

ALMA: *You had to, didn't you? The only person, the only man I've ever loved, and who loved me, and you had to take him from me. Didn't you? Didn't you?*

RUBY *looks at her scornfully.*

ALMA: *Why? Why?*

RUBY (*carelessly*): *Because I could.*

39

Rastrick had eschewed his normal sombre suits for a navy blazer and a pair of mustard-coloured cavalry twill trousers that had last seen active service somewhere deep in the last century. A pair of highly polished brown brogues completed the outfit, together with a somewhat crumpled shirt and green-and-blue striped tie. Whatever had possessed him to make this sartorial switch on this particular morning of all mornings – intuition or mere coincidence – it afforded him the opportunity to strut, peacock fashion, about the building, colour, for once, flush on his normally sallow cheeks, his eyes agleam.

'This,' he announced, pushing open the door to Will Grayson's office, 'will have the ACC struggling so hard to swallow his own words he'll end up with a hernia of the fucking oesophagus. Threatening to hang me out to fucking dry, the bastard. Bottle of Scotch on my desk by the day's end, I'd not be surprised, and some snivelling little billet-doux to go with it.'

Continued pressure on the lads from Newmarket and

their counterparts in Heanor had paid off. By lunch-time on the preceding day, they had been so anxious to pass off blame on to one another, they had scarcely noticed, some of them, that they were miring themselves with the same dirty business. Early that morning, a series of coordinated raids on addresses in Cambridgeshire and south-east Derbyshire had resulted in no fewer than fourteen arrests, including those of the presumed ringleaders.

'Congratulations, Malcolm,' Will said. 'Job well done.'

'How're things going your end?' Rastrick asked.

Will made a face.

'Here, then,' Rastrick said, taking a couple of folded sheets of computer paper from the inside pocket of his blazer. 'Take a look at this. Sandridge finally made a match from one of the prints on that bit of wood we took from the river.'

Will opened out the paper on his desk, looked, and shook his head.

'Jesus,' he said in wonder. 'Jesus H. Christ!'

'Amen to that,' Rastrick said, and left chuckling.

Mark McKusick was also in especially good humour that morning. Confirmation had come through of his holiday to Tangier and one of his customers had agreed to purchase an upgraded Living Control sound server, so as to store in excess of a thousand CDs without the compression, and consequent loss of sound quality, that comes from using MP3 files. Another twenty minutes or so and he would slip out for a coffee, a chance to glance at the paper, relax.

436

Will took Nick Moyles with him, a squad car with three officers outside; he wasn't expecting trouble, but you could never be quite certain. Keep your arse covered, a good motto in this job as in many another.

McKusick recognised him, of course, the moment he came into the room, and with only a slight hesitation, he stepped forward and, smile in place, held out his hand. 'Inspector. What can I do for you this morning?'

Ignoring McKusick's outstretched hand, Will took hold of him, firmly but not roughly, by the upper arm. 'Mark McKusick,' he said, 'under the Police and Criminal Evidence Act of 1984, I am arresting you for the murder of Stephen Makepeace Bryan . . .'

McKusick's upper body tensed and as he pulled his hand away Will slowly released the grip on his arm. Moyles moved a shade closer, watching for any sudden move towards the door.

'You do not have to say anything,' Will continued, 'but it may harm your defence if you do not mention now something which you later rely on in court. Anything you do say may be given in evidence.'

McKusick's face was suffused with surprise and barely concealed rage.

'Is there anything,' Will said, 'you want to say at this time?'

'Fuck you!' McKusick said.

'Make a note of that, Nick,' Will said, 'then see him to the car.'

* * *

Within the hour, McKusick had been informed of his rights by the custody officer, shown a written notice confirming these, read and signed the custody record and telephoned his solicitor.

McKusick's tie was taken from him, as were the laces to his shoes; his wallet had been surrendered, tagged and locked away, along with his small change and his keys. Officers were already searching the apartment where he lived.

The cell in which he was put before interview was small and basic, the smell of disinfectant sharp on the stale air. McKusick accepted water and refused either a warm drink or any food. When he spoke his voice was low and dull and without emotion.

From his office, Will telephoned Helen and told her the news.

'I don't believe it,' Helen said.

'Neither did I. But it looks as if that's what happened. Killed him and then later, when he'd calmed down, got a grip, did his best to make it look like a robbery.'

'I don't bloody believe it,' she said again, louder this time.

'Steady now,' Will said, a smile in his voice. 'Don't want you suffering a relapse.'

'Fuck off, Will.'

'That's what McKusick said, more or less.'

'Who else is doing the interview?'

'I thought Nick.'

'Lucky bastard.'

'I'll keep you up to speed.'

'Do that.'

Will broke the connection. Christine Costello's BMW was easing into a parking space outside. For the first time in a long while, he wanted a cigarette. Swallowing down the last dregs of lukewarm coffee from his cup, he popped an extra-strong mint into his mouth instead.

Time to move.

The interview room was windowless, the slight hum of the air-conditioner prone to break, at intervals, into a brief asthmatic stammer. McKusick sat upright, staring at a point somewhere above Will's head; his cream shirt was unbuttoned at the neck and at the cuffs, the sleeves rolled back above his wrists, his arms resting on the wooden table, fingers touching.

Alongside him, Christine Costello's leather jacket was the colour of dried blood. Her hair was in brittle reddish curls and her make-up sculpted into place. There was a silver ring superimposed with the head of a snake on the second finger of her left hand and a single earring in the shape of a crucifix, also silver, dangling from her right ear.

She might have stepped, Will thought, from the cover of one of those battered Hell's Angels paperbacks he'd nicked from his older brother and read under the blankets as a kid. Mick Norman. Thom Ryder.

Will switched on the recorder and identified everyone present in the room. At a nod from him, Nick Moyles took an eight-by-ten coloured photograph from a manila envelope and slid it across the table towards McKusick.

'Can you tell us,' Will said, 'how your fingerprints

came to be on this length of wood that was recovered from the River Cam seven days ago, between Magdalene Street and St John's Bridge?'

McKusick tapped his fingers together and took his time in answering. 'No comment,' he finally said.

'You recognise it?'

'No comment.'

'Part of a hockey stick, isn't it? A broken hockey stick?'

McKusick said nothing.

'Your game? Hockey?'

No response.

'Stephen's maybe? Bit of a hockey nut when he wasn't at the cinema? Mark, is that it?'

'No comment,' McKusick said.

He said the same for the best part of thirty, forty minutes, either that or nothing, his eyes fixed on a scarcely visible mark near the mid-point of the table or on the line, beyond the top of Will's head, where the wall and ceiling met.

From time to time Costello nodded her approval; once she glanced across at Will as something close to a smile slid down her face.

Keeping his temper, level toned, Will pegged away like a swing bowler trying for the channel just outside off stump. Line and length, line and length. A different sport from hockey, more patience required. All he needed was a snick, an outside edge.

Every once in a while, he sat back and let Moyles take over.

Still nothing. No comment. No comment. No comment. The same straight bat.

'My client . . .' Costello began.

'Your client wants a break?'

'Exactly. A drink and the opportunity to stretch his legs.'

'All that talking,' Will said. 'His throat must be in danger of seizing up.'

Costello's eyes were green, a deepish green Will didn't think he'd noticed before. A new pair of contact lenses, perhaps. 'Shall we say fifteen minutes?' she asked.

'Why not?' Will said. They had more than twenty hours left from the permitted twenty-four and, as long as they came up with something else, there shouldn't be too much difficulty in applying to extend that to thirty-six if necessary. The officers searching McKusick's flat had failed to find anything relevant so far, but there was still plenty of time.

He was on his way back to the interview room when his phone rang. 'All right,' he said, listening. 'Let me get back to you.'

When he dialled Helen's number and she didn't answer on the fourth or fifth ring he thought she might be out or resting, but instead of her answerphone cutting in it was Helen herself, slightly breathless. 'Just doing a little gardening,' she said.

'I thought all you had was a couple of window boxes.'

'So?'

'Lesley Scarman rang. She wants to talk to you. Something about the book her brother was working on.'

'Fine. I'll give her a call. You got a number?'

Will had. 'If it's anything important . . .'

'Don't worry, I'll let you know. How's it going with McKusick?'

'Slowly.'

'I've got a pair of secateurs here, if you think that might help.'

'If it gets that desperate, I'll be sure to call.'

There was a pause in which he could clearly hear her breathing.

'Take care,' he said, and hung up.

Helen listened to Lesley's account of her visit to Orkney with a mixture of fascination and disgust.

'At least it makes some kind of sense,' Helen said, 'of Prince's reluctance to let your brother go ahead. His wife being the product of an incestuous relationship. Not exactly the kind of thing you want broadcast if it can be avoided.'

'I keep thinking about the state she was in that time that I saw her. Lily.'

'You think she knew?'

'According to Irene she did. She reckons they told her the day of the accident.'

'I wonder why?'

'Why what?'

'Why they told her then? After all that time?'

'Maybe they never intended to. Perhaps it just came out.'

'Or they couldn't live with it any longer. One of them, at least.'

Lesley hesitated, letting a thought run through her mind. 'Natalie asked Irene pretty much the same thing. Why she was willing to show the paintings now, let it all out into the open. Irene said it was stifling her, stopping her from breathing. "I had to let it go before I die," that's more or less what she said.'

'How was Natalie?' Helen asked. 'She must have been devastated.'

'Gobsmacked. Physically sick. And then . . . I don't know. Stunned. Silent. I've never known her so quiet.'

'Poor girl.'

'She'll get over it. Come to terms. Under that flaky exterior, she's made of pretty strong stuff.'

'I hope you're right.'

'What you said earlier,' Lesley continued, 'about this being reason enough to explain Prince doing whatever he could to keep it all under wraps . . .'

'Yes?'

'You think it was reason enough for him to have had Stephen killed?'

Helen took a breath. 'We've just made an arrest.'

'Prince?'

'Mark McKusick.'

'For . . . for Stephen's murder? That's crazy. I don't believe it.'

'That was what I said. But I'm afraid you're going

443

to have to get used to it. There doesn't seem to be much room for doubt.'

'But Mark . . . I don't . . .'

There wasn't anything else she could say.

'I'd better go,' Helen said and ended the call.

She made notes of the conversation so that she could pass them on to Will and was checking through them when there was a ring at the bell. A short woman in a smart green apron was standing at the door, holding a bouquet of flowers, predominantly yellow and purple.

'Yes?'

'Helen Walker?' the woman said.

'What of it?'

'These are for you.' She held out the flowers, but instead of taking them, Helen reached instead for the attached card. One glance and she pushed it back from sight.

'Wrong address,' she said.

'No, it's . . .' The woman began fumbling with her delivery book. 'I'm sure it's . . .'

'Take them. Give them to a hospital, an old people's home, anywhere. Just get them out of here. Go, go on, go.' Stepping back inside, swiftly she shut the door in the woman's startled face.

Two hours later he phoned. 'Hope you liked the flowers.'

Slamming down the phone, she disconnected it at the wall, then switched off her mobile. Dar Williams was still on the stereo and she pressed Play, the volume turned high. The last vestiges of gin were in the bottle, some slightly flat tonic and half a lime in the fridge. Helen made herself a drink, pulled the curtains closed, stretched out on the settee and closed her eyes.

'I want you to look at these,' Will said.

This time the photographs that Moyles set carefully in front of McKusick were of Stephen Bryan's battered body in the shower, three showing him from the waist up, the remaining pair close-ups of his head and face.

'Take a look,' Will said again.

McKusick refused, his eyes focused once more above Will's head.

'Look,' Will said. 'Take a careful look. This is the man you loved.'

With a flurry of hands, McKusick swept the photographs from either side of the table to the floor.

Lightly, Christine Costello touched his arm.

Nick Moyles retrieved the photographs and replaced them.

'I should tell you,' Will said, 'that before we came back into the room I had a call from the technicians who've been analysing the piece of wood on which we found your fingerprints, and they say that it matches the splinters of wood that were found embedded in Stephen's skull.'

'No!' McKusick shouted.

Reaching forward, Will gently tapped one of the photographs. 'This is what the blows did to him,' he said evenly. 'This is what they did to his face, you see? His nose and mouth and eyes . . .'

McKusick jerked back in his seat, a harsh guttural sound choking from his throat as if he were about to be sick.

'You see?' Will said, in the same almost pleasant tone.

'Detective Inspector,' Christine Costello said, 'I must protest . . .'

But McKusick had already slumped forwards and the tears were beginning to slide down his face. His voice, when he started to speak, was so quiet they had to strain to hear the words.

'I called round, that evening. I know I shouldn't have. I'd promised Stephen I wouldn't, but I hadn't been able to stop thinking about him all day – you know, the way something sometimes gets into your head and won't let go. I had a couple of drinks after work and then went home but it didn't get any easier. I thought about phoning him, but I knew I'd probably get the answering machine, or he'd hang up, so in the end I went round. It was late, I suppose, quite late by then, and I thought he wasn't even going to come to the door, and when he did he was in his dressing gown and he just stared at me, not saying anything, and then, after an age, he said, "What is it?" and I said, "I just wanted to talk," or "I needed to talk." I can't remember exactly, and he said, "You'd better come in."

'And I almost didn't, he seemed so hostile, but he held the door open and I followed him through into the hallway and he said, "I was just about to take a shower." So I told him to go ahead and he shrugged and said okay, he wouldn't be long, so I went upstairs and waited in the study. I was really tense, I don't know why. I mean, I was happy to be there, but at the same time it wasn't the same. Stephen, the way he was acting towards me, it was different.'

McKusick paused and looked round for a moment at Christine Costello before carrying on.

'When he came out of the shower, I followed him into the bedroom and asked him what was wrong and he said, "I thought we had an agreement." And I told him I'd really needed to see him and he didn't say anything, and then I said, "I shouldn't have come, should I?" and he said, "No." And then, I said, sort of making a joke of it, I said, "Anyone would think you'd been expecting someone else," and he said, "Maybe I am." Not serious, you know. But then he looked at me and said, "I have seen someone, Mark, I think you should know. Just once so far, but I think I might see him again."

'I was shaking, I remember, really shaking, and I asked him how it was, how it had been, with somebody else, and he smiled this gorgeous smile and said, "Wonderful. It was wonderful." And I hit him. With my fist. Punched him and kept on punching him till he managed to wriggle free and shut himself in the bathroom.'

'I think you should stop,' Christine Costello said. 'I really think you should stop now.'

McKusick gave no sign of having heard her. 'Stephen's hockey stick was in the dressing room,' he said, 'leaning up against the wall. He hadn't played for years, not since he was at university. Just hung on to it for some reason. Used to keep it there, out of the way. I grabbed hold of it and followed him into the bathroom. He pleaded with me not to hit him any more.'

McKusick's breathing was wayward and harsh, broken now by sobs.

'I couldn't stop.'

He buried his face in his hands.

'I loved him,' he said. 'I loved him so very much.'

Helen woke with a start and pushed herself up from the settee. Her left shoulder was numb where she had been lying on it awkwardly and there was a slight crick in the back of her neck. The digital clock on the DVD player read 23:17.

Easing back the curtains, she could see the car parked down at the kerb, the vague shadow of a man behind the wheel. When he moved, she could see the white blur of his face. She let the curtain fall back into place, crossed the room and went down the short hallway towards the front door, slid the bolt across and double-locked it with the key. Not any more.

40

Six weeks after McKusick's arrest, just a week before Irene Bast's exhibition of new paintings was due to open, a four-page piece about the show, illustrated with copious full-colour reproductions, appeared in the *Observer* magazine. Irene was, after all, a publicist's dream: a sudden, vivid flowering after years of silence; works of art with what could be termed sensational content. Add to that a father and sister who'd died together in a tragic accident and a film-star grand-daughter with a reputation for wild behaviour, and placing the story was relatively easy. The *Observer* piece was followed up in the *Guardian*, the *Sunday Telegraph* and – with much moral tut-tutting on behalf of middle England – the *Daily Mail*. BBC 2's *The Culture Show* wanted to film a five-minute segment once the show had opened, and there were rumours that Tim Marlow was interested in doing something for Channel 5.

Ideas of voyeurism, paedophilia and possible incest were mentioned in connection with the paintings, and although no direct links were made with Irene's own life and family, the dots were there for readers to link up if they wished.

Howard Prince shut himself away in his house in the South of France, leaving Lily in the care of the housekeeper, a rotation of nurses, and two security guards hired to keep the media at bay. One press photographer, even so, managed to snatch several long-lens shots of a distressed and bewildered Lily in the garden, before one of the nurses, none too gently, persuaded her back inside.

Natalie spoke volubly about her family's artistic legacy and what a thrill it was to be working with Woody Allen. There were new plans for a remake of *Shattered Glass* and rumours that she might take over the Juliette Lewis role in Sam Shepard's *Fool for Love*. It was at least a month since she'd fallen foul of nightclub bouncers or hurled abuse at the paparazzi; almost as long since she'd appeared in a half-drunken state in the pages of *Heat*.

Prince's lawyer, Quentin Anstruther, contacted Will quite soon after Mark McKusick's arrest. Was it reasonable to assume that, now a suspect had been charged in connection with Stephen Bryan's murder, his client was no longer a suspect?

'Was he ever a suspect?' Will asked.

Anstruther made no reply.

'There are a few things I'd still like clarified,' Will told him.

They met again in Anstruther's office, Prince less

edgy than previously, more relaxed, the faint smell of a lunch-time drink or two on his breath.

'No one holding your hand this time,' Prince observed.

'Sorry?'

'Your colleague – Walker, was it?'

'DS Walker, yes.'

'Fine-looking woman. Sparky.'

'She was injured,' Will said. 'Line of duty.'

'Nothing too serious?'

'Serious enough.'

'I'm sorry.'

Will nodded.

'Well,' Prince said, leaning back, 'let's get on with it.'

'This is just for the record,' Will said. 'Not even that, really. My own satisfaction. Loose ends, they trip you up sometimes.'

'Fire away.'

'That phone call to Bryan's home you denied making . . .'

'Denied?'

'Pretty emphatically, as I remember.'

'Look, son . . .' Prince leaned energetically forward again, '. . . this was murder you were talking about. Some poor bastard has got his head bashed in. You think I'm going to utter a bloody word that's going to tie me into that?'

'You lied.'

'Of course I bloody lied. You take me for a fool?'

Fool or liar, Will wondered, which was best? Prince, he thought, had made up his mind long ago.

'And the man seen outside the house, that was you as well?'

Prince glanced in the direction of his lawyer. 'Quentin here allowed as how he didn't reckon the letter he'd sent was going to be worth the paper it was written on. Certainly not worth the fee I paid him to dictate it to his bloody secretary.'

Anstruther chuckled.

'So I called round, just on the off chance, thought if I talked to him, face to face, explained a little, he'd see reason, back off. Course, he wasn't there.'

'Either time?'

'There was only the one time.'

'We had a witness, claimed to have seen you in a car, a Range Rover, just a few days later.'

'Well, they were wrong.'

'You do have a Range Rover.'

'So what? So does half the fucking population. How else are they going to get their stuck-up brats to school?'

'I don't understand,' Will said, 'why, if you thought it was a good idea to talk to Bryan, you didn't try again?'

'Because,' Prince said, with another glance towards Anstruther, 'someone persuaded me it wasn't a good idea to get personally involved. And by the time I'd changed my mind about that and thought, to hell with it, I'll see him anyway, talk some sense into him, the poor bugger was dead.'

He sat back heavily and waited.

There were other questions Will might have asked, what involvement Prince had had with the attack on Lesley for one, but he knew he would only deny any connection out of hand. And without proof, it would just be so much empty air.

Down on the street, the two men shook hands and went their separate ways.

Helen came back to work ten days before the first article about Irene Bast appeared. Restless as she'd been at home, returning to the front line was stranger than she'd anticipated. People tended to go overboard about what had happened, some of them anyway, asking her eternally if she were okay, slowing down if she came alongside, even offering her, for Christ's sake, their chair when she came into the room; either that, or they ignored what had happened completely, which, while it was preferable, she found herself, nevertheless, resenting.

On the first occasion the possibility of putting herself in physical danger presented itself – the arrest of a drug dealer who was known to be desperate and likely to be armed with a knife – she had to fight back a feeling of intense nausea.

And at night, sometimes, and always when she was least prepared, she would find herself catapulted back there, the fists flying all around her, the angry shouts, the boots, the knife.

'You are okay, aren't you?' Will said, around day three.

'Yeah, fine. Why?'

'Because you look like shit,' Will said, and laughed.

Helen punched him, none too gently, on the upper arm.

'At least I've got an excuse.'

When the exhibition opened, Lesley accepted an invitation to the private view. Somehow, in the crowded gallery, Irene Bast's paintings looked less like personal confessions, and more like what they were, works of art. By the same token, Irene herself looked less like the wicked witch of the north and more like a serious artist, pleasantly surprised if confounded at the attention she was getting.

Natalie arrived late, half out of her head on something or other, wearing a pair of tight-fitting black-and-white hound's-tooth shorts, a beaded vermilion top and a pair of thigh-length boots that would suit her if she ever played principal boy at the Hackney Empire.

She embraced Irene, kissed Lesley on the mouth, drank two glasses of champagne and a bottle of Dos Equis, enthused loudly about the fucking brilliant paintings, then fell asleep in the toilet and had to be carried to a taxi and transported back to Primrose Hill.

Lesley, after several conversations with her late brother's erstwhile publisher, was toying with the idea of writing the biography Stephen had started, and wondering, none too idly, which of Irene's paintings would look best on the cover. Perhaps now that everything was out in the open, Prince's objections would be more muted.

Uneasy spring became early summer. The nights started to shorten and now Will could run most mornings without having to wear a fluorescent vest. Lorraine had settled into her job well enough, though despite his willingness to help, with the hours Will worked she found herself struggling to squeeze more and more into less and less.

She found time, though, to take Jake swimming and loved his spluttering, feverish attempts to keep himself afloat, the glee with which he punched water with his pudgy fists, splashing all and sundry. Susie was into everything now that she could crawl, pulling books and CDs from shelves, dragging sheets and cushions to the floor, digging her fingers into the dark garden dirt and then poking them in her mouth and ears.

Things between herself and Will had levelled out into an easy come and go, any tension between them soon released by a quick laugh or a child's need. Most nights they lay close but barely touching, but when, by accident or design, hand or arm fell against breast or thigh and they woke, they made love with an urgency they had rarely known since the early days of their marriage and before.

She really did love him, she realised, safe and a little alarmed by the strength of her feeling.

She was in the kitchen readying Jake's tea, radio playing in the background, when she heard the news:

the body of a woman had been recovered from a drainage ditch in the Cambridgeshire Fens. Will heard the same bulletin on his way home, away early for once and thankful for it. He switched from the local to the national wavelength and back again, but there were no more details, beyond the fact that the woman had drowned.

By the time the main television news came on at ten, it was the second item, squeezed between rising tensions in the Middle East and England's preparations for the World Cup. 'The body of the woman found drowned in a roadside ditch in fenland between Ely and Isleham, has been identified as that of fifty-year-old Lily Prince, mother of the actor, Natalie Prince.' A photograph of Lily, taken some years before, came on the screen, superimposed over what looked like library footage of the Fens. 'By some macabre coincidence,' the voice continued, 'the dead woman's aunt and grandfather were killed in an accident on the same stretch of road a little over twenty years ago, when the car in which they were travelling went off the road and into the drainage ditch that runs alongside.'

'That's incredible,' Lorraine said.

'The deceased's husband,' the newsreader said, 'the businessman and property developer, Howard Prince, who was out of the country when the incident occurred, is believed to be flying back to England from the couple's holiday home in France. A statement issued by Mr Prince's solicitor said that Mrs Prince had been beset by medical problems for some years and was undergoing treatment at the time of her death.'

'Poor woman,' Lorraine said, and reached for Will's hand.

At Howard Prince's request, Will met him some ten days later. More loose ends causing him the occasional stumble, a succession of broken nights. They walked from the house by the back lanes towards the fen, a grey, featureless day on which the sky seemed to press low against the land.

'This is the way she must have come,' Prince said. 'She'd never managed to get quite so far before.'

Mist rose patchily from the deep water as they approached. The earth immediately above the ditch was slippery underfoot, the exact edge partly hidden amongst the russet reeds rising up from the bank. It would be easy for a person to lose their balance, slip and fall. Even though Will doubted that was what had happened.

'They had instructions,' Prince said, 'never to let her stray too far.' Sighing, he turned up the collar of his coat. 'I should never have gone away, not then, not with all the publicity.'

'She saw the papers?' Will said.

'I tried to keep things from her,' Prince said. 'Protect her. Perhaps it was the wrong thing to do.'

Will looked back along the line of the ditch, cleaving straight as a die towards the far field end.

'Is this where the car came off the road?' he asked.

'More or less. Some fifty yards back along.'

'What happened?' Will said.

Prince shook his head. 'All of it, I'm not sure. Stella,

she'd arranged to visit her sister months before. Friends she was going to see over in Norfolk, and she was going to call in here. That was fine. Only Adam, he always was a contrary son of a bitch, for some reason he took it into his head to come with her. I never could stand the bastard and he never could stand me. Two bull stags, I suppose, always needing to lock horns. I kept out of their way as much as I could.

'As the time wore on, they started to argue, pick scabs the way families will. Lily said something about Irene, I think, how her mother never bothered to visit, didn't as much as phone to see how she was, whereas Stella, who was only her aunt, was always so good about staying in touch. And that was when Stella told her. I don't think she'd intended to, I think it just came out, and when it did, the whole sorry story came with it.

'Lily was sick, physically sick, started screaming at them they had to leave. I came down to see what the hell was going on and got into something with Adam; Stella, meantime, she was trying to comfort Lily, but Lily wasn't having any. In they end they left, the pair of them, and within minutes Lily went running out into the yard, jumped into her car and went off after them.' His heel pressed deeper and deeper into the damp soil. 'I thought she'd changed her mind, wanted them to come back, smooth things over.' Prince looked into Will's eyes, then away. 'That wasn't what happened. By the time Lily got back and I raised the alarm, it was too late. I watched them hauling the car out of the ditch,

458

water streaming off the top and sides. Dead faces pressed up against the glass.'

He looked away as, with a booming call, a bittern rose up from the far side of the reeds.

'Did she say what happened?' Will asked.

Prince shook his head. 'Other than that they'd gone off the road, no. But I looked at the car. Lily's car. There were scratch marks at the front and a small dent. The glass on the offside front light was cracked. When I asked her about it, she said she panicked driving home, veered into a tree.' He opened his arms wide. 'Can you see a fucking tree?'

There were a few, Will saw, not many; the chances of hitting one by mistake not high but not impossible.

'I couldn't get her to say any more. I made sure the car was out of the way before the police arrived. Had the bodywork knocked out, resprayed. Told Lily to keep her mouth shut. There was an inquest, of course, and when the coroner came down with a verdict of accidental death, I thought that was the end of it.' His breath was raw on the misted air. 'It wasn't, of course. Lily, she'd not been well before and after that she just, I don't know, closed in on herself. Sometimes I don't even think she knew who I was.'

A sort of smile came to his face. 'When we were first married, not right off, but after the first year or so, I played away all the fucking time. Fucked anything with a hole between its fucking legs. Didn't care if Lily knew or not. But after this, after she went strange, I never strayed, not the once. Couldn't, somehow. I don't know, I don't understand it myself, except I loved her, I suppose. I suppose that's what it was.'

Prince looked down at the water, dark between the reeds.

'Now fucking this.'

He pushed his hand up through his hair and turned his head aside.

'You can find your own way back, I dare say. I think I'll stay here a while on my own.'

Will offered a hand and, crossing the narrow road, set off back across the fields. When he turned and looked back, midway, Howard Prince was lost, more or less, to the mist.

It was Lesley, that autumn, who tore the page from the *Nottingham Evening Post* and sent it to Helen; Helen who showed it to Will that lunch-time, the sun bright for once and clear, a temperature of twenty-one degrees, the pair of them eating a snatched lunch near the cricket pavilion on the edge of Parker's Piece, Helen with a crayfish and avocado sandwich from Pret, Will enjoying a cinnamon Danish with his double-strength coffee. Half of the page was taken up by a photograph of Howard Prince, surrounded by assembled dignitaries, receiving his award as East Midlands Businessman of the Year.

'All right for some,' Helen said, lighting a cigarette.

Will finished his coffee, gave the article a second glance, then screwed it up into a ball.

'We'd best be getting back to work,' he said.

121. INT. DRESSING ROOM. NIGHT.

PHILIP *is standing, at the mirror. As we hear the last bars of 'I Must Have That Man', he picks up her lipstick from the dressing table, uncaps it and turns the bottom so that the lipstick itself, dark and lustrous, slides out. The song finishes and as he hears the applause,* PHILIP *winds the lipstick back from sight, recaps it and sets it back down, just as* RUBY *enters.* PHILIP *glances at her in the mirror, but fails to turn around.*

RUBY *goes up to him and slides her arms around him, resting her face against his back.*

PHILIP *doesn't respond and after a moment, he steps away.*

Close shot of RUBY'S *face.*

RUBY: *You're going back to her, aren't you?*

461

PHILIP *looks at her, but won't hold her gaze, as if lacking the courage to answer.*

RUBY: *Aren't you?*

PHILIP: *Yes.*

A snort of derision from RUBY.

PHILIP: *All this, you and me, it's wrong. (Beat.) It's over, Ruby. I'm going to marry Alma. If she'll still have me.*

RUBY *(dismissively): She'll have you. (As if shaking herself out of a mood, she smiles and steps forward brightly, her hand on* PHILIP'*s arm.) Come on, I'll drive you over.*

PHILIP *(uncertain): There's no need . . .*

RUBY: *A chance to play Cupid. Bring you lovebirds back together. You don't think I could resist that, do you?*

122. EXT. COAST ROAD. NIGHT.

In a shot we recognise from the pre-credit sequence, the car is seen hurtling along the narrow, winding road.

123. INT. CAR. NIGHT.

An expression of fierce concentration on RUBY'*s face as she drives.* PHILIP'*s face, in contrast, shows alarm and concern.*

PHILIP: *Don't you think we're going a little too fast?*

In response, RUBY's *eyes narrow further as she increases pressure on the accelerator.*

124. EXT. COAST ROAD. NIGHT.

A squeal of brakes as the car just negotiates a bend.

125. INT. EXT. CAR. NIGHT.

PHILIP *(pleading) Ruby! For God's sake!*

RUBY: *Did you really think I'd give you up? For her?*

PHILIP: *Ruby!*

RUBY *starts to laugh, and, as* PHILIP *reaches across and tries to take control of the wheel, her laughter becomes more hysterical.*
   Through the windscreen, we see a sharp bend ahead, the road swinging right away from the cliff.

PHILIP: *Ruby!*

Laughing, RUBY *wrenches the wheel to the left and we see the horror on* PHILIP's *face.*

126. EXT. COAST ROAD. NIGHT.

From the rear, we see the car plunge over the edge of the cliff and hear it crashing down the rocks towards the sea.

127. EXT. CEMETERY. DAY.

A clear, cloudless day. Faint organ music and the sounds of rooks from the bare, surrounding trees. We see ALMA *from the rear, dressed entirely in black, standing in front of two open graves, a coffin on the earth at the far side of each.*

Cut to a close shot of her veiled face, pale and wrought with tears.

Hold the shot and superimpose . . . .

THE END

Acknowledgements

My thanks for expert advice which, in a cavalier fashion, I plundered or, when it didn't suit, shamefully ignored, go to Frances Finn, Carole Fleming, Raymond Flynn, Tony Kennedy, Phil Nodding, Liz Simcock and Mike Walker. Amongst other Nottingham-based writers with whom I swapped tales of trials and tribulations during the making of this novel, I'm especially grateful to William Ivory for his encouragement and common sense, leavened with ardent gossip about the fate of Notts County and the goings-on at Meadow Lane. Thanks also to Susan Sandon and everyone at Random House for once again going that extra yard – or metre – and to Otto Penzler and all at Harcourt in the States; to Mary Chamberlain for her speedy yet diligent copy editing, and to my agent, Sarah Lutyens. Beth Orton's performance at Rock City on 19 February of this year was an inspiration.

John Harvey
London, September 2006

Also available, John Harvey's
gripping and atmospheric bestseller

cold
in hand

Read on for an exclusive extract . . .

ONE

It was that curious time, neither day nor night, not even properly dusk, the light beginning to shorten and fade, the headlights of a few overcautious drivers raising a quick, pale reflection from the slick surface of the road, the main route back into the city. Past Ezee-Fit Tyre Change & Exhaust. Quality Decking. Nottingham Building Supplies. Carpet World. The occasional small parade of shops set back to one side: newsagents, florists, Chinese takeaway, bookies, Bargain Booze.

Lynn Kellogg was driving an unmarked saloon that jolted slightly when she changed down from fourth to third, the Force radio whispering sweet nothings through a field of static. She was wearing blue jeans and a pair of scuffed Timberlands, her bulletproof vest still fastened beneath a red and black ski jacket, unzipped.

There were school kids all along both sides of the street, spilling over the pavements, pushing, shoving, shirts hanging loose, rucksacks slung over their shoulders, sharing, some of them, the headphones from their MP3s and iPod nanos; a covey of girls, no older than thirteen or fourteen, skirts barely covering their skinny behinds, passing a joint between them. Another day, Lynn might have pulled over, stopped, delivered a lecture. Not today.

February 14th, Valentine's Day, a little after four p.m. and she wanted nothing as much as to get home at a reasonable time, strip off these clothes and soak in a hot bath. She'd bought a present, nothing fancy, a DVD, *Thelonious Monk, Live in '66*, but it still needed to be wrapped. The card she'd left propped up against the toaster where she thought it might get found. When she glanced in the mirror, the tiredness was all too clear in her eyes.

She had been sitting with her second cup of coffee that morning, half-listening to the early news: another fifteen-year-old had been shot in Peckham, south London, the third in almost as few days. Payback. Bravado. Respect. Some part of her thinking, at least this time it isn't here. She knew the number of senior detectives currently investigating gun-related incidents in and around Nottingham was such that the Homicide Unit were having to consider bringing in officers from outside.

As the newsreader moved on to the prospect of more job losses in the industrial sector and she reached for the off switch, the phone cut in.

'It's okay,' she called through to the other room. 'It's probably for me.'

It was. A man holding his wife and children prisoner in Worksop, north of the county, threatening them harm. Almost certainly armed. Lynn swallowed another mouthful of coffee, poured the remainder down the sink, and grabbed her coat from where it was hanging in the hall.

'Charlie, I've got to run.'

'I'll see you later,' he said, hurrying to the door.

'You better.' Her kiss just missed the side of his mouth.

'The table's booked for eight.'

'I know.'

A moment and she was gone.

Nine months earlier, Lynn had finished her training as a hostage negotiator, ancillary to her main role as Detective Inspector on the Homicide Unit, and since that time she had been called out twice, both incidents being peacefully resolved. In the first, a fifty-five-year-old man, forcibly retired, had held his previous employer captive for eighteen hours, under the threat of trepanning his skull with a sharpened scythe; Lynn had eventually talked him into setting his weapon aside and releasing his prisoner with promises of a hot meal, a probable maximum of seventy-two hours' community service and a personal interview at the local Job Centre. Her second call out had been to a twenty-four-hour grocery store, where an attempted robbery had resulted in one youth being arrested as he tried to flee the scene, leaving another inside with a Stanley knife to the throat of the terrified Somali shopkeeper. Against Lynn's advice, the incident commander had allowed the youth's mother to talk to the boy directly and her pleas for him to surrender had succeeded where Lynn's had so far failed. Bad practice but a good result, the shopkeeper unharmed, the youth walking out into his mother's arms and the waiting police in tears.

This particular morning it was a thirty-four-year-old engineer who'd returned from a six-month stint in Bahrain to find his wife in bed with his ex-best mate, the three kids all downstairs, clustered round the television watching *Scooby Doo*. The mate had legged it, leaving his trousers dangling from the bedpost and the wife to face the music. Neighbours had registered a lot of banging and shouting, but not thought too much of it, until, in the early hours, the oldest of the children, barely seven, had shinnied through the bathroom window and gone running to the nearest house. 'My dad's gonna kill my mum. He's gonna kill us all.'

By the time Lynn had arrived, the street had been cordoned off, the house surrounded, anyone with close knowledge of the interior and the family debriefed, both the layout and the names and ages of those inside clear in their minds. Firearms officers were already in position, ambulances ready and waiting. What the boy had told them was halting and confused; some of the time he seemed to be saying that his father had a gun and sometimes not. They weren't about to take any chances.

The incident commander was Phil Chambers, a detective superintendent Lynn had worked with once before, a murder-suicide out at Ollerton: a husband and wife who'd been together for forty-seven years and wanted it to end the same way. Ben Fowles was the senior firearms officer at the scene, a good thirty pounds heavier than when Lynn had first known him, the pair of them young CID officers working out of Canning Circus station; Fowles moonlighting most weekends, fronting a band called Splitzoid that somehow never seemed to have made the grade.

There was telephone contact with the house, but after the briefest of conversations – little more than grunts and curses – the connection had been broken and the man had so far refused to pick up again. Lynn was forced to resort to a loudhailer, self-conscious despite herself, knowing that all of the assembled officers would be hearing what she said, how she handled the situation, listening and judging.

The man had stepped into clear sight several times, once with what looked like a kitchen knife held against the side of his wife's throat, not an easy shot but possible, nine times, maybe, out of ten. Not a risk they were anxious to run. Not yet, anyway. Lynn had seen Chambers and Ben Fowles several times in close conversation, weighing up the pros and cons, the decision to shoot theirs and not hers. Neither of the remaining children, a girl of five and a three-year-old boy, had been seen for some little time.

'Let the children go,' Lynn said, her voice echoing across the late morning air; the sun up there somewhere, trapped behind a bank of cloud. 'Let them come outside.

Their gran's here. She can look after them. Let them come to her.'

The grandmother was standing off to the left of the cordon with other members of the family, agitated, distraught, chain-smoking Silk Cut; a deal had already been struck with a local reporter who was a stringer for one of the nationals – *My Little Angels: a Grandmother's Anguish*. Should the worst happen.

'Let me see them,' Lynn said. 'The children. I just want to be sure they're all right.'

A short while later, he held them up awkwardly to the window, both crying, the boy squirming in his hands.

'Let them go now,' Lynn said. 'Let them out and then we can talk this over. Nobody's hurt yet. Nothing's happened. You should let them go.'

Half an hour later, the front door opened just wide enough for the girl to squeeze through; for a moment, out there on a square of cracked paving, she froze, before running towards a female officer, who scooped her up and carried her off to where her grandmother was waiting. Another minute and the little boy followed, running, falling, scrambling to his feet and then falling again.

The mother's face showed, anxious, at the upstairs window, before she was pulled away.

'Let your wife out now,' Lynn said. 'Then you and I can talk.'

The window was thrown suddenly open. 'The only way she's coming out's in a fuckin' box!'

And the window slammed shut.

'Could've taken him then,' Ben Fowles said softly at Lynn's shoulder. 'Back home in time for *Countdown*.'

'Not my call.'

'I know.'

'What's the thinking on the gun?' Lynn asked. 'He armed or not?'

'No sign.'

'Maybe the boy was wrong.'

'Seven, isn't he? Six or seven? Old enough to know what a gun looks like, I should say.'

'He must have been frightened out of his wits, poor kid.'

'Doesn't mean he made a mistake.'

Lynn shook her head. 'I think if he had a gun we'd have seen it by now. His situation, he'd have made sure we did.'

'And if you're wrong?'

She looked at him squarely. 'Either way, unless you and Chambers have got something cooked up between you, we carry on waiting.'

Fowles smiled. 'Till what? He sees the hopelessness of his position? Walks out with his hands above his head?'

'Something like that.'

Out of the corner of her eye, she saw Chambers checking his watch and wondered what calculations he was making.

Not so many minutes later, the man picked up the phone. Lynn was pliant but firm, letting him have something to hold on to, something that could lead to a way

474

out. Little by little, bit by bit. She shook her head, some old song ringing like tinnitus in her ears. Retro nights at the Lizard Lounge. Some white soul singer, she couldn't remember the name. Back when she was a young DC. Before she'd met Charlie. Before everything.

It was close to two and a slow rain was starting to fall.

'Let your wife out through the front door. Once she's outside she should turn to the right where she'll see a female police officer in uniform. She should walk towards her with her hands well away from her body. Is that understood?'

Come on, come on.

The front door budged open an inch or so, then swung wide and the woman stumbled out, blinking as if emerging from the dark. As she began to walk, less than steadily, towards the waiting officer, the door behind her slammed shut.

Lynn gave the man time to get back to the phone.

'All right,' she said. 'If you have a weapon, I want you to throw it out now. Then, once that weapon is secured, you can come out yourself. Walk towards the uniformed officer with your hands in the air and follow his instructions. Lie down on the ground when you are told.'

Moments later there was the sound of a gunshot, muffled, from inside the house.

'Shit!' Lynn said beneath her breath and for a split second she closed her eyes.

Fowles looked across at Chambers and Chambers shook his head. Instead of sending the troops charging in like some SWAT squad on late night TV, the incident commander was content to bide his time. The man was alone in the house now and a danger only to himself. Assuming he was still alive.

Time was on their side.

When the man failed to pick up the phone, Lynn used the loudhailer instead. Firm but fair. If he could hear her, this is what he had to do.

She repeated it again, unflustered and clear.

Nothing happened.

And then it did. The door opened gradually and a handgun was thrown out on to the grass.

'All right,' Lynn said, 'now step outside slowly with your hands in the air . . .'

Halfway across the patchy square of lawn he stopped. 'Couldn't even do that,' he said to no one in particular. 'Couldn't even do fucking that.'

'Pathetic,' Ben Fowles remarked.

There was a scorch mark on one side of his face; at the last moment he had pulled his head away.

One of the children tried to run towards him, but the grandmother held him back.

Not for the first time, Lynn caught herself wishing that she still smoked.

Chambers came over and shook her hand.

Fowles nudged her on the shoulder with his fist. 'Good job,' he said.

Lynn did her best not to smile. Dusty Springfield,

she said to herself on the way back to the car, that's who it was.

Little by little, bit by bit,
Should stop caring, but my love won't quit.

She tried Charlie's office number but there was no reply; his mobile seemed to be switched off. No matter, she'd be home now soon enough. A table for two at Petit Paris on King's Walk. Paris, Nottingham, that is. Moules, steak frites. A decent bottle of wine. Try to leave room for dessert.

Lucky?

Her hands were still shaking a little when they touched the wheel.

Like a tooth you couldn't stop probing with the tip of your tongue, the song was still nagging away at her as she made a turn on to Woodborough Road and eased into the outside lane. She heard the call over the Force radio nonetheless: disturbance on Cranmer Street, near the junction with St Ann's Hill Road. Only moments away.

'Tango Golf 13 to Control.'

'Control to Tango Golf 13, go ahead.'

'Tango Golf 13 to Control. I'm on Woodborough Road, just turning into Cranmer Street now.'

Lynn swung sharp left across the traffic, cutting off a mud-spattered four-by-four and causing it to brake sharply. Cranmer Street was only narrow, barely a two-car width, vehicles parked down the left-hand side making it narrower still. A builder's van with fading

Forest stickers in its rear windows made to pull out in front of her and then thought better of it.

'Control to Tango Golf 13. Response units are attending. Advise await their arrival.'

There were several small blocks of new-build flats high on the right and beyond those an old municipal building that was now student accommodation. Behind fencing along the near side, the ground was being cleared, deep holes being dug; council housing demolished and replaced. Just opposite the intersection with St Ann's Hill Road, a crowd of youths, many of them wearing hoodies – what else? – had gathered in a rough circle that spread out across the street.

As Lynn cut the engine, she heard the sound of shouting, raucous and angry; chanting, like a soccer crowd baying for blood.

'Control, this is Tango Golf 13. I'm on Cranmer Street at the scene. A gang of fifteen or twenty youths fighting.'

Lowering her window she heard a scream, urgent and shrill, the one followed almost immediately by another.

'Control, this is Tango Golf 13. I'm on top of the incident and shall have to intervene. Immediate back-up required.'

'Control to Tango Golf 13, advise . . .'

But she was already out of the car and running towards the crowd.

'Police! Police, let me through!'

As she pushed her way into the circle, an elbow

struck Lynn in the ribs and an outflung hand caught her high on her cheek, a signet ring breaking the skin.

A few of those standing at the front turned to see what was happening and she was able to force her way to the centre. Faces, all shades, stared at her, showing everything from indifference to pure hate. Young males mostly, wide-leg jeans slung so low it seemed as if their crotch hung somewhere down between their knees. More than a few wearing black and white, Radford colours. A gang thing, is that what this was?

'Fuck off, bitch!'

A head arched sharply back then jerked forward and the next second she was wiping a gobbet of spittle from her hair.

Jeers. Laughter.

More shouts, more threats.

The two young women – girls – who'd been at the heart of the fighting had broken apart when Lynn pushed her way through.

Fifteen, she guessed, sixteen at best.

The one closest to her – thin white face, head close-shaven like a boy's, leather jacket, black and white scarf, skin-tight black jeans – was bleeding from a cut high on her left cheek, a slow trickle of blood running down. Her adversary, facing Lynn, was most likely mixed race, dark hair tied back, denim jacket and jeans, a short-bladed knife in her hand.

Lynn took a step forward, focusing on the girl's eyes.

'Okay, put the knife down.'

Two steps more, then three. Slow, measured, as

assured as she could be. Somewhere in the middle distance, the sound of a police siren coming closer. Overhead, the street lights seemed to be getting brighter with each second.

'Put it down.'

The girl's eyes were bright, taunting, only the merest flicker of fear. Of doubt.

The crowd almost silent, scarcely moving.

'Down.'

Another half-step and the expression on the girl's face changed, her shoulders seeming to relax as she shifted her hold on the knife and lowered it to her side.

'On the ground,' Lynn said quietly. 'Put it on the ground.'

The girl began to bend as if to obey, Lynn reading too late the widening of her eyes, too slow to counter the movement, lithe, as she sprang past, the blade slashing at the right side of the other girl's face and opening it like a ripe plum.

The girl screamed.

Lynn pivoted on her left foot, seizing the attacker by the sleeve and swinging her hard round, one knee coming up into the small of her back, her fist chopping down on the girl's elbow and the knife tumbling to the kerb, the girl continuing to struggle all the same.

The police siren was closer still, the sound of an ambulance in its wake.

Lynn had forced the girl's right arm high behind her back when, from the corner of her vision, she saw the youth step forward from the retreating crowd, arm raised. Time enough, as she swung towards him, to note the black and white bandana wound tight around his head, the pistol held almost steady in his hand, the contempt in his eyes. The force of her movement took the girl round with her, propelling her forwards, the first shot striking Lynn in the chest and seeming to lift her off her feet before sending her stumbling back, legs folding beneath her, falling away even as the girl, still standing, free hand outstretched as if to ward off what was to come, took the second bullet in the neck, immediately above the gold chain she wore with her lover's name engraved, a wash of blood arcing over the mottled ground and into Lynn's mouth and eyes.

Easy Meat

John Harvey

Why would a fifteen-year-old boy commit suicide?

Mind you, who cares when he's a no-good kid on trial for bludgeoning an elderly couple to death? But when the senior investigating officer is then found brutally murdered, DI Charlie Resnick is put on the case, which leads to some sinister and startling revelations. It also brings Resnick into contact with Hannah Campbell, with whom he finds himself unexpectedly and awkwardly in love.

'This novel has joy, warmth and extreme violence. The compulsion to turn the page is almost painful.'
Mail on Sunday

'A first-class story with a clever plot and believable characters, crafted by a writer on top form'
The Times

ALSO AVAILABLE IN ARROW

Flesh and Blood

John Harvey

Fifteen years ago Susan Blacklock disappeared. Although Detective Inspector Frank Elder has taken early retirement, the case still plagues his mind. Prime suspects, Shane Donald and Alan McKeirnan, were convicted a year later of the brutal rape and murder of a young girl, and now that Shane has been granted parole, Elder feels compelled to revisit the past.

Then Shane disappears and another young girl is murdered. Elder's involvement is now crucial. Taunted by postcards from the killer, an increasingly desperate Elder battles to keep his estranged family from being drawn into the very heart of the crime.

'John Harvey is lights out one of the best and with this book the word is going to spread far and wide'
Michael Connelly

'A gripping and powerful thriller'
Mark Billingham

'A sinister thriller . . . one of Britain's leading masters of atmosphere'
Guardian

arrow books

Ash and Bone

John Harvey

When the take down of a violent criminal goes badly wrong, something doesn't feel right to Detective Sergeant Maddy Birch. And her uneasiness is compounded by her belief that someone is following her home . . .

Retired Detective Inspector Frank Elder's daughter, Katherine, is running wild. Elder's fears for his daughter are underscored by his guilt – it was his involvement in a case that led directly to the abduction and rape which has so unbalanced Katherine's life.

Persuaded out of retirement, Elder reopens a cold case which could have devastating repercussions for the crime squad itself. Elder's investigations take place against the backdrop of his increasing concern for his daughter. He must battle his own demons before he can uncover the truth.

'Harvey once again gets everything right, jangling the nerves and plucking the heart-strings . . . another marvellous read'
Reginald Hill

'Immaculately engineered thriller . . . Harvey's book is fast, fluent and exciting, with a pace and assurance that never lets up'
Literary Review

arrow books

Darkness & Light

John Harvey

A phone call intrudes on retired Detective Inspector Frank Elder's solitary life in Cornwall. It's his estranged wife and she needs a favour. A friend's sister, Claire Meecham, an unassuming widow in her fifties, has gone missing.

Elder agrees to return to Nottingham to try and track her down. Then Claire is found – dead. The killer has arranged her body meticulously, almost lovingly, forcing Elder to remember another dead woman, arranged in an almost identical way. It was his first case with the Serious Crimes Unit. His first case and never solved.

It's clear to Elder that this is the work of the same unbalanced individual and, to find the killer, elder must shine a light into the darkest recesses of human behaviour, that dark and twisted recesses of a disturbed human mind...

'*Darkness & Light* is crime fiction at its best'
George Pelecanos

'Gripping and heartbreaking in equal measure, this is a must-read'
Mark Billingham

arrow books